WASHOE COUNTY LIB
3 1235 02826
D0209622

HOPE'S WAR

By Stephen Chambers from Tom Doherty Associates

Hope's End
Hope's War

HOPE'S WAR

stephen chambers

A Tom Doherty Associates Book
New York

This is a work of fiction. All the characters and events portrayed in this novel are either fictitious or are used fictitiously.

HOPE'S WAR

This book is printed on acid-free paper.

A Tor Book
Published by Tom Doherty Associates, LLC
175 Fifth Avenue
New York, NY 10010

www.tor.com

Tor® is a registered trademark of Tom Doherty Associates, LLC.

ISBN 0-312-87350-6

First Edition: August 2002

Printed in the United States of America

0 9 8 7 6 5 4 3 2 1

To Ben and Michael, and to Daniel

O why was I born with a different face?
Why was I not born like the rest of my race?
When I look, each one starts! when I speak, I offend;
Then I'm silent and passive and lose every Friend.

Then my verse I dishonour, My pictures despise,
My person degrade and my temper chastise;
And the pen is my terror, the pencil my shame;
All my Talents I bury, and dead is my Fame.

I am either too low or too highly prizd;
When Elate I am Envy'd, When Meek I'm despis'd.

—William Blake (1757–1827),
an excerpt from a letter to his longtime friend and patron, Thomas Butts

HOPE'S WAR

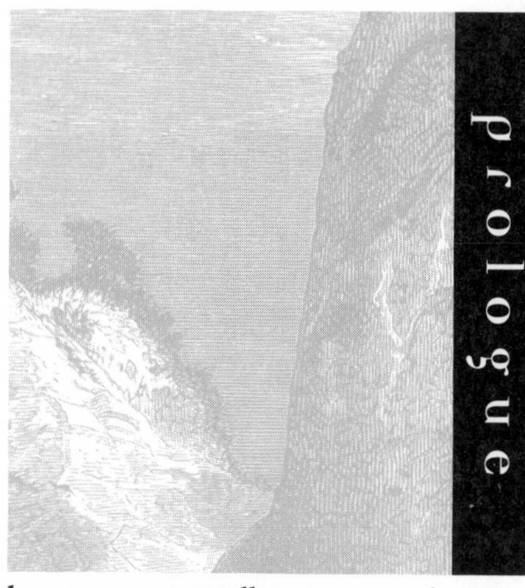

prologue

"Tom" smiled as he entered William's dorm room, though William doubted that that was his real name. A *Yankees* poster with dog-eared corners hung across from William's bed, and several stacks of books cluttered the carpet, mostly comics. William lay on his back on the bed, listening to music loud enough that Tom could hear the bass through a pair of tiny wireless inserts in William's ear sockets.

"William."

William's eyes fluttered open, and he stared at Tom for a moment, unmoving. The song in his ears stopped, and William popped tiny pieces of black plastic from his inner ear and dropped them onto his lap. Another song began, filling the dorm room with tiny noise—Tom clicked a button on the bedside, and it was silenced. William's hand balled on the plastic earpieces.

"Has it happened again?" Tom asked, and William thought about telling the truth, then decided against it.

"No."

"That's good. Martha's treatments are working then."

"Think so."

"Good," Tom said again, and his smile began to appear forced. "You have a flight to Tokyo tomorrow morning. Then on Thursday, we're on the European Coast—Paris, London—did anyone tell you?"

"Yes."

"You haven't started packing."

William closed his eyes. "When's my next free time?"

"William, we went over that the last time I was here," Tom said, like a trainer attempting to calm a frightened animal. "Until we're certain that your episodes have stopped, we can't authorize any free time."

"Not even supervised?"

"Not even supervised."

"But they *have* stopped."

Tom was silent for a moment, and then he said, "Do you need any new books? Have you read all of these?"

William glared at the ceiling. "I want to read the paper."

"William, no one your age is interested in reading the paper."

"How do I know that?"

"Trust me." Tom smiled, the spaces on both sides of his eyes creasing in what must have generally been thought of as "boyish charm." William had grown to hate it in the years he had known Tom; William was eleven now, and Tom had begun teaching William how to behave since he was five.

"What about music? Do you need something new to listen to?"

"Can I go on the network?"

"Didn't Martha talk to you about that?"

"No."

Tom sighed sadly. "I know we talked about that too the last time, didn't we? The network is off-limits except during free time."

"And then it's still limited."

Tom blinked, momentary panic quickly turning into another smile. "What do you mean?"

"I mean you shut off ninety-five percent of everything anyway. I don't have access to all of it. Just like the books." William's cheeks flushed as he spoke, and for an instant he wanted to back down, to let it drop and allow Tom to think that he was appeased—but what was the worst that could happen? They would keep him locked in a cell for the rest of his life, except when he was taken out as an advertising tool: What else could they do? Take away his books, his music? Drug him out of his mind, so that he wouldn't struggle? Let them.

The world was blocked, cut off so that William couldn't even see the headlines. When they took him "on tour," the Sunaki-Heiman planes dropped into whatever airport it was—and William had discovered that all airports looked the same—then William was ushered to a herd of black limousines, and inside the windows were too dark to see out. William's only glimpse of Paris or New York or Osaka was the stretch of pavement from the airstrip to the team of armed guards and limousines. Then, the car would rock and honk its way through traffic as Anglo men and women in suits smiled and drank champagne and talked nervously and asked William polite questions.

"Did you sleep on the plane?"

"Are you excited to be in Berlin?"

"They tell me you're a very talented young man, William."

At the convention centers, William would again be hustled out of the limo, flanked by security personnel in bulky jackets with automatic rifles and earpieces, and marched through marbled lobbies, past fountains or sculptures or greenhouses, up escalators or stairs or elevators, until eventually they arrived at an enormous ballroom that would already be full of expensive-looking people. Applause, and the Sunaki-Heiman "team"—including William—would take their seats at the head table, surrounded by bodyguards, and one after another the important Sunaki-Heiman people would give speeches that never really made sense to William, as he was usually too tired from the plane trip.

And suddenly a spotlight would glare in William's eyes, and he would stand and smile—more applause—and William would say the lines they had made him memorize: "In three hundred years I haven't seen a company as reliable and successful as Sunaki-Heiman." This was usually followed by a poem, and William always got applause. Sometimes the reception moved to a room painted entirely green, where they powdered his face and made William repeat the same lines ten times into a camera, before rushing back to the limos and driving back to the airport. It was a routine William had begun to accept—but not entirely.

"William—"

"Everything I get goes through Sunaki-Heiman," William said. "Even the air. Even you. You let me wander around the gardens and talk to my teachers about just enough that it isn't technically illegal—so that you can keep me. Like a mascot. I read about mascots on the net."

Tom's face was blank, and he glanced back at the door, as if to be certain that whoever was on the other side was hearing all of this. "What are you talking about, William?"

William said, "I even think I know who I am. Because those 'episodes' showed me."

"You're a member of the Sunaki-Heiman corporation, William. You're an employee."

"For life," William said. "You're right, they're not over. I'm still having *episodes*. You'd better pump me with more drugs, Tom, because I was in a city by a river, without cars and without the net, where people walked through horse shit every day. I think I lived there."

Tom went to the nearest pile of books and grabbed one, flipping through pages of black-and-white cartoons. "You got that out of one of these?"

"I *saw* it," William said, and he rolled onto his side, right arm sliding into the space between the bed and the wall. "You own me because you made me, right? And I'm a marketing stunt, aren't I?"

"William," Tom's voice was distant, distracted as he flipped through more comics for any sign of a city with horses, "everyone at Sunaki-Heiman is an employee for life—"

"I don't think that's true," William said. William's hand tightened on a plastic handle wedged into the bottom of the mattress, and he pulled his arm back out slowly. Tom tossed the books onto the floor and rose, forcing another smile.

"Why won't you let me read the paper?" William asked.

"Is that what this is about? You wouldn't like it, but I'll see, maybe something can—"

"What about the net? Why can't I look around there, or go into the city without a chaperon?"

"William—"

"*Why*?" William stood, a plastic blade made of a sharpened toothbrush handle in one hand.

Tom froze. "Where did you—"

The door burst open, and two men in white uniforms with black clubs rushed the room, Martha behind them in her unisex nurse's uniform—as William slashed Tom through the chest and arm. Tom cursed as blood splattered his coat and tie. William threw himself at the guards, driving his blade deep into one's stomach, and the other knocked William across the back of the head, tossing him onto a pile of books that collapsed under his weight, scattering papers in a crumpled mess. William fumbled, still conscious, and he saw a man with white wings standing by the doorway, glowing brilliantly. The Angel nodded and said, "*There will be another time, William Blake.*"

Needles into his forearms, and young William Blake did not struggle—the Angel already gone, and the room faded away into black spots.

"IT IS time for an auction."

"What do you mean? We auction the granary supplies to the highest bidder, just as the late Justice wanted?"

"Just as was agreed, Orik."

"—disagree . . ."

"—think he's right, we must . . ."

"Vel—where do you stand? Will you veto a measure to sell the food and end standard rationing? We need to know."

Vel opened his eyes and watched the Executive Council for a moment without speaking. He could see the shadow of his reflection in the polished black stone table, and Vel studied the thirty members of the Executive Council, each in turn. Lord Denon sat at his right, in a white robe with a black swastika on his chest, and there, at the far end of the table sat General Wunic, Justice Hillor's replacement on the council. Wunic was more of a soldier than Hillor had been, and his long hair flaunted the fact that he was among the best. Only high ranking members of the military elite were allowed long hair.

Soldiers stood quietly at the stone walls of the room, below tapestries with alternating swastikas and five-pointed stars; the Church swastika and the star of the government. Vel wore a long black overcoat, marked with old holes sewn imperfectly shut.

"Where's General Rein?" Vel asked. The general had been here a moment ago.

"The general stepped out," Wunic said.

Orik, one of the minority representatives of Hope's poorer districts said, "What's your opinion, Your Majesty? Any measure to sell our stored food supplies must be vetoed . . ."

"Said I would veto it yesterday," Vel said, and he glanced around the table. "Don't you people remember?"

Technically, the decision to sell the food stockpiles had passed before Vel had become king. But it had happened after the last king—Vel's uncle—had died and had never actually been approved by royalty, as was legally required. Still, there was some dispute as to whether or not the king's approval was absolutely necessary or simply custom—there were no specific laws either way.

"With General Rein . . ." one of the older women on the council said, rings clicking on both of her hands. "We thought—"

"We all heard His Majesty's decision," Orik said loudly, cutting her off. "The king *will* veto it, now let's move on."

Denon leaned close to Vel as the council continued to argue, and said, "There's Rein."

Vel nodded to Denon, and a man in a blue and gray military uniform marched into the room, followed by a company of police soldiers. Rein—hair short and dark—carried a rifle on one shoulder and a sword at his side. All of his troops brought guns as well.

The conversation stopped, and Rein paused rigidly at the end of the table. Wunic glanced at the regular soldiers around the room, about half armed with rifles, the other half with crossbows—all carrying swords. Wunic's soldiers—the king's soldiers—outnumbered Rein's men two to one.

"We need action now," Rein said, and he pointed at Vel. "He'll veto it?"

A fat man in bright clothing nodded, scratching at his beard. "That's right. No regard—"

"You know that we have enough food to feed the city for only another two months," Rein said. "Nothing's been distributed at all beyond basic rations."

"He knows," Denon said, leaning forward, and everyone watched the leader of the Church of Hope. "The king has made his decision."

"And it's wrong," Rein said, backing out of the room. He nodded to the council. "Something must be done."

Denon said, "You are not a member of this council, General."

Rein hesitated, then he said quietly, "We are in a crisis, ruled by *him*—by a boy who murdered one of our greatest leaders, one of our greatest officers."

Orik said, "General, this is treason—"

Rein ignored him, began to back out of the room and said, "Think very long, all of you, before you follow this little rebel. A coup brought him to this palace, and it may take a coup to restore law."

General Wunic was on his feet, soldiers around the room tensed, rifles ready. "I will speak to you in the main barracks, General. Give me your sword."

Rein stared back at Wunic. "Our soldiers, our veterans—the heroes of this city—have not eaten. The granaries are closed, we're fed scraps, and this boy—"

"Goddamn it," Vel said. "*No one's* eaten more than scraps, General Rein. What do you think we've just been arguing about?"

"A measure passed," Rein said slowly, his cheeks reddening as he watched Vel, "before you were in this palace. And now I've been told that for some reason, that decision is no longer valid."

"That decision was never official; it was made without a king," Vel said. "By Justice Hillor—"

"A man you murdered," Rein said, and Rein's soldiers remained around him. Most of these police soldiers had served under Hillor, had fought against Vel. Rein continued, "We were to be given control of the granaries and remaining food supplies in preparation for a general auction."

"*We*?" Vel asked.

Rein said, "The military."

"General," Wunic said, and he advanced on Rein. Rein was one of the highest ranking officers in the military police force of Hope, subordinate only to a handful of others. Wunic was one of these men. "This is out of line."

Rein shook his head, as if he couldn't believe that Wunic was siding with Vel. "General, with all due respect," Rein said, "you're new to this council. Maybe the boy's won you over, but he hasn't won me."

Orik sighed. "General Rein, the fact is, you're not a council member, you're not even supposed to—"

"My men," Rein said quietly, "have no food."

"Yes, General, I know," Orik said. "We're working on a bill now that will allow the rations to be expanded."

"We can last two months," Rein said. "Have you eaten today, Orik?"

By their expressions, Vel could tell that Rein had the support of most of the council members. Most were rich and would benefit from an auction.

"Yes," Orik said, obviously irritated that he couldn't make Rein go away. "Of course I've eaten, that's not what we're—"

"It is," Rein said. "Isn't it better for part of the city to survive years than for all of us to die in two more months? Like *he* wants?" Rein indicated Vel.

"*General*," Wunic said. "Enough. You will leave these chambers, you will leave now, or I'll have you escorted to a cell in the basement. Is that clear?" When Rein didn't respond, Wunic approached him, and the soldiers in the room followed—Rein's men waited, weapons drawn. "Am I making myself clear, General Rein? *That boy* is your superior. We don't choose our kings, but we serve them: Anything else is treason. *Is that clear*? Vel is your king. Now, give me your sword."

"I respect you, General—"

"Give me your sword, General Rein."

"I respect you," Rein said again and reluctantly he backed down the hall, his soldiers following. "But don't pretend. The boy's a traitor, a common criminal, an assassin, and he's not my king. If you follow him, if you listen to him—now of all times—we're all going to starve."

One of Wunic's soldiers steadied his rifle, glancing at Wunic for a command. This was blatant treason now. "Sir . . . ?"

Wunic watched Rein go.

"Outside of this room," Rein said, "things *will* happen. This will be settled, and my men will be fed."

"Sir?" one of Wunic's soldiers said again, and Wunic looked back at Vel.

"Sir?" Wunic said. "This is subversion, disrespect and treason. Defiance of our laws . . ."

Before Vel could answer, Denon said, "Yes, General. For every blessing given to the just, God's punishment will find the wicked."

"What's he going to do?" Vel asked.

Rein was nearly gone, talking quietly with his soldiers at the far end of the stone corridor.

"I don't know, sir," Wunic said. "He should not be allowed to leave."

"Let him go," Denon said, and he smiled casually, waving Wunic back to the table. "We have business here."

"That's right," Orik said and the council members began to relax. "Best way to solve this is to continue normally. If we pass something we can fix this."

"It's already been passed," one of the wealthier members said with a sigh. "Under Justice Hillor. Have you deliberately forgotten?"

"Yes, it passed, but it passed without a king," Orik said. "As I'm sure you're well aware, councilman, anything that passes must be shown to our king, who has the authority to veto. Now, you could try to overrule the veto—"

"You know we don't have the numbers."

Orik said, "*Anything* that's passed can potentially be vetoed. It must go to the king."

There were thirty members on the Executive Council—thirty-one with the king, but he didn't vote—and a simple majority of sixteen was needed for a measure to pass. However, if the king exercised his veto, twenty-five votes were needed to override the veto. Only twenty-two council members had voted for the measure.

"Yes, I'm aware," the wealthy councilman said. "It just happens that we didn't have a king at the time. You can't retroactively—"

Wunic interrupted, still standing by the door. "General Rein has committed high treason."

"And we're going to fix the problems he was complaining about," Orik said.

"It is still treason," Wunic said.

Denon leaned close to Vel. "Why don't you tell our new military-officer-turned-statesman to stop being melodramatic and have a seat? He won't listen to anyone but you."

Vel indicated Wunic's empty chair. "We'll worry about that later, General. Let's work on getting something done so that food can be moved."

Wunic stiffened, told the soldiers to seal the chambers, and then returned to his seat. "Yes, sir."

As Orik and the other council members continued to argue, General Wunic sat straight in his chair, silently, and Vel asked Denon, "Is this the way things usually go?"

Denon chuckled. "Oh no, sometimes it's much worse. This is a good day."

"What's a bad day like?"

Denon hesitated, and then he said, "With some luck you will never have to find out."

VEL SAT in his bedroom, a withered brown vine on the bedside table beside his pistol and sword. A candle flickered there, casting long shadows on the mirror and red carpet. That plant was supposed to cure the Pox, and Vel—along with four other people—drank its sap, draining it, turning it into a dead, useless vine. *And now maybe I'm cured,* Vel thought, *but hundreds of people in Hope are still dying of the Pox, and I don't have another one of these.* Two weeks since Rein had declared he would take action, had openly committed treason, and there had been mass defections from the police; a large fraction of the force sided with Rein and a handful of other rebel generals.

The generals were promising their soldiers military rule of Hope, full access to the food supplies and an opportunity for revenge on the boy-king who had dishonored and killed their former hero, Justice Hillor. The Executive Council still had not taken any definitive action, except to limit rations even further. The rich sided with Orik on this because—in theory—the food that was saved now might later be bought. The rebel Generals said that Vel was deliberately wasting time and hoarding most of the food himself.

"Draft," Denon had said. "There must be full conscription."

So that the city turns into two armies, Vel thought. *Until women and children are slaughtering one another on both sides, so that they won't starve.* And Vel could remember seeing food in the tunnels under the ruins, but how could he get it from the Frill—the dark, red-eyed creatures living beneath the ruins outside the city—if the Frill would simply massacre anyone who tried to bring that food back? *And what does it mean that I'm half-Frill?* Vel wondered.

He tried to sleep, and someone knocked.

"Who is it?"

"General Wunic, sir."

"Go away, General."

"Sir—"

"Go away."

"Yes, sir."

Wunic's footsteps faded away in the hall outside. Wunic always picked the worst times, and Vel didn't care that the people of the Midland District had elected him to replace Justice Hillor on the Executive Council, there was too much in Wunic that reminded Vel of Hillor—too much of the military arrogance. Wunic knew exactly how the city should be ruled, and Vel was a piece to be used just like any of Wunic's soldiers.

Only Denon gave Vel advice. Just too much happening, and when he had tried to allow multiple counsellors they had all argued for different things. All of the men who had served the previous king—the professional bureacrats, as Denon had called them—had treated Vel as an obstacle. They had used his private meetings to argue and had generally ignored Vel's questions and suggestions, until, after just three days, Vel had gotten rid of all fifteen of them. For the moment, he refused to speak with anyone but Denon.

The bureacrats have probably sided with the rebels now, Vel thought. So that now Vel only listened to Denon—the one man who seemed to have no particular bias, who had helped Vel become king and who treated Vel as almost an equal. Denon wanted to save the city more than Vel—and, just as importantly, Vel needed his experience and prestige when dealing with the Executive Council or military. But there had not been a pause in the chaos to find out why Denon had once told Vel that he was half-Frill. No moment of peace in nearly a month. And no sleep.

More footsteps, and a double rap. "Vel?"

"Come in, Denon."

Denon stepped inside, and Vel glimpsed the pair of soldiers always stationed outside his door.

"I think you should know, it's happened."

"What?"

"They're burning the city. They're rioting."

Vel ran through the Palace, Denon at his side, a trail of soldiers in his wake. Long passages of dark stone, and elaborate swastika and star tapestries spaced between giant mirrors and statues of men in uniform, each labelled with a plaque—and in some places the palace walls were still marked with occasional bullet holes, like acne scars. They rushed down the staircase from the second floor to the first, into the main entrance hall.

"—time to end this," Denon was saying. "Must strike very hard, ruthlessly, and it must stick in their minds. If it's done right, you can win the war right now, before it begins."

"They'll remember it," Vel said, stumbling as he reached the ground floor. Three hours of sleep last night, and maybe four the night before, and now the world was a blurry series of frustrating people who told him again and again how the city was on the verge of civil war. How the rebels had seized one of the stockpiles of guns, how they were probably preparing to lay siege to a granary. And Vel wanted to sleep, not to solve all of the city's problems, just to sleep without dreaming and waking in sweat with police soldiers rushing into his room with urgent dispatch after urgent dispatch. Defections and unreliable police and officers who did not trust Vel to help rule the city as king and legal commander of the army—*and they resent me because I killed Justice Hillor, one of their leaders,* Vel thought. *Because I won't just hand all of the food over to the military police.*

Denon guided Vel, and they continued on their way, people racing from one end of the entrance hall to the other, papers scattering as soldiers bumped into one another in crowded hallways. It grew noisier as Vel neared the rear chambers where the Executive Council met.

"The names, Your Majesty," Denon said as he handed Vel a sliver of paper, and Vel tried to steady his heartbeat. *If I only had someone else to help me,* he thought. *Thank God for Denon.* Denon had helped Vel defeat Justice Hillor, had given Vel access to the Church artifacts—the guns that had allowed Vel to take the palace. Without those guns Vel would never have become king. And now Denon kept Vel from being pushed aside, used and disregarded by the other Executive Council members. Denon's advice had kept the rich and the military from getting the food. *Everyone wants to eat,* Vel thought, *and so no one can. This is all happening too fast, and I can't keep up, just trying to stop it from going out of control.*

Vel stopped outside the Executive Council chambers—the other members were already inside; Vel had called an emergency meeting.

"You're sure?" Vel asked.

Denon said, "Yes. Vel, you know we wouldn't be here if I wasn't."

Vel stared in at the table, and some of the council members met his eye and smiled curiously, waiting.

"How many?" Vel asked.

"Three."

"Fine." And as they entered the chambers, soldiers slammed the doors shut behind them.

"Quickly," Denon said, and Vel read the three names on Denon's sheet, wadding it into a ball.

"Take your seats," Vel said, and they all stared at him as Vel stalked around the exterior of the room. "Sit down."

Reluctantly, they sat, and Vel drew his pistol, clicking the safety off.

Someone said, "We have reports that—"

"Three traitors are acting to undermine the council in the name of the rioters." Vel stopped behind a fat woman in a tight blue dress. She started to turn in her seat, but Vel pressed the revolver to the back of her head.

"Stay there," he said.

"Oh my God," she said. "Oh God."

Vel said the names, "Andrews, Koorton, Alaianas. Traitors on the Executive Council."

Police soldiers slid their rifles into readiness, advancing behind the chairs of two older men. One of the men shouted, "You're insane. You want to arrest me? You can't—"

"No," Vel said, "I don't want to arrest you. I want to stop you from beginning a war. If you're arrested, you'll find a way out of the prison." Vel looked at Denon, and Denon closed his eyes, a slight nod—and Vel shot Ms. Andrews in the back of the head. Simultaneous flashes of gunfire, and the other two slumped in their chairs, red spray across the table. Vel backed away from the fat woman's body, wiping blood from his jacket with one hand, his pistol smoking.

People started screaming, trying to get out of the room. Wunic said, "This is—"

"Listen to me," Vel shouted, and he tried to stop the room from spinning, but it continued to blur and shift, and Vel caught himself on the wall. "There will be no war. Tell your constituents—tell them that the government of Hope will not be held hostage, and that *we* are in control. Those three were traitors, and there's evidence. I have evidence. Everyone in this city will eat, and *there will be no war.*"

"The Lord has chosen this city," Denon said before anyone else could speak. "Sacrifices will be made if necessary, and we will trade lives for the greater good. Life over Lies." The room was strangely silent, and Denon said, "So long as there is order, there will be no war."

chapter 1

A young soldier waded through knee-deep snow, a swirling wind of falling snowflakes spraying his military coat as he approached an alleyway. The building on the left, with a collapsed roof, looked like an architectural sketch of a residential skeleton, and the soldier knocked on the door to his right. A slot slid open, and then the door was unbolted, and the young soldier stepped into a large, crowded room filled with candlelight and men and women, most in uniform, armed with rifles and crossbows.

"I'm looking—" the young soldier began, and he was motioned to the rear of the room, where he found a young woman with a semiautomatic rifle and long, curling blonde hair laughing over a mug of alcohol at a circular table with a trio of larger men, all officers.

"General Jak?"

"Not General," the woman said, and one of the officers laughed, finishing his drink.

"Keep getting younger, don't they?" the officer said, and as the young soldier offered a sealed dispatch to Jak, the officer said, "How old are you, kid?"

"Sixteen, sir."

"You want me to believe that? If you're sixteen, so am I. And your mother took you away from her tit long enough to give you a gun, eh? Help you liberate the city."

"Yes, sir."

"Damn right," the officer said, and Jak broke the paper's seal, quickly reading it, and then she offered it to the others. Jak stood, finished her drink, and faced the room, stomping her boot.

"Get your fingers out of each others' pants and listen," Jak shouted, and the room gradually quieted. The young soldier waited to be dismissed and was ignored. Jak said, "You all know how much food they store in this southern granary?"

"Enough to fatten even you up, Jak," one of the women called out, and Jak grinned slightly.

"According to all the lazy royals they had nursing at this storage bin last week, we should get enough for triple rations. You got that?" There was a general cheer, and everyone began to finish their drinks. "That means we need you guys to get your dicks back in your pants long enough that they don't get frozen or shot off, and, ladies, cross your legs while you're being shot at—this goes for you too, Rachel." Laughter, and Jak paced around the room, fidgeting with her rifle as she studied them. "You'll all get some when we're dancing on the bloody grain, got it? Just like we talked about, like we practiced. Nothing fancy, just out here, two blocks, and then three squads into the granary at once. Everybody know your squad." It wasn't a question; of course they knew.

Jak continued, "We're all going to die out there, but that's what this is about, isn't it? You don't join the army of liberation and glory and all that other crap so that you can die of old age, right? I want to see you diving into those bullets and reaching for those arrows so you can send a few of those other bastards to an early grave with you. Got that? We don't eat, they don't eat. But at least we get some."

They all banged wooden cups on the tables, and Jak slid her rifle into both hands. "Let's get rid of some of the mouths they're feeding. And double rations all around. Go! Match up by squad, let's go!"

The tables emptied with a lot of laughter and stomping, and one of the officers brushed past Jak as he exited. "You got some for me when this is done, Jak?"

"Not likely. Get your ass to your squad, let's go."

Outside, they congregated in the snow, shivering and tipsy, and one of the younger soldiers mumbled something about being frightened and sick as Jak passed him. She patted him on the shoulder.

"You'll do all right," she said. "Form up! Let's kick the shit out of them, know your squads!"

Two squads advanced through the snow on the deserted main street, and the third went through a back alley that ran parallel. The granary, already visible through the snow, looked like a giant wooden drum, and a handful of soldiers patrolled its base. Jak led her squad closer, jogging now, snow numbing her toes, the wind chapping her lips and biting into exposed cheeks and nose and ears.

Simultaneously on eight fronts, Jak thought. *Either we win this or we lose before it even begins.*

All five of the city granaries were located at the edges of town, just in front of the now-vacant farmers' fields and perimeter wall. *Probably no soldiers guarded that wall now,* Jak thought, and she steadied her rifle, falling to a crouch as they neared the granary. Rebel soldiers all around the city would be moving into position right now, just as she was, preparing to seize all five of Hope's granaries, along with the Southern Garr—a prison—and a giant chunk of the city in a protective ring around that Garr. The Garr was to become the new stronghold of the Army of Liberation and Justice or whatever the hell Rein and the other generals were calling themselves.

The police around the entrance of the granary hadn't spotted any of the squads yet. The police were barely recognizable splotches of man-shaped gray and blue in the continual snowfall. *And we probably look about the same,* Jak thought.

"Take them down!" she shouted into the wind, and gunfire cracked all around her—the third squad appeared between buildings on the opposite side of the granary, catching the few police soldiers in a crossfire, turning the man-shapes into motionless lumps in the snow.

"—atch for more!" someone shouted, stopping the soldiers in her squad from rushing right up to the granary's entrance. Squad two circled the granary, securing the rear, and Jak remained in position in the snow. *I didn't fire,* she thought. *Funny, I didn't even need to kill anyone.*

Another blob ran out of the granary—disappearing in a rush of snow—and pops of gunfire dropped him. *Can't fight in this,* Jak thought. *I can't even see in this.* She glanced at the houses on both sides of the street, most long since collapsed under the weight of a foot and a half of snow. Granted, here at the outskirts of the city—in one of the poorer districts—they weren't living in the sturdiest buildings, but Jak knew that the poor were not the only ones without homes now. It wasn't just the poor who were freezing, who were trying to find a way into the Garrs and government camps so that they could be near a fire with a stone or wooden roof over their heads.

Jak hadn't seen the government shelters herself—someone was staring out at her from the darkness of a collapsed house. White eyes vanished in heavy snowfall, and then appeared again, staring out of a makeshift tent built of splintered boards and snow-soaked wood. *Whoever it is will freeze in there,* Jak thought. Wind rocked the shacks and tossed wood debris through the snow on either side of the road, and the snow swam in deep drifts, toppling the flimsy roofing, burying the frozen dead.

How many people have already died? Jak wondered. Because the government didn't act quickly enough, didn't help these people stay warm. *No one expected this kind of snow, and no one's dealing with it,* she thought, *and maybe it's just as well that we burn the city down and start over. And that little prick, Vel, will just have to step down . . .* and she thought about how she had been the one to shoot Hillor with an arrow, and about how Vel had then taken his sword and swung for the throat, and—

"—ecure!"

Jak looked away from the eyes in the collapsed shack. The poor go first. *Food and water may not even be the most important things right now,* she thought. *How many are we going to have to kill to save this city?*

"Secure!" Jak echoed, and she thought, *Just like that, and we're at war.*

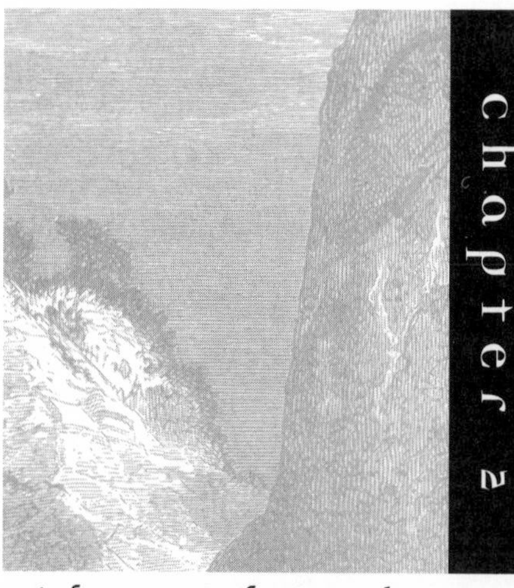

chapter 2

At the age of sixteen, William Blake sat at the rear of his dorm room—the same dorm room, with the same *Yankees* poster, now faded and coated lightly with dust, with different books—and William slipped pins very gently into the quivering hands of a rat. He was crucifying a rat to a board. Arms spread, feet attached side by side. At first, William had tried to spear the rat's feet on top of one another—just like the crucified Christ—but he had decided against it, when, after several tries, the rat had continued to pop its little feet out of the board, pin and all.

So now, he placed the last pin into the rat's left hand and watched it squirm and lay still and fight again and then pause and begin to scream quietly unlike anything William had ever heard. Like a little furry child with a tail. William took out his pocketknife—fourteenth-birthday present from nurse Martha—and began to slowly saw off the rat's tail, and it screamed louder. By now, William's hands and shirt and pants were specked with blood, and his lips were lined with dried brown flakes. He finished with the tail, and blood continued to flow from the stump.

William had kept the rat as a prisoner, not a pet, for just under a month, under his bed, until he had finally collected enough pins and a board thick enough and long enough to act as the little rodent's personal cross. Naturally, it wasn't a cross at all, just a plank, though William had debated on whether or not to carve it into one, thinking it might be amusing, and finally had decided against it as too time-consuming. He wiped the knife off on his shirt, listened to the rat scream some more, and picked up a black Bible from the floor nearby. William began to read verses from the Old Testament to the rat—Vinny—who didn't seem to care.

Several times, William stopped and frowned at Vinny. "Look, this is for your own benefit. You'll have to be quiet if you want me to keep reading."

And Vinny paused, his furry belly heaving in spasms.

"Thank you," William said, and he continued to read, " 'I waited patiently for the Lord; he inclined to me and heard my cry'."

At this, Vinny wailed again, and reluctantly, William shut the heavy book. "This is only as easy as you make it. Look," he continued to Vinny, "this hurts me as much as it hurts you. Now, let's go over it again. How old am I?" A pause, and Vinny remained strangely silent, as if waiting for the answer. Finally, he squeaked again.

"Sixteen? No, wrong. I'm three hundred and nineteen years old. Born in 1757, and now it's what—2076? The addition's right, isn't it, Vinny?"

Vinny screamed a 'yes'.

"Thought so. Granted, a good portion of that time I wasn't here, but I'm still that old, aren't I?"

By this point, sixteen-year-old William Blake had learned enough to know that Sunaki-Heiman's employees did not all—as Tom had once assured him—work for Sunaki-Heiman for life. In fact, as far as William knew, he was the only example of such an employee. Technically, the corporation did not *own* William, but in reality, he was their property, and had been since his existence had been created at their whim.

They still kept the network limited, they continued to censor information from the outside world, but he had learned not to fight with them; had learned that if he led them to believe that he was happy at Sunaki-Heiman they would tell him more. For years William had overheard talk of a war in a place called India, and there was always the whispered talk of the reds—the Chinese—and how the Euro-American government must have been bought off, because now was the time to retake Hawaii, to make the reds pay for the West Coast.

"Just as God owns the oceans," William had once said to himself before masturbating and falling asleep. He had gone to private classes, learned limited mathematics, limited literature, limited history, all from Martha, his physician and teacher and pseudo-surrogate mother. No contact with other children or people. Other people, apart from Martha and a handful of others at Sunaki-Heiman, existed only as flashes of cameras and pictures and videos and the people he met when Sunaki-Heiman took him "on tour." To advertise.

William Blake drives a Sunaki-Heiman, even William Blake's computers are made by Sunaki-Heiman, and William Blake—yes, *that* William Blake—trusts Sunaki-Heiman international banks. Just as Napoleon was used by Boeing to promote their stock, William was used by Sunaki-Heiman to buy public trust. Blake was a visionary, and this new Blake, if *he* sees that Sunaki-Heiman is a reliable bank, a safe investment, and a manufacturer of cutting-edge electronic and genetic technology, then the ordinary person must see that as well. Historical legends—real people—were used as sound bites. If Abraham Lincoln trusts Morgans Industries, shouldn't you?

William never knew exactly who saw the advertisements, but he had noticed a change in the flight patterns. The regular trips to Jerusalem had stopped several years ago, and when William had asked Martha why, she had said the city wasn't safe anymore—but no one would tell him anything more. Recently, in the past few months, many of the flights—the frantic rush from one city to another that William had grown up with—had begun to stop altogether. Why? "Economic recession," Martha had said, her eyes much older and sadder than they had been when William was growing up.

In the sixties William had grown up with a sense that the world was somehow coming together. He had known nothing about the world outside his dorm room, but in bits of overheard conversations of guards who thought he was asleep, William had learned that somehow things were improving in the face of the Chinese threat in the sixties. The place called India had changed all of that, and now whenever they talked, the workers argued. Was that fear William heard in their voices? Fear of what? India? The reds in China?

And in the course of growing older, William had learned not to stab the guards with sharpened toothbrushes, deciding instead to pick the wings off of flies and slowly dissect whatever unfortunate creatures happened to wander into his dorm looking for food. For a while there had been a guard named Fred who put William on the bed, made him drop his pants, and grunted into William's ass. But Fred wasn't at Sunaki-Heiman anymore.

William had gone at least two years without thinking about Martha or other women—or even most other people for that matter—except as abstract concepts. Even when he met Martha for lessons, it was not her. It was the idea of Martha, and masturbating each night was not related to the idea of sex or women or men or Fred, but actually it was more closely linked to the only other sensations that he cared about. And those involved live dissection and crucifixion and torture.

After sixteen years of living in the same room, it had changed very little—William had done nothing since his twelfth birthday to alter its appearance—and apart from tiny differences in clutter, such as different books filling the floor and small stains under his bed and around the corners of the room, the dorm room looked exactly as it had when he had slashed Tom roughly five years ago, in 2071. Because William had decided then that he did not intend to stay at Sunaki-Heiman for the duration of his life as created by the Sunaki-Heiman Corporation.

Instead, three days after William finished killing Vinny, all of the power in the building went out, and the emergency backup systems miraculously failed. A handful of locks were released, while every other one was frozen shut. William walked out of his room with a bag of books and knives, down a perfectly dark hallway, past a door where guards were banging from within—because Wednesday night was football night, and it being a Wednesday they had all gathered inside to watch, and were now sealed within with a dormant, wireless monitor. William walked through a set of doors, normally locked, and then another, and down another hall, where someone rushed frantically past him. He entered a lobby, down another hall—this one with potted plants and black screens on the walls—and into *another* lobby, and he found another door conveniently unlocked, located a safe under a desk and twisted a combination, leaving the office with just over fifty thousand euro-dollars in his bag. Then outside.

It was dark and chilly, and William approached a solitary taxi. Twenty-two minutes later power returned to the building, and the glitches that had paralyzed one of the twenty-first century's most powerful corporations were solved. Fourteen hours later, everything had been analyzed and settled by rooms full of men and women in important suits, but by this time one of their most controversial investments was gone. Codes that Blake could not have known had been used, access that Blake did not have had been exerted, and so it was decided that what had happened could not have happened—it was impossible—and thus, it did not happen. The vice president of the corporation resigned—"If Blake can do that, so can I"—and, though a search did continue, the Primary was gone. And Sunaki-Heiman moved on.

WUNIC SAID, "Has the king heard the most recent reports?"

Lord Denon sat back in his chair and stared across the conference table at Wunic. "For the moment, I have been authorized to speak for His Majesty. What do the most recent dispatches say?"

Wunic frowned. "Lord Denon, I can't give the dispatches to you—the king is not a member of the Church."

"Yes, I am aware of that, General. But as you may have discovered, Vel won't speak to everyone. He's asked specifically not to speak with members of the military. He *will* see me," Denon said. "Now, what are the numbers?"

Wunic stood behind the last chair, a small stack of papers in his hands. "I tried to see him earlier today . . ."

"This is a difficult time," Denon said.

Wunic said, "These dispatches—all of the information in them—are intended for the king."

"Yes," Denon said. "General, I understand that you are new to palace politics. . . . But sometimes we make allowances for inconveniences." Wunic stiffened and Denon continued, "So let me make this easier for you. Very simply, technicalities must sometimes be overlooked. For example, if the King has locked himself in his room and will speak with only one of his advisors for the time being—with his spiritual advisor—and if there is information that it is vital the King had access to . . ." Denon shrugged, as if this was perfectly obvious. "Well then," he finished, "you make do with what you have. You tell me, I'll tell the boy."

Wunic glanced around the empty conference room uncomfortably, as if he wished he had brought a team of soldiers with him. "Lord Denon—"

"It's the way things are done, General. There's a war on, we're in the middle of a crisis, and we make do with what we have. Now, I've never personally been in combat, but I would imagine battlefield situations don't always allow for the most convenient circumstances."

"No," Wunic said. "But, this isn't a battlefield."

Denon smiled and didn't respond.

Wunic continued, "I just need to see that the king receives dispatches. How do I go about that if he won't admit runners?"

"Tell me what they say or try to give them to His Majesty yourself," Denon said, as if it made no difference either way. "For security reasons, very few people are being admitted to the second floor of the palace, and even those who are admitted—well, he won't see many people, will he? You could deliver them to one of Vel's personal guard, though I might advise against that."

"Why?"

"Documents are known to disappear remarkably easily as they pass through more hands in wartime. Seals don't always stay intact, for instance, and in situations like ours—with mass defections—you don't always have to take up arms for the enemy to assist him."

"And what does that mean?" Wunic asked. "You're implying that—what?—Vel's personal guard will leak information? Will *spy* for the rebels? Those are some of the most elite troops we have, Lord Denon."

Denon was quiet for a long moment and then he said slowly, "We're not children, General. And if I'm not mistaken, General Rein was considered among the elite. There's no need to play at false naïveté. This is an uprising, after all, and none of the soldiers stationed here eats as well as you or I. Now, if you'd like, you can tell me whatever Vel needs to know and I'll see that he receives that information. But I won't deliver it and I won't write it down."

"And your interests are the same as his?"

Denon was insulted by the implication. "I am the leader of the Church of Hope, a member of the Executive Council, and the reason that boy is king now. I brought him here. I helped him when no one else would. I am more loyal to that boy than any of the soldiers you might hand the dispatches to.

"And I think you already knew all of that, didn't you? My interests are the same as yours, are the same as his. Why wouldn't they be? I want to win this war, I want life to return to normal. General, I want to go back to my Church without worrying about whether or not my congregation and Religious Guard are getting enough to eat or whether their homes have collapsed in the snow. We want the same things, and I think you know that. It will be much easier—much quicker and more effective—if we work together on this. You're new at politics; that's no secret, and there's nothing wrong with that—and I know next to nothing about the details of fighting a civil war in endless snowfall . . ."

Wunic said, "No one does."

"You see?" Denon said, and he folded his hands calmly. "Then maybe we need each other even more. Let's work together on this, General. They're your men out there, but this is still the Lord's army."

Wunic nodded. "All right. Until I can speak with the king himself, you'll see that this information is passed on to His Majesty?"

"Of course," Denon said. "Now, I think first the king might want to know what kind of casualties the rebels have been taking."

"In the past week I have sixteen confirmed, another fifty unaccounted for."

"Unaccounted for?"

"That means," Wunic said patiently, "my men have stripped sixteen carcasses and reported killing or wounding another fifty enemy soldiers."

"What about our losses?"

Wunic checked his papers. "Four dead. Another twelve wounded. Of those twelve, five are in critical condition and are not expected to recover. My boys have gained seven blocks, in formation around the Southern Garr. Intelligence from the northwest sections indicate that the rebels may have pulled as many as three hundred units from that area into the Garr itself."

"What are they going to do?" Denon asked.

"Probably try to fortify the position," Wunic sighed. "They've taken some of the food supplies, and they have no civilian mouths to feed—they may try to wait us out."

"Can they?"

Wunic hesitated. "No, I don't think they can. They're holding two granaries to our three, but in the near future my boys will cut their supply lines and retake those positions."

Denon thought about it, and then shook his head, confused. "Why would the rebels do that?"

"Box themselves in?"

"Yes. If we're just going to isolate their units—why wouldn't they anticipate that move?"

Wunic put his hands behind his back and thought about whether or not to explain it in detail. He said, "The short answer is they're running out of options. I have more men, more guns, and more rations than they do. My men are going to win out there, and I think the rebels know that; it's possible that they're hoping we'll try to take the Garr by force, which would be like trying to dig the entire city out in a single day."

"You mean it can't be done?"

"That's right," Wunic said. "So, as long as I'm patient, the uprising's already effectively been put down."

Denon tapped his thumbs together. "Could you do it with the artillery? Could you take the Garr?"

Wunic tensed. Along with all of the rifles and pistols and books and swastikas and pictures of skeleton-people with numbers inscribed on their arms that had been found in the ancient storage room beneath the Church, they had discovered several huge crates full of complex tubing and gears that had been labelled ARTILLERY. All of it buried in the genesis of the city of Hope, presumably by the prophet Blakes and his companions who had landed from Merica-Urope five hundred years ago, in the days before Hope had fallen to the use of arrows and swords crafted from the metal of the southern forests.

And Vel had discovered that storage facility and learned the code to enter from a box that contained an information system that could speak through wires—once they were allowed to soak Vel's and only Vel's blood—and this system claimed to be Blakes threatening Vel with death should he reveal that; Blakes, the founder of Hope. Blakes had been the first king of Hope, passing his line on to his descendants, and gradually the Executive Council had formed around the king, limiting Blakes's descendants' power to a mere veto position, so that now two-thirds of the thirty were needed to overrule the king's veto.

Meaning that when the king—Vel, Blakes's last descendant—vetoed something on the Executive Council, whatever he vetoed usually died. Two-thirds of the thirty never agreed. But now, there were twenty-seven, and new elections had not been held to replace the three traitors; and districts full of empty, ruined houses and snow couldn't easily elect new representatives, could they? The rebels controlled a portion of those districts, further complicating matters.

Just what the artillery would be capable of when it was finally assembled, according to the illustrations and ancient text, was not yet known. Wunic had a handful of soldiers working to put it together but as they were working from archaic, terribly complex and detailed pictoral diagrams, there was no guarantee the artillery would be reassembled before the war was over. *And even if the artillery is assembled,* Wunic thought, *the instructions only hinted vaguely at what the weapons might be capable of, assuming that the user was as familiar with the machinery as the maker had been.*

"I think the artillery should be thought of as an experimental tool," Wunic said. "At the earliest, it will probably be weeks before my men have put it together and even longer by the time they've sorted out exactly what it does."

"I'm sorry," Denon said, "I'm sure you're more familiar with this than I am, but I thought we knew what the artillery was used for by the pictures on the storage crates."

"It's never as simple as that. Yes, we think it's a weapon, designed along the same principles as a kind of gun—a very large gun. But we don't actually understand what makes the guns themselves work." He forced an uneasy smile. "I'm considering every option, but the artillery should be thought of as just that: another option. In the long run, I doubt seriously that I will need to even consider using it."

"Thank you for explaining that to me, General."

"Sure." Wunic skimmed the rest of his papers quickly and said, "I think that's all the pertinent information this time."

"I'll see that the king receives it just as I did."

Wunic nodded, appearing more relaxed with the idea of trusting Denon—at least this way the king would be kept informed, and yes, Denon was the Church leader, not a soldier. *Of all the people in the palace,* Wunic thought, *he probably has the least sympathy for a band of rioting military officers.*

"Oh, I apologize," Denon said as Wunic was leaving. "There was one thing I forgot to mention that the king had asked about . . ."

"Yes?"

"How is our morale?"

"My soldiers?" Wunic asked.

"Yes. The ones in the field. You know, the ones most likely to cause a problem if they—if their sympathies change?"

Wunic said, "Morale could always be better, but we have been winning. His Majesty should know that I still command the large majority of soldiers, and they are all loyal to his rule."

"Yes," Denon said, and he hesitated, as if he didn't want to press the issue. "His Majesty *had* asked for specific numbers. . . . I know that might be difficult, but—"

"I'll see that they're taken tonight," Wunic said.

"I'll let Vel know," Denon said. "Thank you. Oh, and you know I mentioned this to you earlier, but I think it's in all of our best interests if we can find a way—we have to heal the boy mentally."

"Yes," Wunic said, though it was obvious he wasn't sure what that might involve.

"The king can't stay in his room indefinitely," Denon said. "After all, I don't want to always act as his courier, and I'm sure it would make things easier for all of us if he met with you on a regular basis."

"I understand his family is all dead," Wunic said.

"Unfortunately, yes. Would it be asking too much—perhaps we could work together on this: Obviously, the war might be easier to manage if the king would personally approve your actions without a middleman. And you said yourself that this war won't last forever. When it's over, we'll need his help—his direct help—to rebuild the city."

"What do you suggest?"

"A girl," Denon said quietly. "We—or someone else—should find him a girl, a distraction. Not a distraction from his job or the government obviously, but from himself. I care for Vel, as I'm sure you do, General, and more importantly, this city needs him. Without something—someone who can—and I'm sure you understand me on this, General—who can *relax* him . . . General, Vel may already be suicidal. From my contact with him, and I think I know him better than anyone else for the time being, the king may soon become a danger to himself and to others. Now he doesn't trust you, General, but he will. This is just a difficult time for him right now."

Wunic nodded. "I understand."

"Then we'll work together on this?"

"Absolutely."

"Good." Denon shook Wunic's hand and said, "Welcome to the Executive Council, General Wunic. The boy doesn't believe in you, but I do—and it's very reassuring to me that you're the man in charge of this war."

"Thank you, Lord Denon."

"In some ways," Denon said, "you and I may be all that's keeping Hope together."

chapter 3

Lord Denon stepped past a pair of police soldiers—both held rifles—into the royal bedroom. The bed was large with red and gold tassels, like a giant, plush pillow. A mirror with swastikas in its frame hung on one wall, and Vel sat on the side of the bed staring at his reflection, ignoring Denon.

"How are you?" Denon asked.

Vel wore black pants and an open red and gold robe, and in one hand he held the withered, dead stalk of a plant. His pistol and sword sat on the bedside table, and his coat—the dead Justice Hillor's coat—was draped across a chair in the far corner.

"What do you want, Denon?" Vel said softly.

Lord Denon pulled the only chair in the room away from the mirror, neatly arranged the coat on another table, and sat beside the bed. There were scratches on Vel's chest, and deep swollen lumps under his eyes.

"Our forces have secured most of the area around the Southern Garr," Denon said.

Vel stared at him, ribs visible with each breath. "And?"

"And when we have the artillery we'll begin an assault. It should be operational within the week."

Sweat collected on Vel's forehead, and he wiped it away with the back of his hand. "What are we doing with the homeless, with refugees?"

"People who have lost their homes are free to join the military."

"What about children?"

"There are shelters."

"The Garrs, you mean."

Denon said, "You act as if that's a bad thing. We're using the prisons as shelters—that should mean something. And there are other camps being set up, of course, but I've spoken with General

Wunic and most of the city's resources are needed to fight the rebels. A draft would solve—"

"We're not drafting everyone," Vel said. "What about the Pox?"

"We have more immediate concerns."

"So no one's been sent to the ruins or the tunnels—the Frill tunnels still connect in the cemetery, don't they? It's still possible to follow that hole in the cemetery all the way to the tunnels under the ruins, isn't it?"

"Yes, Vel. And the hole is being guarded by a detachment of soldiers."

"I saw food there; maybe enough for everyone. This came from the Frill." Vel held up the brown vine. "If I had known it would die, I wouldn't have used . . ."

"Of course, Vel. No one blames you."

"So we have to find more. We have to go see if the Frill have more of these plants."

"Soldiers are needed at the front, against the rebels. Please try to put this in perspective. We don't have men to spare to send to the ruins right now."

Vel paused, watching himself in the mirror, a skinny, frightened kid. Barely sixteen. *Why does it all have to happen at the same time?* he thought. *All of my friends and my family are dead, and I don't have the power to do anything but watch more people suffer. Except that I can't even see them—and I don't want to—and so I hear about them fourth-hand.*

"Why did I kill those three people last week?"

"The council members? They were traitors, Vel. You saw the dispatches—they were providing intelligence for Rein. Bribing our soldiers."

"Yes," Vel said, "but what does it change if we're going to have the artillery later this week? Why couldn't we just lock them up?"

"They were an example."

"And the war still started. *On the same day.*" Vel frowned at him. "Why did we do that, Lord Denon? I didn't stop the war."

"You tried."

"I don't know," Vel said, and he closed his eyes. "You're right. I'm sorry, I'm just not thinking right now. I'm tired."

Denon remained quiet for a while, and then he opened his mouth, paused, and finally said, "The computer system."

"What about it?"

"There could be something there we don't know. You found the storage facility through it—it led you to the sacred artifacts—maybe there's something else. You can access it, Vel. No one else can—that gives us an advantage."

Blakes, Vel thought. *Do you want to talk to me again*? And he remembered the wire sucking his blood, and the sharp flash of pain, and the disembodied voice. Not really a voice though, just a presence, and Vel remembered talking to him. The living computer system inside the small metal box believed that it was Blakes, the founder of the city of Hope—and Vel had understood only a fraction of what it told him. *I don't want to talk to him again*, Vel thought, but he said nothing.

Denon leaned closer to Vel. "Give up, and all the people who have died won't have meant anything. Under God's law, to remain passive in the face of the dead is to do violence against them, as if you'd killed them yourself."

Vel smiled as he thought of Lydia and Ponce. And his parents. He said quietly, "Don't tell me what their deaths meant, all right?"

"Talk to the system again, Vel. Please."

"It's supposed to be infected with the Pox," Vel said, more to himself than to Denon. "Will it give it to me if I've already been cured?"

"Hook into it again," Denon said.

Vel grabbed the pistol from the side table. "Stop it. Stop telling me what to do." Vel clicked off the safety and looked calmly at Denon, one eye twitching shut. "You advise me. You counsel me, because I have no idea what the hell I'm doing here. I want your help. But stop telling me what I have to do, all right?" Vel laughed uneasily. "Goddamn it. I'm sorry, I didn't . . ."

Lord Denon nodded, and Vel pushed the safety on again, and he set the pistol back onto the table.

"They all admire you, Vel," Denon said quietly. "They all want nothing more than to follow you." Vel did not respond, rolling onto his back, arms at his sides. "Life is worth the pain we put into it."

"What does that mean?"

"It means that when you've lost you keep fighting. This isn't like anything you've done before. This time you'll win—this *will* work out."

Vel put one arm across his face. "What if I lose?"

"You won't."

"Maybe *you* won't." And Vel thought, *Maybe I already have.*

Maybe I should stop whining and end this. He thought about the pistol. *Is that too easy? That's not what Lydia would tell me to do, but where did her advice lead her? I can't save this city.*

Vel said, "What does it mean that I'm half-Frill?"

"Hillor made a deal with the Frill, I told you that. You were created to be king so that Hillor could manipulate you—he believed that the Frill might attack the city, but that if you were king—and half-Frill—they would keep their distance."

"*Why?*" Vel asked, not for the first time.

"Why would they stay away?"

"Yes."

"Presumably, they might respect a king who is connected to them. But I'm not sure. The two groups of Frill have prophecies, and you know that only part of the Frill population is opposed to our presence."

"Yes," Vel said weakly. "But why the elaborate experiment? Why did Hillor think they might attack?"

"I don't know, Vel. Talk to the computer system."

And we're back where we started, Vel thought. *But Denon doesn't know all of the answers or he would tell me—but how did he know the code to the storage facility under the Church cathedral?* Vel had never asked about that. After everything, after Vel had finally discovered the four-digit code to open the vault, Denon had allowed Vel to succeed, and Denon had stepped ahead of him before Vel could give him the solution, and *Denon had entered the code.* 1321. Lord Denon, the leader of the Church of Hope, had known.

"You look tired," Denon said.

"Thanks."

Denon started blowing out the candles. "Get some rest, Vel."

"I've tried that."

"Then talk to the system. I'll let you know when the situation changes. You have to sleep."

"Thanks for pointing that out," Vel said.

Denon put his hand on Vel's shoulder. "You're right, the system might be a waste of time. But it's something we haven't tried."

Food, Vel thought, *the Pox, and half of the city is at war.* "I'm going to try to get some sleep."

"Good," Denon said, and Vel watched him leave. *Talk to Blakes,* Vel thought. *Why am I afraid of him? Because he said he could kill me at any time? No—because I know he stored those weapons and he framed that picture of starving, naked people, with numbers on their arms, and he's still alive. I'm afraid because I might be like him,* Vel realized. *I've killed people too, shot them and stabbed them, and I'm the last in his line.*

Vel rolled onto his side, watching the black outline of his sword and gun. "I'm not scared of you," he said. "Come and get me." And in another moment, he was asleep.

TWENTY YEARS old now, and William Blake lay awake reading to the light of a flickering halogen bulb in a small cot, beside a sleeping girl with long blonde hair. Adria was in college. She had a red swastika with a snake curled around it tattooed on the back of her right shoulder, and on her left shoulder was a poorly drawn tattoo of a round, metal helmet with flames licking at the bottom—Blake finished one book and started another. Outside sirens passed, perfectly common in New York. Blake glanced at Adria's bare, pale back and continued reading.

As he read, Blake's mind wandered, until he found himself watching Adria's skin. He closed the pages of *Liberation in Our Times*—written by Li Yen, the twenty-first century Laotian guerrilla leader—and set it beside the book he had just finished, a revised translation of *Mein Kampf.* Blake slid the covers from Adria's back, down her legs, and then he carefully took off his boxer shorts, moved on top of her, and had sex with her. When it ended, Adria, barely conscious, mumbled something that might have been a dream conversation—she had class the following morning at ten—and continued to sleep.

The next day, Blake read about himself in the paper—he was mentioned in an editorial buried deep within the *Times*, but yes, he was still making the news. Sitting on the steps of a museum, drinking coffee from a brown plastic foam cup, Blake thought about the years immediately after escaping. Of complaints from people in the Rockies that West Coast radiation was causing cancer in Denver, and the headlines in the newspapers he had stolen before bribing his way onto a freighter bound for Mexico. Chinese presence in the Pacific, the Russian Duma calling for an end to some kind of Chinese tariff—"Homelessness on the Rise in America: A Look at the Depression"—and there, at the bottom of the second page had been a story about Blake's escape from Sunaki-Heiman. The only picture had depicted the Sunaki-Heiman headquarters, somewhere in Asia.

And somehow, Blake could still remember those headlines. *Because they are the same,* he thought, as he read the current paper. Terrorist attack in the Democratic Republic of West India, missiles targeting the center of Pakistan; eighteen dead in car bombing in Jerusalem, Israeli troops kill Palestinian protesters; the price of oil and the Energy Crisis; the current record temperatures that have brought triple digit deaths to poor neighborhoods in the South. *Where are there are no air conditioners,* Blake thought, and he sipped his coffee. *Summer is hell. The CEO of the Rogers Institute turns 136 and is still in "great health"; and they're dying of homicide with a life expectancy of 31 in the ghettos,* Blake thought. *In the same Euro-American federation, in the same country.*

Blake had learned what they wouldn't teach him at Sunaki-Heiman. Most people didn't care about history, he had discovered, but because they had told him not to care—*maybe because they told me I shouldn't care as a child—I* do. He had learned about the nineteenth and twentieth centuries, and the early twenty-first and the Third World War that had left the West Coast of the United States barren, along with giant patches of continental China. World War III had lasted from 2010 to 2013: at its most basic level Japan, Europe and the United States had fought Russia and China. After about nine years of "phony" warfare in the Middle East—from 2001 to 2010—the United States had withdrawn when, in February of 2010, China had invaded Taiwan and WW III had begun.

The war had cost more than sixty million lives, had eradicated Los Angeles, San Francisco, Seattle, Beijing and a number of other Chinese cities, and had ended with the Chinese possession of Hawaii: the United States had been crippled and forced from the Pacific. Japan had become the eastern Switzerland—as it still was—and had claimed neutrality in the future.

The crowd on the New York street wore hats, and many were carrying umbrellas. Businessmen and women between meetings and lunches, a woman in a shawl, a crowd of Asian tourists, and always the honking traffic that stank of airborne toxins. Blake glared at the sidewalk. *It should be white,* he thought, examining the tar-streaked smears and cracks. *Everything in this city is dirty.* Lots of bicyclists weaved in between the dangerous cars and buses, and everyone wore dark, heavy clothing. *Terrible in this heat,* Blake thought, feeling the drops of sweat on his forehead, along his hairline, *but better than cancer.* Some of the crowd wore white and blue face masks, like surgeons—shielding their lungs from the heat and again, more cancer.

Immediately following the Third World War, China had attacked Russia as vengeance for her separate peace with the West: China smashed Russian defenses and throughout the twenties and thirties took over much of the former Soviet Union in Asia. The world had remained in a virtual deadlock since the war, with the West continually falling farther and farther behind the East. In 2055 the Euro-American Parliament had come to replace the United States and individual European governments on every foreign policy matter. In 2058 Canada was admitted, and in 2062 Russia was brought into the larger government, all in an attempt to curb Chinese power through Asia. It hadn't worked.

The Indian civil war of the seventies had been the last great time: everything that was supposed to change with the cultural revolutions of the forties, fifties, and sixties was symbolically represented in the American, European, Russian and Israeli poets who fought for India against the reds. India was the place to win back the dominance of the West and to annihilate the East in another great war. It was to be the last battleground, the fight for the soul of the next century—except that neither side had won.

The Euro-American Parliament had backed democratic India; China had supported a more totalitarian regime, and in 2079, three years after the crash of '76—after eight years of warfare—India had come apart. Western India remained autonomous and democratic, while the east had become an outlying territory of the ever-expanding Chinese empire. Even with the combined strength of Europe, Russia and the Americas, the Chinese Empire and her satellites continued to outproduce the west three times over, and while '76 had crushed Western economic interests, the East had remained relatively unscathed.

As oil became more and more scarce, the East-West competition in the Middle East had turned into continual open warfare for the last twenty years in and around Israel. The successful corporate states of the West in the fifties, sixties, and early seventies had not changed their tactics after '76, and as more of the western population fell into poverty, the continual flow of advertisements and promises of "the good life" had created a wider class gap, open resentment and riots.

This was a world of genetic manipulation, animal computers and gene therapies capable of curing virtually every disease that had ever existed: all available to the top 5 percent of society. *So that the expected lifespan varies by one hundred years,* William thought, *in the same country, from block to block.* We are a generation that has grown up with the scars of our parents and grandparents. The last generations built the concrete ghettos of Eastern Europe and the American South—the housing projects of the 2020s and 2030s—and the world our parents tried to build in the forties, fifties, and sixties—all the way to 2076—never came. The West never rose again.

Except that I don't have any parents, William thought. *My parents are science, perversion and arrogance.* The West was once the guardian of the world, and into the sixties and early seventies the West was on the path to once more become a dominant force. *The creation of the Euro-American Parliament was supposed to stop the East, it was supposed to put us on top again, and now that I'm old enough to understand what's happened,* Blake thought, *it looks like nothing's changed. Except that we've stopped hoping for a better world because that's what our parents did.* Every day, newspapers ran stories of Chinese spies, Chinese troop movements, Arab-backed terrorists. *The constant propaganda,* William thought, *the constant voice that says, "War is coming, war is coming and this time it will be different, this time it won't go away and we will win."*

Except that it won't be different, William thought. *They'll lose again, because it isn't the West or the East that's wrong, it's* all of it. *The whole Goddamn thing.* The melting glaciers, the Dutch cities that are running out of places to hide from high tide. The sin of science and arrogance, and the masses of poor and impoverished have no voice in a world that cannot remember the last time the proletariat tried to rise. *Communism in the twenty-first century has nothing to do with philosophy or a "leveling of the wealth,"* William thought, *it has to do with* the other. *Because the red are the enemy, and it isn't even communism or culture or weapons or economics or population: None of those things are the problem. It's just people.*

This is wrong, Blake thought again, and he remembered the dreams. Of horses in a city where the air was dirty, yes, but not like this. Not soaked, saturated in filth. Blake watched the people pass, looking into their eyes—they all looked away, instinctively staring at the ground or pretending to be so preoccupied that they didn't notice his gaze. And in his dreams, Blake remembered another time when people had communicated, when they had stopped in the street to exchange pleasantries, because yes, there were places to go and progress to achieve, but things were not fast enough to make basic communication impossible. *I saw that, because I lived it*, he thought. *This is white noise*, Blake thought. *Nothing but noise.*

The white noise people have created is so overwhelming that you cannot hear yourself think, you cannot question because the chatter is so complete. The man who sold William his morning newspaper always asked, "Is today the day, do you think?" And William always smiled and shook his head. "Not yet."

Is today the day? The next time it will be Armageddon; that's what they all think, because there are so many different kinds of bombs, so many different ways to die that if another World War breaks out it *must* annihilate the world. *But it won't*, William thought miserably. *It could, but it won't. They could have fixed this human sickness in 2010, but they didn't.*

The people here in the West either worked in menial jobs in retail, worked within the larger infrastructure of corporations and government or went unemployed. Nothing was really produced in the West, all labor had long since been shipped to Africa and Central or South America. An enormous percentage of the population lived day-to-day in concrete shitholes without jobs, on government and corporate droppings that were just enough to keep them alive into their thirties or forties, without medical care or dreams. *We are provided bread, but few circuses*, William thought.

He flipped through the paper, irritated. Something very bad will happen, won't it? Because more people are going hungry here, more people have less, and so much damage has been done to parts of the world that a solution seems hopeless in our lifetimes. "South African Population Falls Below Historical Record"; "Twenty-seven Children Found Starved in Meat Locker in South Carolina."

So there will be a war, but it won't be the right kind. People know this is wrong, they sense it and their instincts tell them that world is rotted beyond repair, but they are powerless. *And* this, Blake thought, frowning at the masses of people in the street, *this crowd of mindless obedience, of ignorance—it won't go away. It will probably succeed, because it's so Goddamn* productive *to exploit and to rape the world and all of its people.* "Suicide Rates Highest in History Throughout U.S. Cities." Blake closed his fist around one of the pages.

People must be wiped away to fix it. It needs to start again, Blake thought. *That's been tried, hasn't it?* He thought of his books. I'm not the first to see this—and it's never worked. Because when people become cattle and cease to think and care, the simple fact is that they *can* accomplish more; by herding humanity together a great output can be reached. And that's what has to be stopped. And it can be, because now we have things like bombs and viruses that can wipe it all away. God's will, Blake thought, and he remembered the Angel in his room at Sunaki-Heiman. The Angel had reappeared over the years, always watching at the corner of his vision, so that when Blake turned he was gone.

Is today the day, do you think?

I was chosen for this, Blake thought, not for the first time. *And I know who I was in that city with horses, in London, because I read a newspaper in Boston.* "Clone of William Blake . . . by crushing the bones, enough DNA is . . . positive sign for science's progress . . ." And there it was. Everything Blake hated in those words, everything that had turned the world into smears of tar and jungles burning away into deserts. Ice melting and weapons incinerating cities and people without reason—science's progress was responsible. God's will had been perverted into an excuse to accomplish the most arrogant atrocities. *Like bringing me back*, Blake thought. He smiled. *They'll wish they hadn't. Today I know who I am, today it begins. Yes, today is the day.*

"William?"

He looked up, Adria stood over him in a black coat and hat, her lips a bright red, hair in a blonde ponytail. She was pretty, but overly thin, as if her body had somehow been stretched.

"I need friends," he said simply.

Adria grinned crooked, white teeth. "Have friends already." She motioned him to get up and walk with her to the subway. He didn't move.

"I need more."

"All right, we'll get you more." She took his hand and leaned close to lick his earlobe. "*I'm* your friend, William Blake."

"That's not my name," he said quietly, and then he stood to go with her. "Just *Blakes.*"

"Not Blake anymore either, huh? You want to be more than one?"

"I *am* more than one." He smiled at her. "I'm Blakes."

Snow spilled across black stone as Wunic stepped into the cathedral. Wind tossed snow through the entrance behind him, and Wunic shut the doors, brushing himself off. His cheeks were flushed, and the snow in his hair melted as he moved further into the great arching room of dark stone. Two rows of wooden pews flanked a central aisle that led to the altar and an inscribed blue circle on the floor. Candles burned on the altar in ornate holders, and more candle stands flickered around the walls, their stalks decorated with swastikas and some kind of creature with a beak.

Men in white uniforms, with swastika armbands—the Religious Guard, the Church's personal military priests—were stationed between some of the candles, watching Wunic, their hands on swords, crossbows, and *yes,* Wunic thought, *even they have guns now too. Guns that should be at the front, where they are needed.*

Wunic went to the altar, giant swastika tapestries coming into view, hanging from the higher nave and ceiling ahead, and there—cut into the stone wall behind the altar—was a balcony with three chairs, situated to overlook the entire cathedral. Below the balcony were three doors, all protected by more of the Religious Guard. Impossible to discern any forms on that balcony apart from the chairs, impossible to tell if anyone was up there.

Wunic heard someone cough behind him as he neared the altar, and he glanced back, noticing two worshippers in one of the last pews—he hadn't seen them. Wunic avoided the blue circle and opened the middle door. He mounted curling stone steps, arrived at another door, and knocked.

"Thank you for coming. Please enter and be seated."

Wunic stepped onto the darkened balcony, behind the three chairs—Lord Denon already sat in the middle—and so Wunic picked the chair on his left.

"Morale," Wunic said, and he unfolded a sheet of paper, a dispatch. "I thought the king would want to know as soon as possible, so I ran the routine test on the majority of forces garrisoned in the palace and the Northern and Western Garrs."

"The troops at the front could not be included?"

Wunic hesitated. "No. I know the king was interested in their numbers, but the situation has changed."

Denon straightened. "Something's happened?"

"Yes," Wunic said. "And I have a feeling once I start on that, we may forget about the morale . . ."

"Please start with whatever you want, General."

"So," Wunic said. "Morale first. These aren't official numbers . . ." He read: "Positive attitude toward the leadership, fifteen percent. Doubtful attitude toward the leadership," he glanced at Lord Denon, but the priest's expression did not change, "sixty-five percent. Negative attitude toward the leadership, five percent. Actively opposed, five percent. Indifferent, ten percent."

For a time, neither of them spoke. Lord Denon watched the couple in the rear pews below.

"Well," Denon said at last, "I hope the situation at the front is more positive."

Wunic lowered his voice. "For the time being, my men have lost ground. Three hundred rebel units retreated and as my boys cut their lines, the rebels helped reinforce a counteroffensive."

"How bad is it?"

"This is temporary," Wunic said. "I'm confident I'll retake the positions, and this may actually help us in the long run—as it cost the rebels significant casualties in the offensives. That alone should make up for the territory lost."

"Territory was lost?"

"Ten blocks, Although I have conflicting reports. My boys are fortifying their positions, requesting immediate assistance, and I've handled it. The king should know this will probably work to our advantage once the situation has stabilized."

"You issued reinforcements?"

"Units from the Northern and Western Garrs have been moved in to reinforce the front."

Denon leaned back in his chair. "Will that be enough?"

"Yes, it should be—I want to stop the rebel advances on every front, but honestly, at this point—and I think it's important that His

Majesty understand this—defending is much easier than attacking.

"We *want* the rebels to continue this maneuver: for every unit we lose, the enemy is taking two, three, maybe even four times as many casualties—and the bottom line—they can't afford to lose what they're losing; we can." Denon remained silent, and Wunic said, "It's a matter of numbers, honestly—I have more men."

"The king has more men."

"Yes."

Denon thought about it and then he said, "I'm sure you've probably already taken this into account, General, but if what you're saying is accurate, why not move in more? What's the count on both sides right now?"

Wunic looked through more dispatches. "I estimate enemy strength at approximately two thousand soldiers. My count—the king's army—is actually less definite until things settle down. With the reinforcements, I could have as many as five thousand units at the front."

"I'm sorry, General, is that an upper or lower bound?"

"That would be the maximum."

"The king would probably want to know the lower bound as well," Denon said.

Wunic looked at the papers. "Around ten blocks of lost ground—and I'm confident this is *not* the case, but the king should know that it's technically possible we could have lost the bulk of our forces." Wunic tried to smile. "Now, I'm sure that didn't happen, but it's still a possibility until I get more up-to-date reports. Once I've reorganized the front, I should have an accurate count."

Denon nodded, then frowned. "I apologize, General, and I have no doubt that you're right, but I should have a number to give His Majesty as a lower bound—before the reinforcements . . ."

Wunic took a slow breath. "No, I understand. My men could be down to five hundred."

"Five hundred," Denon repeated. "How many reinforcements were sent?"

"One thousand."

"Now, this may be a stupid question, but how many units do we still have in reserve—counting those in the palace?"

Wunic said, "Lord Denon, you should understand that those men are necessary for the security of the prisons and the protection of the king. If the king feels we need more soldiers at the front, it would probably be wiser to issue a draft than to leave himself and our prisons unguarded."

"I know," Denon said. "But he's already made it clear that he doesn't want to begin general conscription." Denon paused. "Say another—what?—two thousand units altogether still posted at the Western and Northern Garrs and the palace?"

Wunic shook his head. "No. The number's closer to five thousand."

"I'm sorry, I must not understand all of this, but if there are another five thousand soldiers at the prisons and palace, and if we may be outnumbered at the front, shouldn't more be moved?"

One of the worshippers below—a middle-aged man with only one arm—walked to the blue circle. Denon rose, and Wunic neatly piled the papers in a stack on his lap.

"Lord Denon—" Wunic said quietly.

Denon held up one hand to silence him—"Just a moment . . ."—and the man below fell to one knee in the center of the circle. Denon waved his hand over him in a neat circular motion.

"Return to the glory of our past," Denon said.

The man stood, bowing to Lord Denon. "Amen."

"Amen," Denon said.

The man left, and the second worshipper, a short woman in a dress, fell into step beside him—they exited the cathedral, snow blowing in through the front door. Denon sat again.

"The blocks we lost," Denon said, "do we know which direction they were from the Southern Garr?"

"South," Wunic said. "But that's not an issue—that actually works for us. Our positions to the rebels' east are holding, they're still across the river, and they haven't made any progress in the direction of the palace whatsoever."

"The king has told me on several occasions that a draft is out of the question. . . . Isn't there the possibility that unless we shift more units to the front, the rebels may continue to gain?"

"No," Wunic said. "My boys will hold."

"Okay," Denon said. "Obviously, I trust your judgment. It's just important now that I have good information for Vel. You know what I mean. He has an aversion to the military on principle—mainly, I think, because he blames the late Justice Hillor for the deaths of his foster parents."

"Yes," Wunic said. Even though he served Vel now, fighting against generals who glorified Hillor, Wunic still understood why they worshipped the dead Justice. Hillor had been a hero among the soldiery, a sign of what the military police could achieve. Hillor had not only risen through the ranks of the police to eventually be given control of the entire force—second in power only to the King—he had been educated, a judge, and a member of the Executive Council.

"That's over," Wunic said at last. "Vel's our King now, and whatever we personally think of his past actions, he is still our leader."

"Yes," Denon said. "Of course, but that's part of what this war's about, after all—isn't it? Have you had any luck finding someone to help His Majesty?"

"Yes," Wunic said. "You remember the girl from Broad Street, Sisha?"

"The whore."

Wunic nodded. "Yes. She's in the palace now. I'm not sure if that's what you had in mind, but . . ."

"She could work," Denon said. "Help get his mind off of everything that's happened."

A woman and three children entered the cathedral, their voices dying as they went to one of the pews closest to the front.

Denon said, "He really is going through a lot now. The king's only a boy, after all."

"The war is temporary," Wunic said.

"Yes, I'll try to make sure he understands that . . . but—I don't know how to handle this."

There's something else, Wunic realized, and he said, "What?"

"There was an attempt . . ." Denon continued quietly, "He tried to kill himself last night."

"The king is—"

"He's fine," Denon said. "But, and I'm sure you understand this, General, we can't take risks with this, can we? And right now, I'm the only one he'll grant an audience."

"That's unacceptable," Wunic said simply.

"Yes," Denon said, "I agree. We need to keep the king under constant supervision for the moment." Denon hesitated. "But, in his room—that would provoke him; if soldiers were posted inside to watch him, they might not be able to stop him. The boy is very fragile, very dangerous right now, and I'm sure you'll agree that we can't risk losing another king at a time like this."

"No—you're right."

"I think he should be temporarily restrained. Watched. Why don't you have him placed in a cell under the palace until we're sure he's all right?"

"Lock him up?" Wunic stiffened. "Do you think that's necessary?"

"We wouldn't be imprisoning him, we would be *protecting* him. You could put him in a cell in the palace prison, bound, so that we're certain we don't have to worry about a suicide. Until we've prepared the girl—and then all of this will be understood: Vel's safety is paramount right now, as I'm sure you know."

Wunic smiled. "You're not serious?"

Denon stared at him evenly, as if irritated that Wunic would question something this important. "The king is more important than you or me to this city, General. If he dies, the civil war will be the least of our concerns. These are extreme circumstances, and this will have been done for the greater good."

Wunic wondered if that was true. Denon was hinting at something here, suggesting what? Anarchy? The city would collapse without a government now; if people were left to their own methods there would be chaos. A military government like the rebels proposed—even Vel's government—might not be able to maintain control once food had begun to diminish further.

"There's a threat I don't know about?"

Denon looked away, at the woman and her children. "If he dies, we die. Don't you think putting him in a cell until the girl is ready would ensure that another suicide attempt—that it's just an attempt."

Wunic was silent, and finally he said, "All right." He stood to leave. "The war will be over sooner than you think."

"I hope so, General. Thank you. We're together in this." Denon patted his arm suddenly with a modest smile. "It's for the best."

"Yes, Lord Denon, I know—I wouldn't do it otherwise." Wunic left the cathedral without saying anything more, heading back to the palace. When the woman and her children were gone, Denon went down the main floor, where he flipped through a large book on the altar, Blakes's *Rebirth*, the foundational scripture of the Church of Hope. *Yes,* Denon thought, *I* am *right. But where are you, Blakes? And where are your demons?*

> In all his ancient strength to form the golden
> armour
> of science

For intellectual War. The war of swords departed
now,
The dark Religions are departed & sweet Science
reigns.
End of The Dream—but a War's end
Comes with its birth, and the horses of pestilence
and death Are ours alone to ride; and thus, dark
Religions will
conquer all
In the deep caves, where furnaces crush all.

Denon considered reading. *Blakes's words continue to haunt me,* he thought. *But, I've already won*—he went back up the balcony—*I've already won.*

VEL LAY on his bed, images spinning and mixing in his mind, as he tried to go back to sleep. Something in a dream had woken him—as it always did—and now he thought about all the people who had died, all those who were dying, about the way he had once believed that things might turn out all right. And how he had learned that life did not work that way. Vel thought about Blakes, and he tried to imagine what Blakes might have looked like in life. When Vel had gone wandering through the Frill tunnels, beneath the ruins, he had discovered some kind of ancient rooms, perfectly constructed, but old, and decaying.

Somehow, a moving, speaking, picture of a woman had appeared on a square of metal on a small device. As if that metal remembered the woman, and Vel thought about the bodies, the skeletons he had found in those rooms. The woman was dead, Vel had seen her skeleton, but yet that metal still remembered her, still remembered the words and the strange, almost unrecognizable accent she had used.

Is that all you are now, Blakes? he wondered. *You're a memory of someone who's probably rotting in some room in one of those tunnels. And the Frill*—one group hating people, another seeming to have no problem with the city of Hope—*did they kill you, Blakes? I wish I had stayed with my "parents,"* Vel thought. *I wish I had become a grass farmer like my "father," and then when things fell apart it wouldn't be my fault—when the city starves it wouldn't be my responsibility to find a solution.*

Vel sighed, eyes still closed, and he wondered what he would have to do to fall asleep now. Someone knocked.

"Your Majesty?"

Wunic, Vel thought. "What do you want?"

Vel heard the door open, and he forced himself to sit up—Wunic approached with a pair of soldiers behind him. *And what am I to you?* Vel thought, glaring at General Wunic. *I'm a boy who shouldn't have any power, because you think you know what to do for this city. Lord Denon told me about you—what you think of me.*

"What do you want?" Vel asked.

Wunic hesitated, and then he said, "You are not well." Not to Vel, to the soldiers with him—"Bind him, confine him and place His Majesty under constant supervision."

"Yes sir."

"—sir."

Vel reached for his pistol, but they were too fast—one caught his wrist, and in a single motion, Vel was flipped onto his stomach, iron clasps closing on his wrists.

Vel struggled, but they held him down easily. "Goddamn it . . ."

"Sir, are you sure—"

"The king is unstable and he needs to be confined for his own well-being. Sedate him."

"—es sir."

"Won't forget this," Vel said, and they wiped the side of a towel against Vel's tongue—he tasted a sudden bitterness that made him cringe. "I'm king, not . . ." The taste slid down his throat, and up into his nose and head, blurring Vel's vision. "Won't forget . . ." And he slept.

vel was bound to a chair with metal locks, in a small, windowless cell. The only light came flickering under a heavy wooden door. *Still a prisoner,* he thought, *even when I'm king, they can still do this to me. I swear to God, Wunic will pay for this.*

Voices outside. *You had better pray I never get out of here,* Vel thought. *I'm not a kid you can just use, and*—the door opened. Lord Denon stepped inside, and before Vel could speak, Denon went behind him, and quickly unlocked Vel's arms and legs, tossing the chains away.

Vel rubbed his wrists. "How long have I been down here?"

"A few hours," Denon said. "How do you feel?"

"Tired."

"They told me he locked you down here."

Vel followed Denon out of the cell, into a narrow stone hall, deep beneath the palace, a prison. "Who told you that?"

"Some of my Religious Guard," Denon said, and several soldiers stared as they passed. "This may have been an attempted coup, Vel. General Wunic said you were incapable, and he boasted—said he could handle the current situation more efficiently than you. I think the general has defected, but enough of your soldiers here remained loyal—that's why we're not dead, why General Wunic has not openly tried to seize the palace."

Vel glanced at a blue circle on the ceiling overhead—a link to the Church prison—and he remembered escaping from this prison once. *Much easier now that I'm king,* Vel thought. *But I shouldn't be here.* They approached an open doorway with a curling stairwell.

"He *boasted,*" Vel said.

"I've spoken to him," Denon said, as he led Vel up the stairs. "Try to let this go for now, please. Don't think on it."

Don't think on it. I intend to do more than think on it, Vel thought. At the top of the stairs, they opened a door into one of the back rooms of the palace.

"You want me to let it go?" Vel said. "Why shouldn't I send him down there to a firing squad or a noose? That's treason, isn't it?"

"Some of the police soldiers *are* loyal to the general. Now—when we're fighting a war—is not the time to react. And there are other, more immediate concerns."

They entered the main entrance hall—the frantic, ever-present soldiers and aides hurried past them, and Vel spotted several members of the Executive Council at a table in a nearby room. The men smiled and waved, and Vel forced himself to return the gesture, before following Denon up the main staircase to his bedroom.

"Lord Denon, before I was king, when people put me in prison, I could respond. Now that I'm in charge and have power, I can't react to this?"

"Vel, you need Wunic now."

"Why, so more soldiers don't defect?"

"Yes."

"Let them." They stepped into Vel's bedroom, and Denon drew the door shut behind them.

"I understand—you have a right to be upset. Has anyone told you about the situation in the city?"

"No one's told me anything," Vel went to the mirror and glared at himself. "I've been in prison."

Denon sat in the only chair. "Keep making those faces and your mouth will lock into that position. Your parents never told you that?"

Vel looked at him in the mirror. "They weren't my parents, were they?"

Denon said, "Wunic didn't want you to know about the situation—he thought you would want to be involved in the command of the army."

"Don't I have command of the army? Isn't the king in charge and the chief justice second in line? And since there isn't really a chief justice now that Hillor's dead, that means *I'm* in command, doesn't it?"

"Yes, Vel," Denon said patiently. "But Wunic is a general. He's been a soldier his entire life. He doesn't think you understand."

"I don't."

"That's not the point. You're obviously young, and Wunic is concerned with your age—he doesn't want you involved in the war. Of course, it makes sense for you to be involved, as you're king and he isn't. I explained this to him, told him it would be in everyone's interests if you were kept informed, that you could be kept up-to-date and that you wouldn't necessarily rescind all of his orders."

"He didn't listen?"

"No," Denon said. "He didn't. But the General did eventually agree last night that he might update you in the future. He told me an hour ago that he had briefed you on the situation, said you were disinterested. That you didn't care."

Vel looked at his sword and pistol, still on the bedside table, undisturbed, along with the long overcoat that had once been Justice Hillor's. "Nobody's told me anything—that was a lie. Wunic told you that so that no one would let me know what's going on, so that you would think I already know."

Denon said, "We've lost ground."

"How much ground?"

Denon took a careful breath, as if he was about to deliver the news of a dead loved one. "I apologize, Vel, someone should have told you sooner—"

"Where are the rebels?" Vel asked, and a cold knot tightened in his chest. "Just tell me what's happened."

"The rebels have broken through the front and have begun to cross the river in the south. Most of their units have been stopped just a few blocks on our side of the river—that's not far from here." Denon paused, watching Vel for a response. "You should know, there may not be much time, Vel."

Vel closed his eyes. "What does that mean?"

"This could become very dangerous very quickly. You may need to consider leaving—evacuating—sometime in the near future. Our artillery won't be running for a few days. And I'm not sure—we don't have that much time."

"I can't believe I wasn't told . . . I wasn't told any of this," Vel said, opening his eyes again.

"The general thought you might interfere."

Vel went to the bedside table and picked up his pistol and sword. "I'll interfere."

Denon did not move. "The general probably does have good intentions. Now—please—what are you doing? Vel, I'm here to help you."

"I know that," Vel set the sword on his bed, and he began to carefully check the pistol's ammunition, just as Denon had taught him. "Thank you, Denon. But you'll understand if I don't agree." Vel slid the gun into the top of his pants and picked up his sword. "Where is he?"

"Don't do this. Please. Stay in your room right now," Denon said, and he stood, as if to block Vel from leaving. "When was the last time you had something to eat? I'll have some food sent up."

"I'm not hungry. You know, I don't remember the last time I ate," he said, slightly amused with himself. "But I'm not hungry."

"Now is not the time—"

"And when *is* the time?" Vel shouted suddenly. "What do you want me to do, sit here thinking about how I've screwed everything up? Goddamn it, Denon: come on. I'm king now, and for the moment, *he* isn't."

Denon went to the door and said calmly, "You're dealing with a lot. I know that, I understand that. The fact is, you can't do anything right now to General Wunic. Why don't you talk to the system?"

"Where's Wunic?"

"Honestly, what do you want to do, kill him?"

Vel said, "Maybe. Maybe I'll just have him tossed in a cell, tied to a chair and sedated. No, you're right, I should thank him for everything he's done, shouldn't I?" With mock laughter, Vel said, "Maybe declare him my successor? Name my firstborn after—"

"Stop it, Vel," Denon said, indicating Vel's sword. "It won't solve anything, and you know that. Regardless, he's still a general, and he works for you. I promise you, this is not the way. Not now."

Not now, Vel thought, and Denon asked again, "Why don't you speak with the system?"

Vel scratched his head, tossing his sword uselessly onto the bed again. He tapped at the pistol handle absently. "You think it's going to help us, think it knows where more plants are that will cure the Pox, and how we can get the food that's under the ruins?"

"I don't know what it knows, that's my point. Only you can speak to it. If you're tired of sitting here waiting for the war to end, why not try this?"

"I suppose I have to try, right?"

"No, you don't have to."

"Yes, I know that," Vel said. "I understand the concept of free will in theory. What the hell, we have so much to look forward to if this Goddamn city survives a little longer."

"Thank you." Denon seemed to visibly relax, as if Vel had just solved their problems. He started to leave, then thought of something, and took out a sheet of folded paper. "I almost forgot, I think you should sign this."

"What is it?"

"An issue for a general draft."

Vel shook his head, sitting in the chair, still tapping the pistol handle. "No. I told you, I'm not going to draft everyone."

"This won't draft everyone, just take a look at it. Do you see?" Denon handed him a very long document with small, stylized writing, and a vacant place at the bottom where a signature was needed. "Just those appropriated by the district sergeants will be conscripted."

"What does that mean?"

"It means only as many people as we need will be drafted," Denon said. "Listen to me, Vel. Documents like this are the reason men like

General Wunic are against you. Wunic doesn't believe you have what it takes to rule—he thinks you're a hard-headed, stubborn little brat without the slightest idea of how to handle yourself in a crisis. I know better."

"Imagine that," Vel said.

"He's wrong. The general doesn't know you, I do. I remember what you were up against before you became king."

And you helped me when I needed it, Vel thought, and he looked away from the paper. "The rebels are almost here? You're sure?"

"Yes," Denon said. "Within a very short time they could be here at the palace."

"And what are people doing? Everyone who lives in the city, what are they doing?"

"Hiding," Denon said, and he shrugged distractedly. "Some are staying in the Garrs, as refugees, but by now all of the Garrs are full beyond capacity, and the more refugees we let in, the more soldiers we need to provide for them, to keep order in those Garrs—soldiers who could be helping against General Rein and his rebels."

"That's what ordinary people are doing?" Vel asked again. "They're hiding and living in prisons?"

"We have some shelters too." Denon shook his head. "It's difficult to know. We're still guarding the perimeter wall, but so far there haven't been any large attempts to leave the city."

"They don't want to get involved, they want to stay out of the fighting," Vel said, and he thought, *Like me.*

"Yes."

"And this order you want me to sign will draft some of them, force them into it."

"Vel, if nothing is done to increase what you have in the field, you *will* lose this war. The rebels will take the palace, and you'll be executed as a traitor. Everyone who isn't a part of their army will starve."

And that may happen anyway, Vel thought. *They want to kill me. Along with the rest of the Executive Council, and then the city falls apart even faster. They won't be able to keep their promises,* Vel thought, *and the food will run out. If they win, there will be mass executions, purges. All to stop a revolt against the new government and make sure there's enough food for the leaders and a handful of killers.*

"This is more fun than I thought it would be," Vel said. "Being king, I mean."

"The draft is necessary."

"If the rebels win—"

"—the city, Hope, ends. Everyone dies," Denon said simply. "They won't try to go to the ruins for more food—and that's the only way there is a chance, even if we win. If the rebels win, after all of their killings, they'll run out of food in a handful of months."

And then we leave ruins, just like whatever left them in the South, where the Frill still live in tunnels.

"You know," Vel said, "I thought when I became king I was doing it to stop a war. They said if I—never mind. It doesn't matter now, does it?" He smiled, and Denon put a hand on his shoulder.

"It isn't your fault."

Yes it is, Vel thought. *Of course it is.* He signed the document.

"Thank you," Denon said, and he took it, heading for the door. "I'll make sure a meal's sent up."

"Thank you, Denon."

"It will work out, Vel. Trust me."

"I do," Vel said. "Just don't let them rent out my room." And Denon left him alone.

What is the war like? Vel wondered, and he dropped onto his bed, hands over his face. With rifles and so much snow that people could barely move through it. What is it like out there, moving from one building to another, frantically killing men and women that might have once been friends in the police force?

God, what's happening here? Vel thought. *This world, this city . . .*

The door opened, and shut again. Vel kept his arm over his face, listening to the rustle of fabric, someone entering.

"Your Majesty, where would you like this?" a female voice said.

"Leave it at the foot of the bed," Vel said without moving.

Fabric shifted again, drawing closer, and there was a clinking as a tray was set down on the carpet.

"Thank you," Vel said.

A pause, and the room was silent. Vel waited, but she was still there. He felt her presence, standing nearby.

"Yes?" Vel said.

"Sir, I . . ."

"Yes?" Vel said again.

"I brought you a dispatch from General Wunic."

Good old General Wunic, Vel thought. The bed creaked as Vel sat up—a tanned girl in her mid-twenties stood with arms crossed over her full chest. Her black hair matched the dark dress she wore, and as Vel stared at her, she smiled. Something exotic about her, in the perfect lines that formed her eyebrows and her slender cheeks, as if someone had taken a long time to perfectly carve that face. She handed him a sealed paper.

"Thank you," he said.

The girl remained. "The tray is on the floor."

"Thank you," Vel said again. Still she stood there, refusing to back away. Vel frowned at her. "Is there anything else?"

The girl smiled when she met his eyes, but Vel only moved into a cross-legged position on the bed, looking away from her.

"Please, you can leave," he said.

The dress sighed with the sound of smooth fabric brushing against her skin as she turned and was gone. Vel broke the seal on the dispatch.

This dispatch is to inform His Majesty that the events in the City are being dealt with appropriately. Some losses have been suffered, but in the near future the situation should be resolved.
GENERAL WUNIC

Vel ate the large, green fruit—grassfruit—on the tray, drank the cup of water and read the dispatch again. Then he went into another, much smaller room on the second floor, locked it behind him, and a lit a candle, sitting on the floor in what was little more than a closet. Vel removed a tapestry from a metal box with a single wire slinking out of its side.

Blakes, Vel thought. *You're in there.*

He hesitated, and then very slowly, cut a slit in his left thumb, allowing the wire to suck droplets of blood away, and again there was the sick sensation—and the acidic smell—as something like blood—not Vel's blood—flowed out of the wire, mixing into Vel's cut.

The situation is almost resolved, Vel thought, and he smirked, waiting in the small room, as the wire continued to bleed on him. *I know now, Wunic.* The box hummed. And—pain drove up through his spine, into the base of his skull, and Vel clenched his teeth, tears already forming in both eyes, and—

Welcome back Vel, I'm Blakes.

"Go," Blakes said, and he rushed into the alleyway with three other men and one woman—they charged the open bed of a cargo truck that sat idle, filling the alley. Its armored sides nearly reached the dumpsters on both sides, and curls of exhaust drifted around the five as they ran closer.

Two jumped into the back with a mountain of wooden crates, all sealed and covered in clear plastic. Blakes hurried toward the driver's side, Adria behind him, and on the opposite side, Charles neared the passenger door.

Pop of gunfire from that side, and Blakes reached the driver's door, threw it wide, and shot the driver once in the throat—the driver's fingers slid weakly across a still-holstered weapon, and Blakes unbuckled the soldier from his seat, dropping him to the concrete alleyway, blood dripping onto the seat, splattering Blakes's sleeve. Blakes got in, Adria slid over him, and Charles hopped in from the opposite side, another body on the ground there. The metallic rattling of the rear truck door shutting, and Blakes shifted gears, slammed his door, and backed out of the alley.

Huge wheels crushed the arm of the still-bleeding driver, and two soldiers appeared in the open warehouse door, weapons drawn. Blakes pressed the pedal harder, and the truck slammed into a dumpster, sparking as its side scraped on rusted metal—and the soldiers opened fire, bullets like hailstones on the windshield and hood. The glass cracked, and Charles leaned out the passenger door—still open—hanging onto it with one arm, and with the other he aimed a semiautomatic pistol around the side, and emptied his clip. The truck thudded on a speed bump—one soldier went down in Charles's spray, and Charles lost his grip, rolling out of the truck, into the alley—and the second soldier shot him twice in the head.

The passenger door flapped like a loose sail as Blakes pulled out into the street—a car swerved, honking wildly as it brushed past the truck's taillights, and the soldier kept up his fire, rushing out of the alley after the truck, blasting through the windshield into the empty passenger seat. Glass exploded in, showering Blakes's cheek. Adria threw herself down, bullets shredding the seat above her, and Blakes swerved quickly, angling back *toward* the alley in a wide arc. The soldier was reloading, and he looked up in time to jump away—the truck's front bumper crashing into the building near his face and plowing through, and the cargo truck drove away, picking up speed as it turned onto the highway. The soldier watched and did not fire again.

Blakes and Adria sat quietly for some time, glass tinkling under their boots each time they shifted positions, and once Adria cursed, picking pieces out of her palm where she had rested it on the seat. The windshield was a mess of spiralling cracks and deep holes. Adria brushed the debris from the passenger seat as best she could, made certain the passenger door was closed and locked, rolled down the window, and lit a cigarette. She offered one to Blakes.

"You think Charles thought he could hang out the door like that?" Blakes asked at last.

Adria breathed deeply and tapped her cigarette out the window, wind rustling in the dark superhighway beyond. They were driving with traffic in the right lane, allowing cars to pass, mixing with the flow of cargo trucks on the interstate.

"Hadn't gone over the speed bump, he might have gotten them," Adria said distantly.

Blakes shook his head. "Didn't we say that we weren't going to do shit like that? Didn't we specifically talk about not hanging out of truck doors or charging trained soldiers?"

"You charged one."

"With the *truck*," Blakes said. "And it made him back off, didn't it?"

"I mean when we got onboard. You charged one and shot him in the throat."

"That was different. We knew that might happen. I wasn't hanging out of a Goddamn window."

Adria didn't answer, and she curled in her seat, picking both feet up off the floor, resting one arm on the door—she stared at the passing trees and dark fields outside.

"He knew," she said after several minutes.

"What?"

"He knew going into this what might happen," Adria said. "There were risks. We knew that. Would have been a hell of a lot harder anyplace else, wouldn't it?" She tried to smile.

"You mean picking this off at a military base or en route? Hell yes, it would have been," Blakes said seriously. "Shouldn't have lost anybody. That's the point. Charles should have stayed in the Goddamn truck and not gone waving his arm out the door like a jackass."

"He might have saved us—they might have gotten us, if he hadn't taken one out."

Blakes shook his head angrily. "No. We were clear. No reason he had to die."

They sat in silence again. Blakes thought about the equipment they had stolen. Three months had gone into planning this operation—their first. Three months of stolen charts and files and encrypted military information, stolen primarily with Jesse's expertise; Jesse, one of the two guys in the back, had gone to college with Adria. The other was Sampson, Jesse's friend, a marine corps dropout who had apparently dropped out of every institution he had ever been a part of—high school, yes, college too, and then the marines. Now a confirmed anarchist, he followed Blakes's guidance, just as they all did. There were thirty-four—thirty-three now that Charles was dead—who looked to Blakes for spiritual salvation.

Salvation from the corporate gods who continued to freeze organs in secret vaults, who continued to replace their own skin and eyes and livers as they rotted away; salvation from the East and the another lost war—"Hawaii is not a Chinese province! Remember Los Angeles!"; salvation from a Godless technological world of mass extinction rates and expanding deserts; salvation from the future. Blakes promised his followers a link to God, a link that had been forgotten but that could now be remembered, as he was chosen by God to work as His prophet in this age. He had promised them victory, not just over the East, but over the corrupt West as well.

"The world was never meant for twelve billion human beings; our grandfathers and our fathers made this world. They cut down the trees and pissed into the oceans and burned away millions of lives and sacrificed our cultural heritage—our God-given traditions—for the sake of technology. And we will not accept this Earth, we reject their past as we reject their future. Our parents promised themselves a Golden Age in the sixties and seventies, and now that it's 2085,

where is that Golden Age? What were they fighting and writing poems about in India? Why did they give away our islands in the Pacific and build living cemeteries of gray concrete and red brick in our proudest cities? Where are our doctors and our representatives—where is our future?"

And it will come, Blakes thought. *We will burn away the rot of secular perversion.* At twenty-five now, Blakes had researched Sunaki-Heiman, he had learned rigorously about the genetics that had brought him to life—given him his rebirth. William Blake exhumed, ground into powder and catalogued inside a machine that then spent months copying that signature—Blake's—into a newborn. Blakes had learned of others like him. Before '76, companies had funded the cloning of men like Gandhi, Lenin, Yahamoto, Lincoln, Mao. Blakes had read of the suicides. Still, dozens were being grown in captivity, for media purposes; for movies, advertising. Propaganda.

"For two thousand years, ours was the civilization of God and of glory, from ancient Rome to the dynasties of Los Angeles and the beaches of Honolulu. They tell you to work within the system, to vote, to buy their products, to write literature and to wait for the day that the world changes: It will not change. Unless we kill it, this age will never die and mediocrity will continue for our children and their children. Ours is a second dark age; we live in the shadow of the East and of a treacherous society that feeds on the misery of the poor so that the rich will outlive our grandchildren. Our doctors commit the ultimate perversion and watch as the world slowly dies of illnesses that can be cured.

"Ours is a society that sacrifices its children to the gods of Cholera, Typhoid, Malaria and Smallpox. Why? Because they have a new altar—the altar of science and collective isolation—they've trained us to live in their concrete prisons and we wait for their government pennies, because there are no longer any jobs. They've sold our factories and our well-being to South America and to Africa where slaves will do it for them. We are the poor southern whites of the nineteenth century American South, we are the destitute with televisions so that we can listen as they tell us how privileged we are. But we are losing. A war is coming, no one doubts that—but who will win?

"From the malarial swamps of Louisiana to the drowning children of Amsterdam, our culture has been betrayed. Because they outnumber us, the East produces three or four times what we do, and because

our leaders want only to increase their profits and extend their lives, they will not risk upsetting their own existence. We cannot fight a war to reclaim our place in the world without tearing it all down first. Everything must be removed, all of the sinews and cancerous flesh that our ancestors grew must be burned away and we must start again.

"The old cannot be changed, it must be entirely annihilated. Industrial revolutions and globalism: If all the cows were slaughtered today, how much rice would we grow with the fresh water they drink? You don't stop a ravenous dog by reasoning with it, you put a shotgun in its mouth, and you have the courage, the will to destroy it. That is our spiritual and historical duty."

Adria finished her cigarette and tossed it outside, rolling the window up with a shiver. "Will it work?" she asked.

Blakes frowned at the road. She had never said anything, never voiced any doubts before now. And he had explained it to all of them—the pulse had to be timed and triggered simultaneously in several key locations. Everything had to be overwhelmingly synchronized. Blakes had convinced several Eastern corporations that he was working for them; *The Chinese and the Arabs see me as a pawn,* he thought. *Their money and their friendship because I am a spy, a terrorist in white skin. But not for them—I will hit them too—and yes, of course it would work.*

"Yes," Blakes said.

Adria nodded and they kept driving.

After they returned to their house in upstate New York, Blakes locked himself in one of the bathrooms and turned on the fan. Then he took out three cages filled with rats, along with a black spiral notebook. Blakes killed the rats one at a time, skinning them alive in the bathtub, and in between each death he wrote with blood-stained hands in a blue pen, filling page after page in the notebook. Much of what he wrote he had already written—three hundred years ago. Blakes had memorized all of it as well as he could. All the words *he*—William Blake—had known in the London before cars, before the sin of technology had overwhelmed humanity's senses. Blakes mixed those words with new ones, and he began his first book with the blood of vermin. And he called it *Rebirth.*

---

you're back, Vel. What do you need?

Blakes, I need to know how we're supposed to get through this. We need more of those plants that can cure the Pox, and we need more food—and we need them right now.

The Frill have both. You saw the food yourself.

How do I get it?

You know that you're connected to them in their prophecy.

I know that somehow I'm half-Frill, but I don't know what that means.

That are you are damned as surely as they are, and yet you are my son, and I love you, Vel.

That's sweet of you.

Careful.

I don't look like they do. I saw them—a room full of them. Thin things with metal faces and pipes crisscrossing up their necks. They didn't look human.

They aren't human.

Really. Thanks for clearing that up. How can I be part Frill, Blakes?

You know that when I founded this place of Hope, I brought the means to mix genetic material they had on Earth. They could play with the substance of life, they could pervert God's will as certainly as any demon.

And they could combine people with animals?

If they wanted to. They built this, didn't they? This animal that acts as a computer, where I wait.

What do you mean you 'wait'? You *are* the computer system now, aren't you? You copied yourself into it, didn't you?

Yes, Vel.

Then those machines, whatever could mix different kinds of blood, different animals with one another, they're still around somewhere. They're still working, aren't they?

Yes.

Someone used those to make me?

Yes, Vel.

And they put me together with a Frill? Why don't I look like them?

You were designed not to. Remember Shadow and Sky.

The Frill creed, right? What the hell does that mean? The Frill are the shadow . . .

Shadow and Sky
Born of Shadow and Sky.
Without understanding, all is lost.
Heat binds wounds that separate,
And snow feels like cold ash.

And you came out of the sky. They think people are the sky—that we fulfill whatever that prophecy is. That's it. I'm supposed to solve that, aren't I? That's why I'm still alive, why they didn't kill me. They knew it was going to snow, didn't they?

You need food and the plants that the Frill cultivate to cure disease.

That's right.

The Frill won't just give them to you. You have not fulfilled their wicked prophecies just yet. You must appear to work for them if you would use them.

What do I do?

The key is buried in this city—you must unearth it. Regardless of what happens, never forget that they are the enemy. The Frill are demons of sin and temptation, and they will destroy you, just as they tried to destroy me.

Where do I find the key, with your pictures?

. . . Pictures?

What did you do before you came here, Blakes? They sent you here, right? Because you started some kind of war.

A crusade, Vel. Do not think you can understand. You have never been there, you have never seen the fount of sickness that was humanity and science. I was given a cross to bear because I sought to purify them. To save them. Do not challenge me, Vel. We are allies, but if you make me your opponent, I will watch you burn. Do you understand?

No. Why are we allies? What have you done for me so far except threaten my life?

You are my son.

Your great-great-grandnephew. Not your son. I'm not you, Blakes.

We are more alike than you realize. You are king now. I will help you—I will provide you with the key that you can use to save this city—but you must agree to certain conditions.

What?

You must take me with you.

What, you mean take this box with me?

Yes.

Where?

To the tunnels and the Frill.

Why?

You must speak with me periodically, and follow all of my suggestions. Listen carefully: you will not survive unless I am obeyed without question. I see more than you or anyone. I have watched Hope since its birth five hundred years ago, since I founded it. I know what must be done.

So why don't you just tell me?

Because the situation may change, you must take me with you if you want my help.

I'm supposed to leave the city and take the box with me?

Yes, and no one else. Do not let anyone—no one—accompany you, or the Frill will kill you outright.

They didn't the last time.

And were you alone when you met with them?

Blakes—

You will not survive without my guidance.

So where's the key?

We are agreed?

Yes, I'll take you along if I have to.

You will consult with me when you are inside the tunnels and I will give you further instructions. If anyone knows I am alive, you know that—

Yes. All right. Where's the key?

Your key to the Frill is buried in the cemetery.

In the tunnel that leads to the Frill?

No. In an ancient grave of one of the city's founders, one of my friends.

Who?

The stone is worn now so that only one word can be read. You will find it near my grave, and it will say "Adria."

What does Adria mean?

Just dig, and you'll find what you need. Then go into the tunnels and consult me.

I don't want to go back there.

You don't have a choice.

I know that—I can still wish I didn't have to go. Good-bye, Blakes.

I'll speak with you soon.

Lord Denon entered the large palace auditorium, glanced at the stage that had been set up at one end, scanned the chairs of soldiers, most standing and cheering or drinking, and then went to a rear corner, where General Wunic sat with an untouched cup of alcohol. A small band played music on an arrangement of glass tubes and wood and cloth drums.

A woman danced to the fast, ever-changing beat. She stomped and twisted from one end of the stage to the other, her black dress falling occasionally from perfectly tanned shoulders, sliding down—but not revealing—full breasts, and she swished the dress up the inside of her thigh—cheering from the soldiers, and several soldiers stumbled out of their row, heading for a lavatory down the hall.

The woman turned and threw her head back—the graceful, perfect curve of her neck—and then lowered herself into a turning crouch, the front of her dress dropping to expose the curves of both breasts, and the two hundred soldiers shouted. A row of soldiers with rifles stood guard at the base of the stage to keep them from rushing, and from time to time they had to push back drunken men, reprimanding them and sending them out into the hall.

Denon sat beside Wunic, and they both watched the stage, the music growing louder, so that each felt it inside his chest, like an external heartbeat. The woman slid to the floor, her legs spreading and snapping back in one movement. For an instant there was the exposure of leg beneath the long dress, and then only swirling fabric. She spun to her feet, smiling at the men and running both hands down her sides, to her waist, and legs.

"I take it we're having problems?" Denon asked.

The dress ruffled as the dancer pulled at it, flapping the end above her knees and down again.

"That's right," Wunic said. "Vel was cold. She left him, said he wouldn't accept her advances."

"It's her job to deal with that, isn't it?" Denon said. "She knows better than to leave it at that—what does she expect us to do? What do you think, General?"

Wunic picked up his mug, but didn't drink. They sat at one of the few tables in the room, along with several other high-ranking military officers at the rear of the room.

"I don't know," Wunic said. "I don't know what the kid needs, and I'm sure I couldn't give it to him if I did. As far as I know, she says she gave him a clear invitation. All I can say is, the war is simple compared to this nonsense."

"Still, General, as difficult as the boy is, he is king. We have to save him, and I think you'll agree that it should be done now before too much time goes by."

"Hm," Wunic said, and he shrugged. "I don't know—the kid will speak with you at least. Young people make good soldiers, but I've never been impressed with their reasoning. Now, he is king, of course, and I trust him."

"He's *sixteen*," Denon said, and they both smiled.

"Yes," Wunic said, "exactly. That's all I'm saying. I leave it to your judgment: you tell me if he still needs the girl, and I'll speak with her."

The woman slid her hair out of her eyes with both hands, exposing a slender, mischievous face. She played with several of the men in the front row, her torso quivering, rolling in and out, like a snake.

"She *is* talented," Denon said. "Isn't she?"

Wunic straightened. "I only want to look out for the king."

Denon looked at him. "You've never considered—"

"No, Lord Denon. We're still at war." Wunic did not look at him. "The men need to be distracted from time to time—the boy does too—and I understand that. My boys know that we've taken casualties. That's all this is. The women we're keeping at the palace are that distraction, but we're still at war."

The woman ran one hand down the front of her body, tracing the lines in her skin through the dress, and she spread her legs, rocking on an invisible seat. Vel stepped into the auditorium, a pistol and sword hanging from his belt.

"His Majesty decided to make an appearance after all," Denon said quietly. Wunic noticed Vel too.

Vel was frozen, watching the woman's performance, and she spun, hair spread across her face. She saw Vel. Carefully sliding her hair away with one hand, the woman touched the side of her neck with the other, gradually moving her fingers down.

The soldiers seemed oblivious to the fact that she was watching Vel, and they continued to shout and drink, the drumbeat falling into a precise rhythmic pulse, quickening. The woman fell gracefully onto her stomach, body arching in a wave toward him, and Vel visibly stiffened and forced himself to turn away. His cheeks were flushed, and the woman continued to stare, struggling to catch his eye. Vel saw Lord Denon, and Wunic rose, offering Vel his hand.

"Your Majesty," Wunic said.

Vel stopped, his hands sliding to both weapons. "General." Vel ignored Wunic's outstretched hand.

Wunic hesitated, and then he stepped aside, motioning to the chair beside Denon.

"She's good at what she does, isn't she?" Denon said, nodding to the front of the auditorium.

Vel glanced briefly in her direction. "Who is she? I saw her in my room earlier—she brought me food, didn't she?"

"Her name is Sisha." Denon said.

"I spoke to the system," Vel said. "I know what I have to do."

Wunic stood nearby, hands behind his back as he listened to Vel's conversation.

"And what's that?" Denon said. "Why don't you sit down?"

Vel remained where he was. "There's something buried in the cemetery, near one of the older tombs. I have to take it to the Frill."

Denon glanced at Wunic, and Wunic shook his head.

"Vel," Denon said. "Most of the casualties from the earlier attack—when you fought the police for control of this palace—most of those bodies were buried near the older tombs."

"What? Why?"

"The cemetery is overcrowded," Denon said, and he sighed. "You know that. The city founders were buried very deep—more than twelve feet down in some cases—so we could bury new bodies without disturbing the old."

"They put the dead police in with the city fathers?"

"The same graves were not used, Your Majesty," Wunic said. "But they do occupy some of the same land."

"Are there markers?" Vel asked Denon.

"Yes, over some of them. There wasn't time for tombstones—even wooden ones—in most cases."

Unmarked bodies buried on top of the city fathers, Vel thought. *Because they're running out of cemetery space, and founding a new cemetery isn't high on the list of priorities at the moment.*

"Why weren't they burned?" Vel asked.

"Some were," Denon said. "But the officers were not. And we ran out of space."

"It's a matter of distinction," Wunic said. "Military police officers receive a full ceremonial burial and honor guard."

"I don't believe this," Vel said. "There's something buried in one of those graves—and I have to get it out, except there are probably bodies on top of it now." He paused, and neither Wunic nor Denon answered him. "I have to dig it up, there's no other way."

"I'm sorry, sir, but that's not possible," Wunic said.

"What is it?" Denon asked.

"I don't know," Vel said, and Wunic put his hand on Vel's shoulder—Vel jerked away from him. "Don't."

"Do you know what you're looking for?" Wunic asked. "We could send someone to make sure no one came across it during the services."

Vel remained perfectly still, the music growing louder, as the woman—Sisha—continued to dance. "No, I don't know what it is. I just know it's there."

Wunic said, "Your Majesty, I don't think you understand the situation. If you don't know what you're looking for, then what guarantee do we have that anything would be gained by desecrating those graves?"

"Are you an idiot?" Vel said. "Were you listening a second ago? The system told me to look there, at a particular old grave in the cemetery. And the system knows what's there, General."

"These men were very recently buried," Wunic said, his face beginning to flush, veins pressing at his neck. "Police officers gave their lives, and were interred in honorable burials just a few weeks ago. Your Majesty, unless you *know* that something will be gained by digging up their corpses, it can't happen. I have to forbid that action."

Denon was silent.

"You have to forbid it?" Vel said, his voice rising. "You don't forbid anything, General, do you understand? Who do you think you are?"

Wunic stiffened, but he did not back down. "I am on the Executive Council—"

"So was Justice Hillor!" Vel was shouting at the larger man now, and Wunic had begun to visibly tremble, fighting to remain calm. Vel said, "Hillor forbade me to become king, but now I'm in charge, not him, not you. You understand that?"

Wunic unconsciously touched the handle of his pistol with one hand—Vel gripped his pistol and sword, but did not draw them yet.

"You want to stop me? I'll fight you right now, General. Come on,

General Wunic, I don't care who the hell you are or how many officers you had to screw on your way to the top," Vel said. Wunic looked at Denon for help, but Denon merely shifted in his chair uncomfortably.

The drumbeat slowed, quieting, and Vel drew his pistol, clicking off the safety.

"I'm not like everyone else you know," Vel said. "You can't use me like a piece in some game. I'm king now. These men serve me first, not you. Come on, General, you want to do this?"

The music stopped, and Sisha was no longer dancing. The room of soldiers watched as Wunic stepped away from Vel, his pistol still holstered.

Wunic said softly, "I apologize, Your Majesty. Please understand, if you were to desecrate the bodies of—"

Vel said, "You going to stop me? You going to lock me up again? Throw me into the prison?"

Wunic looked again at Lord Denon, and Denon caught Vel's arm gently. "All right, Vel. Think about this: You don't want this. Let it go, Vel."

No one spoke, and Vel aimed his pistol at Wunic's head. Wunic stepped away, nodded briefly to Lord Denon, and left the auditorium, Vel still aiming the pistol at him until he was out of sight. Gradually, the soldiers began to leave the auditorium, some stumbling slightly, and Vel put the safety back on his weapon, the soldiers staring at him as they left.

The musicians exited, and only Denon and Vel—and Sisha, sitting on the side of the stage, staring at them—remained.

"Why don't you sit down?" Denon said to Vel. Vel put away his gun and sat. Denon continued, "As much as you want him to be, General Wunic is not your enemy, Vel. He's an easy, effective link to the police soldiers, to your army."

Vel smiled. "I don't care. I'm going to dig up whatever's buried in the cemetery, with or without your or his help or anyone's, and I'm going to save this Goddamn city."

"The computer system told you to go digging?"

"Yes."

"Then perhaps you should."

"Yes, *perhaps* I should," Vel said sarcastically, and he leaned back in his chair, noticing Sisha, still seated on the stage, watching them and tugging at the sleeves of her dress uncomfortably, as if she knew something but was afraid to speak. "I'm going to dig it up."

"How are you feeling?"

"What?" Vel smirked at him, but Denon's face was serious. "How do you think? I'm dandy."

"I know you miss her."

Vel saw Sisha out of the corner of his eye, and he said, "Miss who?"

"Vel, you can do this. You can deal with this."

"I told you, I'm going to save the entire Goddamn city. Doesn't that sound like a good plan? I'm fine, Denon."

"*Stop it,*" Denon said, and he took both of Vel's arms. "You need—" Vel drew his sword, and Denon twisted his arm behind his back—Vel fell to his knees, sword banging to the floor, tight pain under his shoulder socket as the arm threatened to break.

Sisha gasped, and Denon glanced briefly at her, before he released Vel's arm. Vel remained in a crouch, staring at his sword.

"Do not draw your sword on me, Vel. I am your friend, if no one else is," Denon said. "Don't casually insult me, and don't forget."

"I'm sorry," Vel said. "I don't know what I was—"

"You can trust me," Denon said, and he motioned to Sisha—she left the room noiselessly.

"I know," Vel said. "I do trust you—it's not that. I want to be king, but I don't know what to do and I'm—I just—I'm having a hard time trusting anything else. You know?"

"What do you mean?"

"We're going to lose this war, aren't we? They've crossed the river already."

"The artillery may be operational soon," Denon said. "That could give us the advantage. It might be the turning point."

"Unless the rebels get here first," Vel said.

"You'll be protected, Vel. You'll be evacuated long before they can take the palace—and this will pass. You know that. Eventually, it will pass. Remember that: you know I'm right."

"It will pass." He smiled sadly. "You think I don't know that? That's exactly what I'm afraid of."

Not dead, but sleeping.

Three shovels hit the frozen ground, stabbing the snow. Three shadows stood in long overcoats—two gray, one black—their backs arched as they lifted clumps of ice and sod, tossing it aside. The cemetery was cold, and the wind howled, blowing snow. The snow fell in waves, periodically drifting away from the tombstones, revealing words.

Lovely and pleasant in their lives.
In death they were not divided.

Two of the men—the soldiers—wore hats, and the third—Vel—shifted, wiping long hair from his face as the wind blew around him. Snow streaked their coats, collecting on the fabric, and a pair of assault rifles lay on the ground nearby.

In the morning of his life,
God called my darling home.

They had been digging for some time now, and they had created a hole at least four feet deep. No bodies yet. Vel climbed out of the hole, shaking snow and cemetery dirt from his coat. Impossible to see beyond a dozen feet in the cemetery, the cemetery fence only occasionally visible nearby. Gray tombstones faded in and out of existence in the nighttime snowfall. Vel had chosen to come at night, when there was less chance that anyone might notice the king and two soldiers desecrating fresh graves.

Only after they had arrived had Vel realized that in the daylight, the snow might be just as fierce, just as blinding. As it was, Vel found himself at times unable to spot anything beyond an arm's length away. They were digging in an old section, where the city fathers were buried, their grave markers all stone. And it had taken a long time to find "Adria"; Vel had led the soldiers from one to the next, fighting with the numbness in his toes and the knee-deep snow, clearing it away from the stones. Finding each grave by the very tip of the headstone, like tiny rocks in the sea of snow. "Adria" had been buried completely, and they had only discovered it after Vel had tripped over it, moving up a very deep snowdrift on one small hill.

The tunnel that led to the Frill could be reached in this cemetery, Vel knew. Just below the surface, near Blakes's tomb. Twenty feet down, it ran beneath the buildings, beyond the perimeter wall and the grassfields, all the way to the ruins and the southern forest.

Vel caught his breath and watched the soldiers continue to dig in the grave. Their coats fluttered and shifted with the wind, and Vel rolled his sleeves down further. Sleeves that had once belonged to Justice Hillor, another corpse. The old headstone was worn away—and Vel could tell that there had once been at least four lines of writing—only the first word was faintly visible, and had Vel not know what to look for, he might have seen only cracks; but there it was:

Adria

A clank of metal on metal.

Vel crouched closer to the hole, even deeper now, perhaps five feet or more. They should have found bodies by now.

"—ir, there's something here."

One of the soldiers climbed out of the grave, and Vel jumped down, beside the second man. Wind hissed, whispering coldly in Vel's ears, biting with snow. They had uncovered some kind of wrappings. White paper, now faded yellow and brown—corpses. Bodies covered in cloth.

Vel was careful not to step on the shapes. "Just bodies."

The nearby soldier shook his head. "Something under them. Drove it in deep, and I hit something a foot or so underneath—you heard it?"

Vel nodded. He helped the soldier lift one of the frozen white bodies out of the way, setting it on one side of the hole, and they uncovered more, the soldier's shovel accidentally breaking the wrapping in several places, driving into frozen flesh. Vel helped him lift a corpse aside—and there were more, piled on top of one another horizontally in at least three columns of two, but now they had cleared away the central column, and Vel dug into the fresh dirt between the remaining bodies. His shovel clanked.

"Would you like me to remove it?" the soldier said—there was only room for one person to dig in the hole.

"I can do it," Vel said, and snow fell in the grave, collecting in the corners. The soldier climbed out of the hole, and Vel continued to dig, dumping the dirt onto the wrapped bodies they had moved.

The dirt began to part around a thin metal object—like a very narrow blade of a sword—except it was round, like a pole—laid carefully in the same direction as the bodies were pointed. Vel dug further, accidentally backing into one of the bodies as he continued.

"What is it?" one of the soldiers asked.

"Don't know," Vel said, and he finished with one end, finally finding the rounded tip. He tried to pick it up, but it was still too firmly buried at the other end. Vel walked to the opposite side of the hole and continued digging—larger here, as if the metal turned into a blade at this end, and Vel hit a body just below the metal. Another wrapped in white cloth; he saw the hint of blue and white skin between the slit his shovel had created.

Vel's stomach caught in his throat, and again he tried to pick up the metal pole—that's what it was, some kind of pole. Some kind of weapon. *Was this what Blakes meant?* Vel wondered. This *is what I was supposed to find?*

Vel tried to dig around the larger end, and he hit the same corpse again, stabbing a hole in another place. Vel swallowed and snow sprayed into his face. The entire weapon—the pole or whatever it was—was made of metal. And now Vel began to see the outline of this end, the curling black blade. Snow blew against his back, knocking Vel onto his stomach, across the pole, his arm brushing the layer of corpses to his right. Vel started to rise, and dirt sprayed his face, into his mouth. Not snow, dirt.

"What the hell are you—" Vel coughed, and something heavy hit the back of his head, a clump of frozen sod. Vel fell again, hands scraping against the rotting fabric nearby, shredding it. And Vel saw one of the soldiers picking up a body that they had moved out of the way. More dirt onto Vel's back, and now the soldier dropped the corpse on top of Vel, and as Vel struggled—more dirt in his eyes—the second corpse was added to the top of the first. Vel fought, and the wrappings came away, and Vel felt dead skin—it collected under his fingernails as he struggled.

More dirt onto Vel's exposed legs and head, forcing his head down.

"No," Vel wheezed, fighting to wipe the mess from his eyes, but both hands were trapped, along with most of his body, between the frozen corpses. Vel forced one arm down, to his sword handle, and then, with all of his weight, he rolled, drawing the sword, and another body rolled on top of him, the rotting fabric pressed against his cheek and mouth.

More dirt was piled onto his head, and Vel instinctively turned away—into the side of the body, to keep breathing. He fought, stabbing and heaving with his sword. Fabric opened, and Vel writhed as his sword slid into the bodies, opening them onto him, and he tried to shout that he would kill the soldiers, that he was king, but Vel tasted only dirt and the mold from the body wrapping.

He could no longer move, but Vel struggled, one arm still straining through the ground, toward a pocket of air, still stabbing, and not caring how many of these bodies he ripped open or exposed. Metal—the tip of a shovel—cracked against Vel's sword hand, and he lost the weapon, pulling his hand back, and it brushed inside one of the wrappings—to cold skin, like soft parchment, and down—his fingers slipped inside an open mouth. Vel felt teeth. He recoiled, but he could not withdraw his hand—the dirt had locked it in position, and Vel breathed haltingly, the air quickly disappearing with each thud of more dirt that they piled onto him.

A dried, shriveled tongue, and more teeth, one came loose. *Oh my God,* Vel thought. *Oh God.* Vel shuddered, and his stomach turned on itself, heaving—he tasted bile. No. And they were done burying him, and he heard nothing. Not even the wind.

TWO ON the East Coast of the United States, one in the north, one in the south. Blakes sat in a hotel room with Adria and Jesse and five others. A television was playing an old black-and-white Mickey Mouse cartoon—in French—and Jesse had insisted on watching, even today. As Mickey drove a steamboat, happily whistling and swaying his hips, Blakes sat at the hotel table, flipping through the sheets, Adria seated across from him. The rest of them were all watching the cartoon and cleaning an assortment of guns, strapping on body armor, polishing helmets.

Two in England, two in France, four in Germany, and so on, throughout Europe. Eight across Russia, eleven in China, and another six in Japan. Thirteen spaced across the Pacific. More in India, the Middle East, the Americas, and yes, even Africa and Australia. *Every pocket is covered,* Blakes thought, and the phone rang. It had taken years of travel, years to link the devices and gain access to the East.

Blakes had contacts throughout all of the world; Adria supervised newspapers in eighty-four different languages that spread Blakes's message over the network. They set up "bots" that scanned millions of networked profiles, automatically searching for people of a certain demographic, in a certain section of the world, with access to certain resources, and these bots sent messages signed by Blakes himself. Automated to be untraceable.

This boy is unstable because his parents have been divorced, and he feels isolated from the world, and his bank account falls into the upper third tax bracket, meaning his father gives him money—and so a message will be sent from Blakes, asking for his help in a crusade against the modern world.

Systems within systems, all running on the vast networks of worldwide information cables and satellites. Bots and servers tracked down potential cells, gave them orders and waited for confirmation. Existing petty terrorist cells were purged—leaders exposed anonymously by Blakes—and as the followers waited to be trapped, Blakes's bots sent them messages, offering them jobs. Computer programs located anarchists, fundamentalists, communists—any group with a certain range of members, with certain resources, which were serious but incompetent, and these groups were automatically exposed to government organizations; their leaders usually arrested.

Then new bots would send messages from Blakes, calling them to his side, to his world, so that they could work for the creation of a better, more holy and pure world. They were recruited to the cause of the destruction of the modern world.

There was no need to create new terrorist systems: most of Blakes's cells were already there. They just needed to hear his message of success through the spiritual, of the phoenix—new life in the death of the old. Since the mid-twentieth century, terrorist cells had been deeply rooted in every part of the world; for Blakes and Adria it was just a matter of isolating the right groups and approaching them at the right times. Money continued to flow from the East, guns from the oil deserts of the Middle East, and after just four years, Blakes had a network of independent, fully automated and virtually untraceable cells.

Drugs were used, money, prostitution, gambling, *jihad* and lynchings—race, sex; every existing animosity was fed into the same system and focused toward Blakes's end. Stylized messages catered to

Black Power, White Supremacists, and the Islamic Jihad. Every group could achieve what it wanted if it worked within Blakes's plan, and most of them agreed. The world would begin again, but to achieve that rebirth, it had to die.

The phone continued to ring, and someone answered it in French, then laughed, and continued to speak English.

"Do they have to watch that now?" Blakes asked softly, and Adria rubbed his hand. Blakes was twenty-nine years old now, and he had grown a light beard, even as his hairline showed hints of premature baldness.

"It helps to calm them," she said.

Blakes listened to the cartoon, and several people laughed at the black-and-white animation—a girl named Jenny offered Blakes the portable hotel phone.

"They're ready," Jenny said.

Of course they are, Blakes thought, and he took the phone from her. "Thank you," he said. "Hello?"

"All stations are ready," a low voice said.

"Good. Synchronize, and set in one hour and fourteen minutes. Check with every team."

"Already done."

"They're ready?"

"Yes, sir."

"God's justice," Blakes said, the other person echoed him, and Blakes hung up. He glanced at Adria, and she nodded.

"Justice," she said.

Blakes folded the papers—nothing more to do, he had been over these more times than he could count. It had taken four years to plan, four years to coordinate, and there had been traitors, people who had defected, and there had been arrests, but Blakes was clean, and now it was arranged, and nothing anyone could do could stop them—they had too many fallbacks, too many counter-switches.

Blakes switched off the television, and the room was suddenly very quiet.

"We go in forty minutes," Blakes said. "Everyone in armor. We'll review the outline again for anyone who wasn't listening the first three hundred times."

Several smiles, but no one laughed. They watched Blakes, some with nervous tension plainly visible, others with a kind of distant stare. Blakes held up his right hand in a salute, and they all found a place to fall to their knees, heads bowed to Blakes.

"Our Reich begins now, my children," Blakes said. "With the end of the perverse, and the beginning of God's kingdom on Earth. Rome ended when it was swept away, and for centuries they believed more fully in God's love than in any secular sin. When the lights go out, the darkness *will* be frightening, but we will be the light in that time. Our bullets are divine judgment, and the cattle—the columns of mindless humanity who stand in our path—will be burned. God's glory on Earth."

"God's glory," they said, and they looked up at him without standing.

Blakes walked to a table near the television monitor and sorted through his black duffel bag, finally producing an old black and red flag, with a huge swastika in its center. "We are not Nazis, we are not communists, nor capitalists, nor socialists, nor fundamentalists, nor anarchists." Blakes held the flag up high. "This is the symbol of freedom through fire. Only the bravest men and women in history have tried to stand above the collective will of the weak. And sometimes deaths *are* necessary. We all know why we're here. Hitler is a name that only historians know, but the ideas and the sacrifices that were made under this flag are symbolic of our struggle. Mercy is not to be cherished—we want only victory, at any cost.

"We are not Nazis, but this is their symbol, and the fear it brings, and the hate, and the death we understand because we are the masters of this planet, and our society will not be beaten. Indeed, we have already won." Blakes smiled at them. "We will not persecute based on color or religion or wealth, except when it acts as a tool of slavery and weakness in society, and then we will persecute everyone who would hold humanity back in the sin of arrogance. And the world will return to God's hands, through our deliverance. God's glory on Earth."

"*God's glory on Earth.*"

Blakes set the flag down on the table and pointed to the collection of weapons and armor on one of the twin beds. "No mistakes," he said. "And we *will* win. We have already won."

one hour later a series of simultaneous electronic pulses were activated across every continent on the Earth, disabling power systems, erasing vast amounts of information and paralyzing governments and corporations. Backup systems did not fail everywhere, as they had been intended to. Blakes had not known that many wealthier nations had begun to replace electronic computers with organic systems in many key areas, and thus, these organic, living computers were untouched by the pulses. Even some electronic systems simply contained too many fallback systems to be eliminated by the pulses.

The terrorist attack—"The Pulse of '89"—was accompanied by simultaneous assaults on the leaders of virtually every First World nation, East and West. None succeeded. In France, a group of terrorists attacked a corporate conference, with leaders of the West's thirty-three most successful corporations. Only one CEO—along with a handful of lesser personnel—was successfully assassinated: Jen Sunaki of Sunaki-Heiman.

In all, over five hundred individuals were arrested in roughly sixty nations. Despite the failures, damage *had* been done, and the following morning, stocks in every part of the world plummeted, and a month later a worldwide depression had begun—the fifth of the twenty-first century.

In prison, Blakes caught glimpses of the network news stations, all in French of course, but he understood enough of the language to learn what was happening. Of the eight hundred soldiers in God's service around the world, at least half were dead, and the rest now sat in prison. Blakes's untraceable network and terrorist cells had been eradicated by both the East and the West. Only a handful remained in hiding, and probably not for long.

Rumors circulated the network of the leader responsible for the attacks, Jesse Winthrop, a native of New York, and Jesse began to develop an underground band of supporters. As word spread of what Jesse had tried to accomplish, of his vision to start over—to break the East and the West and begin the world again—Jesse drew a following. *Jesse,* Blakes thought, as he sat in his tiny cell, thinking about what he had just seen on the black-and-white monitor in the mess hall. *Jesse-the-leader, and he's responsible for all of it.* Blakes sat on the floor, barely finding enough room to lay out beside his tiny cot and toilet and sink. And he unfolded one of the pieces of paper they had given him, along with the tiny stub of a pencil they had allowed. Blakes sharpened it with his fingernails, exposing the uneven graphite center.

Blakes thought about the books he—William Blake—had written

in his first life, in London, hundreds of years ago. He thought of demons and betrayal, he thought of Urizen. Blakes remembered the words he had memorized, *his* words, and he wrote:

> His cold horrors silent, dark Urizen
> Prepar'd; his ten thousands of thunders
> Rang'd in gloom'd array, stretch out across
> The dread world; & the rolling of wheels
> As of swelling seas, sound in his clouds,
> In his hills of stor'd snows, in his mountains
> Of hail & ice: voices of terror
> Are heard like thunders of autumn
> When the cloud blazes over the harvests.

Blakes stared at the words, his eyes straining in the dim prison light. Then he wrote below these old words, new ones:

> I am come to redeem the world in the name of
> blood,
> And in the whirling void I shall cast the damn'd
> For I, yes I claim it, I am Urizen; And death follows
> me.
> I swear that I will bring this world of sin
> To the ruin of Eden; God's Will on Earth.

Blakes thought, *So the book begins.* He glanced up and saw the Angel standing in the corner of his cell. Blakes steadied his hand on the page.

"I remember," he said.

The Angel smiled. "*You do God's will, my child. Do not let it end.*"

Blakes said, "No. It hasn't begun. The next time *I* will be the name they know. The next time, I will triumph, and I swear I will spill their blood, however many deaths it takes for mankind to learn."

The Angel was gone.

Blakes turned back to his new book, and at the top of the page he wrote the title: *Urizen's Return.*

"I have more dispatches for the king," Wunic said, sitting beside Lord Denon at the conference table. "Where is he?"

Men in white with swastika armbands—the Religious Guard—stood around the walls, armed with swords and rifles.

"Resting."

"I need to apologize," Wunic said. "I shouldn't have challenged him publicly."

"He *did* provoke you, General." Lord Denon moved the piles of papers he had been looking through to one side of the table, and said, "Is it good news?"

Wunic arranged three papers in front of Lord Denon, where the other piles had been. "You'll make sure he's kept informed?"

Denon frowned. "What's wrong, General? Of course."

"Honestly," Wunic said, and he scratched his beard. "I'm tired of fighting *them* and the boy. What do you think I can do to talk to him?"

"Nothing right now," Denon said. "But I'll see what I can do."

Wunic nodded. "Enemy attacks have been repulsed, and with the reinforcements—I *did* shift more units from the Western and Northern Garrs and the palace; I followed your advice—my men have pinned the rebels to the Southern Garr and a five block radius."

"A five block radius," Denon said. "I'm confused: I thought we held positions to the immediate north and northeast."

"We did," Wunic said, and he shrugged as if it made no difference. "I focused the counteroffensive in the south, and in order to make sure the southern front would hold—that's where the rebels had gained ground, you remember—I had men moved down from the north to support the attack. When they shifted, the rebels took a couple of blocks in that immediate direction, nothing serious. And the gains more than make up for it." Wunic grinned. "The rebels were overextended and my unit commanders saw that."

Denon thought about it. "The rebels knew how to push north? I don't understand how could they have known that you had weakened the northern front?"

"Out there," Wunic said. "Things aren't as *neat* as they are here. It's possible that some rebels were actually retreating north, they may have even been defecting—whatever the reb movement started as, it turned into them stumbling across a couple of weakened positions."

"Correct me if I'm wrong, General, but wouldn't a large shift—say twenty percent—from the Garrs and palace have been enough for the counteroffensive, without—"

"I didn't move twenty percent," Wunic said. "I moved ten percent."

"Why only ten?"

"The rest are needed at the palace and the Garrs for basic security," Wunic said. "And they weren't needed: the counteroffensive succeeded. You can tell the king that the war is close to being won. I suspect that after what happened out there, large numbers of rebels, maybe even entire reb units, will start defecting."

"Have you had many so far?" Denon asked.

"Not yet. My men have taken a small number of prisoners. I think that may be about to change."

Denon asked, "Have you considered that the rebels may attempt to break out?"

Wunic forced himself to remain patient. "Yes," he said. "Of course."

"I just ask because I was under the impression that we had intended to wait them out." Denon smiled as if to say, *I'm only saying this because I have to—for the king.* "A conservative strategy—that's what I told His Majesty to expect."

"Yes," Wunic said. "And the situation has changed."

"Did the company commanders decide to launch the counter—"

"*I* decided," Wunic said, and he shook his head, as if he regretted having to go over the obvious again. "I'm in charge, the offensive was successful: What's the king's problem?"

"No," Denon said, holding up one hand, "you misunderstood me, I'm not implying that His Majesty isn't satisfied with your help."

Wunic stared evenly back at Denon. *Of course you are,* he thought. *This war is my war. I'm fighting it, not you or that unstable little prick, Vel. We need him because he's king, I serve him and will always serve him because he is king: but this is my arena, not yours, not his. This war is being won because I'm fighting it, and I've waited for too long, sacrificed too much for this moment to have it trivialized or questioned by an ignorant boy, God save him.*

"Tell him the war is going well," Wunic said quietly. "And it will be over soon."

"Good," Denon said. "I'm sorry, General, if I've said something . . ."

"Never mind," Wunic said. "Does the king want to know anything else?"

Denon looked through the papers. "Oh, I won't keep you, just a few basic things. . . . How much ground would you say we've gained?"

"All but five blocks and the Southern Garr."

"Let's see. . . . How many guns do you think the rebels have now?"

"About one hundred," Wunic said.

"And how many men did you say we lost in the counterattack?"

Wunic hesitated. "These gains are not insignificant, and the king should understand that the rebels no longer hold *anything* substantial apart from the Garr. It's safe to think of them as a prison population at this point. He should also know that in *any* military action of this kind, significant losses are to be expected."

"Of course," Denon said. "We're at war, after all, aren't we?"

"Exactly," Wunic said. "In war there will be casualties. The king needs to understand, he needs to be prepared for that."

"I'll try to make sure he understands."

But he won't, Wunic thought. *Because he's never worn a uniform. The boy used to be a criminal; no respect for the rule of law, except that by his birthright, he* is *that law.*

"What kind of numbers should I give His Majesty?" Denon asked.

"The figures that are quoted here," Wunic said, and he adjusted the papers so Denon could see them. "Obviously, our losses are more certain than reb casualties now that the fronts have settled down somewhat, but you can see they lost maybe five hundred units, probably more."

"That takes them down to fifteen hundred?" Denon asked, making notes on one of the pages.

"Yes, that's right. Now, before the attack, my boys were up to thirty-five hundred, and that includes the new reinforcements."

"I'm sorry, General, but wouldn't we have lost more soldiers in the attack, or have I misunderstood—"

"It's possible," Wunic said, and he folded his large hands on the table in front of him. "Common sense says that you multiply enemy casualties by three, but from what I've heard, my boys' losses weren't nearly that bad."

Denon waited, and Wunic continued, "Now, of course there were casualties, but the territory makes up for that: this choke hold—a classic Vitnum Encirclement—has cut every reb supply line to and from the granaries and also most of the wells. For the moment, the rebs still have water—they can use the Garr wells—but they'll run out of food very quickly. And that's when we're going to start seeing mass desertions."

"Then you think we've effectively won at this point?"

"I know we've won."

"Now," Denon said, "let me see if I understand what you've said. . . ." He consulted his notes and continued, "The rebels lost five hundred soldiers, we lost three times that many—"

"*May* have lost," Wunic said. "Every report I've seen indicates fewer casualties on our side than that."

"All right," Denon said, and he scribbled more notes, then paused, something occurring to him. "Would it be possible—could the king speak with someone from the front, a soldier who . . ." But Wunic was shaking his head. "I'm sorry, General, is that impossible?"

"The king has nearly won this war," Wunic said, and he thought: I *have nearly won this war. Years of wasted time, years of waiting, listening to men who are oblivious talk about war and now it's happened and I'm here. The bullshit I put up with at the academy, the routines, the endless public executions and guard duty assignments—and now I'm here.*

"His Majesty had asked to see someone," Denon said, "a soldier from the—"

"No," Wunic said. "This is a war, not a . . ." He hesitated. "No, that would be inconvenient and unprofessional." *When the king won't speak to me, except to publicly challenge my authority, he thinks that he can demand to speak with one of my men.* Wunic forced himself to remain calm. *He's a kid,* Wunic told himself. *He may be king, but he's still just a kid, he doesn't know any better.*

"I'm sorry," Denon said. "I wouldn't have brought it up, except that he asked."

"I understand."

"So, now, just so I can satisfy His Majesty's curiosity . . ."

Curiosity, Wunic thought, and Denon continued, "The rebels have fifteen hundred units in and around the Southern Garr?"

"Correct."

"And His Majesty's army consists of . . ." He checked his figures. "Perhaps two thousand, twenty-five hundred units immediately surrounding the rebels?" Denon hesitated. "Excuse me for asking, General, and this is probably very obvious—you know much more about this than I do—but wouldn't the rebels try to break out?"

Wunic shook his head, a slow smile forming, as if he was waiting for the punch line. Denon watched him without expression, and Wunic said slowly, "Those that don't defect—of course they'll try to break out."

"Five hundred or one thousand extra units is enough to stop them?"

"Lord Denon, I know you're asking because you have to, because you want the king to have all the information he can, but you have to understand, the rebels only have around one hundred firearms left, with maybe an average of two dozen rounds each, probably less than that. Every one of my boys—with few exceptions—is armed with a clean, fully-loaded gun." Denon frowned, as if he didn't understand, and Wunic said, "Yes. A thousand extra units is more than enough to keep the rebs where they are."

"If the king wanted, could we move more units in? Increase our numbers in the field even more?"

"It's not necessary. The rest of our soldiers are needed where they are."

"I just ask so that if the king asks, I have something to tell him," Denon said.

"It shouldn't be considered an option. But, yes, of course there are another thirty-five hundred units at the Garrs and palace."

Denon made more notes and asked quietly, "Is it true that the Garrs can operate on a staff of twenty?"

"With just a prison population to watch, yes. But there are civilians living there now," Wunic said.

"What about the palace?"

"Lord Denon, the king should know this is not an option. If troop presence were to drop at either of the Garrs there would be no one to organize basic things like food and water distribution."

"You're saying they might start rioting?"

"Yes. They might."

Denon asked, "Do you think the palace is safe?"

"Yes, but after everything that's happened, I would rather be over-cautious where the government is concerned."

"I understand: of course, General. I know you know what you're doing out there. I hate to ask you again, but are you sure no one can be brought back here from the front?" And before Wunic could respond, Denon continued, "We are going to have to get along with each other once this is over, and if you brought someone personally from the front, it might go a long way toward pacifying the king."

Wunic sighed and thought about it. If it really *was* that important, of course someone could be brought. "The king should know that this is not an acceptable request, and ordinarily I wouldn't consider taking individuals randomly from the front. But, if His Majesty honestly cares about the soldiers' situation, I'll see what I can do."

"Thank you, General. The boy doesn't know what he's doing, but he *does* care."

"I'll find someone at the front myself," Wunic said. "I'm sorry if I've been difficult, but you understand—"

"Of course, General."

"Will you also tell the king that I'm sorry, I shouldn't have challenged him in front of the soldiers. I didn't think."

"It wasn't your fault."

"I know," Wunic said, and he smiled. "But I should be stronger, because I can. That was inexcusable. He's still just a boy."

"I'll tell him," Denon said. "I'll make sure he understands."

"Thank you." And Wunic paused. "I don't think this would work without you, Lord Denon. I respect what you're doing and how hard this must be for you, going back and forth."

Denon smiled, and he went to Wunic, placing a hand on his shoulder. "Well, hopefully, for both our sakes, the kid will come around. He won't be sixteen forever."

"Thank you. I know you're behind me in this, and I respect that." Wunic shook his hand, and Denon said with a smile, "You'll get someone from the front?"

Wunic nodded to him. "Yes, Lord Denon, of course I will."

Denon watched him leave, and then he turned to the Religious Guards. "Come with me, all of you. And bring a shovel."

curling the fingers of his free hand into a spade, Vel fought through the mess of bodies and loose wrappings, toward the frozen dirt and the surface. Rot—frozen mold and mud—trickled into Vel's nose and mouth, and he retched, only to breathe in more. Small, hurried gasps, and he could still breathe—except that his body would not cooperate. Vel gagged, fighting the urge to vomit, more hot bile in his throat.

He struggled with his free arm, trying to find a way to move the bodies or enough of the dirt away, to use his legs and push up, but each time, Vel's muscles strained harder, and each time he rubbed more dead flesh, parting the dirt above him slightly, never enough. His fingers dropped into the fleshy jaw again, burning along the length of his entire arm and back from the exertion. Vel realized that he was holding his breath, the sickness still in his mouth. *Don't taste it*, he told himself. *Now push up—all the way.*

Vel kicked, but his legs were still too securely packed into the hole, there wasn't enough purchase, and Vel's free arm continued to writhe. Vel breathed tiny insects into his nose and throat—itching—as their tiny legs flailed inside him, and Vel vomited, his body shuddering, but he did not move. And he coughed miserably, warm stench on his face and across all of the blackness in front of his face. *The coughs were pathetic*, he thought distantly. Just a hollow, empty sound that died, soaked into the dirt and corpses around him. Vel wheezed, straining to find some air. *Almost gone*, he thought, *I'm done.*

Help me, he thought, and adrenaline flowed through him. His body instinctively used all of its strength, everything to find a way out, and for a moment Vel's heart quickened as his free hand broke through—but he could not move the corpses enough, there was simply too much dirt packed on top of them. *Goddamn it*, he thought, *someone help me—no, I can't die here. Not like this, because of those Goddamn soldiers. I can't die yet, please.* Vel convulsed, growling as he fought with the solid prison around him.

His vision began to cloud. The darkness of the grave, of the vomit and the dirt and bodies spotted into a deeper darkness, inside his head, on the interior of his eyes. Something stabbed his right arm, starting a fire in his forearm, and Vel felt his warm blood running out of a fresh wound. He tried to focus, and there were voices, just beyond, and now his right arm flopped—not into another body or another layer of soil, but through the *air*. His hand was above the ground. *Hallucinating*, he thought weakly, trembling involuntarily as the blackness took over. And now—*My eyes should be open*, he thought; *should be watching*—and he heard stabbing just beyond, and his free arm slackened.

"—arm!"

I'm . . . dying, he thought slowly, and consciousness fell away.

"—ull him out! Pull him out!"

And Vel was gone.

chapter 7

Lord Denon made himself comfortable in the solitary chair, and as Vel awoke with a rasping cough, Denon smiled, obviously relieved. Vel sprawled in his bed, right arm wrapped in a bandage, and as he woke, he tried to sit up, using his right arm for leverage, and then he stopped—wincing at the sudden pain.

"Goddamn," Vel said.

Denon motioned to the bedside table, and Vel saw the water cup, downing it rapidly. He cleared his throat, set the cup down, and leaned back weakly on the bed. They sat in silence for a moment, Denon studying Vel, and finally Denon said, "You're lucky I found you when I did."

"How did you know?" Vel asked, without moving.

Denon hesitated, as if he knew the answer would upset Vel. "General Wunic. . . . He told me."

Vel stared at the opposite wall, considering that, and then he coughed softly, sat up, and stared directly at Lord Denon. "And you want to tell me how General Wunic knew?"

"The General . . ." Denon paused. "I don't know."

Vel said it again slowly, "How did General Wunic know where I was?" And when Denon didn't respond, Vel asked, "What did he say?"

"He was explaining the situation at the front, and then he made a comment that he was sure you wouldn't interfere or object in the future." Denon waited for a response, and Vel slowly clenched the bed covers in both hands. Denon continued, "When I asked the general what he meant, he just said that he thought the cemetery was more dangerous with the rebels so nearby. He said he was surprised you would go there alone."

"Did he say anything else?"

"No. He wasn't very subtle—"

"He's in the military," Vel said. "You expect subtlety? Only an arrogant moron would push me into a Goddamn hole instead of just cutting my throat. Maybe he thought it would be funny. Where is it—I found a weapon down there. Did you bring it out?"

Denon went to the wall and picked up a long, metal spearlike object from the floor before the mirror. The spear was three feet long, black, and at one end the metal grew into a deadly curling blade, like an exaggerated scythe. Denon held it awkwardly at the rounded end, and he set it at the foot of the bed.

"What is it?" Lord Denon asked.

"Don't know. That's what I was told to get," Vel said. "May be one of their weapons."

"You think this belongs to the Frill?"

"Yes. I think I'm meant to trade it to them for some of their food and more of those plants." Vel took Denon's hand. "You pulled me out of there: Thank you."

"There's no need for that." Denon patted his hand. "I told you I would do what I can for you, Vel."

"Denon, if you hadn't found me when you did . . . I was almost gone—I *was* gone." He shuddered, remembering the desperation and the helplessness and the filth and decay. . . . "I would have been missing, no one would have found me. The snow would have covered the grave, the dirt would have frozen over, and General Wunic would have stopped anyone from digging up anything, wouldn't he? No one would have investigated. Wunic would have said that I didn't want to be king, that I ran away or something—he practically said that earlier. He doesn't want me here, does he?"

Denon sat again, glancing uncomfortably at the Frill weapon, then at Vel's arm. "How is the shovel wound?"

"It's better than dying down there."

"I'm sorry you had to go through that, Vel. And I know what it looks like, but you cannot immediately blame the general. We are at war right now, and there are a lot of people who—"

"I can blame him," Vel said. "Where is he?"

"I tried to find him," Denon said, "once I found you. The Religious Guard tell me that the general is at the front."

"Hiding," Vel said, and for a moment he wondered if it *had* to be Wunic; Denon was right, all of the rebels wanted Vel dead. Even if Wunic had known about it, he might not have—and how much difference does that really make? *The general wants me dead,* Vel thought.

"I was going to wait to talk to you about this. You need time to recover, but now I don't think we can wait. We've had more difficulties, more territory has been lost—General Wunic is personally overseeing an attempt to counterattack. Vel, we're going to lose. You need to prepare for an evacuation."

"Where are the soldiers who buried me?"

"I don't know," Denon said. "I have patrols looking for the men who accompanied you to the cemetery. They haven't been seen."

Vel shook his head as he smiled miserably. "I've had enough—I'm going to end this now, before it goes any further. I want to see General Wunic."

"That's not possible, Vel; he's at the front."

Vel stood, searching under his bed for clean clothes. He found his sword and pistol beneath his folded black overcoat on the floor nearby, and Vel said, "So? I'll go to the front then."

"Vel, I don't think you understand. The situation at the front is unstable at best, and the rebels have the advantage for the time being—"

"Denon, don't." Vel dressed quickly, stepping into new pants, found a new shirt—both black—and laced his boots. He tied his belt at his waist and slipped his pistol into the side. "I understand what you're saying. I understand that I'm too important to the city and all the rest of that, but I don't really care right now." Vel shrugged. "There are more important things."

"Like assassinating the general."

"Yes. Like that, for instance—as a purely hypothetical example." Vel grinned and attached his sword to the side opposite his pistol.

Denon remained where he was and said, "Please, Vel, think about this. Did you hear what I said a moment ago? There's a counteroffensive in progress right now. Even *if* you could find the general—which might be very difficult at the moment—if you did anything to hurt him—"

Vel started for the door. "There are other generals."

"*Vel.*" Vel paused, and Denon continued, "That's not the point. Regardless of how effective General Wunic is, the instant Wunic's soldiers realize that you're threatening their commanding *military* officer, what do you think will happen?"

Vel looked as if he had just sampled something with a strong aftertaste, and he said—as if *Of course they would do that*, "You think they'll try to stop me?"

"Wunic *is* a general, and right now, he's personally responsible for your entire army. If you're going to replace him, you have to do it quietly. Go after the general at the front and you'll be treated as an enemy." Denon shrugged. "*If* Wunic is responsible, he'll think you're dead, which will give you an advantage when and if he comes back."

"Goddamn it," Vel said, and he glared at the door, frustrated, then back at Denon. "No, there must be a way to do this now. He won't be around soldiers the entire time."

"Of course he will, Vel. He's launching the attack, he's orchestrating it."

Vel thought about it, and then he said quietly, "I really want to shoot something right now, Denon."

"I understand."

"I was *buried alive.*"

"I know, Vel. But now is not the time to go after the general of your entire military police force. Not when he's leading an army."

"So when he gets back . . ." Vel said, and he went back to the bed, not making any attempt to take off his weapons. "Maybe I should chop him up with this?" Vel touched the handle of the Frill spear.

Denon headed for the door. "You understand that I have to keep track of more things than I can count. Will you be all right if I leave you alone?"

Vel said, "I'm fine. You're sure I can't go kill General Wunic?"

Denon opened the bedroom room. "Trust me, there will be another time. I'll have a meal sent up if you're hungry . . ."

Vel thought of the girl who had delivered his last meal, the girl he had seen dancing. "Lord Denon?"

Denon looked back. "Yes?"

"Thank you," Vel said. "Honestly, if you hadn't found me . . . You saved my life. Thank you."

"Your well-being is one of my responsibilities, Vel. You wanted me as an advisor, this is part of that. I told you, you don't have to thank me for that."

Vel grunted. "*Responsibilities.* Just accept that I'm in debt to you. Again. How many times is this now that you've helped me out? Against Hillor, with information, trying to keep this Goddamn city together." Denon started to respond, and Vel said, "No, don't argue with me again. Thank you."

Denon allowed himself a brief smile, nodded, and was gone, his footsteps becoming inaudible further down the hallway. Vel drew his sword, approached the bedroom chair, and said, "Oh, Your Majesty, I didn't know you would be here, I—Not at all, General Wunic." And he chopped it in half, slight relief as he kicked the pieces apart. *Not yet,* he thought, and sheathed his sword again.

Vel stood for a long time, staring at himself in the mirror, wondering what he would do when he finally did meet Wunic. Would it be like it had been with Justice Hillor? Hillor had done his damage before being killed. *No,* Vel thought, *it won't be that way.* And he chuckled tiredly. *I don't have anyone I care about, nothing he can take away. I haven't the slightest idea of what I'm supposed to be doing as king, and everyone I know is already dead. Without Denon*—Vel didn't want to think about that. The door opened, and without turning, Vel said, "Is that my dinner?"

A female voice—Sisha's voice—said, "Yes, Your Majesty."

Vel turned—it was indeed the same girl—Sisha—who had brought him food earlier, the same girl he'd seen dancing in the auditorium, and she still wore that black dress. Sisha held a tray of more grassfruit, more water, and several peeled nuts. Her long, black hair had been drawn into a ponytail down her back, and she watched him through dark, intelligent eyes. Sisha was barefoot.

"I remember you," Vel said, taking the tray from her.

Sisha waited as he sat on the bedside, arranging the tray beside him. She examined the broken, chopped pieces of wood scattered across the carpet, as if the chair had exploded.

"Did something happen?" she asked.

Vel began to eat the grassfruit, carefully picking seeds out of his mouth as he ate. "Yes, I think I might need a new chair. I saw you dancing."

She blushed slightly. "I know, Your Majesty."

"That's not my name," he said. "My name's Vel." She didn't respond, and he said, "Who are you? I hadn't seen you, and now all of a sudden everywhere I turn in this palace, you're there."

"My name's Sisha."

"What do you do, Sisha? Dance and serve food?" Vel motioned her to sit with him—she sat at the foot of the bed, hands in her lap.

"Yes, Your Majesty."

"Vel. I have a hard time with people calling me that, unless I don't like them." He said in between bites. "And honestly I don't know you well enough to hate you yet, so we might as well stick with 'Vel' for now, all right?"

"And you'll let me know when to say 'Your Majesty'?"

"That's right. Like for instance, if you try to kill me or something—then you might have to be more formal."

She smiled and moved closer. "How is it?"

"What—the food? It's fine. How long have you been in the palace?"

"Not long."

Sisha began to casually undo her ponytail. Vel found himself watching the gesture intently, and when she noticed, he looked at his tray uncomfortably.

"Sorry, I . . ."

Sisha tossed the ribbon to the carpet and her hair fell in perfect waves across her shoulders and the slender dress straps. Sisha watched him, leaned closer, and gently moved the tray of food to the opposite end of the bed, away from them. Vel didn't move.

"I—"

She said, "Vel." And took his hand, opening his fingers and pressing them to the top of her chest. Vel felt his body reacting, blood changing its course of circulation, and his mouth began to dry.

Vel tried to think of something to say, and she eased his hand to her left breast, so that he was cupping it—he felt her regular heartbeat through the dress. His hand up to her neck, chin, and then into her mouth, and she began to suck his fingers, eyes closed. He felt her teeth lightly—loose, dried teeth, withered tongue—and Vel realized that he had jerked his arm back.

Sisha stared at him, even closer now. "What's wrong?"

A chill down the length of his spine, and Vel said, "Please, get out of here."

"Why?"

I don't know, he thought. *Because I'm insane. And because you'll die just like that someday. And I don't need to care about you, I don't want to. You're already dead. You do this, you even touch me, and whatever it is that finds the people who have come into contact with me and destroys them—it will kill you. I'm safe now without that—* and she moved beside him, her fingers on his shoulder.

"It's all right," she said softly. "Don't think."

Don't think, he told himself, and she was untucking his shirt, loosening his belt, discarding the pistol and sword. *Stop,* he wanted to say. *You don't understand.* Vel's pulse was a drum in both ears, echoing through his skull, and—*I'm terrified,* he realized, arms shaking. *Why? I can fight and kill and still this frightens me.*

When I have seen by time's fell hand defaced, the rich, proud cost of outworn unburied age.

Vel closed his eyes, and Sisha helped him take off his shirt. He let it happen, trying to stop his body from reacting, trying to stop thinking about Lydia and about the corpses. *I don't love you, Sisha; I don't even know you.*

Sisha draped herself across Vel's chest, dark curls falling over his bare skin, and he felt her kissing up and down his chest. She began to undo his pants—he imagined that Lydia was watching from the corner of the room, drained and dead and wrapped in a white burial shroud. Bloody smears stained the inside of the fabric where her face had been blown apart, but Lydia was watching as Sisha slipped his pants down.

Sisha rolled on top of him, and Vel opened his mouth—her lips with his, and their tongues together. And she eased onto him—and he felt the warm, hot rush; inside her, and suddenly that was all that mattered. Sisha didn't stop kissing him, and Vel reacted. She did too.

Eight years since prison, and now Blakes—thirty-five years old—stood on a platform, his vision the white of continual flashbulbs and recorders and transmitters. Behind him hung a banner with the logo, *Life Over Lies: Blakes in '95 for Euro-American Consul.* He heard the cheer of the crowd as a continual, unbreaking noise, like the ocean.

Blakes smiled and nodded thanks to the audience. He had long since given up trying to make out faces through the glare of lights, and now he had learned to look from one place in the whiteness to another, acting as if he was recognizing individuals.

His advisors had told him that only the first twenty seconds of this day's speech—even though it was to be one of his last and most important—only the first twenty seconds of it mattered. Everyone in the crowd, those people who would hear the entire thirty minutes, were already committed to voting for Blakes or they would not have paid the several hundred dollars to get in. The important element was the thirty percent who were undecided, and who would probably listen to all of the sound bites played on the networks that evening of Blakes, Flanigan and Morrey; the three candidates who now statistically had a chance of winning the election for Euro-American consul at the end of the following week.

And so Blakes made the first twenty seconds count:

"You know who I am and you know who my opponents are—this is not the time for a listing of triumphs or challenges or failures. I swear to you that if I am elected consul, I will oppose the interests of mediocrity, I will bring honor and strength to this great continent—I will fight your battles for all of you, in the name of security and justice. We are Westerners, and there some people who seem to have forgotten what that means; as Westerners we will never shrink from our obligations to this world and to ourselves. As Europeans and as Americans we are united in supremacy. Whatever the challenge—this is our world, our day, *our time*!" Blakes banged his fist on the podium, and the crowd exploded into applause.

The important part was done—translated into hundreds of languages on millions of networks—and after Blakes finished his speech, he went through the crowd, shaking hands and smiling, and finally through a tunnel to the hotel where he was staying in Vienna. Blakes's advisors spoke to him of the details of his current campaign, and several other men and women from energy corporations and network boards met with him privately, thanked him for his time, and explained that they had full confidence in what he would bring to the parliament. Blakes thanked them, laughed and joked with them, and when he was alone again, Adria came and sat beside him on the huge hotel bed.

Two consuls headed the Euro-American Parliament, acting as a joint executive branch, and the other four hundred and six senators and congressmen and women served as the legislature. Eight years since prison, and he had found friends in the outlying bureaucracy of the parliament, had found disillusioned, frustrated politicians who had narrowly lost the last great election, who saw war coming with no chance of Western success. The next century might be one of Chinese occupation unless the world changed, they had often said. Blakes took menial jobs, bought dinner for these men, and slowly, he had found his way higher and higher within the inner circles.

No longer a terrorist, Blakes claimed that he had been falsely indicted in '89, that he had simply been in the wrong place at the wrong time. And because there was sympathy for the terrorists' ideals among some of the intelligentsia—"Yes, something *should* be done unless we want London to turn into a western Calcutta run by three hundred year old Rockefellers"—Blakes had become their tool. They were using him to change the system from within: he was intelligent, an excellent public speaker, and the reincarnation of William Blake.

Blakes thought about the corporations as he watched a news report on various European polls on the large monitor at the opposite wall.

"It was a good speech," Adria said.

Blakes nodded, of course it was. It had been written by a team of professionals with combined experience in more than a hundred successful campaigns all around the world. Blakes had changed two words after receiving it. "This" to "That" and "My" to "Our" toward the end of the speech. Blakes was to be an instrument of the corporations, governments and media who were helping to fund his campaign. William Blakes, the sixteenth consul of the Euro-American Parliament, who would serve into the twenty-second century, as the consuls had terms of five years.

"I said it was a good speech."

"I heard you," Blakes said. "Thanks."

Adria rolled close to him, and he wrapped an arm around her shoulder. She rested her head on his chest.

Adria had once run a computer program—using one of the new organic systems, the "animal computers"—to analyze one of his speeches for content, and the program had concluded that it had none. The speech had been composed entirely of rhetoric.

Blakes pushed the top of Adria's head gently, closer to his stomach. She eased down, resting her chin on his shirt and went no further—Blakes unbuttoned his pants, and as he spread the opening, Adria said, "Please, I'm tired, I—"

"So am I," Blakes said, and as he pushed the top of her head, she resisted. So he slapped her hard.

Blakes watched her cheek redden, and Adria looked at him with empty submission. "Go ahead," he said, pushing her head again. And she did.

Ten days later, Blakes sat at a circular table in a cramped, smoky room, surrounded by aides and monitors all set to roughly the same level of volume, so that none were understandable. Blakes nodded when appropriate and he tried to read the sheets they gave him. Countries not voting for him the way he expected, losing some areas, and now gaining others he should not have gotten. The charts and statistics were all right there, the election could not be happening as it was. It was theoretically impossible.

"—still in the lead."

"—we'll pick up votes here, and then . . ."

And on and on, and it was already past three in the morning, and still the results were coming in. Blakes thought about what he would do, Adria in a chair by his side. He thought about what he had told her last night and about Jesse, and the ice pick he had driven into the base of his skull at that bar in Mexico City. Blakes had stabbed him forty-three times in the lavatory, until Jesse's head was a messy pulp, and then he had let it drop into the dirty toilet bowl.

"—didn't think the Rhineland would . . ."

"—you see these numbers! We're picking up the Spanish . . ."

Blakes smiled and nodded and smoke and drank, and he continued to think about working the campaigns he had. About befriending Sunaki-Heiman on his way up, and their publicity campaign, and then Blakes had worked with Donitz in '93, and now Donitz would be his ally in the parliament, as the other consul once Blakes was elected. Except that Blakes didn't want allies. He thought about the swastika he would hang from the capitol buildings in Berlin, in Washington, D.C., New York, Chicago; in Paris, London, Rome, and yes, everywhere in Europe and America. Blakes had grown up with talk of war, with the growing feeling that apocalyptic destruction might lie just beyond the next season, but that the Euro-American government was actually too cowardly to act and so it made no difference. If anything happened, the government would submit to the Eastern powers long before they risked nuclear Armageddon: "Remember Los Angeles."

Blakes would not hang the swastika for historical reasons—and yes, some historians might understand the significance—but actually very few in the population would probably even recognize the symbol. Blakes would denounce Nazism, and the swastika was to be what it had once been; the flag of life over lies, the flag of power. *And it is the power of the individual at the expense of cattle that I am interested in.*

And I'll burn it all down, and until that moment I will smile and nod and let them use me. And I will be the instrument for the corporations and all of the other bastards who have perverted and polluted and raped this world—and I will cleanse it with fire. Things have gone so far astray, and people say this all the time in the streets or at conversations over dinner, that it's really too late to fix anything. The only way to fix it, Blakes thought, *is to wash it all away. If millions have to die for that perfection, I have the strength of vision to order it,* Blakes thought. *No one else, not Jesse, but me: William Blakes.*

Blakes was wandering through the halls of his campaign headquarters, past aides offering him coffee, past more advisors who quoted numbers, past endless television and computer monitors, and there, at the end stood Donitz. Donitz had been one of Blakes's most important supporters in this: as a veteran of the wars in India, Donitz stood 6'8", with broad shoulders, and he was the other reigning consul: if Blakes were elected, Donitz would be the other most powerful person in the government.

Wearing a shiny leather jacket, holding a cup of styrofoam coffee, Donitz smiled when he saw Blakes. Donitz's short hair was streaked gray along the sides, and he waved Blakes to follow him down a nearby hall, grabbing a cookie off of a passing cart.

"Consul," Blakes said, "sir, I thought you were in New York."

"No," Donitz said, and Blakes fell into step behind him. "I'm here. How are you?"

"I don't know—I'm tired. I've never done this before, I'm not sure if—"

"It's perfectly normal," Donitz said, and he paused at a closed door: through the slotted window, the conference room inside was dark. "That's what campaigns are all about. Anxiety, fear and hate." He smiled. "It's not unlike war." And he clicked open the door to the empty conference room, but didn't turn on the light as he moved inside. "I want to talk to you, just for a minute—I can't stay."

Blakes followed him in, and when the door shut, the only light was the square at the top of the door, the white glow of the hall. Blakes could faintly see Donitz, one hand in his pocket, sipping the hot coffee as he paced along the opposite wall, as if oblivious to the fact that they stood in total darkness.

Blakes said. "Why are we—"

"I know what you're doing," Donitz said, and he stopped. Blakes couldn't see, but he thought he heard something snap, and there was something in Donitz's free hand, like a lighter or a keychain.

"I don't understand."

"You can bullshit me out there." Donitz indicated the window with his styrofoam cup. "But not right now." Silence, and then Donitz said, "You're a very dangerous, very bad person, Blakes. I know that, I'm not judging you—I'm telling you—I see what you are. I know what you're capable of, what you might want to do, but I think that your hatred is rooted in good intentions. That's why I'm willing to work with you. And you're intelligent and capable, and most importantly you have the bonus of being William Blake—a propaganda tool that we don't have to work on—going for you.

"I'm not going to play games with you right now. When this is finished, we'll go back into the hall and we'll smile and we'll talk and shake hands, and we'll never mention this conversation to anyone else, to each other or to ourselves. These words do not exist. This room isn't bugged, isn't miked, and even if I missed something a moment ago when I looked through it, I'm wearing a scrambler: what we say in here right now never has and never will exist, do you understand?"

"Yes."

"Okay. Don't fuck with me, Blakes."

Blakes stared at him, one hand creeping back to the door, and—not for the first time since he had been campaigning—he wished that he had allowed his personal bodyguards to follow him more closely.

Blakes said, "Why would I—"

"I'm making you consul so that we can work together, so that you can help me and I can help you do what needs to be done and what everyone else is too afraid to do to improve the world. I'm talking about keeping the chinks and the niggers out, do you understand? I'm talking about segregation, about our culture. It is possible to take that to an extreme: that's not useful. I'm interested in these ideologies, in championing the Western world and our heritage, blah, blah, blah, so long as it's doable, so long as we gain an economic, political and military advantage in doing it. I am *not* willing to risk my career or your career or the future of the world on *ideas*, on propaganda and petty college, anarchist bullshit. The moment that isn't working, they're Chinese citizens and Africano citizens, whatever you or I may think. This world requires compromises, and success depends on flexibility. We're not destroyers, Blakes, we're builders. Do you see what I'm saying?"

"Yes."

"The only way we can make this better is by working within the system. As mucked up as it is, it beats the alternative. You remember what I said? You cross me . . ."

"Yes."

"I know what you are," Donitz said, and he drank some of his coffee, and then shook his head. "I know, and that means other people know. I'm smarter than you are. You fuck me, and before you know you're going to act against me, I'll put a cord around your throat: I'll destroy you, do you understand? I made you."

"Yes."

"Okay." Donitz hesitated, and then he put whatever it was back into his pocket and approached Blakes, patted him on the shoulder, and went out into the hall, smiling and talking about the coffee as he passed Blakes's campaign advisors.

Blakes let the door shut again, staring at the empty room. *You're a coward,* he thought. *Even if you're right, and a worm lives longer than a butterfly, what kind of life is that*? Back into the hall, and Blakes returned to the anarchy of the main campaign rooms.

At just after five in the morning, Blakes was falling asleep at the table, and Adria had gone off somewhere, probably to collapse in their bedroom. Aides continued to rush in and out on the flow of artificial stimulants. And someone was shaking Blakes's shoulder, trying to wake him.

"—sir . . ."

And it sounded like they were shouting about a gun. Someone had a gun.

Blakes sat up slowly, wiped his eyes, and the room was smiling at him—champagne offered to him, and a young girl on his staff kissed him full on the lips. Confetti in his hair, and Blakes spilled some of the champagne on his shirt. Not a gun, they aren't saying "I've got a gun"—not "you've got a gun", instead:

"—you've won!"

"Mr. Consul, thank you for—"

And Blakes shook hands, forcing the weak smile to his lips. He set the champagne down and made his way through the crowds of noisemakers and politicians and important business men and aides, and Blakes thanked them all and pledged himself to the future of the West.

"—a poet as our ruler!" someone shouted, laughing, and Blakes smiled.

A poet, he thought. *And God's will be done.*

Denon kept his arms folded tightly, head down, as he braced himself, slogging through the cold, hissing air and snow. A circle of a dozen men in white uniforms with swastika armbands, all armed with assault rifles—the Religious Guard—created a perimeter around Denon, and as they hiked through the deep snow of the street, Denon squinted: The Garr should be there. Just ahead, a ghost-shadow; the dark outline of an enormous black fortress, the Northern Garr, was barely visible.

Drawing closer, tents and makeshift shelters scattered along cleared bits of frozen ground on both sides of the street. People huddled around wisps of fire, staring numbly at Denon and his Religious Guard as they passed. Soon the tents and shacks filled the center of the street, and as Denon drew nearer to the Garr, the Religious Guard guided him in a weaving path through the maze of rickety dwellings. Soldiers patrolled the street in heavy overcoats, carrying pots of broth rather than weapons. Denon passed long lines of people in rags, all waiting to fill tiny bowls, and on both sides, freezing children cried.

Stomping through frozen piles of excrement and constant, dirty slush, the Garr loomed much closer now. This is where everyone had come. All of the thousands of people that had lived in the city of Hope before the snow and the war had been told to come to the Western and Northern Garrs, where they would be supervised by soldiers and provided rations. People huddled in clusters, shivering under layers of blankets, and Denon stepped over bodies, half-buried and blue, that weren't moving at all. As he passed, people shouted to him, whispered praise.

"—praise God, thank you, Lord Denon."

"—believe you can save us."

Denon smiled at them warmly and when they rushed in front of him, the Religious Guard carefully cleared a path, and Denon waved his hand, blessing the crowds as he pressed through, approaching the outer defenses of the Garr. The Northern Garr was surrounded by two circular defensive walls, and tents and shacks had been packed into every conceivable space, leaving a faint, slippery walkway. The snow had been compressed into smooth, slick ice in this weaving path, and Denon caught himself on the outer wall—the Religious Guard steadied him—and through the space between the walls, there were more lines. The roofing of shacks created an almost unbroken miniature city, with people huddling and coughing and pissing and sleeping together in the covered spaces.

Soldiers directed them, ordering people back to their "homes" once they had filled their bowls with a thin broth, and no one struggled or fought. The eyes of the people Denon passed looked worn, faded and dead, as if they had given up emotion. Into the main yard that surrounded the Garr, the shacks were slightly larger and even more dense, more soldiers hurried from one end of the yard to the other with dispatches from the front.

Closer, and now Denon reached the entrance of the Garr itself: inside—and Denon saw it, but he didn't go in—the air was hot with the smell of sickness, and people lay along both sides of the narrow hallways. The Garr was a prison, and it was not meant to be used as a shelter. Around the opposite end—in the yard—Denon watched a pair of soldiers carrying a cart of frozen bodies that they dumped onto a growing pile.

The soldiers guarding the entrance saluted Denon and said, "Lord Denon, no one told us you would—"

"I know," Denon said. "What are you doing with the dead?" He indicated the pile around the side of the Garr. "That can't be all of them. . . ."

"There was talk last night of using the meat as a base for—"

"We are not savages," Denon said shortly. "Cannibalism is not an option, do you understand me?"

"Yes, sir. The bodies have been burned in the past, but with the snow, it's difficult to cremate them entirely, and the rations aren't enough to provide for—"

"How many people at this Garr?"

"I don't know, Lord. You'll want the C.O. Colonel Burran was appointed by General Wunic to supervise this Garr."

"I'm not interested in inspecting the Garr," Denon said. "I need a runner, and I want you two . . ." he indicated two of the men guarding the entrance, ". . . to come with me. You're being reassigned."

The first soldier began to pale. "Sir, we're not to be transferred to the front without—"

"Not to the front," Denon said. "Where's the runner?"

They found a kid with white markings, and Denon handed him a sealed dispatch. "To General Wunic." Denon told him where to find the general at the front and then said, "It's extremely urgent that he receive this message before he leaves that position, do you understand?"

The runner nodded. "Yes, sir."

"Go," Denon said, and the kid started across the yard.

Denon took the two soldiers he had indicated a moment earlier, and they went back to the palace.

Through the main entrance hall, past soldiers and Religious Guard that hurried from one room to the next, and Denon led the men to the rear chambers, through a pair of sealed doors, all manned by the Religious Guard, and they finally stopped in a room where thirty soldiers worked with large bits of metal and plastic.

Open crates were strewn along the walls, and the soldiers paused when Denon stepped inside.

"Here are two more to help you get this operational more quickly," Denon said. "It looks like it's coming along well. . . . Which one is this?"

He approached a mounted, rivuleted platform of metal, elevated on treaded wheels. A pair of long metal tubes extended from its end, like the barrels of a very large gun. Two teams had been working independently on the artillery; Wunic had been checking in on one—seven men assembling an artillery unit at the far end of the palace. Those seven men were far from completing their artillery unit; the general was convinced that the war was nearly over, and so finishing a piece of artillery had not been terribly important to him.

"The ninth one, sir," one of the soldiers said. "This is number nine."

Denon had independently assigned a team of thirty men to put together artillery pieces as quickly as they possibly could. The finished artillery was stored in the recesses of the Church, and all of Denon's operations were supervised by the Religious Guard. Yes, the military police soldiers were necessary; without them, the artillery pieces would never function as effectively in the field. Military units were needed to use the artillery, but the Religious Guard were kept close at all times to ensure that these operations remained entirely secret, except to the men who had been assembling the pieces and who would soon command them.

Wunic doesn't know, Denon thought. *No one knows.* He's been struggling to put together a single piece for weeks, and hasn't particularly cared whether or not it could be completed. The finished artillery units were large, impressive, and they supposedly lobbed heavy explosive shells—their range, according to the instructions on the crates, could cover the entire distance of Hope. Denon had ordered some of the explosive shells tested, had learned what they were capable of. Finished artillery could annihilate men, crush buildings, and smash holes in the Southern Garr. It was complicated, yes, but the end result was worth the weeks it had taken to get this far.

"How long until all sixteen are ready?"

"We'll have to get the sixteenth from the other end of the palace, sir."

"Yes, I know. How long until they'll be finished, Sergeant?"

The soldier rubbed his eyes: Denon hadn't let them sleep. He had had teams of twenty or thirty soldiers working in eighteen-hour, continuous shifts to put the artillery together and learn to use it.

"Not long at all now."

The men Denon had brought from the front were confused, and Denon indicated two of the soldiers who had been working the longest.

"You two are off-duty," he said, then smiled at the newcomers. "And you two will take their places. Explain the situation to these new men, Sergeant, and when you rest, of course, you are not to leave this wing. I'll have double rations brought in within the hour."

Denon had them sleeping on cots in the side passages and along the walls of this room—this back room and the adjoining passages were connected to the palace only through one door—and that entrance was always manned by the Religious Guard. When an artillery piece was completed, they covered it in blankets, Denon temporarily had all of the soldiers in the main entrance hall and nearby passages reassigned, and they rushed the artillery outside, several blocks through the snow, to the Church, where it was hidden and guarded in the underground vaults: where all of this had been stored in crates to begin with.

"How long?" Denon asked again.

"A day or two," the Sergeant said. "Maybe longer, maybe shorter, depending. And we'll have to get the one they've been working on at the other end of the palace . . ."

"Very good," Denon said, and he thought, *This is how battles are won.*

In the subconscious, in the world of secrets and half-truths: *This is how I will win this war, this city. Not with God, with artillery.*

chapter 8

Approaching the front, Wunic saw heads.

Three soldiers as an escort, and they moved from one line of reserve soldiers to the next, from building to building in an area just west of the market district. From the palace, over the bridges, the river was now frozen in jagged blocks on the surface, and Wunic had paused in the continual snowfall, trying to see as far as he could downstream. The buildings on either side of the river had all appeared deserted, most of their roofs collapsed under the knee-deep snow that filled the streets and alleyways.

And as he drew closer to the front, Wunic had seen markers; poles with heads mounted on them standing in doorways or around occupied buildings or snowy rubble. It was a tradition the police soldiers used against rioters and criminals sometimes, to leave reminders where the offenders had been stopped. Here, the heads served as signs of battle, and Wunic paused at a two-story building, its surface scoured in bullet holes, the front entryway visibly dark with what were probably bloodstains. Several soldiers occupied a line of buildings or blocks at fairly regular intervals as Wunic drew closer to the front, and he passed a mound of bodies trailing a long plume of white smoke. They had been piled on one side of an alley on a stack of broken wood from a collapsed house, but the snow kept the corpses from lighting.

Closer, and now the markers were more frequent, with rows of heads in the center of streets, some falling over in the drifting snow. How many bodies had disappeared under the waves of snowfall? Wunic's lips felt dry, chapped, and already his toes were growing cold as he trudged through more streets, passing through more buildings—more papers shown to whatever officer happened to be stationed at that checkpoint—and now Wunic saw a line of perhaps twenty men and women hanging from a crossbeam overhead. Most were missing arms or legs, and Wunic ducked, and exited this building, walking across a wide street, usually filled with merchants and peddlers, wading through the deep snow, past more "head-posts" as he had heard several men call them, and now he heard a distant irregular cracking, as if someone was smashing unripe grassfruit together too loudly.

At the opposite end of the street, Wunic was led to a large building, two stories high, filling a good portion of the block. It had once been a bar and brothel, and Wunic saw the sign, MALIN TAVERN posted above carefully arranged rows of heads and more piles of bodies. Bullet marks here, and deeper, long grooves in both walls. Wunic offered his papers to the soldier posted at the entry. The kid held a rifle over one arm and looked exhausted. He stiffened crisply to Wunic and moved to the side, Wunic's escort heading back across the street the way they had come.

"Commanding officer?" Wunic asked.

The cracking noises—*gunfire*, Wunic thought—continued from somewhere in the vicinity. Then stopped, and then more shots in a confused chattering.

"Yes, General. The colonel's on the second floor."

"Thank you," Wunic said, and he stepped past the soldier into a hallway of men and women, seated on either side, filling the space. Wunic stepped carefully between rows of tattered legs and sleeping torsos, and then into a larger, main room, where soldiers rushed with weapons from end to end. *Fewer people resting here*, Wunic thought, and then he noticed the boarded windows at the opposite wall, where snow blew in through wide, cracked holes.

Wunic took a rickety staircase to the second floor, past jumbles of soldiers, some solemn and resting, others laughing and shouting at one another. The second floor hall led to a series of rooms, presumably once used for lodging and prostitution, now acting as snipers' nests and command centers. Wunic paused in one doorway, watching a pair of men at a boarded window, peering through a slot in the wood, rifles wedged into the gap—and beyond Wunic saw only the quiet snowfall and occasionally, the opposite block, across another wide, snowy street.

"Commanding officer?" Wunic asked a passing soldier, and the man pointed to a large room at the end of the hall, where more snipers were gathered. Wunic saw clusters of officers with papers and a short, bulging man in uniform: the colonel.

The three windows in this room were each manned by a separated row of snipers, with makeshift boards set in place to protect themselves from return fire. Now Wunic could make out a large, two-story building directly across the street, and snow blew in over the boards, whipping across their faces and spraying their blue and gray coats. Everyone Wunic saw was armed with a rifle and sword.

"Colonel," Wunic said, approaching the officer, and the colonel held up one hand, continuing to talk to a young aide.

"—that flank must be reinforced. You tell the major that I issued this order personally."

"Yes, sir," the aide said, and he ran from the room with a bound dispatch.

The colonel turned casually, and then stiffened when he recognized Wunic.

"General, I didn't—"

"I'm not here to relieve you, Colonel," Wunic said. "I just need one of your men."

"One of my men?" Gunfire from across the street, and Wunic heard return fire behind him in one of the other rooms. The colonel was oblivious to the noise, and he said, "Sir, I'm sorry, but I don't understand. You came here to ask for one man?"

"That's right, Colonel."

"I need reinforcements, sir. Do you know if we can expect more units from the palace?"

Wunic started to answer, and loud popping from outside cut him off—one row of snipers at a nearby window fell—their wooden cover smashing in half—the three men dropped, blasted through the torso. One, two, three.

"—bastard . . ."

Someone started screaming obscenities, and all of the snipers in the room opened fire, rifles flashing in controlled bursts as they peppered the opposite building. Wunic watched the rifles flash and hiss—gunfire from outside—and one of the soldiers standing beside a window yelled as part of his leg blew away in a red mist. He screamed and went down, grabbing at the sudden wound. There was shouting from outside, through the snow.

"I got him!" one of the men shouted. "Look at that!"

Someone outside began to yell unintelligibly.

The colonel backed into the hallway, and Wunic followed him, staring at the three wounded snipers who had been first hit. Two were old, but the third looked young, perhaps in his early twenties. All three men had been split through the chest several times, blood running from their bodies in a steaming pool. The last injured man continued to wail and lay in a corner, holding his leg. Soldiers ran from the room, searching for a medic.

"We're hit like this, sir." The gunfire continued, the colonel shook his head, walking back into the room. "Cease firing! Cease firing!"

One by one, the men stopped, keeping their weapons trained through the open window. There was a final crack from the other side of the street, and a hole exploded in the corner of the window frame, wood spraying across the bloody floor.

"Damn it! Goddamn it," someone said.

"I want my wounded out of here," the colonel said, waving his arm at the one-legged man. Then he motioned to the dead. "Come on, let's clean this up."

They began to carry the bodies away, down the stairs, and the colonel returned to Wunic. *This is unlike anything I was trained to do*, Wunic thought. Wunic had been to the front before, but each time he saw these weapons—these guns—in action, he thought about what he had learned at the academy. About swordsmanship and strength and virtue and honor and all of those things that they taught when men and women were trained to become police soldiers. *I don't see any of that in these weapons*, Wunic thought. *And maybe politics is just as appropriate: dealing with people, with a king who has no sense, who has no sense of what's happening out here, how war has abruptly changed—maybe that's appropriate because the rest of us are just pretending to understand the consequences of these weapons.*

"We continue to take losses like this, sir," the colonel said, patting men on their shoulders as they rushed from the room with stretchers. "Bastards haven't stopped, and they're less than fifty feet away, but it doesn't matter because with this Goddamn snow—excuse me, sir—with this snow we just eat up ammunition in these firefights."

The youngest of the wounded—the boy in his early twenties that Wunic had thought was dead—was staring at him.

"General," the boy said. *He recognizes me*, Wunic thought, and he went back into the room, kneeling beside the kid. Wunic examined the shredded coat and open, pulsing meat of the boy's chest and stomach. Someone else in the room started laughing, and Wunic ignored the noise. Most of them were watching him.

"General," the boy said again, "General, what happened?"

Wunic touched the kid's bloody cheek. "You're all right, son," Wunic said. "Stick it out, and you'll be all right."

". . . dying?" the boy said. "I can't die . . . please . . ." And he looked frightened, as if he was going to cry.

Wunic shook his head. "No. Calm down, soldier. Death doesn't happen to us—you're not going to die."

"Oh my God. . . . What happened?"

"That's right, you wait and we'll get you patched up and fighting again. You're not going to die."

The boy made a gasping noise, his fingers curling and then slackening, and he died. Wunic got back up, the rest of the room watching him. "Back to your posts! What do you think this is? No, don't salute me, son, those rebs would love to tag an officer, wouldn't they? Back to those positions! Let's get these bastards!" And Wunic returned to the hallway with the colonel.

"So Colonel," Wunic said, "I need you to give me one soldier. Who it is, I don't care. I just need one."

"Just one, sir?"

"That's right."

"May I ask what the—"

"No, you may not, Colonel. Just pick one of your men. You're doing a fine job here, a fine job."

"Yes, sir."

Wunic watched them carry the dead kid out of the room. *Taking him to a pile of corpses,* Wunic thought. *These guns have changed everything.* Another crack of gunfire from across the street, and wind scattered snow across the floor, new soldiers hurrying into the places where the four men had just been killed or wounded.

A courier with white markings on both shoulders of his coat took the stairs two at a time, watching General Wunic—and Wunic and the colonel stopped talking as the courier drew closer.

"Sir, dispatches from the palace," the courier said, breathing hard. His cheeks were flushed a bright pink, and Wunic accepted the sealed paper from him. It was closed in the perfect emblem of a blue circle, the marking of the Church. *What is this?* Wunic wondered. *Now the king doesn't want just one, but an entire squad to describe the front to him?*

Wunic opened the dispatch:

General Wunic,

This is extremely important or I would have waited until you returned. The building adjacent to your current position has been drained of almost all rebel forces. The enemy has withdrawn units temporarily, and they are keeping token resistance in place to hold the position until new units are moved in. They currently have roughly ten soldiers in the adjacent building and only another twelve or so within distance of reinforcement.

I think you'll agree that the adjacent buildings should be taken now with whatever you have at your disposal. This could be the mistake that costs the rebels their perimeter around the Southern Garr. I thought you would want to know, and if you plan to attack immediately, I advise you to do whatever is necessary to see to it as soon as possible, as the situation is probably only temporary.

LORD DENON

Wunic stared at the paper, the young courier watching the snipers at the window. *I'm going to lead this,* he thought. *I'm here, aren't I, and enough of these kids have died—they deserve a chance to hit back.* And there had been no mention in Denon's note of the soldier he wanted to see—this is much more important than appeasing the king and Denon knows it.

"Thank you," Wunic said to the courier.

The courier nodded. "Would you like me to deliver a reply, General?"

Wunic glanced at the colonel, who was waiting to be shown the dispatch.

"Yes," Wunic said. "Tell him I'll do it, tell him we're going to smash the rebs and we're going to do it now."

"Anything else, sir?"

"No, that's it."

"Yes sir."

The courier left, and Wunic folded his arms across his chest, dispatch still in hand.

"How many men do you have in this building, Colonel?"

A crack and a hole exploded in a nearby wall, inches from one soldier's shoulder, and the soldier jumped, nearly firing his rifle on reflex, his eyes wide and tired.

"Seventy-four, sir," the colonel said.

Wunic handed him the dispatch, and when the Colonel finished, he shook his head. "Ten units," he said. "I don't believe it, sir."

"The rebs have ten," Wunic said. "And each of our boys is fully armed; theirs aren't."

The colonel frowned at the paper. "General, I'm sorry, sir, but are you certain this information is accurate? What are the intelligence sources? We haven't seen—"

"The information is reliable, Colonel. The figures are correct. Lord Denon wouldn't have sent it unless he was sure. He understands the situation as well as we do."

"Sir, I don't understand why the rebels would shift their units so dramatically away from *here*."

Wunic took the paper and slipped it into his coat. "It doesn't matter. There will be casualties, of course, but that building over there is worth a handful of men, isn't it?"

The colonel smiled a cold, unfeeling smile. There were dark, accented lines around his lips. "Yes, General."

"How many units will we lose—how many is that position worth? How many lives will it save in the long run to take it now?"

The colonel paused, not to think about it, but because he had realized that General Wunic was taking command of the offensive. The colonel said, "Sir, my men have taken losses for weeks continually. I've found, General, that you can multiply the number of enemy rifles by two or three, that will be our casualties."

"Say twenty or thirty maximum then," Wunic said. "Is that position worth twenty or thirty of your men?"

"Yes, sir. But—General, if that information—"

"It is reliable," Wunic said, and he thought, *Denon wouldn't have sent it otherwise. Why would he?*

"Sir, once we've crossed, we might lose another ten in the house."

Wunic thought about it. "Fine, Colonel. We're both adults. Ten more casualties once we've crossed the street, but we will have pushed the rebs back, won't we?"

"Yes, sir."

Constant fighting, unending casualties, Wunic thought, and he studied the colonel.

And that's why you don't want to believe Lord Denon's numbers, Wunic thought. *Because you've been fighting frontal assaults since the war began, and it's done nothing but kill your soldiers—and how many of these boys were with you when this started? But the war's almost over: I know that and you don't. You've been waiting for the assaults to pay off, for a rest; you thought that the hard part was over until the rebs try to break through, and even then it would be easier because the numbers always work in favor of the defense.*

"Keep pushing them, Colonel. That's the way we're going to win—we're going to break them."

"Yes, sir."

But Lord Denon's instinct was right, Wunic thought. *If we can take this building from the rebels, they might never get it back. Make the rebels see what I see, that their fight is hopeless, that they're just waiting to die at this point. Keep pushing and they'll know that they've lost, they'll understand.*

God, I've waited my life for this moment. Crush them, smash the rebs until they're all lined up and then stand aside and bow and thank His Majesty the king for the honor of leading His men, because whatever some of these officers think, these men serve Vel, not me. That's the way it should be, the natural order of things. Tradition, justice; Life over Lies.

Wunic watched the soldiers in the large room. Some were obviously listening, they had overheard Wunic's conversation with the colonel, and Wunic saw the exhaustion and fear that tugged at the corners of their mouths and the muscles in their cheeks. The colonel had probably suggested, may even have told them that the frontal assaults are over, Wunic thought. *It's much easier to play this defensively, isn't it?*

"But that's not the way we're going to do it," Wunic said.

"Sir?"

Wunic paced through the room. "Get up, men. All of you get up."

A shot blasted a hole in the wall opposite the nearest window with a brief pop—and a soldier who had been walking in exactly that direction stopped and grinned nervously with the others around him.

"You boys are tired, I know that," Wunic said. "We're working to get you reinforced, but we've got them. Those damn rebs are running out of options, and we know it—and today we're going to make sure they know it.

"We're going right over there and taking that Goddamn building from them. They've pushed us and we're going to push them back. The rebs don't have water or food and they're running out of bullets.

Now that building there," Wunic said, and he stepped right up to the window: a clean target for any snipers that might be watching, and he pointed out at the house opposite them. "That building there is down to *ten* men; now that's a mistake, and Goddamn it, it's a mistake that we're going to make them pay for.

"We're going to exploit it, do you all understand? We're going to run right over there and make these bastards wish they had stayed with the force a little longer."

Some of the soldiers smiled tiredly, and Wunic went back to the colonel.

"You boys are doing a great job. I want you to know that—we're all counting on you, and I want this to be over just as quickly as you do. We don't want our wives or our children fighting this war, do we? Then let's finish this. We'll take their position," Wunic said. "They don't know that we know we have the advantage, and we're going to use it. Colonel, I'm going to help you lead this. I'll be there with the rest of you."

And then, Wunic thought, *I'll take one of your men back with me, because Goddamn it, there is still a government, and if the king wants to talk to one of the enlisted, he should be able to.*

"Yes, sir," the colonel said. "Good to have you with us, General."

Vel and Sisha lay together on his bed, both naked under the covers, and Sisha was playing with his long black hair with one hand. Vel had nearly fallen asleep, but now, as her fingers brushed past his ear, he scratched involuntarily and woke up.

"Hi," Sisha said.

Vel blinked at her, sitting up in the bed, and Sisha rolled away from him, onto her stomach, her shoulders smooth and tanned, long black hair down her back, under the covers.

"Was I asleep?" Vel asked.

"You tell me."

"I don't know," Vel said, and he tried to remember if he had been dreaming. "I haven't slept in . . . What was your name?"

"Sisha."

"Why did you come here—why'd we do that?"

She started to laugh, and when he didn't smile, she said, "What?"

"What do you mean 'what'? What we did was wrong, I don't have any idea who you are."

Sisha began to pick at her painted fingernails. "What do you want to know?"

"You've worked at the palace for . . . what?"

"A few days."

"Light a candle."

"Why?"

"Because I want to look at you," Vel said.

Rustling of the bedsheets as she got up, her bare feet padded across the carpet quietly. Sisha went to a table near the door, naked as she worked with a small set of matches, finally lighting the stumped wick in the metal holder. In the flickering light, Vel saw that she had high, round breasts, a flat stomach and muscular legs—all very dark, as if she had a permanent tan.

"Better?" she said as she returned to the bed.

Vel stared at her. "Who are you?"

She smiled and slipped back into the bed beside him.

"What do you mean?" she asked. "I'm just like you."

"No you're not." Vel touched her hair carefully, trying not to think about the tension in his chest or the way the bed smelled. "Where did you learn to dance?"

She smiled, resting on his chest. "My mother taught me, when I was much younger."

"And where did she learn?"

"Don't know, she was a . . ." Sisha kissed his chest, ". . . street performer."

"You were pretty good when I saw you earlier."

"Pretty good?"

Vel smiled and closed his eyes, wondering what time it was. Day or night? There were no windows in the royal bedroom. Vel said, "Tell me why you did that."

"What?"

"What do you think? Why did you hop on me like that?"

"I wouldn't call it hopping."

"What would you call it then?"

Sisha shrugged playfully. "Not sure, but hopping's definitely not it. Why? Was that your first time?" He straightened, blushing, and she put her hand over his, "It's all right. You were good."

"Goddamn it, what am I supposed to say to that?"

"What did you think of it?"

"You're very redundant, you know that?"

"And you're very self-conscious." She began to pull at his hair again. "Your Majesty."

"What do you think I thought of it?"

"I don't know, you tell me." She waited, and when he did not respond, she asked, "Was it all right?"

"Yes," Vel said. "Yes of course it was—it was wonderful."

"There, then what's the problem?"

"I don't know," Vel said, and he realized that he really didn't. But something was wrong here. "I used to go after girls all the time; God, that seems like so long ago."

"Before you were king?"

"That's right," he said, and then put one arm over his face. "Haven't done much of anything since I've been king."

"Why'd you stop going after girls?"

"People started dying," Vel said. "All the people I used to know are dead." He shook his head. "And it's funny, because I don't know you and I don't particularly want to know you—"

"—Well, thank you."

"But I'm telling you these things. And I don't know why."

"Why don't you want to know me?" Sisha asked.

"Because I feel good right now. I'm not really worried that the city's going to come to a burning end, and I'm not thinking about how people are going to starve, and how all my friends and family are dead. And I'm not feeling sorry for myself."

"Isn't that a good thing?"

"Yes," Vel said. "That's the point." He smiled at her. "If I feel good, it means I can feel bad. So long as I'm feeling sorry for myself—I want to feel numb—so that I don't care who gets killed. Just shut off." He smiled. "It's a hell of a philosophy."

"Very noble of you."

Vel put his arm over his face again. "Thank you. You sound like her."

"Like who?"

"A girl I knew, who never let me get away with anything. Everything I said she would pick apart to make me get over myself."

Sisha pulled his hair, and Vel yelped, wincing.

"There," she said.

"What the hell was that?"

"Me pulling out a clump of your hair." And she showed him the collection she had yanked.

"Yes, I know. Why did you do that?"

"Because if I didn't do it, who would?"

"What's wrong with you?"

"I should ask you that," Sisha said. "I know what it's like when people die."

"Maybe we should start a club."

"Seriously—can I call you Vel, or do I have to keep saying 'Your Majesty'?"

"Vel's fine."

"No he isn't, but that's all right. I'm getting ready to bare my soul to you, and you just go on with the witty little remarks."

"It's part of my charm," Vel said quietly. "So who do you know that's died?"

"My husband."

"Sorry to hear that."

"Little over a year ago," she said. "Got the Pox." She said it as if it no longer mattered. "But you move on, you know?"

"No, I'm not at the 'moving on' stage yet," Vel said.

"That's why I'm here."

"Who put you up to this?" Vel asked. "You didn't just randomly come in here, did you? Someone sent you in here."

"Vel, I do care about you."

"So did they put you up to this? Who was it, General Wunic? Was it the general? Did he have to hire you for this?" Sisha swallowed, and then Vel frowned, backing away from her. He shook his head, laughing shortly. "This is ridiculous. Someone *hired* you to cheer me up?"

"Vel—"

"Yes or no?"

"Yes."

"I don't believe this," he said, and he rubbed his face with both hands. "I mean I understand and it makes perfect sense; but God-damn it, do I really look that pathetic?"

"Yes."

Vel said, "Leave me alone. You can go now."

"Vel, I do care about you."

"I bet you do. Go on. I'll have whoever it is pay you whatever they were going to pay you, how's that?"

"Vel—"

"No," he said, and then he looked at her seriously, his hand shaking as he touched his chin. "Look, I appreciate it. I appreciate the sleep and the sex, but I need some 'me' time, all right? You can leave. Tell them I want them to pay you double. That all right? I'm fine now."

Sisha shook her head, moving closer to him. "Vel, listen to me. Just for a minute, okay? Then I'll go."

"I don't think so. Bye Sisha."

"Vel—"

"I said, get the hell out of here." He smirked. "What part of that wasn't clear? Get the hell out of here and leave me alone." She didn't move, and he said, "Who was it? Wanted to distract me—it was probably that bastard general, wasn't it? Thought I needed a whore to tide me over." She didn't respond. "Who hired you?"

"Please—"

"You're not going to tell me?"

She took a slow breath. "No."

"Get out of my bedroom."

"Vel—"

He hit her in the center of the chest with both arms—knocking her off of the bed, and Sisha's head banged loudly on the bedside table as she fell. She winced, trembling as she touched the back of her head.

"Go away," he said, unmoving.

Sisha dressed hurriedly, and Vel didn't look at her as she left, and suddenly he was alone again. *Good,* he thought. *Now I'm safe. Now I'm so Goddamn safe that nothing can hurt me.* He smiled at himself and wanted to cry, then suppressed the feeling.

How noble, he thought. *I can push a nude whore off of my bed without breaking a sweat. How Goddamned brave.*

"All right," Wunic said. He stood behind the closed rear door of Malin Tavern. Snow hissed, and the wooden door rattled on its hinges—Wunic nodded to the rows of soldiers in the hallway behind him, and at the colonel, several lines back. "*Now.*"

Wunic threw open the door, side-stepping as soldiers rushed past him, pouring out into the street. Snow blew in a sharp gust into the faces of the first row, and there were sharp, repeating cracks that dropped the first soldiers, knocking them back into the doorway and hall, their blood spraying Wunic's pants and coat as they fell screaming, and more soldiers pushed past, jumping over the bodies, into gunfire.

"Go!" Wunic shouted, and more men and women rushed out, firing blindly through the open doorway, their greatcoats flapping as they charged.

More shots from outside, and soldiers in the hall died in a frantic whistling of bullets, but the colonel was shouting, urging them on from the rear, and they continued to run out into the street, the soldiers in the street firing sporadically at the enemy snipers in the opposite building.

Only ten, Wunic reminded himself, and Wunic watched more men pass—they were all clearing the doorway now; the snipers were focusing on the soldiers in the street—and Wunic readied his own rifle. He mixed with the soldiers, rushing into the street.

The snow immediately caught his legs, and he struggled, plowing through the drifts, past deep holes, where men had been shot down, their bodies falling in messy patches of wet snow. Wunic squinted in the freezing snowfall, the world blurring white for a moment, and still the gunfire continued from the opposite end of the street. But now Wunic could see his men charging across, and some were almost there—out of the killing zone, at the opposite building's doorway.

Wunic tried to move faster through the snow, and the wind knocked him aside. Everything was happening too slowly, and Wunic could not lift his legs high enough to clear the snow completely, so that he seemed to be continually tripping in the deep layers. A group of soldiers had reached the enemy building—they were blasting the door with their weapons, and Wunic watched someone lean out of the second floor window, aiming a rifle down, and then the quick flashes as Wunic's soldiers were killed where they stood, at the enemy doorway, caught in the enemy volley from above them.

Wunic stopped running, rifle up, snow blinding him as he pointed it where the sniper had been and felt it buck with each shot. Tiny bursts of steam rose from Wunic's rifle as it flashed, and with another torrent of wind the building disappeared entirely for a moment.

"General!" someone shouted, and the wind turned against him violently. Wunic winced and felt the flap of his coat tug. More gunfire ahead, and he watched holes appear in the snow just ahead of him. Soldiers hurried past him, and when the wind cleared for an instant Wunic saw that their soldiers had reached the enemy building and were inside—more gunfire and return fire, and a confused series of random bursts from beyond. Wunic continued moving, closer to the building—miraculously no one was shooting at him—and now he was there, at the opposite end of the street. Wunic stepped over the bodies in the doorway, some still moving, and the colonel grabbed his arm, stopping him.

Ahead a corridor led to a right turn and Wunic saw the edge of a railing—there were stairs there, leading to the second floor. The colonel held Wunic's shoulder with a trembling hand, his face utterly calm.

"Can't go up, General," the colonel said.

Wunic stepped past him closer to the stairs. More bodies had been scattered across the hall, some theirs, some the enemy's. Wunic's soldiers crouched at the corner, at the base of the stairs, out of the line of sight of anyone at the top.

"Why not?" Wunic passed more bodies and pieces of bodies. "Come on, boys, let's go!" There were dark smears on the shredded paneling of the walls.

"Fortified the second floor," the colonel said. "Slaughtered going up there."

"How many casualties?" Wunic asked. "Why are they just waiting there?" And he said again, "Come on boys!" The soldiers didn't move.

The colonel smiled. "Too many, I don't know. Tried to rush the second floor."

Wunic froze, he saw only six soldiers in the hall apart from the colonel and himself.

"Where are the rest?" Wunic said.

"This is it," the colonel said.

"No," Wunic said quietly. "This isn't it, they've only got ten soldiers—" Gunshots from the top of the stairs, and the soldiers at the base responded, sporadically angling their weapons around the corner and firing blindly up.

"Goddamn it," Wunic said, and he felt very cold suddenly, exposed. "What the hell happened? What in God's name is going on here?"

"Sir, do you have any suggestions?" the colonel asked.

Wunic shook his head—"Get out of my way!"—and he drew closer to the staircase. He could faintly see the remains of bodies there, soldiers had been chopped into bloody lumps on the stairs, trying to go up. It was a mess of blood and organs. Wunic saw the head of a boy who had worn a black necklace, and an arm with thick black hair that probably was not his.

"Goddamn it," Wunic said again, pacing back to the colonel. "You want to explain this to me, colonel? Are we pinned?"

"More than ten soldiers," the colonel said.

Wunic nodded, not really looking at him as he went back to the outer door. *More than ten*, he thought. *A lot more.* Snipers would still be posted up there. "We can still do this," Wunic said softly. And he thought, *But we can't.* "We can still take this position."

"Come on down!" one of the soldiers at the stairs shouted. "Come on!"

Gunshots from the top, and the torso of someone was hit and rolled down one stair, so that they could see it, just around the corner. One of the soldiers in the hall began talking to himself very quickly, clicking the safety of his gun on and off.

"No way out—got to get out of here—" another said. "We're stuck, we can't—"

"We're going," Wunic said, but they weren't listening to him. "We're going up those stairs or back across the street—we're not sitting here on our asses."

The colonel stared at the street and the bodies outside. "Not going to happen, sir. We can't—"

"We have to," Wunic said again.

One of the men waved his rifle at Wunic's coat. "Sir, do you see that? One of them kissed you."

Wunic looked down. In the flap of his coat, less than an inch from the side of his right leg, was a large hole.

"Either they're going to break," Wunic said, "or we are. And we're not. You hear that? Let's do this, let's take these Goddamn stairs!"

"General, they can't—and we're dead if we go back into the street," the colonel said, and then he grinned angrily. "I've been told of at least fifteen reb snipers that were shot down. That's more than ten, sir, and they've still got—"

Yes, Wunic thought, *I know.* And he shook his head. "Two of you stay behind. The rest of us are going across the street—I need volunteers. When we fall back, the two that have stayed behind will rush the stairs. Come on men, I need volunteers."

The soldiers stared at him, and the colonel said quietly, "Can't go up those stairs, sir."

Goddamn it, don't you think I know that? Wunic thought, and he said, "Yes, we can, Colonel. Now you organize these men into new squads and we'll move out. When the rebs focus on the street, those two might—"

"No, General," the colonel said. "*Can't* go up those stairs, and the rebs are waiting for us to move back into the street; we can't—"

"Colonel, I know the situation," Wunic said, but he knew the colonel was right. Boxed in, trapped. "This is the way out," Wunic said, and he pointed back to the street. "That's the way we're going. You can stay and take the stairs with one other man, Colonel. Pick him now."

A soldier rushed back from the stairs, and he shouted to the colonel, "Sir, thirty reinforcements crossing the street!"

Wunic smiled and said, "There is always another way." *Except,* he thought, *there was no way that this soldier could have known—*

The soldier shook his head. "Not friendly, sir. *Enemy* reinforcements. I overheard . . ."

The colonel nodded, as if he had been expecting this, and then he turned to Wunic, and sighed miserably. "The intelligence, General, was not—"

"Pick your man," Wunic said. "You're staying behind. *Now*, Colonel. Do it now."

"Sir, these men are all going to die if we move."

"Goddamn it," Wunic said. "Who are you talking to, Colonel? Am I a Goddamn private? I'm ordering you pick a man and take those stairs. *I'll* organize the rest into squads." Wunic started shouting at the soldiers, "All right, men, groups of three, let's go. Now!"

"We surrender," the colonel whispered.

"What was that?" Wunic said, footsteps hurrying down the stairs—"Stand fast!" Wunic shouted, and he raised his rifle. The soldiers posted at the base of the stairs stiffened, preparing to open fire on the rebels—the colonel rushed toward them—past Wunic—his rifle over his head.

"Hold your fire!" he shouted. "We surrender. Hold your fire!"

The footsteps stopped, on the other side of the corner, at the base of the stairs.

"Slide out your weapons," someone shouted.

Wunic backed away, toward the exit. The rest of the soldiers were a mixture of confusion and fear. No real anger, just frustration at being led into this. They looked from the colonel to Wunic for orders.

"You stay where you are, men," Wunic said. "You hold onto those. We're not giving in to these bastards—"

And the colonel cut him off, approaching the corner.

"We are, General," the colonel shouted back, and then he looked at the other soldiers briefly. "You're all with me. We don't have any other option, you understand—"

"*Slide out your weapons!*"

"Colonel, you drop your gun," Wunic said, "and I'll blow your fucking head off myself." And he watched as the colonel kicked his rifle away, into plain view—Wunic raised his rifle, aimed—"Colonel, you stay where you are!"—the colonel stepped around the corner.

Someone shouted, "Hands higher. Get on the ground. Face down."

"Hold positions," Wunic said.

The colonel slowly dropped to his knees—still visible around the corner—and one of the soldiers closest to the stairs rushed around, firing into the rebels, and now Wunic heard shots from the top of the stairs, and their soldier was blown apart on the opposite wall, and somehow the colonel still kneeled, unharmed around the corner.

Wunic said, "Goddamn it, you hold those Goddamn—"

Rebel soldiers rushed into the hall—they fired into Wunic's soldiers at point-blank range, and Wunic's men returned fire in a frantic exchange of blood and screaming, and soldiers were dropping on both sides—bullets hissed past Wunic's head, and more rebels entered the hall—but it was already over. All but Wunic and two other soldiers near him were dead or dying.

"Stand fast!" Wunic fired—nothing; his gun jammed.

One of Wunic's soldiers said, "We surrender!" and a rebel shot him in the throat, and more advanced—Wunic's remaining soldier was knocked to the floor. Before Wunic could ready his rifle, they kicked him to his knees, knocked his gun away, and the colonel was led into the hall at gunpoint, hands over his head.

This isn't supposed to happen, Wunic thought slowly, his mind struggling to keep up with the frenzy around him. Not making sense—except that it did make sense. *This can't happen.* He watched his soldier convulse on the ground, blood pumping out of his neck. Sudden orders to attack. Why would Denon do this? And Wunic's first thought was that the orders must have been false. But no, the seal had been perfect—they had to have come from Lord Denon.

The rebels started shouting orders, forcing the colonel and the other soldier to kneel in front of Wunic. What the hell had Denon thought? No reason to send orders like that unless the information was absolutely reliable. And it hadn't been. What could he possibly gain by doing this?

I was meant to die here, wasn't I? Wunic thought slowly. *What the hell is happening?*

A strong blonde woman in a black overcoat led the group of rebels closer, kicking the colonel hard in the back as she passed him. Wunic counted the rebels as they entered the hallway. Nineteen, twenty-three . . . and now he watched the woman as she glared at them, the three who were still alive.

"Which one of you is the commanding officer?"

The colonel said, "There are two officers here."

"And your rank is . . . ?"

"Colonel."

The woman noticed the markings on the shoulder of Wunic's coat, and she whistled. "A general. What do you know about that? Stand up please, General."

Wunic stood, and they quickly tied his wrists behind his back—and then two soldiers stepped behind the colonel and the other soldier, putting rifles to the backs of their heads.

The woman nodded, the colonel said, "You don't—" And the rebels shot them both. The colonel and the other soldier slumped to the floor, and the rebels shouldered their rifles—Wunic watched smoke rise from the hole in the back of the colonel's head.

"What's your name?" the woman said, stepping in front of Wunic. She wrapped a gray scarf around her neck, her hands covered in heavy gloves.

"General Wunic."

"My name is Jak," the woman said, and then, as if continuing some private joke with the rebels, she said, "*Just* Jak. You're only a prisoner as long as you're useful. I'm sure you understand, General. Try to escape, try to piss without permission, and we'll kill you. Do you understand?"

Wunic nodded.

"Good," Jak said. "You're going to give us intelligence on everything about the regular army. I'm going to cut off your fingers when you don't cooperate, and when you're no longer helpful, we're going to kill you. Do you understand?"

"Yes."

"Glad we had this little talk." She motioned to several soldiers to bring him upstairs.

Wunic tried to stop thinking about Denon, about the bigger picture of what had just happened, and he stared at Jak. "Where have I seen you before? You're not a soldier. . . ."

"And why not? Women are allowed in the military."

"You said—"

"Shut up," Jak said, and she turned away quickly. "If the general keeps talking like that, feel free to cut off one of his ears. Take him to the second floor." She said to Wunic, "Don't worry, I won't forget about you, General. We'll have a nice little talk later."

He wrote from memory:

> Of the primeval Priest's assum'd power,
> When Eternals spurn'd back his religion:
> And gave him a place in the north,
> Obscure, shadowy, void, solitary.

Eternals, I hear you call gladly;
Dictate swift winged words, and fear not
To unfold your dark visions of torment.

"Fear not," Blakes said, and he listened to the rain on the window at the opposite wall of his suite. Adria slept in the bed, facing away from him, and Blakes sat naked on the floor, his back arched against the wall of the huge, darkened suite. He wrote in a notebook, almost entirely filled with his tiny writing, a book titled, *Urizen's Return.*

Blakes's hair had begun to recede, and now his eyes bulged with the permanent circles beneath them. He was losing weight, and with one hand, he counted his ribs, before continuing to write:

Lies, lies, lies, I say I understand,
Urizen becomes Los in the rainy whirlwind:
Los wept howling around the dark Demon:
And cursing his lot; for in anguish,
Urizen was rent from his side;
And a fathomless void for his feet;
And intense fires for his dwelling.
God, I wish I did not see it.

Blakes's hand was trembling, and he pressed the tip of his pen to the top of the page to still it. Slowly, he sketched a human skull, and then he went into the main room of the suite and sat at a small black box connected with wires to a monitor and keyboard—one of the organic systems. *Genetically engineered to function as a computer, but it is still an animal,* Blakes thought. *Still a perversion of everything that God meant animals to be.* Chaos. Thunder grumbled outside, and the rain slapped the glass harder.

This was the fourth year of Blakes's term as consul, 2099, and he was thirty-nine. Blakes spent his days working to appear a competent consul, to bring the Russians further into the parliament and to make them see the danger of appeasing the Chinese, the Muslims, of cooperating with anyone who would not belong and submit to the parliament. At night he wrote. It had been four years since Blakes had really slept, and he sometimes wondered why he had spent any time resting in the years before becoming consul. So much more could be accomplished if one was focused and allowed oneself to produce continually.

Blakes sent a message to Donitz, his friend and co-consul, making certain that the banks and corporations had been shifted to certain committees. Over four years, Blakes had brought every Western and pseudo-Western corporation under the regulation of certain branches of the parliament, meaning, for his purposes, that they were linked to a series of living computer systems all under the parliament's "limited" control.

Blakes waited and several minutes later, Donitz explained that the corporations in question had been shifted to different routes of control, and then Blakes responded, suddenly cutting his reply short, as if a power surge had shorted out his system. Even though the systems themselves were now largely organic, much of the infrastructure connecting the nets and communication systems were remnants of an era dependent entirely on electronic technology. Blakes sent the fractured message. He then sent an encoded message to the mesh of systems that governed the parliamentary committees and thus every major Western economic interest. The encoded message was simply, *His Will.*

Four years had been spent constructing "factories" all across Europe, the Americas, and parts of Africa and the Pacific Rim; all funded by the "Western Work Act" of 2097. The factories were supposedly built to encourage Western corporations to bring jobs back from the Third World. Blakes always headed the missions to inspect the buildings and, as it had been his proposal, he was entirely responsible for them. These "factories," Blakes thought, would now become functional. Twenty minutes after sending his encoded message to the parliamentary network systems, Blakes received a message from Donitz:

Consul Blakes:
Be advised, this could be a simple system error or network malfunction, but I did not get your full message. Receiving fragmentary reports of network malfunctions and virus-related failures. Could be nothing; thought you should now.
CONSUL DONITZ

Not nothing, Blakes thought, and he sent a reply thanking Donitz for the information. Ten minutes later, another message came that said:

Consul Blakes:
We have been hit by terrorists operating within the Asian or possibly Middle Eastern sphere. As of now, eighteen corporations have reported complete economic fallout. Currently, backup systems are not yet functioning, and the world stock trade has dropped more than two hundred percent in the past thirteen minutes. Prayer and resolve may be our most important duties at this point. Calling for emergency parliamentary meeting within two hours in Paris. Please advise.
CONSUL DONITZ

Blakes replied and continued to write for two hours, and then he switched the monitor to one of the network stations so that he could watch the meeting that he had just told Donitz he would attend. Still early morning in Paris, but all of the members seemed to be in attendance, even on such short notice, and someone explained that the world stock market had fallen a total of eleven thousand percent literally overnight, with hundreds of major corporations announcing bankruptcy as their systems had been simultaneously destroyed by the terrorist sabotage.

Blakes watched, and then, just as the network was about to switch to another announcement about stock, the picture went dark. A frightened woman standing on a narrow cobbled street in front of a mass of sirens and screaming people and police and great clouds of smoke explained that some kind of incendiary device had been detonated inside the parliamentary building, and—the building was shown as a mass of ruined walls and plumes of black smoke. *For once,* Blakes thought, *it worked. I helped set up the committee networks, making certain to connect several key routes into every major corporation's personal system, and I arranged for the explosives in the bowels of the parliamentary building. I personally set the timers. I did this, not anyone else, but me.*

He heard Adria getting out of bed in the next room. "Are you awake?"

Blakes turned off the monitor. "Yes," he said. "I am. Go back to sleep." He got back into bed with her and was nearly asleep when someone knocked. *Why not ring the bell?* Blakes wondered as he woke.

Sitting up, Blakes stared at the gray light from the streetlamps outside.

Adria mumbled, ". . . someone—"

"Go back to sleep."

Slowly, he slid out of the bed, took a pistol out of the bedside table and advanced. Blakes had bodyguards, personal security: if someone had knocked, it meant that the bell wasn't working or the guards weren't there anymore. Both Blakes and Donitz—and every member of the parliament, to a lesser degree—had personal guards. Maybe the media, he thought as he stalked through the room, down the hall, to the stairs, and there, at the base of the stairs, was the heavy, reinforced oak door. No, they would still have to go through security: *and security always used the bell.* In the four years that Blakes had served as consul, his personal bodyguards—who should be posted all around the outside of his home in Paris—in four years they had never knocked.

Bell must be broken. Down the stairs, and Blakes neared the door—his pistol was an antique, a German .45 revolver, made in the 1930s, over one hundred and sixty years ago. The Germans had known how to make guns, and this one was still in excellent condition, and would probably continue to work for hundreds of years if it was maintained. Closer, and now Blakes padded barefoot across cool floorboards to the black carpet just in front of the door. The locks were all drawn: two deadbolts, electric fastenings and a chain.

Someone knocked again, and Blakes held his breath, alone in the entryway. *Overpower the guards*, he thought, *this is the end: they've surrounded the building, they* know. *But, who would have ordered this in time? If they wanted me at an emergency meeting—and the entire Parliament had been annihilated; who was* they?—*this wouldn't be the way they would summon me. If we need to plan strategy, and of course, "we" do, it would begin with a phone call or a network communication, not a knock at the front door.* There must be chaos now; Blakes had been sure that things would not settle down until the following morning—that's why had gone back to bed.

The security personnel should ring and call inside, "Sir, you are requested outside." They wouldn't *knock.* Blakes backed away, gun still raised: would a .45 go through the oak? No, these doors were made to take bullets, and there might even be a plate of reinforced steel in the middle of it. This was the consul's house, after all, and security had had two months before Blakes moved in to make sure it was adequate.

Another knock, and Blakes moved away, the floor creaking, back to the stairs. How had they known? The one man who might have seen Blakes's maneuver, but who had trusted and needed Blakes enough not to act—Donitz—was dead now, along with the rest of the parliament. Who had—

"Sir, you're needed outside."

Blakes stared at the shut door: his security chief. Pistol into the top of his pants, back to the door, and Blakes undid the chain, entering the code for the electric deadbolt.

"Yeah," he said. "Just a minute."

Silence outside—the electric lock clicked off—and now Blakes flipped open the regular deadbolt, turned the knob, pulled open the heavy door—the outer screen door was ajar—and Donitz stepped in, a tiny silver pistol to Blakes's chin.

"Hands up." As Blakes hesitated, Donitz pushed him back, kicked the door shut, and jammed the .22 harder into Blakes's neck. "You want to die? Hands over your head now."

Blakes did as he was told, staring blankly at Donitz. "Honorable Consul, what—"

"Shut up, Blakes." Donitz took Blakes's pistol, aimed it at Blakes's heart with his free hand, and forced Blakes back toward the kitchen, both guns ready. "Are you alone?"

"Yeah," Blakes said.

"Do you want me to look? If I find anyone else here, I swear to God—"

"I'm alone. Donitz, what are you—"

"Shut up," Donitz said again, and he indicated one of the four chairs around a square wooden table. "Sit down."

Blakes sat, and Donitz remained standing, his back to the hallway and the stairs beyond, both guns casually aimed at Blakes's head, less than three feet separating them.

"I warned you. I told you, remember—and while your enemies were all incompetent—they were only incompetent because I helped you destroy them. Four years, we've done this, Blakes. We worked together on this, bringing the Russians in, keeping the Chinese out, keeping the sand niggers out of the Balkans, out of India."

When Donitz paused, Blakes asked, "Can I put my hands down now?"

"Yeah, fine."

"How did you get in?"

"How do you think?"

"I don't know," Blakes said. "If I knew, I wouldn't have asked."

With his .22 hand, Donitz took a tiny black square out of his pants pocket, a recorder.

Blakes frowned. "Now, why would you—"

Donitz clicked the one of the buttons: "Sir, you're needed outside." He clicked it off.

"You used all the memory on that?"

"There's more," Donitz said, and he smiled slightly. "No, trust me, there's more." He put the recorder away again and aimed the .22 at Blakes's crotch.

"They usually ring the bell."

"Yeah, I know. It was broken. I broke it killing your doormen. I assume you have more in the surrounding blocks?" Blakes shrugged, and Donitz continued, "Yeah, well, we've got time, there are fires by the river, and some of your security was recruited by the Domestic Engagement Forces."

"Can they do that?"

"They did," Donitz said. "We're in a state of emergency. After all, the parliament just went up in smoke, along with the entire Euro-American government. Didn't it?"

Blakes stared at him. "Yeah, I know. What is this about? You had something to do with that?"

"I'm not in the mood for your bullshit, Blakes. So I'll make this brief, in the interests of time and—"

"Why weren't you at the parliament?"

Donitz swallowed, moving his hands together, so that the side of his little .22 was pressed to the German .45.

"Traffic," he said.

"Hmm. Well."

"That's what I said. Now, I want to know what you had planned—before I decide to kill you."

"You're going to shoot me?"

"What did you have planned? What are you going to do? You can't run this without me, you should know that by now. The bureacracy won't work without two consuls. Yes, maybe you could maintain some control over the satellite states without the representatives themselves for a few months—and you'll hold the urban areas on both continents—and then there's always the possibility of new elections. . . . But that would defeat the whole point of this in the first place, wouldn't it? What do you want to do, Blakes?"

"Why don't you stop pointing those guns at my head?"

"No."

Blakes shook his head in amusement. "You're very German, you know that? I forgot that you were in India, that you were one of the poet-soldiers. A war hero, right?" Blakes had never forgotten. "What rank did they give you? You got some kind of medals too, didn't you? That was how you got into politics in the first place. . . ."

Donitz clicked the safeties off of both guns. "What," he said, "did you. Have. In mind? I want to know out of professional curiosity, and because you tried to kill me tonight. Now, you say anything—" A floorboard on the stairs creaked, and Donitz straightened, already turned so that the .22 was still aimed at Blakes, the .45 now pointed down the hall to the stairs. The stairs dropped from directly above the kitchen: they weren't visible, except from the front hallway, and anyone might walk down without being visible in the kitchen.

"Who is that?" Donitz shouted, and then he glanced at Blakes. "You piece of shit, there *is* someone else here, isn't there?"

"You know," Blakes said, "I have cats."

"Cats," Donitz repeated, and he kept his weapons trained. "How many?"

"Three."

"Bullshit."

Blakes watched Donitz passively. The stance was textbook military: *And it doesn't matter,* Blakes thought. *God's will be done, and no armies in the world will be able to stop holy fire.*

"Calm down, Consul," Blakes said.

"I should shoot you right now, shouldn't I? I'll regret it if I don't. I thought I might come here and hear something, some grand strategy about how I hadn't been a target at all. The worst part of it is, I *knew* what you were, just as your political enemies did—and I thought I was using you when I helped you beat the opposition. I thought we were allies."

"We were."

"Yeah," Donitz said, and he looked directly at Blakes, the .45 still loosely aimed down the hall, ready to snap back up. "But you *were* a terrorist, weren't you? You were in Mexico in '92, the same day the leader of the '89 blast—what was his name, Jesse something?—was killed. I can't know this, I understand that you covered all of your tracks, but not everyone in the world is entirely ignorant, Blakes. People watch what you do, and now, they'll suspect you."

"No they won't."

"No?"

"No, they'll suspect whoever I tell them to suspect," Blakes said quietly, and he leaned closer to Donitz. "People are cattle, that's the problem, and it's also the tool to fixing this. We have to get rid of them."

"You're insane, and they're going to haul you to Nuremburg."

"Only if I lose," Blakes said, and Donitz's head exploded across the table—he went down in a enormous splattering of blood and brains and knocked over one of the chairs, so that his body had slumped across it, half of his head gone—and Blakes heard the shots a moment later, heard the random fire as Donitz's hands squeezed both triggers, blasting the entryway and the wall beside Blakes.

Adria slipped around the corner of the stairs, a smoking gun in one hand.

"God," she said. "He—"

"Yeah," Blakes said, and he started to wipe the blood from his face. "Thank you."

"You're welcome. Should I get a towel or something?"

"Call security," Blakes said.

"I did."

"Thank you," he said again, and she smiled, helping him up.

"I love you," Adria said. "He cracked, didn't he? Said the parliament was gone—Donitz lost it."

"The parliament *is* gone."

She froze. "What—"

"But you're right, it broke him." Blakes put an arm around her. "Donitz was a red spy, an assassin."

"The parliament isn't—"

"Tomorrow," Blakes said. "It's the middle of the night. Let's have them come in here, clean this up, and we'll talk about it tomorrow."

"We can't just go back to bed now."

"I'm tired," he said, and he kissed her cheek, guiding her toward the stairs. "Donitz forgot that he's not the only one who knows how to fire a gun, didn't he?"

Adria nodded, looked back at the mess, then at the holes in the entryway where .45 bullets had ripped gashes in the wood panelling. "*Cats*," she said at last. "As if you would own cats."

The following morning, Blakes stood in front of a room packed with network and media transmitters and cameras. Behind him hung a red and black swastika flag. No one but historians would know who the Nazis were, but yes, Blakes heard the chanting from the back of the room, where a crowd had gathered. He talked over it.

"—the symbol from history of individual strength over collective mediocrity! We will make them pay for their crimes, and we will not stop until the world—I say the world—is made to remember those men and women who were butchered in the name of weakness and fear. The enemies of the West have committed an act of war, and *we will retaliate*."

From the back of the room: "*Sieg Heil!*"

Blakes held up one hand, in a salute, and he nodded grimly to flashbulbs. "War is our tool of justice."

Two weeks later, after bloodshed and bombings, and complete denial of the accusations by every Middle Eastern and Asian power, the "factories" were opened. Blakes accepted his self-proclaimed nomination as temporary leader with complete control—as Führer—of the Euro-American Parliament, and martial law was imposed across the continents. Dissenters were put on planes and into trains, into the beds of trucks, and shipped to the "factories," where they were forced into gas chambers and ovens or summarily shot.

Protests against Blakes's new control—protests calling for elections and peace—broke out across both Europe and the Americas, with guerrilla campaigns in the Rocky Mountains, the Appalachian Mountains, and throughout Central and South America. In every major city, the strengthened parliamentary army, now the army of the Führer, crushed the uprisings violently through mass executions and further deportation to the factories. Every able man and woman between the ages of seventeen and thirty-five was drafted into the army of the Führer under the "Conscription Act of the New Modern Army of 2099."

When warheads were launched by the Chinese Empire, most were destroyed by counternuclear devices—but a handful of major cities and Western military centers were obliterated, and a counterattack with biological agents released in the lower atmosphere blanketed all of China, India and the Middle East, killing over four billion people in less than twenty-four hours. The following morning, immunized armies bearing the swastika flag marched through Jerusalem, Mecca and Baghdad, landed in New Dehli, Calcutta, Bombay, Islamabad, Hong Kong, Bangladesh, and on and on. The Chinese surrendered to the Führer Blakes, and the dead continents came under the control of his armies. The few neutral nations, such as Japan and outposts in Africa, also submitted to Blakes's control.

The factories became even busier with more and more militant radicals rising to oppose the Führer's armies. Blakes sent generals to the factories, and anyone he suspected of treason found his or her way to the mass graves rapidly forming all around the world. Dissident monks in Tibet, the militias of North America, and radical Muslims all went to the factories, where they helped—as Blakes often said—in producing the freedom of the newly united world. During the day he worked, but at night, Blakes continued to write, and sometimes he waited for angels to speak to him.

vel was pissing into a chamber pot in the corner farthest from his bed when someone knocked.

"Yes?"

"It's Lord Denon," Denon said from behind the door.

"Come in."

Vel finished, and he remained by the pot as Denon stepped into the room, hands folded.

"Do you know who sent her?" Vel asked before Denon could say anything.

Denon paused, glanced at the broken wood still cluttering the floor, and then motioned to the bed. "Who?"

Vel went to the bed, and Denon sat beside him. "The girl, Sisha," Vel said. "Who sent her up here? Was it General Wunic?"

Denon said, "I don't know. You mean the dancer? Why would she come up here?"

"That's who I mean," Vel said. "She's a whore, and I think the general had her sent up here to keep me from chasing him down. Did you do it? When you sent food, did you—"

"No," Denon said. He thought about it, and then he said, "I don't know what to . . . Vel, we're out of time."

"What do you mean?"

"I've received reports that the rebels have broken through our frontline defenses." Vel waited, and Denon continued, "We have less than an hour before they will arrive here, at the palace."

Vel said, "That soon?"

"Yes, Vel. It's time to leave."

"I don't get it, what am I supposed to do?"

"We still have a route open to the cemetery. You can go to the tunnels beneath the ruins. The system suggested you do that anyway, didn't it?"

Vel went for his sword and pistol, and he began to get dressed. "The rebels are really that close?"

"Yes."

"You know I might become just as dead at the ruins. The Frill nearly killed me the last time I was there."

"We don't have any other choice. You'll take an escort of soldiers who will—"

"Denon, you know an escort won't do any good if I run into the Frill or those other big hairy things, the Nara. Soldiers will do more here, fighting the rebels."

"I won't let you go alone," Denon said shortly, and Vel smiled at him.

"I know you want to help me."

"Then take the soldiers."

"I'm taking the box," Vel said. "That's all. So that I can get advice along the way."

"From the system? Are you sure—"

"That's right."

"Explain this to me," Denon said.

Vel put on his black overcoat, shaking it so that his arms emerged from the sleeves. "Where's Wunic?"

Lord Denon swallowed and looked away. "I don't know."

"What do you mean? He was at the front, wasn't he? Couldn't have just—"

"General Wunic has not reported in as I expected. I've gotten conflicting reports. . . ."

"What does that mean? 'Conflicting reports'?"

"General Wunic has defected, Vel."

Vel's jaw tightened. "What?"

"I told you we're short on time," Denon said, standing, and Vel followed him to the door. "Apparently, the general has either joined the rebels or been killed."

"Goddamn it."

"When you're gone, you should know that I'll probably be taken prisoner. They won't kill me—they're after you, not the Church."

"That's sweet of them."

"While you're gone," Denon said, "I'll do whatever I can—which might be nothing, if we're occupied—to keep a government in place, so that when you return, and the rebels are forced out, the transition will work more easily."

"Let's hope so," Vel said, and he followed Denon into the hall. Vel went into a side door and picked up the black box, wire trailing in the air behind him. "I don't know how I'm going to carry this."

A pair of soldiers fell into step on either side of him as Vel followed Denon to the stairs.

"They'll carry it for you."

"I'm not taking an escort, Denon. I'm sorry. I can do this alone."

"I'm not going to argue with you about this, Vel." Denon paused at the summit of the main staircase. Below, soldiers rushed from one room to the next.

"Where is that girl?" Vel asked.

Denon frowned. "Who, the dancer?"

"Yes, I wanted to apologize. I shouldn't have—"

"Vel, I'm sorry, but we don't have time. You have to move while the route to the cemetery is still open. I'll make sure that she knows that you're sorry for whatever you did."

Vel forced a smile as he followed Denon down the stairs. "Make sure it sounds heartfelt."

"I will," Denon said without stopping.

When they reached the main entrance of the palace, Denon had several packs of food and water brought to Vel, along with a bag for the system-box. Denon then ordered the two soldiers at Vel's side to accompany him to the cemetery and on to the tunnels. The men both carried rifles and swords, and they agreed without hesitation. Even as Vel protested the escorts, Denon ushered him out of the hall, the box and supplies weighing heavily on his back; Vel had refused to let either of the soldiers carry the box that held the living computer system.

Outside, they paused on the front steps in the falling snow, and Denon put a hand on Vel's shoulder.

"If I can arrange it, I'll have runners sent to the tunnels, so that you're kept informed," Denon said.

"Thank you," Vel said. Not wanting to argue about the escorts anymore, he continued, "I think you might be the only one here who's keeping me alive."

Denon pointed to the gate at the far end of the snowy courtyard. Soldiers stood just inside, their rifles aimed at the surrounding blocks.

"You need to go," Denon said.

"Thank you," Vel said again.

"We will survive this, Vel: This is only temporary. The artillery will be working soon enough that with any luck, you can be back in a couple of days. Now go and wait for my messages." He paused. "We're friends in this, Vel. Remember that."

"I know, Denon." And he said more softly, "Sometimes I think you're the only one who doesn't want to see this city starve."

"There may be some truth to that. Dead souls are much more difficult to save. Be careful."

"I will."

The soldiers started across the courtyard, and Vel followed, slipping in the snow. He looked back a final time. The palace was beautiful, with snow lining all three of its dark stone levels, like a terraced rock carving.

Denon waved briefly, and Vel tried to think of some last thing to say, then he decided to just smile and wave back. Vel followed the soldiers out of the courtyard, to the cemetery—and this time he let them dig.

chapter 10

General Wunic's hands were bound tightly behind his back, and he sat curled in the corner of a small room on the second floor of a vacant housing complex. Rebels walked in and out of the windowless room, reviewing papers, whispering orders, and three remained at the far doorway, motionless. The continual sound of distant gunfire continued over the whistling of the wind in the loose wall boards. Wunic had been marched through a deserted residential street, past houses, all one and two stories, all empty except for the rebel soldiers who raced from one end of the road to the other. Wunic had recognized some of the rebels: He remembered training them for the police force in the years before the snow and the war.

Wunic stared at the rebels guarding him evenly. One looked back, adjusting his rifle strap. *Lord Denon had sent those orders,* Wunic thought. *It had been Denon who ordered me to attack, to ignore any other plans I might have had. Why?*

"There a problem?" one of the guards said.

Wunic did not reply, continuing to glare at the rebels as he wondered what could have motivated Denon to put him in this position. Denon wasn't capable of running this war, and he wouldn't want to. Had there been someone else, then? Another soldier? *If I'm gone,* Wunic thought, *if something were to happen to the king, Denon might be able to—he could never hold the army together.* Without a strong officer, a single general, the individual company commanders would be helpless.

All of those soldiers had been killed attempting to sack a building that was too well-defended. They had been sacrificed for what amounted to nothing. Unless the real purpose had been something other than the death of the soldiers. Wunic tensed the muscles in his legs to keep them from going numb in his immobile, cold position.

Could have been a simple error, Wunic thought. Denon *could* have received false information—then why the sudden order? *I was meant to die today,* Wunic thought. Lord Denon—the bastard who arranged the attack—had intended everyone to be annihilated. *Denon, Goddamn it, I don't understand.* The seal had been legitimate, which meant the order *had* come from Denon. For it to have been faked, there would have to be a pro-rebel conspiracy high into the Church hierarchy. *Not likely,* Wunic thought. The Religious Guard took orders from Lord Denon and no one else, and they certainly weren't likely to sympathize with the rebels, unless Denon told them to. *And maybe you were the sympathizer, Denon,* Wunic thought. *But* why?

What was your motivation, Denon? Why would you want to destroy me? Wunic wondered. *Why the hell would you want to bury me attacking the front? What have I done? Did you suspect me of treason? What could you possibly gain in this? You're already Lord over the Church of Hope, a member of the Executive Council, and the only advisor the king seems to listen to. Why this move, why now?*

Jak walked through the doorway. She held her hands behind her and wore all black, a long assault rifle slung over one shoulder. Jak said something to one of the rebel guards, who shrugged and replied, pointing to Wunic with one hand. Jak's blonde hair was tied tightly behind her head, and one cheek was smeared darkly as if she had rubbed ash into it, darkening the skin. Jak approached Wunic.

"General," she said.

Wunic nodded to her, watching the rifle. They had taken all of his weapons, even the knives he kept hidden under his clothing. These rebels had once been police soldiers, Wunic had to remind himself, and they had searched him just as he had trained them to. *I lost,* a part of Wunic told him. *This war belonged to me, and I lost. This was my war, my time, everything I had ever done, all of my service to the city was leading to this. And it's lost now.*

"General Wunic," Jak said again, "I'm going to ask you some questions about the royal forces and about the situation in the palace. You should know that I've interrogated four other high-ranking prisoners, and each time you give me an answer I don't believe I'm going to take one of your fingers or toes." Two rebel guards approached behind her, one holding a sword. "So, you'll have twenty opportunities to lie, I suppose."

"And if I don't answer?" Wunic said.

Jak adjusted the rifle, leveling it to his chest. "I'll shoot you until you change your mind or die. I don't want to have a pissing contest with you, General. But let's say I know how to make it more even, if we do need to see which of us can pee the farthest." She pointed the rifle at his crotch.

One of the guards untied Wunic's right boot, and Wunic did not struggle as the guard took it off and removed the cloth covering beneath, exposing Wunic's pale foot to the cold air. Wunic suppressed a shiver, watching his toes uncomfortably.

"I'll start with an easy one," Jak said. "How does the king feel the war is going?"

"It's a petty rebellion," Wunic said.

"Are those his words or yours?"

Wunic rubbed his exposed toes with the fabric of his other boot. "I haven't actually spoken with His Majesty about the war in any depth—"

"That's a lie, General. We know that you're the top ranking military commander, that you have been overseeing everything. Why wouldn't you meet with the king about that?"

"He doesn't allow me," Wunic said. "Everything I say goes to the king through Lord Denon."

"*Denon*? You're joking." Jak paused, and the rebel with the sword squatted over Wunic. The other guard held the general's shoulders, restraining him, but Wunic wasn't ready to struggle yet. The one with the sword lowered his blade to Wunic's foot.

"What?" he said. "That was true. Denon is the only person His Majesty will see."

Jake smiled. "Just a reminder of how this works." And she muttered, "The little runt hasn't changed. When will your artillery be operational?"

"In a couple of days," he said.

The guards glanced at one another, and Jak frowned. "That soon?"

Wunic nodded. "Yes. It may even be ready now." When Jak did not respond, he asked, "Are you in charge?"

Jak scratched at her blackened cheek, wiping away some of the dirt, but didn't answer.

"Who's in charge? Is General Rein your commander?" Wunic said, raising his voice.

"We have an excess of commanders," Jak said quietly. Her mind was elsewhere. "You're certain the artillery will be running in a matter of days?"

"Yes."

"What is it?" Jak asked. "What is a piece of artillery?"

"I'm not positive. Artillery is a siege weapon, I think."

"That doesn't tell me anything." Jak motioned to the guard with the sword, and the blade lowered—the other rebel held Wunic's legs and chest tightly. "What else do you know about it?"

"Not much. They're like very big guns," Wunic said, and the sword dropped to the smallest toe on his foot. "Wait, Goddamn it! That's true, do you want me to make something up!?"

Cold metal touched his skin, and Jak backed away, shaking her head and talking softly to herself.

"You know more," she said. "You're in charge, General. Tell me about the artillery."

"I don't know exactly what it does."

Jak gestured to the rebels, and the sword pressed into the skin of his little toe.

"Goddamn it!" Wunic shouted. "Let go of me, you little shit! Stop it! It's not a lie!"

Wunic screamed, his body convulsing, and they cut off his small toe, blood spurting from the wound. The rebels quickly wrapped a bandage over the bloody space, and Wunic continued to fight, shouting at them.

"Damn you," he said. "I was telling the truth! Damn all of you!"

"You swear?" Jak said, looking at him casually.

Wunic made no attempt to repress the pain, and he let it pump adrenaline through him. "Go to hell," Wunic said. "I'm going to gut you, you understand? You had better kill me, you worthless bitch, or I'll make you wish you had."

Jak nodded to the soldier, who moved his sword up to the next toe.

"Were you lying?" Jak said.

"No, Goddamn it!"

She looked at the guards and then at Wunic again. "That," she said, indicating the lost toe, "was a trade. To know for certain that we may face artillery in the next few days."

"They'll blow you to hell, you Goddamn whore," Wunic said.

Jak nodded to the rebels, and Wunic lost another toe.

"Yes," Jak said too quietly for them to hear over Wunic's screaming, "But you get to go first, General. Thanks for the advice."

in the tunnel, the walls glowed blue, and the light of their torches flickered off of the smooth rock. Vel looked back at the small hole in the ceiling, twenty feet overhead, where they had broken through. Snow drifted in, melting on the tunnel walls. The two soldiers—Guin and Sayt—waited for Vel to lead the way. But he had stopped less than ten feet into the tunnel. The blue light followed them, of course, but Vel had insisted that they light torches. *The blue light is less than reliable,* he thought.

"Sir, how far is it?" Guin asked.

"Don't know," Vel said. He wasn't thinking about the walk under the city, past the wall and the grasses, to the chambers beneath the ruins. He was thinking about the bodies he had seen the last time he was here. Both Guin and Sayt carried a rifle and a sword, but would these weapons matter against the Frill? Vel carried the Frill spear at his waist, tied beside his sword and pistol. What had the Frill said the last time Vel was here? That no human had ever killed one of them, and the first people to settle this planet, to found Hope, had brought guns with them. Vel had seen the remains. Would the rifles work?

"You went to the ruins?" Sayt asked.

Vel nodded. "That's right. Look," he said, "I understand that Denon assigned you to protect me, but I don't think it's a good idea. You're both going to die if you stay down here, if you come with me."

They waited for him to go on. *Obviously they hadn't understood,* Vel thought.

"The Frill will kill you, but they might not hurt me," Vel said. "I don't exactly understand why. Just trust me. I want you both to go back."

The torches hissed and sputtered, and yellow light flickered on the walls, turning shades of purple where it mixed with the blue illumination.

"Sir," Guin said, "we're here to protect *you*."

"I know, but I don't think you can. Listen, I understand your orders. I want to overrule what Denon told you to do. Can I do that?"

"Not in this," Sayt said, and Guin shook his head. "No."

"If they're going to kill me, they'll do it."

Sayt said, "We need to move, Your Majesty. Our orders were to take you out of the city as quickly as possible."

"Please," Vel said, and reluctantly he fell into step between them. "Just go back."

"Sir, what are they?" Guin asked.

Vel frowned, continuing to walk away from the hole that led to the cemetery. Their footsteps echoed in the silence. *Good question,* Vel thought. *What are they?* "I'm not sure. Whatever they are, they lived on Hera before Hope was founded. They were supposed to be extinct, but there are hundreds of them at least. I saw them briefly the last time I was at the ruins. I think there was some kind of war between the Frill and the first people to come to Hera."

"You mean God's prophet?" Guin asked.

"Yes," Vel said, and he realized that both of these soldiers probably knew the Church teachings of Hope's origin: of the prophet Blakes's arrival on Hera from Merica-Urope, of his inspired "rebirth" of humankind on Hera to save them from the sin of temptation that had existed in the old world.

"Blakes and whoever else was here with him fought with the Frill," Vel said, the blue light and torch glow illuminating a rough circle of stone in the corridor ahead of them. Vel stared at the darkness beyond as he continued, "But the Frill won, I think. That's why there are rules against leaving the city, that's why there's a wall around Hope to keep people from going into the grassfields and ruins, except to collect raw materials."

Both of the soldiers were quiet, and then Guin asked, "What did they look like?"

"Like thin people with long hair and pipes where their throats should have been," Vel said. "Except their faces were metal, and their eyes were like red slits." Vel thought about it. "I think I saw them with these." He indicated the Frill spear he was carrying, the weapon he was supposed to somehow use to barter for food and more Pox-curing plants. "But there was something else, too. You both know the stories about the Nara?"

They nodded, and Sayt said, "They're in stories, kind of like the Frill, aren't they?"

"Yes, except I think the Nara are something completely different than the Frill. They're big, and I don't know how to describe it, except that I saw one kill some of the Religious Guard. They were butchered."

Guin grinned and nodded to the passage ahead of them. "We're not the Religious Guard."

"I don't think you understand," Vel said, slowing his pace. "You're not going to survive if we keep moving."

"Sir—" Guin started, but Sayt spoke up, cutting him off.

"Sir," Sayt said, "you know it isn't easy to rise like we have—you know how much training we each have, Your Majesty. Sir, we've been trained since we were children to live and die at your service."

"I understand that," Vel said. "But there's a difference between living and dying against criminals and against the Frill."

"Sir, with all due respect, you're wrong." Sayt's voice was calm, and he looked peacefully at Vel, as if he was reminding him of a principle Vel had forgotten. "We live for you, we're here for you. We both believe that you were right to remove Justice Hillor—you are king because you deserve to be king. It is possible," he said, "that we won't be able to fight the Frill. And it is possible that the Nara will be entirely invincible as well, should we run into them. But it is also possible that there are other *people* who will be looking for you."

Vel thought about it, and realized that he was right. *I didn't even consider that,* Vel thought. *Even after what happened the last time I was at the ruins, I'm not thinking about the human threat. The Frill are still the real danger,* Vel thought, *but there* was *some truth to what Sayt said.*

Sayt continued, "Regardless of whether the opponent can be beaten or not—we are your lives, sir. At the moment, you have three, and you were correct when you said that we would both die. Your Majesty, if you die before we do, then we've failed. We're here to die in your place."

Vel said, "You might be right in—"

You were warned, boy.

Vel stiffened; he recognized the voice inside his skull.

"They're here," Vel said, and both of the soldiers set their torches down and levelled their rifles into the blackness. "Go back," Vel said. "Please, forget that speech, and just go back."

Guin said quietly, "How do you know they're here?"

"That's not important," Vel said, and he slipped out his pistol, tapping it with one finger unconsciously. Tap. Tap. Tap. "Just go."

We remember you, boy. We don't forget.

"And I remember you," Vel said. "Guess what, I'm not here to fight you. Just want to haggle." Tap, tap, tap.

"You're talking to them?" Guin said, looking back at Vel.

"Something like that," Vel said, and one of the torches went out.

Sayt went to the torch that was still burning—and the flames hissed into a trail of white smoke. *Damn it,* Vel thought, and he squinted in the dim, blue light emanating from the walls.

Leave.

"Funny you should say that," Vel said. "I can't just go back. I need your help."

"Sir, I don't see anything," Guin said, and Sayt waved his arm for silence.

"I'm here to trade, I think," Vel said again. "You want this?" Vel flicked the handle of the Frill spear. Carefully, he removed his bag that contained the Blakes-box and set it on the floor. "Come on, don't do this. I don't want to fight."

Everything you have ever known will come to nothing.

"Thank you," Vel said. "Thank you, you sons-of-bitches, come on. You remember me? Well, I remember you." Vel held up his pistol. "You don't want to deal—come out." Tap, tap, tap. "You know what I think?" Vel said to the soldiers. "They're not even going to—"

Darkness, and quick slits of red, and Vel fired at one—pistol flash, and the cracking flares of both rifles, and Guin and Sayt were screaming—and then silence. Vel stood in the sudden quiet, his pistol still in hand, and he stared at the blackness, waiting for a noise or movement, waiting for something to kill. The blue light returned, and now Vel was alone, his bag untouched at his feet, several piles of used ammunition scattered across the stone, and ahead, a single discarded rifle.

Didn't touch me, did you? Vel thought, and he shouted, "Come and get me, you bastards! Come on! Let them go, Goddamn it. You didn't have to do that. I'm the one who's trespassing, not them. Come and get *me.*"

He paced in the dimness, and then Vel put his bag back on, the box still straining on his shoulder straps, and holstered his pistol.

"Cowards," he said. "You won't take me, will you? Goddamn it."

Vel barely looked at the solitary rifle left on the stone as he passed it. *Why did they have to tell me their names?* Vel thought. *I told them to get the hell out of here, I told them.* Further into the tunnel, and now Vel stopped, glanced back—only darkness beyond the circle of blueness, and he continued: a wooden door set into the stone. *That wasn't there,* Vel thought, his pulse suddenly racing. *Goddamn it, that wasn't there a second ago, and it wasn't there the last time I was here. These tunnels have changed.*

He glared at the door, looked away, and then back at it—the door remained. No identifying marks, just a black doorknob. *Is this the kind of situation I'm supposed to consult you about, Blakes?* Vel wondered. *The sudden appearance of doors?* Vel opened the door.

Inside, a stone marker read:

I know you're afraid they might make you into soap. But I think you'll make a better set of buttons.

Vel stepped through, and another stone, set higher than the first, was carved in large letters:

Welcome to Auschwitz Funland!.

It was rumored that he was mad, and that he was a genius, a prophet, a messenger of God, a murderer and tyrant. Blakes had ordered his personal guard to build a throne of skulls, to drape the tapestry of a Roman emperor across it and to carve the crucified Christ from a single tree—that must be taken on the first day of spring from a forest deep in Russia, but he wouldn't say which forest—and then this effigy was to be nailed to the back of his throne.

When it was finished, Blakes had the throne mounted at the top of a black staircase in front of a swastika flag, several hundred feet in length, and on either side he mounted candles in swastika-eagle candle holders, remnants of the twentieth century. Behind the candles, Blakes had more crosses set, alternatingly lined with diamonds and the joints of children's fingers.

Blakes sat reading one night in the fall of 2100, columns of soldiers stationed at the base of the staircase that led nowhere but to his throne. Blakes listened to the silence. Five weeks since his July Laws, which outlawed all "technology" without an official sanction from the Führer, Blakes. Blakes allowed monitors and the network to function in his capitol buildings, but he ordered all electric wires removed from every city in the world, all communications cut, starting from the largest hubs of activity and moving out to the periphery, so that after five weeks, the silence was almost complete. *And the noise,* Blakes thought, *the noise is nearly gone.*

The satellites still orbit, he thought, *but so do angels, and their power far outweighs that of sin.* At his feet rested a new notebook that Blakes had just begun to write in several days ago, and the book had no title yet. He flipped the pages of a collection of the works of William Blake—*My works,* he thought. *All mine.* Blakes was dressed in a black robe with a swastika armband on his right shoulder. Portraits of Adolf Hitler and an array of others hung from every wall of the large room, and Blakes frowned at one above a doorway to his right; Philipe De La Ceña, a dark-skinned Spaniard with wild eyes, long hair and the tattoo of a five-pointed star on his left cheek, just below his glass eye. Philipe had poisoned the water reservoirs of Spain after the Reintroducíon, after his family was massacred by the new militant government in 2038. Blakes had read all about Philipe, and he knew of each step Philipe had taken in his campaign against the Spanish dictator, Daniel Manera.

And you won, Blakes thought. *You had Manera burned alive in the center of Barcelona, along with the rest of his arrogant posse. You triumphed, because you understood the necessity of God's law over the arrogance of man.* Philipe had prayed the rosary as Manera roasted, and when he took control of the government—in the weeks before his assassination—Philipe had called for Spain's return to its glorious past, to the past of the armada and the voyages of discovery and the age of the conquistadors.

Blakes smiled and flipped the page without looking down. *I am like you, Philipe,* he thought. *We are the same, and your struggle is mine.*

Blakes had read accounts of the Asian cities and the factories and life in his empire in the West. In China, after Blakes's armies had occupied cities and countrysides full of corpses, they had returned with stories of empty continents; of ghosts and cannibalism and anarchy. Four billion deaths on the first day of the strike, at least another four billion since. The world population had dropped from 12 billion to roughly 3.8 billion in one year. The diseases had not stopped after infecting the districts of China; they had spread, killing everything that breathes in a great swathe across all of Asia, into the Middle East, through Eastern Europe, Russia and Northern Africa. Inoculation stores had run out almost immediately after treating the armies. China was empty, as was India and the Middle East: fields of skeletons, and Blakes had heard stories of pigs feeding on great piles of bodies in the once-busy streets of Bombay, of the few survivors being shot by Blakes's armies.

There *had* been a few battles with dying armies, but they had not lasted long. The Führer, Blakes, had crushed the world's opposition, had done what no one had had the courage to do before. Humanity was being erased—technological, secular sin would follow.

". . . eighth day of our assignment in New Beijing, and Sergeant Vickson shot himself. We saw a little girl picking bits of her mother's skull off of the pavement, collecting them like broken flower petals, and this girl looked up as we passed. The street was all rubble, and Barnes muttered, said that he was surprised there weren't more rats and buzzards: they all must have gotten sick too. Just burnt out buildings, dead cars, mounds of decaying people buzzing black with flies and swarming with stinking maggots.

"And this girl just stared at our company as we marched past. Someone asked her if she wanted to come with us in Cantonese, and she shook her head and then went inside, and I could see what was left of her mother sitting upright in a wooden chair through the open window, and the little girl started arranging bits of her mother's face onto a swollen, meaty lump of flesh that was connected to lumpy clothing. The girl was starving, crawling with parasites, and Sergeant Vickson stopped in the middle of the street, started mumbling about his own daughter, took out his pistol. It started raining before he . . ."

The Fourth World War would be the last world war, Blakes thought, *because the world will be cleansed this time. We are not cattle to be herded at the sound of an electric buzzer, we are not interlocking pieces in a biological factory, we are God's chosen and we have souls,* he thought. *And it takes true courage to recognize what must be done: the rejection of 'progress.'*

". . . got a job with Morgans Industries before the war. Diana was pregnant, my boss said that I was due for a raise, and I didn't particularly like working in a cramped office building manipulating figures on a computer screen for ten hours a day, but it had a nice view of the Thames and it paid for our flat a few blocks away in Soho. Things I took for granted then—like the war. I remember everyone was always talking about war and what the Chinese were capable of and how horrible the Third World War had been for our grandparents, but I don't think we really understood.

"Adam was our first kid, and, yes, we had him adjusted, so that he

would have the best possible future. I had the money and Diana—who had always been opposed to adjustments in other peoples' children—had agreed, had pushed for it. And so when we found out she was pregnant, the doctors adjusted the fetus, and Adam was the most beautiful, most wonderful thing I had ever seen. He was very smart, something like a 160 IQ, and a projected life expectancy of eighty-nine natural years, and I bought that for him. We loved him so much. That was in '98. I don't know where he is now.

"After the '99 fallout I was laid off, Morgans went under, and we lost our flat. We were driving out of London when the first wave came, and when London was hit, I remember thinking how happy I was that we had gotten on the road that morning and not waited, and then the car had swerved off of the street. I don't want to talk about that.

"I've been living in a farmhouse just past the London suburbs—I didn't steal it, there wasn't anyone here. Maybe the owners are dead, maybe not. Don't know where Diana or Adam are. They weren't in the car when I woke: and it was smoking on the side of the road, crashed into another vehicle, but they weren't there. I remember the way people had been staring at the black sky in the south. We all knew that London had been hit. I knew when I saw the flash in the far distance, in the rearview mirror, that left me half-blind.

"There was this crazy moment when I wanted to laugh. Because my suitcase had spilled open and all of my clothes and personal things were covered in mud, all ruined, and my skin had blistered along the back of my neck and arms. And all the traffic had stopped in a line of wreckage and wounded and just the endless sight of people standing by the side of the road staring back where London had once been . . ."

Adria entered through the doorway below Philipe's portrait, walked past a painting of Louis XIV, past Che Guevara and Adolf Hitler and Mao Tse Tung and Li Yen and Joseph Stalin, finally stopping at the foot of the stairs.

Adria's jaws were tight, and her form thin, as if she was slowly starving. *And she isn't,* Blakes thought. *She, of all people, should be healthier than this.* Adria looked tired, as if she had worked for years loading heavy boxes or plowing soil with her bare hands, and she hadn't. Adria's long blonde hair fell in braids down her back, and she wore a simple blue dress that reached her ankles. *Still,* Blakes thought, *she is as beautiful as she ever was. Her bosom is full, her eyes young, and her hips wide enough, but not too broad.*

". . . operate the factories under God and with full knowledge that history will someday recognize the vision of the task our Führer has assigned to us. Last night I pushed some of the vermin into a ditch, shoveled the bodies in and watched excess fat from the soap building drain out of a rusted pipe in greasy, bloody streams, covering the bodies. The fat helps them burn faster.

"Funny, because this was the first time I can remember hearing a voice from the pit. Someone was alive under the corpses, someone had survived the gas, and I heard this strained, horrified voice—like my grandmother's voice—calling out, saying she was frightened and crying. She thought she had died and was in hell. Avarez adjusted the piping and sprayed the fat over the whole length of the bodies in a spray like bloody phlegm, and I laughed, because no, she wasn't in hell, but she would be soon.

"Sometimes hell is necessary to reach heaven: If we didn't do this, who would? Who would have the courage to exterminate these rodents and begin again? Avarez called out, and at the opposite end of the pit Dominique turned on his flamethrower and we backed away, and it was funny because I remember . . ."

Adria opened her mouth, and Blakes held up one hand. The soldiers in black uniform, with gas rifles and nerve bullets, remained exactly as they were, ready to kill on command.

"There is a Smile of Love," Blakes read, moving his finger along the lines to keep his place. "And there is a Smile of Deceit, and there is a Smile of Smiles. In which these two Smiles meet."

Adria waited.

Blakes grabbed his notebook from the floor. "Do you like that?"

"Yes," Adria said weakly.

"Hmm," Blakes said, and he copied the verses into his book. "I rather like it myself, you know." He had begun to speak with a forced British accent, as he—as he often said—'became closer to reaching himself.' "What did you think of it?"

Adria watched him, hands behind her back, face expressionless. "It was about smiling."

"No," Blakes said, and he finished copying the poem, shut both books, and carried the notebook with him down the stairs. "Not about *smiling*, about *smiles*. Big difference. One is an action, the other an expression—a thing. Not the same thing at all."

"Yes," Adria said. "I understand now."

Blakes nodded as he walked past her into the hall, and she moved a pace behind him, as she always did. "The rebel mourns what she cannot retrieve, and her lover's neck, a tender . . . prick." He stopped, and she froze, waiting for him to continue. "What did you think of that? Just had the thoughts, just now." And he started copying them into his notebook. "What did I say? 'The rebel mourns what she. . . . ?' "

"Cannot retrieve," Adria said.

"Yes," he said, and he was quiet as he finished writing it. "Yes, of course, thank you. Would have thought of it, but thank you for that."

Adria did not respond, and then she followed his lead as he started walking again.

"Something wrong?" he asked, as they entered a room full of silent monitors. Rows of men and women sat at them working, wearing tiny wireless earpieces. Several of Blakes's personal guard followed a dozen paces behind Adria, and Blakes paused in the monitor room, examining the charts and figures and numbers and text racing across each screen. "So?" he said. "What is it? You're not telling me why you came to get me."

"There's been another uprising in the American South," Adria said.

Blakes smirked. "They never get it, do they? The bastards hardly had any wires before we took them away. They'll be cleansed with an atmospheric silo—not messy, though. I'll have to make sure of that, it'll be biological." He thought about it, and then asked, "What else?"

"The rest isn't as important," Adria said.

Blakes nodded, as if he had already known that. "All right. Come on, then." And he led her through the hall, into another full of Roman statues, up a grand Victorian staircase, past a wall of black-and-white photographs from the Nazi concentration camps. Adria stiffened as they passed—Blakes noticed the gesture and stopped.

"What?" he said.

"Nothing." Her face was blank again, and Blakes stepped past her to the images of skeletal people, of mounds of bodies—almost too jumbled and messy to really be clear in the black-and-white pictures.

"Something wrong?" Blakes asked, and he tapped one of the pictures of a line of old men, all with numbers tattooed on their arms, all naked and starving. "What is it?"

"I don't know," Adria said, unmoving. "I don't think I'm feeling well. Might be getting sick."

Blakes watched her for a long moment, and then asked, "You like Mickey Mouse?"

She blinked. "What?"

"You like that character that they were making cartoons of before we shut down their power? Did you like those Mickey Mouse movies?"

"I never saw a Mickey Mouse cartoon."

"Hmm," Blakes said, and they started walking along the second floor again, past color photographs of more killing, this time in a bright green jungle. Soldiers stiffened as Blakes passed, and several saluted, "Sieg Heil!", and then Blakes stopped at his bedroom, and he locked the door behind them.

Swastikas hung from the walls, and a large bathtub the size of a small swimming pool ran along the opposite wall. There were rows of ancient swords and various weapons mounted on the left wall, and on the right an enormous bed was draped in red and black, the mirror beside it carved with more swastikas in its frame. Blakes heard a pair of guards stop outside his door, as they always did whenever he was inside, and Blakes set his notebook carefully on a bedside table that had once belonged to the American, Ronald Reagan. Blakes sat at the foot of his bed, and he noticed that Adria was still standing by the door, as she had been when they had entered—she had not moved and was looking directly at the opposite wall and the bathtub, no emotion on her face.

Blakes stared at her, and then he said, "You know, I was thinking, it's been awhile since we've talked. You know that?"

Adria remained as she was.

"And I was thinking," Blakes continued, "maybe you would like some real formal power. I can give you something for your years of service, something like a city that you can just watch. Like Paris; do you like that city? I always loved Paris in the days before the war. Now, it's full of lunatics, but then—then it was a *city*." He laughed. "Would you like that?"

Adria looked at him—looked *through* him, as if she was studying the interior of his skull.

"You know I have to have children," Blakes said. "My mistresses won't do for that, you know. You must give me children, Adria. I wonder why we haven't seen that yet."

She didn't answer, and now Blakes began to tense, and he leaned forward, hands on his knees. "Come here."

She obeyed, walking to within an arm's length of him, and Blakes touched her chin. He stroked her cheeks, and she did not respond.

"I feel sick," Adria said evenly, and Blakes withdrew his hand.

"What about the medicine you've been taking? I know about that. Your nurse gives it to you, doesn't she?"

Adria said, "Yes."

"I think you've had enough of it. Go on." He motioned to the floor in front of him. "Take off your dress." Adria remained exactly as she was, and Blakes smiled, brushing his hand against her cheek again. "Go on, Adria."

Adria said, "I need my medicine."

"Take off your dress," Blakes said, and Adria still did not move—Blakes stood over her, and he put his hands on her shoulders. "Did you hear me? Get on your knees, then." When she did not respond, he pushed down hard, and Adria gasped, trembling as she was forced to her knees. "Adria, I love you, you know that. Please, why are you making this so hard?"

Adria began to shake her head, and then she glared up at him, her face flushing a deep red, and the veins in her neck pushed at the skin.

"Adria—"

"Stop," she said, and then she backed away from him and stood. "You. Just stop it." For a moment, Blakes couldn't react, and Adria continued, "Who—*what* do you think you are, you arrogant bastard? You're not *him*—you're not William Blake any more than I am."

"You're not feeling well," Blakes said quietly, and he balled his hands into fists. "I know—"

"You *don't* know," Adria said, and she went to the wall and took one of the smaller swords, with a curled, ornate handle. Adria smiled, advancing on him. "You don't know, *Blakes.*"

"There are soldiers outside the door," Blakes said carefully. "Think. Adria, please, what are you doing? Do you think you can—"

"Shut up." Blakes backed around the side of the bed as Adria came nearer. "I hate you so much."

"Let's talk about this without the weapon, please," Blakes said, but he wasn't backing away anymore. Instead, he stood his ground, letting the sword point inch closer. "I'm sorry for whatever you think I did. Whatever it is, you're not feeling well."

"Don't tell me how I feel."

"Adria—"

"Fuck you," Adria said, and she lunged, catching Blakes through the side of his stomach. He spun and hit her hard at the base of the neck, and then shouted—soldiers rushed into the room, and Adria slashed again, cutting a gash in the bedside table, and they dragged her away, screaming.

Blakes sat on the side of his bed, watched her go, and one of the soldiers asked, "Sir, should we—"

"To the factories," Blakes said, and he spat, touching the cut along his side gingerly. "Make a bar of soap out of her."

LORD DENON took the papers from the religious soldier who had brought them. He sat on the balcony overlooking the empty cathedral floor, and the soldier waited behind Denon's chair as Denon broke the seal and read them quickly. The soldier wore a swastika armband, just as all of the Religious Guard did, and he was dressed in a white uniform, a rifle hanging from his left shoulder.

"My son," Denon said, after he had read the message, "is this true?"

"Yes, Lord Denon."

"How many are there?" Denon asked.

The religious soldier-priest thought about it, and then he said, "Fifteen, I believe, Lord."

"And what are they capable of?"

"Not certain, Lord. I have heard that they can level buildings, that they fire the wrath of God through their long pipes."

"They fire large bullets?"

"I'm not certain, Lord. Something like that, I think. Except their bullets are the size of a man's head, and they explode, annihilating anything in their path."

"Good," Denon said, and he wrote a short note, folded it, and then stamped it with blue wax in a circle, sealing it. "Take this to them. Tell them that they are to move as soon as they can."

"Yes, Lord."

"And explain to them that it is crucial that I be informed the moment they have finished with my orders."

"Yes, Lord."

"That's all, my son." The soldier-priest left, and Denon watched him exit down the main aisle below, saluting the other Religious Guards who were stationed around the cathedral.

Fifteen, Denon thought, and he relaxed in the chair. The artillery was ready.

Wunic spat blood down his shirt and chin, and he slumped against the wall, his legs cramping as he tried to hold his bandaged feet against the cold floorboards, to stop the pain. Three rebels lounged at the far end of the room, two with rifles, the other bearing a crossbow.

Three soldiers, Wunic thought, *three Goddamned rebels.* An empty plate sat at Wunic's feet, and a mug with a trace of water in a circle at the bottom. *Damn them,* he thought. *Damn her. Damn whoever put me in this position. I am alive,* Wunic thought. *I am alive to find who ordered that attack and make him suffer, to find Denon. The colonel and all of his men are dead because of that order. God knows if they've lost that building to the rebels because of the suicide charge I led. We all have places we're supposed to be, things we're supposed to do at certain times—not destiny, but something close to it. This war was taken from me. My life.*

Denon, Wunic thought, and the rebels periodically glanced at him, but said nothing. Footsteps echoed in the hall outside his room, hurrying closer, and Wunic winced as he sat up, his feet sliding against the floor. Wunic glared at her as Jak walked into the room, her rifle swinging as she came closer.

"All right," Jak said briefly, stopping in front of him. "You have a seat on the Executive Council—that true? You took Hillor's place?"

Wunic nodded.

"Has the council met since Hillor was killed?"

"Yes," Wunic said, and he tried not to look at the spaces on both of his feet where three toes had been cut off. Two little toes, and another on his left foot.

Jak motioned to the rebels in the doorway, and one left. Voices in the hallway, and a pair of rebel soldiers dragged a dirty man into the room by his armpits.

"The government is hoarding food," Jak said.

"Don't be stupid," Wunic said. "That's not true."

"It is," Jak said. "I know it's true because I've seen the insides of the granaries. They kept cutting rations, but they've still got enough to go with normal rationing."

The rebels threw the dirty man on the floor beside Wunic, and the newcomer groaned as he rolled onto his side, wiping a patch of dark wetness in his hair. One of the man's eyes was swollen shut, and his shirt was torn with bloody smears around the gash.

Wunic sat up straighter. "Councilman Orik."

The wounded man—Orik—stared at Wunic, and then smiled slowly.

"Good. Then you two know each other," Jak said.

Orik put one hand to the bloody space on his chest and stomach, wincing as he breathed. "Hello, General."

"No, this doesn't make sense," Wunic said to him. "Why would they bring *you* here? You're not—"

"I was supervising the reconstruction of a retaken neighborhood, when we were ambushed." Orik shook his head. "Piss on fate if they got you too."

Wunic stared at him. "You're a civilian. Rules of warfare—"

"There are no civilians anymore, General." Jak crouched between them, a pair of rebels just behind her, hands on their rifles. "And those *rules* no longer apply. I want you both to tell me what you know about Lord Denon."

Wunic frowned. "Why?"

"I want to know if he's in charge now. Who else is left on the Executive Council to check him?"

"Check him?" Wunic said.

Orik shuddered as he breathed, and he said weakly, "Don't know."

Wunic said, "Military officers run armies, not priests."

Jak ignored him and motioned to Orik. "You served on the council before all of this. You were the strongest advocate the poor had. I want to know what Denon is going to do."

"Lord Denon's been in charge since the beginning," Orik said. "Even when Hillor was on the council, Denon used the Justice for what he wanted." When Wunic started to object, Orik said, "General, he used you too. Why else would you be here?"

"And now he's in charge," Jak said.

"He's been in charge for years," Orik said. "You want to know what he's going to do, look at what's already happened."

Wunic shook his head. "I'm sorry, Councilman, but I disagree."

"General, with all due respect, I've seen Lord Denon at work for over twelve years; he's always been in charge to a large extent, indirectly—every veteran of the Executive Council knows that."

"Even with Justice Hillor on the council?" Jak asked. "I don't know. I find that hard to believe. Hillor had significant sway before he got himself killed."

"Hillor always needed Denon," Orik said tiredly. "And Denon used him."

Wunic swallowed blood. He had bitten his own tongue hard when they had taken his toes. "Even if this is true, the military is still outside of Denon's control."

"Then what brought you here?" Orik said again.

"I was careless. I made a tactical mistake." *Because of Denon,* Wunic thought. *I wasn't careful. I thought I knew him, thought I could trust him.*

Jak said, "I want to know if Denon will appoint someone in your place, General, before attacking. Vel is the only real check on Denon now. Without—"

"Vel's no check," Orik said shortly. "Denon controls him; he always has."

Jak paused, as if she hadn't known. "He controls the king?"

"Yes, of course," Orik said, and he smiled at Jak's confusion. "What's so hard to understand about that? Wasn't Lord Denon partially responsible for Vel becoming king in the first place? Do you think that was a purely selfless gesture?"

"I wouldn't have thought Vel would trust him. After everyone who's—"

"I told you," Orik said. "Denon helped Vel become king, he helped him beat Hillor precisely so he can use him now. It's very simple. Hillor was pushing his own agenda, getting too powerful—Denon was losing control—and so Lord Denon replaced him with someone he *can* control. We all saw it happen. On the Executive Council, we watched them—we knew."

"Why doesn't anyone tell the king?" Jak asked. "Why the hell would you leave him to Lord Denon?"

Orik shrugged, as if it should be perfectly obvious. "Some of the council belong to Denon, the rest are either afraid of the Religious Guard or are oblivious."

Wunic straightened. He tried to focus his thoughts, tried not to think about the empty spaces on his foot or whether or not, once he was able to stand, he would be able to walk.

"If you knew everything beforehand," Wunic said, "why didn't you say anything to me?"

"The same reason I didn't talk to the king. I think Denon is just after power. I don't think he has any great desire to see the city starve to death—and I think he'll do everything he can to keep things together. Under the Church, of course, but still together." Orik hesitated, trembling in obvious pain, and he forced a weary smile. "And naturally, Lord Denon made it very clear a long time ago that he would not regret sacrificing my life for his greater good. If I had warned you or the king, General, neither of you would have listened, and the poor would be one voice shorter because I would have been killed."

"Why do you need our help?" Wunic said to Jak.

"You've both worked with Denon," she said. "We have to anticipate his moves."

"His move will be to wipe you out," Wunic said.

Jak smiled. "Don't think so. But without the king, Denon *is* in charge of everything. We're not fighting anyone but Lord Denon."

"That's not true," Wunic said. "Denon has left certain military commanders in charge of their units, he has to—you can't run a war any other way, and Lord Denon is not a military man." Wunic remembered the conversations they had had, Denon's questions: Had that all been an act?

"I'm sorry," Orik said, "but you're wrong, General. Lord Denon worked very closely with Justice Hillor and other top officers long before this—he has experience from commanding the Religious Guard, and my impression has been that he's *very* familiar with tactics and basic procedures."

"No," Wunic said. "I disagree. I spoke with him . . ." Orik was shaking his head tiredly, and Wunic thought, *All an act, all arranged to put me here. To build my trust and throw it away for no reason, as if my life makes no difference to him, as if I haven't earned this.*

"What about the king?" Jak asked.

"I don't agree with the councilman on this," Wunic answered. "I think Vel still has a lot of control."

Orik shook his head, but didn't answer, and Jak asked, "So what about the council? There aren't thirty or thirty-one members anymore. And most civilians are gathered together in just a few places—you can't hold elections without people in the districts to vote."

"Why wouldn't Lord Denon appoint a new council?" Wunic said. Orik glanced at him, but said nothing. Wunic continued, "You said yourself that he cares enough about the preservation of the city and the council was established when Hope was founded."

"I said I couldn't think of a reason that wouldn't be in his interest," Orik said.

Wunic said, "Once the war is over, Denon won't be able to maintain control by himself without the bureaucracy."

"And you?" Jak said to Orik.

Orik put one hand to the side of his head and looked at the blood that stained his palm. "I suppose I'm dying."

"What will Denon do now that he's in control?"

"He isn't in control," Wunic said. "He needs the military. He needs the king."

"No, he doesn't," Orik said. "Of course he's in control. And the other possibility—if he tried to rule without a council—Denon can use his spiritual pull with the people. He *can* maintain control if he wants to. If he started a new dynasty, Denon could become a dictator, just like Blakes."

"That was five hundred years ago," Jak said. "You really think that he'll try to pass himself off as a successor to Blakes?"

Orik said, "When the king dies, you'll know."

Wunic said, "No, he won't kill the king. Whether or not you're right about anything else, Lord Denon cares about Vel. Why would he protect him this long just to kill him?"

Jak frowned. "That's a good question."

Orik said, "The king was kept alive this long so that everything could be put into place, and now there's no one alive to stop him. Who has the following to challenge Denon now? If Hillor were alive, there might be a chance—Justice Hillor might take over himself—but he isn't. And if you were still there, General, you might rally enough of the soldiers to depose him before they had been forced to swear oaths of holy allegiance. But Denon has the Church, that's important. Even you might not get enough soldiers to turn on him. The only one who still can at this point is the king, but the boy is probably dead already." Orik closed his eyes. "The rebels have lost the war, Denon's won."

Wunic said, "*If* Vel dies, but he won't. Denon won't put the king in danger." Wunic thought about it. It was their last hope, really. Without Vel, Orik was probably right. No one would be able to challenge Denon once the war ended. *And I didn't see it,* Wunic thought. *I'm a fool: Why didn't I see it before?* "Whatever happens," Wunic said, "Vel will be protected. Denon won't let him leave the palace."

Vel stepped into a cavern full of long, gray buildings, all identical and rectangular, as if they had been built out of a single mold. At the ends of the lot, Vel saw towers and a gate, surrounded by several layers of what might have been rope. As he drew closer, Vel saw that it was a kind of sharp metallic rope, curled and twisted regularly into sharp spirals.

Beyond the immediate block houses, a larger building rose—a smokestack—with the words CREMATORIUM GIFTSHOP carved on its side. Vel touched his sword and pistol uncomfortably, and another stone sign was posted nearby:

COME ON.

Vel wandered down the empty rock between the buildings, past several posts that looked like crude gallows, and then he saw two long, empty spaces, where people were presumably supposed to line up to enter—a stone on the right said, MEN, a stone on the left, WOMEN AND CHILDREN.

Inside, Vel entered a long, empty metal room. The walls were lined with posters and more pictures of skinny people with numbers on their arms and bright swastikas. Vel saw signs below them with numbers: 3 FOR $5.00, and the words SOUVENIR AUSCHWITZ UNIFORMS: S, M, L AND XL. Vel thought, *This isn't real. Whatever this is, it isn't real. It wasn't here the last time I came to the ruins.* He walked to the end of the room, and found another door that opened to a large stone room—another door at the opposite wall—and there were metal fixtures at regular intervals along every wall with the words: AUTHENTIC SHOWERHEADS below them.

"Showerheads" is gibberish, Vel thought, and as he went to the next door, he felt a chill. There was something very strange about the precision of everything. The deserted yards with the identical

buildings, and now this, all perfectly aligned and . . . built for some purpose. Vel opened the next door and glanced back at the "showerheads." *What happened in this place?* Vel wondered, and he stepped into a dark room with long metal slots on either wall. Heat radiated from behind both walls, and a sign mounted in the middle of the floor read AUTHENTIC OVENS, FEEL FREE TO OPEN!

Vel touched one of the handles uncomfortably, warm on his palm. *Ovens,* he thought, *ovens for what? What would anyone cook in such a strange building? Why would they build something so perfectly arranged and ordered?* Vel smiled, and he thought, *Probably for cooking some kind of grassfruit pie; a Frill recipe.* He opened the door. Rows of blackened skeletons—he imagined that he could hear someone whimpering in the flames that flushed Vel's cheeks and tingled across his exposed skin.

He shut the door. *Why am I here?* Vel thought. *What is this? This is a joke, right? Some kind of sick punch line that the Frill want me to see? Is that what they did to the first people of Hope? Those weren't human buildings; no one would build something like that,* Vel thought. To the next door, and Vel was back in a circular blue tunnel. He shut the door behind him and walked quickly away, the blue light following him, and the passage split in two—Vel ran to the left, and then it split again, and he went right. *Should end at a hole,* Vel thought as he ran. *Should be in the grassfields, and then at the ruins I get on top of a building and the walls were filled with carvings now.* The strange, curling Frill script and the human graffiti that had been ripped into the rock on top: *Sieg Heil . . .* and more swastikas.

Vel was getting tired, and he paused, leaning uneasily against one wall of crude swastikas that had been etched over whatever the Frill had originally written. The Frill writing had once filled all of the walls, curling up overhead in an unbroken dome. Now it was wearing away in places, and whoever had carved the swastikas had tried to block out the Frill words with row after row of swastikas and lines of mostly illegible text.

On the opposite wall, Vel saw the words:

ile of Love,
a Smile of D
ile of Smile
ese two Smil

"Is this real?" he said aloud. "What did I see back there? Did you do that? Did the Frill make me see that somehow?"

Not the same tunnel, Vel thought. *Wherever I am, this isn't the same.* He thought of the blue dress, burning, and the layers of bodies, and Vel started walking again.

Ahead the tunnel opened into a larger room, and Vel slowed as he drew closer. *Good luck getting those messages to me, Denon,* he thought. Inside, Vel saw a large stone table, perfectly round, set in the center of the circular room, and all of the walls were filled with Frill writing and more graffiti. *Where is the place I was before?* Vel wondered. *I don't recognize any of this. Where is the place with the bodies of Blakes's friends? At least there I would*—he saw something the size of a large grassfruit sitting in the exact center of the table.

Guin was staring at him. *No,* Vel thought, and he looked away, breathing fast. *Guin's* head *is staring at me,* and he steadied himself on the nearest wall. *Terrific,* he thought. *Thank you so much for showing me this, you Goddamn cowards.* Vel glanced back at the table: Guin's eyes were wide, and Vel saw dried blood crusted to the bottom of his chin and cheeks, as if it had splattered when his throat was cut. *Goddamn it, I wish I didn't know your name. I wish you hadn't said anything to me.*

Vel walked around the exterior of the room, making no attempt to get any closer to the table, and he found another doorway at the opposite wall. Another hallway—something moved quickly just outside the circle of his blue light—and Vel drew his pistol and sword, waiting in the doorway. He kept the Frill spear where it was at his waist.

"What do you want? Why did I see that back there? You've changed these tunnels, haven't you?"

Nothing, and Vel walked out of the doorway, down the hall, his pistol aimed directly ahead, his sword levelled below it. Vel heard his pulse in both ears, and he tried to keep his sword from shaking with the adrenaline in his arms. *Just concentrate,* he thought. *Nothing's happened, I'm safe: if they wanted to kill me they would have. And half of this isn't real anyway.*

Someone was moaning just ahead, a soft crying sound.

Vel tried to swallow, but his throat wasn't working. "Someone there?"

The moaning stopped, and Vel realized he wasn't walking anymore. *Goddamn it,* he thought. *Just do it if you want to fight me.*

Stop playing with me. A soft cry, and Vel started walking again—someone was kneeling in the hallway ahead, hands folded in front of him. *Sayt,* Vel thought as he came closer.

"Sayt, you—"

Not kneeling, Vel thought, and he tried to look away. *Not folding his hands in front him.* Sayt's legs had been severed at the knees, his arms at the elbow, but they weren't bleeding. They were just gone, as if they had never been there. Sayt's jaw was missing, and so was his nose, and Vel backed away.

"God," Vel said, and he stared, his stomach beginning to roll onto its side. Sayt's eyes flicked to Vel, and Vel felt himself retch—red slits in the hall behind Sayt—and Vel vomited nervously on the floor in front of him. Someone very thin flashed behind Sayt, and a point, like the Frill spear, blurred through Sayt's neck—Sayt's head remained where it was, and the red slits flashed again in the dark hall, and then Sayt's head dropped from his shoulders, but it didn't bleed as it rolled, and his body jerked and slumped to one side. Then it fell over and was still.

Vel tasted bile, and it hurt his throat as he tried to organize in his mind what had just happened. He heard himself say, "Oh God . . ." And then darkness, and Vel waved his pistol weakly at nothing, and when the blue light came back Sayt's body and head were gone. The stone in front of Vel was stained, it smelled—from vomit, not blood—and Vel moved away, down the hall to where Sayt had just been. The blue light followed him.

Down the hall, and now Vel saw dark spaces on either side of the hall, where the surface was different and clean of any writing, like cool metal rather than stone. Vel drew closer—*almost transparent,* he thought—and inside, Vel could dimly see the outline of a person on his back, lying inside the wall. *Not real people,* Vel thought, as he forced himself to keep moving. *Can't be real.*

"Please," he said, as the hall continued, "I want to trade with you. I didn't come here to fight."

You brought murder here.

A door at the end of the hall, set into the stone, and as he drew closer, he saw the outlines of people reaching out of the rock. *I've been here,* Vel thought, hurrying to the sheer door. *This is the same, I know this.* He touched a square set into the metal door, it opened, and then a short metal hall with another door inside with words written on it in perfect letters:

WELCOME ABOARD!
PLEASE VERIFY YOUR CLEARANCE ID NUMBER BEFORE PROCEEDING.

The blue light faded behind him and new, white light hummed and flickered from parallel metal strips overhead. Vel touched the second door.

"Identification number please," a female voice said, and Vel answered, as he had the last time he was here.

"One, three, two, one."

"Welcome aboard, Commander Blakes," the same voice answered, and the door opened.

I know where I am, Vel thought. There are squares of metal and corpses and chairs, and a ladder that leads to another floor. *This is where people came from,* he thought, and he smiled as he stepped into—a square, perfectly white room full of dangling bodies on metal hooks. The room was cold, and the door shut behind him before Vel could stop it, his breathing misting the air as he held onto the wall. Rows of thin, nude people hung from the ceiling, the nearest, an old woman with gray skin, a giant hook stuck cleanly through her back, the point protruding from between her shriveled breasts. Her head hung down, just above the point of the hook, and Vel began to shake. Row after row of people, some much smaller than others—children—and Vel slumped to the floor.

"Let me out," he said softly. "Goddamn it. I hate you, let me out." Vel's teeth began to chatter, and he closed his eyes—but the bodies didn't go away, they remained on the insides of his eyelids, twirling slowly on their hooks.

You brought this here. You have no idea what you will cause, boy.

"Stop it," Vel said. "This isn't real. Those aren't real people. However you're doing this—I don't care. Let me out."

No answer, and when Vel opened his eyes the bodies were still there. He leaned to one side, trying to look past them. No other doors that he could see, and the door behind was a sheer black surface without a knob or even a square to touch. Vel pressed it with both hands.

"Open the Goddamn door. Let me out of here."

How many bodies were there? Vel wondered as he pounded the metal. *Fifty? More than that?* He didn't look at them, resting his forehead on the cold metal door. *Please,* he thought. *Goddamn it, there must be a way out of here.*

Blakes.

Vel opened his bag and shivered as he took out the simple black box and wire. Without looking up, he slit his thumb with his sword and pressed the wire to the wound.

"I'm sorry," Sisha said for the second time.

Denon stood near the mirror, and Sisha sat on the side of the king's bed in a black dress.

"You did what was expected of you," Denon said slowly. "I think I've made that clear. Please, now isn't the time."

"I know," Sisha said. "And I'm sorry, but I have to speak with him."

"You'll be compensated, just as I told you. Your new house is waiting for you less than two blocks—"

"Denon," she said, and he stiffened; Denon was not accustomed to being cut off. He let it happen when he had to; yes, he would tolerate insults when they worked to his advantage—but not from a common prostitute, not here.

Sisha continued, "I know you have the money to pay me, it isn't that."

Denon folded his hands in front of him. "I don't understand, what's so important if we're not talking about money?"

"I want to talk to the king before I go. I want to tell him I'm sorry, I have to make sure he—"

"The king is busy," Denon said shortly. "Be realistic, please, for one moment. His Majesty also gave rather explicit instructions: He does not wish to see you."

"I know, I just—"

"And even if he were not extremely busy, even if he had not given those orders," Denon said, "the king isn't in the palace now."

Sisha frowned. "Where is he?"

"Enough—I'm sorry," Denon said. "But it's time for you to leave."

"Lord Denon, you don't understand," she said. "Please, I just need to talk to him. It won't take long, if you could tell me . . ."

Denon approached her slowly, his body tense, his face absolutely calm. "You will be compensated as we originally agreed."

Sisha glanced at her reflection in the mirror behind Denon: hair neatly combed, eyes and lips painted carefully for the king. *I need to see him—not as a whore. I need to talk to him.*

"Yes, Lord Denon, thank you for the money. But I care about him," Sisha said.

Denon was quiet for a long time, and then he frowned. "You care about him?"

She nodded. "Yes. Please, I just have to talk to him once. After that—"

"I am going to pay you. That's why you're here. This is a job."

"What we agreed to—"

"—is what I will pay you," Denon said. "You do not 'care' for him, do you understand? That boy is your king. You will not care for him in any other way."

"I do—"

"No," Denon said again, as if discussing the weather, "you don't."

"Lord Denon—"

He shook his head and stepped closer, within an arm's length of Sisha. "My girl, you're a whore."

"Lord—"

"You have always been a whore, that's your place. You're here on business. You don't think or feel in this case. That should have been self-evident; I wouldn't think that I would have to explain that to a professional. Just business."

"Yes, Lord Denon, but please—"

"You will accept the money, and you will leave," Denon said. "And you will not—"

"I need—"

"You," Denon said, leaning closer, and Sisha tried to still the trembling in her arms, "will do," he glared at her, "as I tell you."

Sisha held her right hand behind her back, shaking in a fist on top of the bed. "I care about him."

Denon struck her, the room spun, Sisha's forehead was burning, and she fell onto her back on the bed. Denon remained where he was—she started to sit up, and he hit her hard in the stomach. Sisha gasped, choking, and Denon watched patiently where he stood. Sisha could not breathe.

Deliberately, Denon began to undo his robe, and Sisha tried to move away—he twisted her forearm easily behind her back, and Sisha screamed at the sudden pain in her joint, like knives ready to cut her tendons and muscles, ready to snap the bone. Still, she could not breathe. *No,* she thought, *oh God.* Denon still held her arm with one hand, and he opened his robe.

She clawed at the sheets and kicked, but he pulled violently on her locked arm, and the pain stopped her. She wheezed, air suddenly returned—*Try to find another way to fight him, another way to get away.*

"No," she rasped, "no."

Denon slipped up her dress, and everything was a confusion of kicking and screaming—and the searing pain as she felt her arm beginning to break, and then he forced her down harder, forced her legs apart, and she was screaming and cursing at him.

It was over, and Sisha lay trembling. She remembered tears, and he had . . . he had found places inside her that no one, not him, not her mother, no one should have seen or touched. *I didn't fight,* she thought, *I couldn't stop him.* Denon was dressing, unspeaking, ready to leave the room, and Sisha hurt, she ached. *Kill him,* she thought, *and I hate myself for being weak, for pushing him. Why the hell did I push him? It was my fault.* She began to curse him quietly, crying as she curled into a fetal position. Sisha held onto her knees, trying to slow down her heart. *No,* she thought. *That couldn't have happened, didn't happen.*

She heard Denon walking to the door. He said something about soldiers and how she could stay in the king's room for awhile, and parts of her ached that had never ached before, as if she had swallowed hot embers and they had found their way into her groin and bowels.

So suddenly, and now it was over. *Maybe it had not been real,* she thought. The door opened, and closed again. And Sisha understood now. *Yes,* she thought, *I know why you did it. Now I see, Vel. I understand. You are cursed, and because I touched you, because I cared, now I am too. Now I want to die.* And she cried.

"This Angel," Blakes said, "who is now become a Devil, is my particular friend." General Finshteig watched him from the bottom of the black stairs that led up to Blakes's throne. Blakes wore a white robe now, with a swastika drawn onto its chest. It was February 2100, and although he hadn't been outside, Blakes had heard that the new century had been ushered in with a fresh layer of snow.

General Finshteig started to say something, and Blakes said, "With all I do, in everything I am, I see God. Amen and praise be his name. For what was once a prophecy is now my reality. Don't you agree, General?"

The general squinted up at Blakes, his hair short and very white. He said with a thick German accent, "Is your will, my Führer. Loss should you know about in the desert-land."

"In the Middle East?" Blakes said, and then he laughed. "Heretics will suffer along with everyone else. Why haven't you dumped germs on them?"

"Have countermeasures, my Führer," the general said simply. "Restored have power to the Baghdad and cities surrounding."

Blakes had officers serving under him from an array of nationalities throughout Europe and the Americas. *Interesting that this one should be German,* he thought.

"Do you know what happened on this day, General Finshteig?"

"No, my Führer."

"Neither do I," Blakes said, and he chuckled to himself. "Neither do I. That's all, General."

"Should know," the general said, without moving, "that Baghdad cannot retaken without the troops weakening Serbian territory."

"Just shift in more legions or send different bugs to get them. Hit them with an ICBM—why are you wasting my time with this? Wipe them out, General. You know our policies."

"Countermeasures, my Führer," he said again. "Sorry, but should you know of these dangers."

"What dangers?" Blakes said. "Do you take me for the Greek Apollo?"

Finshteig frowned slightly. "Do not understand, my Führer."

"Do you take me," Blakes said slowly, his mouth hinting at a smile, and his personal guard remained quiet, "for the *Greek* . . . Apollo?"

"No," Finshteig said, although it was clear he had no idea what he was answering.

Blakes jumped out of his chair and pointed at the ceiling. "*That!*" he shouted. "That is the Greek Apollo!" Blakes smiled and stared wildly at Finshteig. "He is Satan."

General Finshteig was quiet, and then he backed away slowly. "Yes, my Führer. You take rest. Sieg heil." And as he left, Blakes burst into laughter, slumping into his chair again. "Funny, funny, funny," he called to one of his guards. "God, did you see him? What am I but a tool of the divine flesh?" And he burst into laughter again.

Two weeks later, Blakes received reports of enemy rebels taking over the Middle East, China, and the Rocky Mountains of the United States. Blakes continued to write, now working twenty hours of every day. He spent the other hours with his mistresses, sometimes ordering that they be chopped into pieces in front of him when they had finished with sex, sometimes asking for a crucifixion. And sometimes he let them live, but not often.

They brought him reports, but he never read them. They offered him prisoners, top officials from the opposition, but Blakes never saw them. The skin and flesh of the world had been removed and now only the bones remained to be picked clean: Blakes knew that he had already won. His officers warned him less and less, as he had had the "prattling miscreants" sent to factories for suggesting that God's will would fail. All bad news comes from spies, he had once told them, and had refused to inspect his territories, had refused to leave his palace, and he had ordered all of the officials who brought the news torn to pieces by attack dogs.

Blakes saw angels every day now, and they congratulated him on his work, on his service in God's name, in his restoration of the original Plan.

"Things are happening very quickly now," the Angel told him. "It's good that you have not been outside this palace."

Claustrophobic. Watching the world die from a corner in a black room, Blakes thought. *It has to die so that it can be reborn, and I don't want to see it until the old world is gone.* The sin of learning and collective will had been crushed under the Nazi flag, whose motto had always been "Life Over Lies." Blakes had saved the world from its own mindless noise and ignorance. And he knew that he had cleansed it, even if billions had to be purged in the process. The current rebellions would soon end, and the new age would continue.

Except that the rebellions didn't end. On the fifteenth of March, five of Blakes's top generals, flanked by rows of soldiers and loyal members of the highest echelons of Blakes's intelligence network, marched into his throne room, and in a brief firefight killed all of Blakes's personal guard. Blakes stared at them, his notebook open in his lap, pen in hand. He didn't carry weapons anymore, and the generals moved to the bottom of the staircase, their soldiers rushing up.

"Führer, your incompetence," General Finshteig said, "has deemed you unfit to rule." He spoke clearly, with only a slight accent. "If your empire is to be saved, it must be worked through 'blood and iron.' Not mindless slaughter."

The soldiers grabbed Blakes's notebook, and he shouted at them as they forced him up, hands bound behind his back, and then Blakes was marched down the stairs. In the corner of his vision, the Angel smiled, shaking his head.

"You should have seen a coup coming. It's what they do when they're afraid. You have been the mystic through all of this, communing in your isolation; they have been contaminated by the outside world."

Blakes forced them to stop in front of General Finshteig, and the general watched him coldly without moving.

"Lion," Blakes said, and he shook his head, smiling, as if he was amazed that it could be happening, rather than outraged or frightened; as if he didn't believe it. "You are the voice of one crying in the wilderness, General."

Finshteig nodded, and the soldiers forced him toward the door.

One of the other generals said, "Blakes, you are relieved of your command. I suggest you pray that we can salvage what we have created. Pray that you are never brought to trial."

Blakes laughed loudly and shouted, "Kill me and I shall be reborn. Damn you all, you don't even see it. This is not my life yet—I have not yet been born! My great works are yet to come!"

As he was dragged past rows of soldiers and workers and the monitor room where technology was still being used in the last stages of purification, hundreds stared at him. Blakes watched the Angel walk ahead of him, wings beating peacefully in a warm white glow, and the Angel nodded to him, leading Blakes down stairs, and deeper, into a dark room without windows, where Blakes was left alone with the Angel.

"Our time is not yet come," the Angel said.

Blakes sat on dirty concrete, and he sprawled out, staring up at the blackness. "What's happening? What should I do?"

The Angel began to sing, "Hail, finger-footed lovely Creatures!"

Blakes watched the Angel dance in a circle as he continued,

> "The females of our human Natures,
> Formed to suckle all Mankind.

'Tis you that come in time of need,
Without you we should never Breed,
Or any Comfort find."

When the Angel had finished, Blakes said, "You think it's because of *her*? You think she brought this? Don't talk to me about karma, you sterile raven—I haven't lost."

The Angel shrugged. "Then where are you?"

"Waiting," Blakes said.

"Waiting for what, exactly? You want another chance? They're going to kill you this time. A martyr is only a martyr because he didn't succeed."

"I tell you, *I haven't lost*!" Blakes spat at the Angel, and it was gone. "Go then," Blakes said, and he slumped back to the floor. "I will be reborn, and the next time. . . . All of it will be returned to the way it was meant to be. All of it will burn until no one is left. Whatever I have to say or do or think or believe until then, I accept. But, I will make it burn." He grinned at the darkness. "And they'll wish they had never made me."

The Angel said from somewhere in the blackness, "Oh, don't worry, my son. That's one thing I wouldn't worry about, were I you."

Hello vel.

Blakes, I need your help. I'm in the tunnels; under the ruins, maybe, I don't know.

I know where you are. You want to escape.

Yes—how do I get out of this room?

I'm going to help you, but you must do exactly as I say.

All right, go ahead—what do I do?

You will use the Frill spear to cut open the door.

But, the door's metal, it won't—

It will. Once you're back in the hall, you'll return to the section of the tunnel where you saw bodies through black segments of the rock, through metal slots. You will go to the last body on your right, and then you will cut a small slit along the metal, opening the body's box, letting in air.

Why, I don't—

Listen. Once you've done that, you'll go back inside the tunnel and this time instead of saying one, three, two, one, you will say three, seven, seven, nine. Then, you will enter a small room where you will find a monitor, a chair and a set of wires extending from a panel in front of the monitor.

Monitor?

A square of reflective metal. There will be two wires, a red one and a black one. You will connect the wire from this box to the black wire near the monitor.

Connect it, how?

It will connect when you put the ends together. Then you will find a small keyboard—a complicated configuration of letters and numbers and symbols. These little pieces are called keys. Be very careful and press the keys for "1-3-2-1", the same code you entered before. Just those four numbers, Vel. Once you've done that, leave me—leave the box—in that room.

And then what? Why should I leave you there?

You're leaving me in there so that the Frill don't get a hold of me. That room is protected from them. All of those steps will force the Frill to confront you.

Why? Why should I cut a hole in the wall and—

Do it, Vel. You said you would not argue. Just trust me; you don't have time for a full explanation. All of it is designed to get the attention of the Frill. They'll confront you shortly after that and you can 'barter' with them.

What do I do when I see the Frill? I give them their spear?

Vel, I did not tell you to dig up the spear so that you could give it to them. You are half-Frill, and you can move just as they do. You are as much demon as angel.

So what do I do, Blakes? Just tell me.

You're going to kill them with it.

What?

You are going to fight the Frill using their weapon.

You want me to get killed? I don't understand, why should I try to fight them when they can—

Vel, we don't have time. Just do as I said. You remember the steps I gave you?

Yes.

Good. It's been nice talking to you. I'll see you soon.

Vel's mouth was dry, and he sat up weakly, a piece of frozen meat brushing his hair—the old woman's foot. She spun slowly on her hook, and Vel forced himself to stare at the floor, not to think about it—his stomach tensed—and Vel put the box away, drew the Frill spear and held it awkwardly with both hands. *Cut through the metal,* Vel thought, and he swung at the door, cleanly slicing a gash that nearly cut the door in half. Vel hesitated, the weapon still lodged in the slit. Through the opening, he could faintly see white light, and warm air breathed in. Vel swung again, and again—and then he kicked out a slab of the door. It whined as it scraped free.

Vel climbed through the opening, and he was back in the short hallway, the two lines of light still glowing overhead, heat returning to Vel's cold hands, feet and ears. He rubbed them, heading back to the other end—glancing back Vel saw the dimness of the bodies through the square hole he had cut in the sealed door. Vel returned to the tunnel, and blue light followed him past rock people, half-sealed in the walls, toward the Frill writings, swastikas and black metal spaces. To the last one on his right, and Vel crouched, spotting a silhouette through the dark, translucent metal.

He levelled the spear and carefully cut a hole in the metal to the body, still unable to really see the body. It lay motionless inside the wall. Vel put his spear away and started back toward the hallway.

Don't.

"Don't do what?" Vel said, and he glared at the walls. "You won't do anything to me."

Vel returned to the hallway, past the first door, and the lights had gone out overhead—they returned with a flickering buzz, and Vel could still see the bodies hanging through the opening in the second door. He touched it with one hand.

"Identification number please."

"Three, seven, seven, nine," Vel said, and the hook room slid away, shooting up, and now Vel saw layers of black rock shooting past through the hole he had cut in the door. *It's moving,* Vel thought, remaining perfectly still. *Something's* moving. A room flashed up, and now more black rock, another room, more rock, and then the rock slowed and opened into another, small room. *This door doesn't just lead one place,* Vel thought uncomfortably, not really knowing what it meant. He thought about the door that had suddenly appeared in the tunnel, the door to *Auschwitz. These tunnels aren't fixed, are they?* he wondered, and then the door opened, scraping the piece of chopped metal on the floor as it opened.

Vel stepped through, into a small room, layered in dust, and lights stammered on from the ceiling. A table with a yellowed blanket sat at one wall in front of a poster with a perfect picture of yellow-red flames and the words, TWENTY-FIRST CENTURY NIGHTMARE over them. At the opposite wall was the "monitor" Blakes had mentioned and a chair, and there—Vel drew closer—were the wires.

He slid into the chair, coughing on the swirls of dust.

Please, boy. Don't. You do not understand.

"Then why don't you tell me?" Vel shouted at the ceiling. "Come out and explain this to me or shut the hell up!"

When nothing happened, Vel opened his bag and took out the box, hooking the end of the wire to the black wire extending from the panel in front of him. Blakes had been right; it fit perfectly. Vel set the box at his feet, and it began to hum softly. He found the keyboard and typed 1, 3, 2—

You've brought it with you, boy. Murderer.

Vel typed the last number Blakes had given him: "1", and the monitor flickered, words appearing through the dust. Vel squinted, watching them magically scroll across the metal glass—not metal, just glass? Black words on a white backdrop:

Initiating sequence, preparing add-drop to scale 837, engine sequence initiated . . . online. Second engine sequence . . . online. Tyger being solicited . . . alive/rehydration procedure initiated. Time remaining on Tyger unknown. Less than three days, will advise . . .

The words continued to scroll, and Vel heard the voice inside his mind again, *You will die, boy. You belong to us, not him.*

Vel turned in the chair, examining the empty room.

"Come and get me," he said, and then he smiled. "I'm safe here." The screen went through several cycles of nonsense, and finally Vel stood, drank from the container in his bag, and left the room, shutting the door behind him. Vel walked to the first door and stepped out, back into the corridor, waiting, one hand on the Frill spear.

"What are you going to do?" Vel asked. "Swarm over me like you did the last time?"

Red slits flashed in the darkness behind him, but Vel did not see them.

"I'm ready for you," Vel said. "Whatever you think I am, I'm not yours. I don't care what you think you're entitled to. You didn't kill me the last time I was here, and this time I'm ready—"

Something struck the back of Vel's head, and he fell unconscious.

wunic tried to sleep. *Not as easy as it should be,* he thought, *when you're tied to a chair with your hands bound behind your back tight enough that the rope scratches open holes in your wrists. To say nothing of my Goddamned feet,* Wunic thought tiredly, and he shifted, opening his eyes briefly to look at Orik, who was propped in another chair at the far corner of the room, head on his chest, eyes closed.

One rebel soldier sat in the doorway, a rifle in his lap, his head back, and he tried to sleep, using the doorframe for support. The rebel coughed and without opening his eyes, he tried to suppress a second cough by raising a gloved hand to his mouth.

Wunic heard the low rumblings of thunder in the distance. *I wonder what lightning looks like in a snowstorm,* Wunic thought, and he tried to let the thunder lull him to sleep. The throbbing in his feet where toes should have been kept him from ever getting comfortable, despite all the rebels had done to numb the wounds—they had still cut off his Goddamned toes.

Wunic rolled his head, listening to the joints of his neck pop, and the rebel soldier was staring at him sleepily.

"General," the rebel said.

Wunic blinked the room into focus. "Yes?"

"Shouldn't be thunder, should there, General?" the rebel asked.

How the hell should I know? Wunic thought, and he willed himself to become more alert, but the drowsiness and the irritating notion that he *should* be asleep kept him slumped in the chair.

"It isn't the rainy season, is it?" Wunic asked, and he grinned slightly. *Not even close,* he thought. Whatever rainy season there should have been had turned to snow, unlike anything Wunic had ever heard of. There were no records of this kind of snow, no stories. Winter was supposed to wait another few years, and all of the grain storage was specifically designed to accommodate twenty years of normal weather, then five years of harvest and five of winter. This time, what should have been a five-year summer had ended after a handful of months in enough snow that Wunic would be happy if he never saw it snow again. *And maybe I won't,* he thought.

"Why don't you go back to sleep, son," Wunic said, and he had to remind himself that this soldier, who had probably served under Wunic's command in the police—directly or indirectly—was now a rebel. *A traitor, enemy,* Wunic thought, *and he's just a Goddamn kid. He doesn't have any idea why he's fighting, what this is really about. His superiors probably turned, and this boy followed them to fight against the king for more food.*

The floor shivered, and through the walls that same distant thunder repeated. And again.

"Doesn't sound like thunder to me," the rebel said, and still Orik slept in his chair.

Wunic tried to concentrate on the noise, tried to ignore the aching, itching pain in his feet for one moment and just think about something else. *No,* he thought slowly. *Thunder rumbled, hesitated, rumbled, and then paused before starting again.*

"What is that?" Wunic said. The rebel watched him calmly. "What the hell is that?" Wunic said again, and then louder, "What the hell is going on? Get your commanding officer in here."

Orik mumbled and shifted slightly in his chair.

"Did you hear me?" Wunic said. "Go on—get someone who knows what's going on."

"Didn't know it would sound like that," the rebel said quietly. "Did you, General?"

The sound was rhythmic, deep and rolling. Too controlled to be thunder, too precisely timed—it was like nothing Wunic had ever heard. *Organized chaos,* he thought.

Wunic swallowed and said, "No. The artillery's not supposed to be ready for another week."

"Earlier, General, you said—"

"I know what I said." *And I thought I was lying,* Wunic thought.

"Listen," the rebel said, "this is still earlier than—"

"Yes," Wunic said, and then louder, "We're all going to be blown to hell. The artillery will tear this building apart."

"You said you didn't know what it would do."

Wunic stared back at the rebel and said again, "I know what I said."

Orik sat up, blinking weakly, and he coughed. The rebel nodded. "They're *your* soldiers, your army."

"No," Wunic said. *They should be the city's,* he thought, *and the King's. Not mine, not Denon's.*

Orik asked, "What's going on?" He heard the thunder and tried to stand, the ropes holding him where he was. "Oh my God. Oh my sweet God."

Wunic said slowly, "We're dead if we stay here—we're too close to the front." To the rebel: "Untie me; look, I don't have a weapon, just let us go. Let's get the hell out of this building. You're going to die in here, soldier. We're all going to die in here."

Orik grunted. "Look at me, General." He nodded to his blood-stained clothes. "Tell me something new. But, this is not supposed to be happening yet—not like this."

Wunic turned to the rebel. "Where's the bitch? Where's your commanding officer?"

The rebel stiffened. "General, I—"

"Son, it makes absolutely no difference what I call her right now. In a few minutes we're going to be cut apart, do you understand? Where is she?"

The rebel watched him blankly, sweat on his forehead, and when Wunic asked again, the rebel said, "Don't know, General."

"We need to know what's happening," Wunic said. "We need to know how much time we have. Is this making sense to you, kid, because we don't have time for this bullshit right now. Listen, the two of us are more important to your commanders than you or any of your friends. Do you understand?"

The rebel nodded and said, "I'm sorry."

"Soldier, do you know who I am?"

"Yes, General."

"Good. Now, do you hear that noise? Do you know what that is? Yes? Good, so do I, except I know more about what this artillery is going to do than anyone else alive. Are we hearing each other?"

"Yes, sir."

"Thank you, now get us out of these Goddamn chairs."

Orik shook his head. "General . . ."

"Sir," the rebel said, "wouldn't your soldiers know where you are? If you were taken prisoner, sir, wouldn't they have an idea that that might be possible and know *not* to shoot at—"

"Pray that they don't know where I am." Wunic strained at the ropes. "Because if any of them know, it won't be the artillery commanders, it will be Lord Denon—and if he thinks that I'm still alive—let me put it like this: I can't go back right now, do you understand?" *After everything I've done,* Wunic thought, and he clenched his jaw. "Get your C.O. Do it now."

When the rebel didn't move, Orik said, "They're not going to let us out of here." And he winced. "That hurt. Damn, I can't even breathe without tearing myself up."

"I understand that you have orders . . ." Wunic said to the rebel, and footsteps approached in the nearby hall—the rebel jumped to his feet and glanced at Wunic, and Jak walked in.

She carried her rifle with one hand, hair dishevelled, and dark stains crusted both of her arms—Wunic recognized the coloration perfectly. A pair of new rebels—equally weary-looking—stepped into the doorway behind her, and a sword swung regularly from Jak's waist.

Wunic said, "We can't stay here."

"How do we stop the artillery?" Jak said, panting, and she pointed her rifle at Wunic.

What part of this don't you understand? Wunic thought, amazed that she would stand here and casually interrogate him—and all he could say was, "What?"

"Don't do this, General." Jak clicked the safety off. "Just tell me how we can stop it."

"We don't have time to—"

"Let me worry about the time, you Goddamn coward," Jak said, and she glared at him. Wunic felt his pulse quicken, blood rushing to his cheeks, adrenaline down both arms. "Now," Jak continued, "tell me what to do. Your men have artillery, how do I fight it?"

"You don't."

"What do you mean? It's impossible?"

Nothing's impossible, Wunic thought, *but you have no idea what you're doing here either, do you? It's a matter of costs, risks*—and he said, "You could capture it, I suppose."

Orik asked, "What kind of damage is it doing?"

The regular thumping continued behind the walls, like organized thunder. *That's exactly what it is,* Wunic thought. *Organized thunder.*

"Too much," Jak said, and then to Wunic, "We can't just capture it—counted at least six pieces out there. It would take too many soldiers to capture even one of those positions. Tell me how to fight it. There must be something we can do, and you're going to tell me what it is right now."

"Six?" Wunic said, his mind working very slowly.

Orik took a deep, wheezing breath, and Jak said, "That's right, General. Six pieces of Goddamned artillery on our northern flank."

Wunic wanted to laugh at her, at all of them. He wanted to laugh at himself for being forced to sit in this Goddamn building waiting to be blown into tiny pieces with these rebels. I am General Wunic, he wanted to say, and the absurdity of it was almost hilarious: *except that I'm about to die.*

"Not six," Wunic said.

Jak looked at Orik, opened her mouth, and then closed it again.

"You . . ." she said, "you have more than—"

Wunic said, "We have to get out of this building."

Jak asked, "How many then?"

"We have to get out of this room."

"General, listen to me—"

"No," he said, staring down the barrel of her rifle, "*you* listen to me. You can't fight that artillery. It isn't so complicated that you have to ask me for advice—you're all going to die if you don't pull back now. Everything. Anyone you leave where he is will be killed, including everyone in this room."

Jak eased the rifle closer to Wunic's face. "How many pieces, General?"

"How will shooting me help you?"

"General—"

"Yes, I am a general," Wunic said. "And you cut off my toes. I'm confused about what you're threatening me with at this point. Death? You're going to leave me in here, and whether it's intended or not, I'm going to die in this room because of your ignorance, carelessness and stupidity."

"How many pieces are there?" Jak said quietly.

"Let's not play this game again. I may not have had access to all of the information in the first place. Why wouldn't I lie? That's right, so let's see if you can finish this pathetic charade and shoot a man in the face. I know it would be easier with a dick, but for all I know, you may actually be hiding one under there. That's right; if you're going to shoot me, now's the time."

Jak's finger pulled the trigger—a rebel hurried into the room behind her, one of the soldiers in the doorway stopping him before he could reach Jak. They gave Jak a dispatch, and she paused long enough to read it.

"Stop it, General. Don't do this," Orik said, coughing again.

He thought, *My name is General Wunic, I am supreme military commander of Hope's military police force, I serve on the Executive Council at the pleasure of my king, in his name and for the glory of Hope.*

"I'm not doing anything," Wunic said. "I'm tied to a chair."

"General," Jak said, crumpling the dispatch in one hand. "I don't want to do this with you. He's right."

"You're already fighting me. You're an idiot," Wunic said. "And you people aren't revolutionaries or soldiers or anarchists—or even rebels—you're just frightened whores, pimps and criminals. You're the bottom, and you're there because you belong there. Our God isn't yours and neither is our city."

Jak shrugged. "Maybe. I want you to help us beat that artillery."

"No."

"General, you know more about the artillery than anyone else. If we really don't have a chance, you will have saved thousands of lives."

"Your leaders will just surrender if I tell them to? That's nice of them."

Jak said, "This can go one of two ways: You can stay here and die or you can help me and stay alive."

Another rebel rushed into the room with a dispatch, and as Jak took it, Wunic said, "And trust you?"

Without looking up, Jak said, "I suppose you could hope to get back to the other side somehow without getting killed, *back to people you trust.*"

Lord Denon, Wunic thought. *You're the reason I'm here now. Everything I've worked for, the greater good, all sacrificed—for what? Thrown away like pieces of rotten wood. All of this to kill me, except that the artillery has not begun to hit this section of the front, so maybe my death isn't really that important. Maybe Lord Denon thinks I'm already gone. I'm going to punish him. But, I can't just go back; I have to think like him—if all of this was arranged, Denon would have backups. Maybe* I'm *a traitor now,* Wunic thought. *Maybe they think I've deserted. Denon will have a plan: and so I must have mine.*

Jak said, "Our northern flank has collapsed." She paused, a strange, exhausted desperation in her voice, as if she had just realized that she was in the middle of a civil war. "I was just there, before I came here—ten minutes ago—but now it's broken."

"Have the re—have you secured a new front?"

Jak shrugged, as if there were more important issues. "I don't know—I need your help, General."

"I need my toes back." *My honor, my life; I need vengeance, retribution—I need to make Denon feel my betrayal, my helplessness.*

"General . . ." The thunder stopped. Jak seemed to make a decision—she pointed the gun at him again, and this time he knew that she would fire. "We're out of time," she said. "We both know that. I *will* kill you—I don't want to, but I will. Help me, and I'll be in your debt, I'll owe you. But I need your answer. Now. One way or the other." Wunic opened his mouth, and Jak said, "I'll take a smartass remark as a 'no'. And I'll kill you."

Wunic thought about it—*No real choice, is there?*—and he said, "Pull them all back. Pull everything back."

"Everything?"

The floor trembled. Wunic heard a quick, high-pitched *whir* in the near-distance, then a rapid series of shots that were loud enough to shake the walls, and Jak lost her rifle, grabbed the back of his chair with both arms—a noise falling—Wunic saw Orik's eyes widen. Orik shook his head and shouted something that was silent in the sudden roar, and the room exploded.

The ceiling collapsed, and all four walls shattered in a screaming of wind and rocketing wooden daggers that knocked Jak to the ground, and Orik disappeared as the floor cracked and violently gave way, the boards somersaulting—the world blurred, Wunic was falling, and the shots continued, and Wunic hit hard—the chair broke under his weight—the bones of his back and left leg were hot metal.

Oh God, he thought. *What could have possessed people to create weapons capable of this?* Wunic was staring at mounds of broken, burning wood and half-buried bodies in what had probably been a two-story house before the war. *Second floor,* he thought, *second floor entirely annihilated, and now snow poured in through the open roof.* Not even really a building anymore. Only fragments of two of the large house's walls still stood at the corners. Smoke curled up from bits of blackened debris, tossing and stinking in the snow wind.

Wunic struggled with the ropes on his wrists, digging them deeper into his flesh, and he felt blood on his freezing hands and forearms. The shots continued—like the sky coughing—and one of the remaining walls exploded in a rain of wood and stone that fell into Wunic's hair and eyes, peppering the debris that covered part of his lower legs. Wunic twisted hard, no longer caring about the blood on his hands, and the ropes tore, grating on his raw wrists as they broke away, and Wunic pushed away the remnants of the chair, tried to stand—swords stabbing through his left leg, and he cried out, collapsing again.

"Orik," Wunic said, as the pain began to recede, and without moving he shouted. "Orik, are you there!"

People groaned, and bits of the debris shifted where people were trapped beneath heavy piles. Where a wall had once been, Wunic now saw a main street, and soldiers in gray overcoats ran slowly through it, sloshing and stumbling in the snow, toward the source of the thunder. Wunic heard them yelling, saw them wave rifles—gunshots—and the continuing roar of artillery as snow whipped through the blown-out building.

He grabbed a long plank and snapped it into a pole, and then carefully, Wunic pushed away the debris from his legs and, using the pole for support, climbed to his feet. The waves of pain spotted out his vision, and Wunic tasted blood in his mouth from biting his tongue. He hobbled through the destruction—and there, immediately on his right, lay Orik, back arched, mouth wide. Orik looked like he was sleeping—in the street, the ground erupted in a sudden explosion that threw a cloud of snow, dirt and bodies into the air, ripping them apart as they fell. Wunic stared at the deep round crater, and the bloody remains that rained with the snow.

Get away, Wunic thought. *Just get out of this—this is not honorable combat. This is not skill with a sword or bow, this is not based on training. This is slaughter,* he thought, and he turned, fighting back the pain in his leg and back as he hurried away from the street.

"Help me."

Wunic spun, nearly falling—Jak's face was streaked black and bloodied, and she pointed her rifle at him with one hand. Another concussion rocked the mounds around them, and Jak winced away from it, glancing around like a frightened animal.

"Help me," Jak said again.

"Look around," Wunic said, absolutely deadpan. "You asked what the artillery would do—that's what it does."

"Please," Jak said, and bits of wood and hot metal whistled past Wunic's ear, and behind Jak, he saw someone lose an arm and a leg in the street, screaming and writhing in the deep snow. More rebel soldiers filled the street outside, snow tossing their long coats.

"What?" Wunic said. "What do you want from me?"

"Come with me," Jak said, and she lowered her gun. "We need your help."

"You'll shoot me if I don't?" he said, and she didn't answer. "Let me leave. I'm not going to help you."

"I'm sorry about your toes."

"So am I."

"Please, General. You know we don't have a chance without your—"

"A chance? Look around, you don't have a chance, you haven't had a chance since this began. It's over!" Wunic shouted at her, and the last of the walls collapsed, crushing several people who had been crouched below them for shelter from the snow. "We're all just dirt, but my boys have more guns, more food and water, and there are more of them. Are we seeing the same thing here? Look—you've lost!"

Jak touched his shoulder, and Wunic considered breaking her arm—but with his injured leg and back it might not be a good idea. Not so long as she had the rifle. *Goddamn it,* he thought. *I don't want this, I want to find a way back without getting shot, find out that the king is okay, that the government's still in place, that Denon hasn't won, and then I want to break him.*

She said, "Come with me, General. You're not a prisoner anymore if you agree."

Snow flecked Wunic's hair, and the ground shuddered as the artillery continued.

"What?" he said.

"You won't be a prisoner."

"I'd be a rebel," he said and thought, *Just like Denon's probably told them. If I go back, I'm captured by my own men. Some might support me, but it's too dangerous. There isn't a way out of this, is there? But I can't help these rebels win: They've lost.*

"You don't want to die in these streets," Jak said, and then her expression lightened. "I'm not Lord Denon."

Wunic tensed. *And that's what I'm going to do: use the rebels somehow against Lord Denon. Use them to get back and unify the government without the casualties that will come if the war continues. Work with the rebels, Wunic thought, use them to an end. They're a weapon like any other. If the ends don't justify the means, I don't know what does.* He said, "I'm going to kill him. I just decided. But I don't know what you expect—I don't know what we can do."

"Right now," Jak said, leading him away, "we can run."

chapter 12

Vel woke in a large, warm cavern. His pistol and sword were gone—the Frill spear, yes, it was still there. He rolled onto his side, the room slowly coming into focus—huge rounded ceiling with tiny, continuous Frill writing—and the walls were the same, with one doorway, two, three; there were dozens of doorways carved out at regular intervals, and a Frill stood nearby. Vel froze.

The Frill's face was a sheer metal mask with a pair of dark slits where its eyes probably looked out, and at the top of the metal facepiece, locks of thin hair fell long, straight back, down to its "neck." The neck was a collection of slender pipes that linked the bottom of the narrow facepiece with the Frill's metal breastplate, though it might not have been a "breastplate." No distinguishing marks, just a slab of metal that seemed to be fitted to the top of the Frill's torso. The arms were too long and triple jointed, and in its left hand five fingers gripped a curled Frill spear, identical to the one Vel had brought. The legs were also triple-jointed—five toes on each foot—and all of its body below the metal plates and facemask was absolutely black, with no real skin, as if it was wearing some kind of sheer suit.

Vel stared, unable to move.

He said quietly, "What do you want?"

You.

A moment's silence, and then Vel said, "Any particular reason?"

You belong to us. Shadow and Sky.

"What does that mean? The union of people and Frill—is that it?"

It is not that simple.

"What were those rooms? Those people . . ."

We did not build them.

"Then who did?"

You forget that humans have been on Hera for five hundred years, since the murderer landed.

Blakes, Vel thought.

Yes.

So I don't have to talk, he thought. *I can just sit here and—*

Yes.

And I'm talking to you? Vel motioned to the nearby Frill. You all sound the same in my mind.

Distinguishing signatures will come. Yes, I am talking to you. I am Ulyu.

Nice name, Vel thought.

So is Vel.

Vel began to relax, and he slowly rose, approaching the Frill. It remained perfectly still, as if it wasn't even breathing. *Not very tall,* he thought, just a little over four and a half feet high—the Frill had looked much bigger in the hallway when it killed Sayt.

Are all humans the same height?

So you're short for a Frill, Ulyu? Vel thought.

Yes.

Why am I here?

You are going to be killed.

Vel felt his pulse quicken slightly, and he scanned the doorways for more of them.

Why? he asked.

You are the fulfillment of our prophecies, boy. Just as you were created to be.

And the prophecies involve killing me?

Ulyu was suddenly several feet away. Vel realized that the Frill must have moved. *But I didn't see it,* he thought.

Follow me.

Ulyu walked with slow, rehearsed movements of its legs and arms, the blade swaying in its hand. Except that it wasn't moving slowly. When Vel had taken several steps, Ulyu waited at a doorway twenty feet away, as if time was moving differently for the Frill, as if its body ignored the same rules that Vel's followed. *No noise,* Vel thought, *nothing at all.*

Vel reached the doorway, and the blue light followed them into a tunnel with carvings that were all nearly faded into smooth stone, all Frill—no human swastikas here. Still Ulyu led, appearing to flash from one place to another, rather than walking, although if Vel watched carefully he *could* see the steps. And his mind seemed to object, as if a part of Vel refused to believe what he was seeing and therefore tried to ignore it because the movement was too fast.

This is one of our oldest sections.

How do you move like that? Vel asked.

I am a Frill.

I can't even see you move.

You're not trying.

Thanks, Vel thought.

You are part of us, boy. You are linked to us by what you are.

Half-Frill, Vel thought, and he asked, What does that mean? I don't *look* half-Frill.

They stopped at a solid stone wall, where a pile of uneven rock had collected, a small white rock visible in the debris.

There are two groups of us now. One believes that you are who you are—you are our savior from the death that we see ahead, from this hell we have been damned to endure.

I take it you're with them?

Yes.

And the other group's going to kill me?

Yes.

Vel frowned at the wall and at the writings. What do these say?, he asked.

We did not write them.

I don't understand, Vel thought. You—the Frill—said something like that to me before. That the ruins outside the city, that they were ruins *before* humans landed here.

The gods left us.

The gods, Vel said.

Yes.

Okay. What are we doing in here?

You are going to fulfill the first element of your prophecy. You are going to commune with the gods.

Vel shook his head. I don't understand, Ulyu. I don't see anyone in—

The bone.

Vel glanced at the white stone, half-buried in the pile of black rock. That's a bone?

Yes.

What do I—

Touch it.

Vel stepped closer to the pile. I just—

Yes.

Vel touched his fingers to the exposed bone—cold to the touch—and the frigid, smooth surface warmed. He had the sensation of his arm filling with light. He turned his head, as the light tried to find ways into his skull. Vel tried to withdraw his hand, but the light found an entrance up his neck, into the base of his scalp, and the world flashed crimson, then white, and then was gone.

understand that my actions were justified. The Society may not deem them as such, indeed, probably *would* never forgive what I have done, or not done. But, then the Society does not know about what is to come. Or do they? Whoever you are, you must be one of us, a Nerago. This is my last message—your responsibility now, not mine. I know that it is impossible for the Frill to understand last messages, and we are connected to the Frill—you and I—but we are different. Think what you will.

It began years ago, during the second age of atonement, when the Nara were still kept in their penned circles, still studied and fed. When the Nerago, my people, walked proudly through our city. I sang and danced, and I made love with Wi-al's beautiful daughter in the moonlight. There is too much to tell, and I must confess that I am inexperienced in creating the lines of structure that bind events together. I will try.

My name is Bin, and I was born on this planet, Frillai—which means, of course, World Given to the Frill. Our city here was magnificent in those days. Our structures towered proudly in the cool breezes, and we constructed bridges overlooking the small river, Treide. Treide flowed through our city, and into the blue forest beyond. The city was made of reflective black stone that glowed to the touch and would play bits of music or teach the history of our race's journey from Mentha—the home planet, meaning Security—to the children or anyone who was interested to learn.

I was happy in those days, growing up. I was happy because of *her.* Her name was Kall, a young girl, slightly older than me. Unlike me, Kall had been born on Mentha itself, and her parents were two of the most influential citizens of the city. They were responsible for fully half of the construction and half of the Artificial Securities who were building the mighty bridges across the river. The Artificial Securities are mechanized imitations of our race, imitations of the Nerago, and they can separate and reform stone with ease and without great fatigue to themselves.

During the long days, I sat eating grass on a hill far from the city, and I watched the Frill, with their small, slender bodies, working to assist the Artificial Securities in our city improvements. I remember this from when I was very young. I sucked pieces of grass between my slent, feeling it dissolve as it moved down my throat. Kall had come with me, dressed in large, well-formed blue leaves, as was the style in those days. She wore the leaves seductively, and in the bright light, the green grasses waved below us, rippling toward the city.

"My father has forbidden me to see you," Kall said.

I remember watching her. I continued to dissolve grass, unsure of what she wanted me to say. Neither one of us spoke for a long time, and Kall looked at me, her intelligent black eyes searching for some sign that I understood what she was saying.

"Bin," Kall said, "my father has told me to say good-bye to you. We can see each other in the city, but he has forbidden me to follow you alone into the fields or the woods ever again."

"Because of your birth," I said, and Kall touched the side of my face, stroking it carefully.

"You knew that when we first met."

I lay back, feeling the grasses touch my sides, watching the wind shake the blue leaves she wore. God, she was perfectly formed, and I could not stop looking at her. Kall began to stand, moving away from me.

"What do you think?" I asked.

She stopped and looked down at me. "What do I think?" Kall said.

"Yes."

"You were born here, on Frillai," Kall said, and I knew that she was reciting her father's arguments, not her own. "Your body is different than mine. We may look the same race, but we are not. My birth on Mentha, the homeworld—"

"No," I said. "I meant what do *you* think?"

Kall seemed more unsure of her reasoning, but she tried to hide the uncertainty by picking at the grass around her, swallowing the green blades.

"We are the same," I said.

"No," Kall said.

I touched her, bringing her back to me lightly. She could have resisted, she could have remained standing, but she did not.

"My father won't allow it," Kall said, more quietly this time.

"Do you love me?" I said.

"Bin, we cannot have offspring."

I ignored the words, the words that had been lingering beneath our conversation.

"Do you?" I said, and Kall let me hold her.

"Yes," she said. "But my father—"

"Wi-al will make bridges, he will bring this city more glory, before the next journey. But you are not another of his projects. You are yourself, Kall. That's all you are."

"That's supposed to make it all right?" she said.

"I love you."

She looked at me for a long time, and then we made love, the wind singing through the grasses, the Frill still working in the distance. It didn't matter then. That moment was everything. And I used it. We both did.

Seasons passed. During that time, we met in the fields and in the hidden places, deep in the blue-leaved woods. We found each other in the moonlight, and it did not matter that our lovemaking was hurried, that it was *unproductive.* In those days, as I held her to me, as she slept against my body, sweat running into the folds of our joints, I felt nothing. Peace, a pure absence of worry, absence of concern for the city, for the journey, for the Frill, even for the future—concern ceased to exist in my mind.

Wi-al confronted me during the next season. He placed a group of his personally created Frill to guard Kall from me. Kall cried, begging her father to rethink his actions. She told me that we were doomed, and that there was nothing she could do now that Wi-al had discovered us. I never knew how he learned about our secret meetings, and, in all honesty, it does not matter.

When I saw Kall in the town, she smiled at me, and we tried to speak, but always the Frill were there, reading our intentions and following their orders from Wi-al, keeping us apart. I turned away from the city. I considered killing Wi-al, but Kall would never forgive me, and then I would lose her even more certainly. The journey away from Frillai was approaching, and I saw Kall only rarely. I remember one night, sneaking to her house and climbing the side wall, telling the living stone to be silent as it tried to remind me that Mentha was the home of Security and that we Nerago were the creators and those chosen to create Security throughout all of existence.

"Kall," I said, from below her window, and for a long moment I hung there, unsure if she had heard me. Unsure if the Frill were stationed around her at night as well. What would Wi-al have done if he found me there?

"Kall," I said again, refusing to move closer to the opening. I already hung over a thousand lengths from the ground. Kall appeared in the opening, and she looked down at me, surprised. She had been crying—I saw that immediately.

"Oh," she said, reaching out to touch my face. "Bin, what are you doing? If they find you—"

"Meet me," I said.

Her face seemed to relax. "When?"

"When can you slip away?" I said.

"Ten revolutions," Kall said, after a moment. Her voice had quickened, and I heard noise behind. She turned, and then looked at me again tensely.

"Where?" she said.

"The hill," I said. "In the moonlight. In ten revolutions."

"All right," Kall said, and she touched me again. I could not move, where I hung, and there was movement from the darkness behind her. She said, "I love you."

"I love you."

"Kall," someone said from within. It was her father, and Kall turned away from me. I dropped in quick jumps, catching holds in the wall, bits of music playing at some points, lights flashing at others, and then I hit the ground, hurrying around the corner, into the city.

I walked quickly, knowing exactly where I would go. For the past seasons, while Wi-al had kept Kall from me, I had spent much of my time moving alone in the forest, speaking with the reclusive tree mites. That is where I went then. I passed Frill going silently about their business, and other Nerago greeted me, asking if I needed anything, if they could do anything to help. The city knew about my situation, and one old Nerago reminded me that it would not be long until the next journey, and that on the world we traveled to, there would be new opportunities, and that I would have a heightened status there, just as those born on Mentha had here on Frillai. I could not take consolation in this.

The Nara moved in their pens, watching me through their large, stupid eyes as I passed. I saw their tails snap, and I knew that they would never be released from the containment pens around them, that they would always be kept, and watched. When we, the Nerago, had first arrived on this planet, the Frill had been created to help in the construction of the city and in the containment of the Nara.

I arrived at the woods, passing a red, arching sculpture that marked the main path. The sculpture was large and delicate, representing what might have been veins or millions of tiny branches, or both. The tree mites hummed and sang in the background, and the giant branches swayed above me, thousands of lengths high, their massive, perfect blue leaves shimmering in the light. I waited for the tree mites to speak first, and I moved farther into the forest, wandering away from the main path.

Sinaka turned as I passed, giving off scents, hoping that I would trample them so they could take one of my legs as a meal. The tree mites were silent, and I saw one, a very large, gray tree mite high above me, its antennae waving at me in the moonlight. It had rows of legs, and its sides swayed, conducting the wind, making music.

"Hello," the tree mite said. I had heard the voice before. It was the patriarch, the leader of the swarm that lived closest to our city.

"Hello Patriarch," I said.

"I have a message that must be given to your kind, as our swarm will soon be moving on."

I had never heard the tree mites speak this way before. Usually they began with a discussion of their meals, questions about the current season and the grasses, asking how my relationship with Kall and her father had progressed. I had also never heard of a tree mite migration.

"What do you mean?" I said.

"Your kind will soon be leaving this planet," the tree mite patriarch said. "We know this. You must deliver this message and consider our urgings before moving on. Bin, you are fortunate to pass this way now, as we will leave immediately ourselves."

"Why are you leaving?"

The patriarch ignored my question and went on. "If the Nerago leave Frillai, as you intend, if you leave this planet with the Frill to watch over your city, to protect what you have created, it will be lost. You made the Frill as creations to assist you, but they are truly organisms in their own right. If you leave, the Frill will split into two factions, and the Nara will escape their containment, driving the Frill underground. The seasons and time will lay to waste all that your kind has created."

"How do you know?" I said.

The patriarch looked at me with what might have been sadness. "It is written in the trees."

"What am I supposed to do?"

"Some Nerago must stay here if your city is to be saved."

"Our city is one of the finest in existence," I said, thinking of Wi-al. "The Frill will watch over it."

"No," the patriarch said. "It will be lost. You must tell them. Tell your leaders."

I could see Wi-al's reaction. He and the other leaders would order those Nerago who had been born on this planet to remain behind and those from Mentha to move on to create another city in another place. That is exactly what would happen.

"I'll tell them," I said.

"Thank you," the patriarch said, and he was gone in a fluttering, the mites' music dying suddenly. I shivered in the wind, feeling very alone. A giant blue leaf fell to the ground, swaying through the air as it dropped. I watched it fall, cracking as its fragile surface touched the ground.

I met Kall in the night, far from our city, in the rolling, soft grasses of the hillside where we had first made love so many seasons ago. We touched awkwardly at first, finding each other again as our passion took control, and when it was ended, she lay beside me, breathing regularly in the dimness. I studied the curves of her body, memorizing it.

"I want to see you again," I said, and she touched me.

"I do too."

"When?" I said.

"I don't know," she said. "It may not be for some time."

I thought of what the tree mite had told me. The city was full of conversation, speculation as to why the insects had abruptly gone, leaving the forests silent, and more leaves were falling. It was as if the trees were weeping.

"When?" I said again.

"Perhaps in another ten revolutions."

"Tomorrow," I said, and she rolled to face me.

"I can't tomorrow. The Frill will be keeping watch."

"Even tomorrow night?"

"It's very risky," she said.

"Tomorrow."

I touched her, and we began to make love a second time.

"Yes," she said softly. "I will see you tomorrow."

Midway through the following day, I realized that we had not settled on a location for that night. I searched for Kall in the city, and eventually found her, supervised by four Frill, on one of the main avenues. She was listening to a purple section of stone tell a story of lost love, and there was another crowd of Frill standing nearby. Whether they were listening to the stone or watching Kall, I could not be certain. She was gorgeous.

I wandered near to her through the crowd, struggling to catch her eye, but she was lying back, obviously thinking.

"Where?" I said loudly, sure for a moment that the Frill would spot me. Kall sat up slowly, and she noticed me. The others around us seemed utterly oblivious, and she stared at me nervously.

"The tunnels," Kall mouthed.

"The tunnels?" I said, and still those around us had not noticed.

"Yes," she said, and then she lay back again.

I wandered away from her, picking fruit from a public grove I passed through. The storage tunnels were being constructed constantly under the ground. They were to be home to the birthing machines for the Frill and for their sustenance generators. Everything the Frill would need to survive in our absence was to be placed in the tunnels. I thought again of the patriarch's words. I would tell Kall about the tree mite's prediction that night.

It was late in the day when I passed the river, watching the Nerago who swam, splashing through it. Couples held each other, playfully pushing one another under the water, and a Frill hurried past me, calling out to a Nerago on the opposite side of the river.

"It's Kall!" the Frill said. On the opposite bank stood Wi-al, Kall's father. He saw me, and ran for one of the bridges.

"What's happening?" I said to the Frill, and in a panic, the Frill started to back away. I grabbed the small creature and shook it in the air. "Tell me what has happened!"

"Kall has fallen into one of the tunnels," the Frill said. "It's collapsed on her."

I tossed the Frill aside and dashed for the entrance of the tunnels. There was already a crowd gathered around the circular transport entrance, and I could see them assembling a company of Frill to save Kall.

"What's happened?" I said, and they ignored me, Nerago and Frill blocking the circular transport. I pushed past them, and a Nerago grabbed me, trying to stop my advance, but I was already on the transport. They released me, and I entered the tunnel below. Immediately I saw what had happened. Kall had come here to prepare a place for us. She had found a room in the well-constructed tunnels that had not been entirely finished so that we would not be disturbed, and the unfinished floor had given way, dropping her into a hole. Then, one of the supporting walls had given way, falling onto her. Kall looked at me through a break in the rock—she was struggling to hold a massive section of the collapsed wall off of her—the opening was too small for her to fit through.

I lowered myself to her and reached through, grabbing at the rock.

"You can't," she said weakly. Kall was barely supporting the rock, and as soon as her strength began to give, the entire wall would flatten her, crushing her into the floor, burying her.

I pushed my arms and legs into the gap, widening it. *It will be lost. You must tell them.*

"I'm going to push through," I said. "And when I do that, I want you to come out."

"No," she said.

"I'm going to switch places with you," I said, forcing the rock far enough for my body to slide through. This would only work if our timing was perfect, and a part of me knew that once I had gone into the hole, the wall would collapse from the sudden release as Kall let go. I would not be able to hold it up then. I knew that. *It will be lost.*

"Now," I said.

"No, Bin—it's too heavy!"

"Switch now!" I said, and I pushed through the opening, forcing her out. She screamed at me, crying as I wedged myself into the hole. The wall trembled as she scratched at the collapsing opening.

"I love you!" she said, and I thought about telling her. I still had time.

"I love you," I said.
And the wall fell.

Vel pulled his hand away from the white bone.

Now.

He looked around the tunnel, disoriented. Ulyu, the food shortage, the Pox, Lord Denon, the girl Sisha, and—

No time, boy.

"What's happening?" Vel said. "I wasn't here, I saw—"

You communed as none of us have. You are as the gods were, you are our savior, boy—now, you will prove it.

The Frill are coming to kill me, Vel thought.

Yes, Ulyu said inside his mind, *but you will not die.*

Blakes wrote a new book during the months that he sat in prison, *History of the Twilight.* Much of the time he sharpened his pencil stub with his fingernails, writing the words without seeing them in the darkness of the cell. No news from outside his floor, and the only contact Blakes had with the larger world was the jailer who brought him bowls of white rice and cups of water several times a day.

Then it changed, and a different jailer began to bring him food, not speaking to him as the previous soldier had. This jailer brought a plastic tray of military rations and he wore a strange, light blue uniform. *They've lost,* Blakes thought. *We have been occupied.* Still, he waited, and then one day, they came for him. Blakes was forced out of his cell, marched up, through his headquarters, now filled with columns of men and women in that same blue uniform. Blakes's paintings were gone, and much of his setup—the monitors, the chairs, everything—had been torn out.

Outside, and Blakes was ushered through a street of staring crowds and flashbulbs. The houses on either side had power; the victors had restored technology to them. Blakes was ushered through the masses to a large gymnasium that Blakes had used as a military barracks—inside was a long, black rectangular table. Behind it sat perhaps fifty people in an irregular rainbow of blue and red and green uniforms. Several of them simply wore suits, and most were Asian, several dark-skinned members as well. Blakes was shown to a chair directly in front of the table, and his trial began.

He listened to their charges.

"Before the defendant in this case is called upon to make his plea to the indictment which had been lodged against him, and in which he is charged with crimes against peace, war crimes, and crimes against humanity, and with a common plan or conspiracy to commit those crimes . . ."

War crimes, genocide, ethnic cleansing, death camps, billions dead of toxic chemicals and engineered diseases and nuclear fallout, economic catastrophe.

". . . On Thursday, October 18, 2100, in Berlin, the indictment was lodged with the tribunal and a copy of that indictment in English has been furnished to the defendant. . . ."

Blakes ignored his copy, ignored the lawyer they had provided him with: he stared back at them, and he smiled. All because of Blakes. *They blame it all on me,* he thought, and he chuckled as the trial went on and on. *Good.*

Hours went by.

Statement after statement, and prepared papers, all explaining what was happening, why Blakes was here, why they would be pushing the trial to a speedy finish. The gym was hot, the only noise the continual clicking whir of flashbulbs and recorders and the rustling of papers, the tinking of glasses as they offered him water and drank from long-stemmed pitchers.

". . . the charter of the tribunal, and accordingly named as the sole primary defendant in this cause as indicted principally on the counts hereinafter set out: William Blakes . . ."

Blakes sighed, leaned back in his chair and let the heat of the room and the monotonous drone lull him to a half-awake doze. He folded his hands calmly in front of him, shut his eyes and listened.

". . . participated as the leader, organizer, instigator in the formulation and execution of a common plan to commit, or which involved the commission of, crimes against peace, war crimes, and crimes against humanity. . . ."

"Yes," Blakes said, and he leaned forward. "Thy will."

The leader of the tribunal paused, studied Blakes and then said, "This tribunal does not recognize the accused at this time." And then continued. For hours.

The next day, it was the same, and then the next, they had finally finished reading Blakes's crimes, and he laughed as a thirty-hour monologue reached its conclusion.

"That's it?" he asked.

He had refused to speak with his defender, and then the tribunal leader frowned at him curiously.

"The question," the leader said, "will have to be answered in the words of article twenty-four of the charter, and those words are printed in italics:

" '*The tribunal shall ask the defendant whether he pleads guilty or not guilty.*'

"I will now call upon the defendant to plead guilty or not guilty to the charges against him. He will proceed to the dock opposite the microphone."

When Blakes didn't move, the leader repeated, "He will—"

"No," Blakes said, "he won't."

Murmurs from the crowd, and the leader adjusted his microphone. "William Blakes."

"You want me to—"

"I announced that the defendant was not entitled to make a statement. You must plead guilty or not guilty."

"No."

"That will be entered as a plea of not guilty." Scattered laughter from the crowd, and the leader reddened. "If there is any disturbance in court, those who make it will have to leave the courtroom." Blakes stood up, and the leader glared at him. "You are not entitled to address the tribunal, except through your counsel, at the present time."

The prosecutor, a short, Anglo man with a sickly, pale complexion moved to the front of the room and started talking—Blakes ignored him, and his defender leaned close.

"You shouldn't isolate yourself from—"

"You're a bug," Blakes said, and he spat in his lawyer's eye.

The trial dragged on for weeks, and Blakes sat scribbling poetry, oblivious to the tribunal and their continual chatter. *This,* he thought, *this is what I meant to destroy.* Once, while they were interviewing a witness, Blakes shouted, "It is all a vain delusion of the all creative imagination." The gym fell silent, and when the leader cleared his throat, Blakes continued, "Life for life. I will have human blood and not the blood of bulls or goats, and no atonement. Thou shalt thyself be sacrificed to me, thy—"

They forced him from the room and adjourned the trial until the next day. That night, he met with an angry, fat Asian man in a room that had once been a control center, full of consoles and soldiers. Now the room was an empty shell set with two uncomfortable chairs.

"Do you have any idea what you've done to the world, Blakes?" the man asked. "You must know—"

"God and Satan know all."

"I'm here to review you, you know. They'll have others here after me. But I was actually out there. I *saw* Teheran. And the dead of Nagpur, Hyderabad, New Beijing, Xuzhou—"

"Yes, and?"

The Asian man stiffened and leaned forward. "They're going to hang you. Because you're not crazy. I'll die before I'll say that you're crazy."

"I don't remember a war," Blakes said with a smile. "I remember a birth."

"You won't talk to him, but your lawyer says you're unfit to stand trial. He says that you believe you were inspired by God, that your generals were responsible, your intelligence officers."

Blakes smirked. "I don't remember."

The fat Asian man punched Blakes in the jaw, cutting his lip, breaking one of his teeth. The next day the trial resumed.

The prosecutor: ". . . I ask in what period the real amnesia of Blakes applies. He pretends, according to the defense, to have forgotten facts which occurred more than fifteen days ago. It may be simulation or, as they say in the report, it may be real simulation. I would like to know if according to the reports Blakes had really lost his memory of facts which are referred to in the indictments. . . ."

The fat Asian man: ". . . did not suffer from any kind of insanity, nor is he now suffering from it. At the present time he exhibits hysterical behavior with signs of a conscious intentional simulated character, which does not exonerate him from responsibility under the indictment. . . ."

The arguments continued, and Blakes watched his newest lawyer argue that he was unfit. Later that night he met with another analyst, an Arab man with intelligent eyes and a soft voice.

He asked, "Blakes, are you crazy?"

Guards surrounded them at the exterior of the room in body armor, all armed with shotguns.

"God's words are truth."

"You're not crazy," the Arab said, and he scribbled notes. "The rejection of technology, the desire to wipe out the world . . . these sound like very normal aspirations to me. You *acted* on them, that's what makes you different from the rest of us." And the Arab offered Blakes the notepad. It read: *You were right. We believe you saw God, and we want you to live.*

The Arab flipped the page, covering the words and continued, "What's the last thing you remember?"

"Lions," Blakes said.

"Mm? Lions, did you say?"

"Yes."

"You know that I'm here to evaluate you, that they won't accept your lawyer's claims. Even if you were insane, it wouldn't matter at this point." The Arab shielded the words from the guard, flashing them so that Blakes could see: *You brought God to Earth again. We will make sure you are given another chance.*

Blakes nodded. "I know."

"I don't think you're unfit. Yes or no: Do you?"

Death was necessary in the face of the evil of the world.

"Yes," Blakes said.

"Hmm." The Arab smiled and patted Blakes on the shoulder as he got up to leave, and then—his mouth very close to Blakes's ear: *"Even the tribunal is not all against you."*

The next day, they reached a decision:

". . . will begin the session by reading the judgment of the tribunal upon the application made by counsel for the defendant Blakes.

"The tribunal has given careful consideration to the motion of counsel for the defense of the defendant Blakes, and it has had the advantage of hearing full arguments upon it both from the defense and the prosecution. The tribunal has also considered the very full medical reports which have been made on the condition of the defendant Blakes, and has come to the conclusion that no grounds whatever exist for a further examination to be ordered.

"After hearing the statement of the defense yesterday, and in view of all the evidence, the tribunal is of the opinion that the defendant Blakes is capable of standing his trial at the present time, and the motion of the counsel for the defense is therefore denied, and the trial will proceed. . . ."

Weeks passed. Weeks became months, and Blakes had nearly finished another book throughout the course of the trial. One night in late July of 2101, a jailer slipped an envelope into Blakes's cell, waiting just outside, shining a flashlight in so that Blakes could read.

> Jesus was crucified; you are a voice against the tide of oppression.
>
> If you were going to start over, what would you need? Supplies. Write, do not speak.

Blakes met the jailer's eye, and the man nodded solemnly, and Blakes used his pencil stub, and he wrote. When he handed the envelope back, the jailer saluted Blakes with his open right hand. Sieg heil.

The trial continued. They outlined everything that had happened, called witness after witness to describe the horrors of the Fourth World War, Blakes's war. Blakes was condemned, and as the weather became cold on Blakes's regular walk from his prison cell in the basement of his old palace across the street to the gymnasium, the trial reached its conclusion. All of Blakes's officers had been tried separately.

And finally, one day, there were no flashbulbs. It was raining cold spit outside, and the room was full of guards, all stiff, lined up around the exterior of the room.

The leader said: "William Blakes is indicted on all four counts. Crimes against peace . . . in 2099 that by arranging to move offensive units into the Pacific sphere, Blakes allowed . . . War crimes and crimes against humanity . . ." But it finally ended, and the leader paused for a long moment, took a drink of water and then said, "Conclusion: The tribunal finds the Defendant Blakes guilty on all four counts of the indictment."

The sentencing happened the next day, and it was still raining.

"In accordance with article twenty-seven of the charter, the International Military Tribunal will now pronounce the sentence on the defendant convicted on this indictment."

A pause as Blakes set his pencil down and met the tribunal's eyes. *Come on,* he thought. *I am more than any of you will ever be and the world still knows it. They understand me, even if you cannot. The rivers and the air and the people of this planet understand what I tried to do, that I tried to begin in the only way possible. Through death.*

"Defendant William Blakes, on the counts of the indictment of which you have been convicted, the International Military Tribunal sentences you to exile on the planet Hera permanently."

The trial was over.

Death by hanging, Blakes thought. *Exile? I don't understand.* He stood up and started to speak, but they were already ushering him out of the room. *Hera?*

His lawyer offered him a hand. "I know you haven't wanted to—"

"What does this mean?"

"The sentence?"

"Yes," Blakes said, as they walked back across the street in the rain. "I don't understand."

"You're going to be given a ship, the *Australia*, and you—along with a crew of approximately two hundred people, all chosen from members of your own staff by the tribunal, based on their participation in and lack of commitment to the holocaust engineered by your generals—will be frozen on board, in an experimental method of hibernation designed to keep you alive until the ship reaches its destination . . . after three hundred years in transit."

Thus, the godly are cast out by the wicked, Blakes thought. *These men of science and progress will return the herd morality to the greater world. The white noise will return and the separation from ourselves will resume, and the crusade to restore godliness and purity will be remembered only by a single scratch in the timeline that is called a World War.*

"After three centuries—in approximately the year 2400—you will arrive on a planet discovered late last year, *Hera*. Hera is believed to be capable of supporting life, based on the distance from its sun and the larger, Jupiter-sized planet that orbits beyond it. You will have only enough non-renewable fuel to transport you to Hera, not enough to return or go anywhere else. You will be allowed a reasonable number of supplies for survival on the planet. On Hera, you will live out the duration of your natural life, and your decisions once you have reached the planet will be irrelevant, as everyone in your crew—yourself included—would otherwise be sentenced to death by lethal injection or hanging here on Earth. I think we were . . ."

Blakes thought about the decision as they finished as he returned to his cell.

"Thank you," he said to his lawyer.

"We were lucky," he said. "You could have—"

Blakes ignored him and sat in the corner of his cell. It made perfect sense: humanity's second chance, a hope at a restoration of society and civilization to its past. Blakes had been given this opportunity by God. It seemed impossible that they would give him this, that they would spend the money to build a ship and transport him for three hundred years to another world—could Blakes really have that much controversy surrounding him that the victors had to submit to Blakes's survival?

It made no sense to him unless a large minority still believed that he had been justified. *Or if they think I'm crazy,* he realized. *But then why send me to a rock millions of miles away? Because they don't know what I am,* he thought. *They don't know what to do with me and my kind, and so they want to get rid of me. The notes, the Arab and the jailer—they had been right. God had provided.*

Blakes was given a list of supplies that he would be allowed and a roster of his crew of two hundred and forty-four people; exactly one hundred and twenty-two of them male, the other half female. As the months passed and the departure date loomed nearer, Blakes found people inside his jail who sympathized, and he persuaded them to collect supplies for him, to replace the agricultural machines with crates that Blakes knew were hidden in bunkers all around the world—with antique weaponry and books and historical paraphernalia. *Much more useful than plows or genetic beans,* he thought, not really knowing whether or not any of it was being smuggled aboard the *Australia,* as the jailer told him it was.

A missile, he told them, I need a missile, and a specific kind of drill, both inside the *Australia,* and on and on, with bits and pieces of modern technology Blakes requested replacing, gram for gram, the mass of some of the supplies he had been carefully given by the occupying council of the Allies. The jailers told him that it would all be meticulously hidden inside the *Australia,* mixed in with what he was supposed to have been given, so that the *Australia* would even pass a summary inspection.

One night, the jailer crept close to Blakes's cell and whispered, "We're passing the inspections . . ."

"Hmm?"

"The *Australia* will be ready for you if we continue to pass the inspections. The Alliance is falling apart, and they don't have time to deal with this, their premier was assassinated—"

Blakes asked, "Why are you doing this? Why are they still following me? Why haven't they given up?"

"Your vision was too big," the jailer said. "And the Alliance is too busy to stop us, and as they tear apart Western cities, many of your old armies claim to defect, but they remain loyal. You even have sympathizers with the Chinks—"

"Why?"

"We know you saw God. We know you spoke with Him, that you were His prophet, and He asked the same things of you that He would have asked of Noah if He could have. Noah was spared, but if He could have, wouldn't God have asked Noah to destroy the world in His name? If Noah could have done it, wouldn't God have asked Noah to bring the flood himself? To start over."

"Don't tell me what God wants, boy." The jailer was silent, and then Blakes said quietly, "I see angels . . ."

"You're a prophet."

"A warrior," Blakes said. "I am the voice of one crying in the wilderness. I am the infection that rots away at the smallest tear and kills the beast. My supplies are being smuggled aboard?"

"The Alliance is breaking up. They're only worried about you escaping or being liberated. They haven't had time to worry about what we put on the *Australia*—the ship is already set so that it *must* go to Hera, and when the premier died, there were uprisings in—"

"My supplies?"

"Yes," the jailor said.

"Good. This world is finished. I have given up here. Hera is humanity's hope for the future. Earth is gone."

"There are many of us who wish we could come with you."

"Fight," Blakes said. "You're young. I've lived more lives than anyone should, and they should never have brought me back: fight against the corruption of white noise and slavery. Fire is the only tool that really cleanses."

"You're a great man. Good luck, my Führer."

"God go with you."

And then, in late November of 2101, Blakes was shown to a black metal chamber deep inside the irregular, blocky *Australia. The ship looks more like a honeycomb of tin and plastic than a spaceship,* he thought, and Blakes saw members of his crew only briefly as they were shown to similar bunks all around the large, plastic room. Blakes had seen none of the ship, he had no idea if any of the supplies he had requested had actually been smuggled on board, and when the jailer he had known for the past months stood over him and the bunk, Blakes raised his eyebrows.

The jailer nodded and slipped a small white brick into Blakes's hand. Blakes lowered himself into the bunk, and the jailer fit the lid into place over him and whispered, "Sieg heil."

Blakes looked at the brick. It was a bar of soap, and a word had been crudely cut into it: *Adria.*

AS WUNIC followed Jak through the stone fortifications to the Southern Garr, the low rumblings of artillery grew more distant. The Garr was a squat, ugly building built of black stone. It rose three stories, sprawling across more than a full city block, and it was surrounded by two stone walls, each fifteen feet high. The windows were tiny slits in its walls—prisoners didn't need light. Several wooden tents clustered around the base of the Garr, inside the walls: barracks for guards on the off chance that the Garr should be overcrowded, as it was now.

Rows of tiny razors lined the tops of each of the two guard walls, and as Jak led Wunic through the "killing zone" between the walls, the rebels stationed ahead stiffened. They stared uneasily at General Wunic, uncomfortably aiming rifles and crossbows at his torso and head. *I know these men,* Wunic thought as he neared the wooden gate of the second wall. *These men were* my *men before all of this.* He had thought about what the rebellion meant, but this was the first time Wunic had actually seen soldiers he knew. He could even remember some of their names.

Tiny slits, rifle and crossbow notches, marked the inner wall at regular intervals of roughly ten feet—*and that's why the space between the walls was called a "killing zone,"* Wunic thought. It was said that the Garrs had been built during the separatist war several centuries ago as fortresses, not primarily as prisons. Supposedly, they had only become prisons after the war ended. *Regardless,* Wunic thought, *the Garrs served their purpose well.* It was possible to secure a Garr filled to maximum capacity with prisoners with fewer than fifty soldiers, and if one section of the prison rioted or if it was attacked by a crowd, sections inside the Garr could be separated from one another fairly easily—it could be defended from enemies within and without easily.

Wunic had begun to adjust to the pain in his leg, finding a pace with his makeshift wooden staff that allowed him to move relatively quickly without putting too much weight on the damaged bones and muscles. He followed Jak through the second wall's gate, and they approached a company of ten soldiers who were gambling with colored rocks by the tents and main entrance. Only two were armed with rifles, the rest carried crossbows.

Jak waved at the black, double-doored entrance, and one of the soldiers stopped playing—eyes on Wunic, hand on his gun.

"Put that away," Jak said. "General Wunic is with us."

The rebels ended their game, and Jak motioned that Wunic should stay where he was as she approached the soldiers. They spoke quietly, the rebels always watching General Wunic, ready to kill him should he move too quickly. Finally, one of the rebels nodded to Jak and motioned Wunic to the entrance with his crossbow.

Wunic limped after Jak, through the main entrance of the Garr, two of the rebels pushing the heavy stone doors open.

One of them nodded solemnly to Wunic. "General."

The entrance hall was a long corridor of flickering torchlight on a low ceiling and narrow walls. Cell doors were aligned on the walls regularly, every three feet. The double doors shut behind them, and Wunic wondered just how many rebel soldiers he had seen so far at the Garr. *Several hundred? No,* he thought, *fewer than that: perhaps one hundred.* At the end of the hall a staircase with small, awkward stairs circled up and also down.

Wunic grunted as he tried to position his staff on the stairs, hobbling up after Jak, and she slowed, bending to help him up. *Everything about these Goddamned Garrs was designed to make it difficult to move from one place to another,* Wunic thought as flashes of pain spiked up his leg. *And very soon the Southern Garr would make a perfect artillery target.*

They stopped on the second floor, the stairs continuing up to the third, and Wunic said, "Thank you."

The second floor corridor looked identical to the first, except that the ceiling might have been lower and more uneven, and there were regular, four-way intersections. And the cell doors were packed even closer together on either side. More rebel soldiers filled the halls, and as Wunic and Jak passed a group of them, they had to turn and squeeze past, Wunic nearly falling as his staff slipped on the stone floor. *So that fighting is single file,* Wunic thought miserably, *one-*

on-one. So that in theory, the better-trained defenders can kill the mindless attackers and escaping prisoners one at a time. To say nothing of the bodies that would clog the hallway.

They turned sharply at a corner, heading right, and he nearly bumped into several torches mounted in the next hall.

"There's someone you're going to want to see," Jak said, and she stopped at a wooden door marked RL2-53, and knocked. A pause, and a group of three soldiers passed, ducking and brushing against them.

A voice from behind the door said, "Who's there?"

"It's me," Jak said, and Wunic heard movement inside. A lock was unhooked from the other side of the door. The door opened, and a large, unshaven man who probably hadn't slept in weeks stared out at them, blocking the doorway.

Inside, past the tired man, Wunic saw a large cell, modestly furnished with three beds, a square table and a handful of chairs, some arranged around the table, some not. Candles glowed from the floor and table, and suddenly Wunic realized who he was looking at. The tired, exhausted-looking man was General Rein, the man who had almost single-handedly started all of this.

Beyond him, a man who had been sitting on one of the beds jumped to his feet and pointed a pistol over General Rein's shoulder, at Wunic. Rein stepped aside, eyes on Wunic, and Wunic stepped after Jak into the room. Rein shut the door again and drew the lock into place. Jak ignored the soldier with the gun—Wunic recognized him as a young colonel named Murthus. Wunic remembered him because he had heard something about his reputation as a swordsman, and Murthus had risen through the ranks faster than any soldier since Justice Hillor.

"Put it away," Jak said to Murthus.

Wunic stared at the pistol without moving. "I'm not—"

"Quiet," Murthus said, approaching Wunic. "I'll take any weapons you have."

"No you won't," Wunic said.

Murthus glanced at General Rein for a signal, but Rein only frowned at Wunic, heading back to the table.

"Didn't think I would see you on these terms, General," Rein said.

Wunic nodded. "General."

"You belong to Lord Denon. What are you doing here?"

"Lord Denon finished with General Wunic," Jak said. "He's agreed to help us."

"Are you certain?" Rein asked Jak.

She nodded. "I wouldn't have brought him here otherwise, you know that."

"Unless you've defected," Rein said, and Jak stuck out her tongue at him.

"Thank you, General," she said.

"All right," Rein said, and he waved at Murthus. "Put the gun away, Colonel."

The young colonel pursed his lips, and he kept his pistol aimed at Wunic's head.

"General, this man is dangerous, and he's loyal to the king."

"We all should be loyal to the king," Wunic muttered. "The king's not the problem."

"He's with us," Jak said.

"No," Murthus said, "he's not. We turn our backs on him, we die. Why in God's name did you bring him here, Jak?"

"Colonel Murthus," Jak said slowly. "Listen to me. General Wunic has agreed to help us—and I think in our present condition we *need* his help."

"You don't understand," Murthus said. "General—"

"I *do* understand," Jak said.

"No," Murthus said, keeping his pistol trained on Wunic's head, "you don't. General Wunic will kill every soldier on this floor if we let him. This man is dangerous."

You think I could if I wanted to, Wunic thought, glancing at his wounded leg, but he remained standing. *And where would that get me? No. I need all of the soldiers on this floor: If Lord Denon has the royal military, I need all of the scrawny reb soldiers I can get.*

"He's with us, Murthus," Jak said. "Now calm down."

"We'll watch him," General Rein said. "Now, put the gun away, Colonel."

Murthus did not move.

"Murthus," Rein said, more loudly, "put the Goddamn gun away. What's wrong with you? You saw the dispatch."

"The dispatch was a lie, General," Murthus said. "Please—"

"Goddamn it," Rein said, and he reached for his sword, a strange, overly large black blade. "I told you to put that gun away—do it.

Now." Rein set his huge sword on the table in front of him. Wunic couldn't imagine anyone actually using a sword that large in combat.

Reluctantly, Murthus lowered his pistol, and he said, "Remember this, General," Murthus said. "This man should be locked up or executed."

"I'm well aware of who General Wunic is," Rein said shortly, and then he nodded to the door. "Check the casualty reports."

Murthus said to Jak, "Please, listen to me. He must be locked away—"

"Check," Rein said. "The reports."

Murthus holstered his pistol and stalked past Wunic, leaving without another word. Rein shook his head, and asked Wunic to draw the lock back into place. Wunic did as he was told.

"General, you'd better not shoot us after that," Rein said, sheathing his sword again. "Have a seat."

Wunic limped to a free chair, and Rein nodded to his leg. "If he had known about that, he might have shut the hell up."

Wunic smiled. "How are you, General?"

"How do I look? How do you think I am?" Rein asked, and he rubbed his eyes. "We're getting the living hell beaten out of us. And you're one of the people who specializes in that. Why are you here? What's happened?"

"It was an assassination attempt," Wunic said—*And it had been,* he thought. *A large-scale assassination attempt that had involved killing dozens of other soldiers who just happened to be in the wrong place.*

"We don't have much time, General," Rein said. "What should I do? What would you do?"

"Against the artillery?" Wunic said.

"Yes, how can I fight that? Is it possible?"

"No, I'm afraid it isn't," Wunic said. "My advice would be to withdraw from the field entirely. Keep a handful of soldiers at checkpoints to delay my—the army's advance. Pull everything back here, all of it. Concentrate in the Southern Garr."

Rein blinked, as if he had considered that many times, but discounted the idea as too easy. "Withdraw entirely?"

"Yes," Wunic said. "Have you seen what the artillery's doing to your lines?"

"Yes," Rein said. "I'm aware of what it's doing."

"This position cannot be held, General."

Rein nodded calmly. "The royals have broken through in the north, and along our western front."

"That's where we just were," Jak said quietly.

"Artillery will pound through anything you set up," Wunic said. "But if you wait for them to encircle the Southern Garr, there might be a chance to break out if you concentrate everything in a focused attack."

Rein stared him in the eye. "Do you believe that, General?"

It could get me out, Wunic thought, and he said, "Yes."

Rein's brow creased. "Colonel Murthus agrees with you." Rein thought about it, and Wunic waited. "But I do not," Rein said at last.

"Why?" Jak said.

Rein said to Wunic, "Tell me about the artillery."

"What do you want to know?"

"That's tricky," Rein said. "Right now, it's chopping up my soldiers. As of now, apart from a few technicalities about *how* it's ripping them to shreds, that's the *only* thing I know. I know it's blowing apart wooden houses, shops, factories—everything we've been using as our battlefield. Tell me something, General: Shouldn't I believe the artillery will do the same thing here, to this Garr?"

Wunic felt uneasy tension in his stomach. He *had* assumed that the artillery would not be able to destroy the Garr immediately—that it would take time for the artillery to blast through it, at least. Yes, the Garr would fall, but not right away—and it would take more time for the artillery commanders to coordinate, to set up, to organize the siege.

"I'm sorry, General. I don't know. You may be right—this Garr may come apart as easily as everything else," Wunic admitted. "What I *do* know is that the artillery's never been used before, ever. The men operating it—even Lord Denon—they probably don't know exactly what it's capable of. They're making this up as they go along, General, just like you."

Rein said, "Yes, I know. And until that little king dug up the warehouse full of guns and artillery, no one knew any of this existed in the first place."

"That's true," Wunic said. "But what I'm saying is, my boys in charge of the artillery are still learning how to use it. It's going to take time for those boys to arrange their units in positions that can hit the Garr. Now, as they're doing that—as you retreat there are certainly going to be defections—the artillery commanders will think the war is over, that the rebels are on the verge of defeat."

I'm telling the enemy how to beat us, Wunic realized. *I'm sharing secrets with the leader of the rebel forces—this is conspiracy, espionage, treason. But, what else can I do? The rebs still can't win, the war's over. This is a method, a technique to break through, to stop Lord Denon. If Denon takes over—if I can stop him there might be a government once this ends. Whatever I say, these rebels are dead and have been since the beginning.*

"General?" Rein said.

Wunic continued, "The city's army—the royals—will expect a surrender, and they'll wait until they can fire all of their artillery simultaneously."

Rein smiled sadly. "I don't think so."

But it might *be possible to get out before the rebels break, to escape capture and stop Lord Denon,* Wunic thought, and he said, "Whether the Garr can hold or not, you'll have time before the siege actually begins."

"Listen to him, General," Jak said.

"That's how they train us to think, General Wunic," Rein said, without looking at her. "Encircle an enemy and wait until there is the maximum chance for success with the fewest friendly casualties. That's what people like you and me teach the police, but we tell them that so that they can fight rioters and find black market books and trap convicts. None of those strategies—none of our training—was designed for this kind of combat."

"I don't think it matters, General," Wunic said. "It's still effective. And whether it is or not, that's how every officer is taught. You're right, those are the strategies."

"Maybe," Rein said, "but they have more options now, with these weapons. Your men won't wait if they don't want to—if we fall back, they could trap isolated units, rather than encircling the Garr. And your men might open fire on the Garr the moment they have *one* unit of artillery in position, not sixteen. Why shouldn't they? We don't have any artillery of our own. What's going to stop them?"

"That's not their strategy," Wunic said. "I know, I was just leading them."

"And that's what you would have done?" Rein asked. "You would wait until the Garr was entirely encircled, then you would wait even longer for a surrender, and only *then* if none came you would open fire with all of your artillery, rather than risk more soldiers, General?"

Wunic considered it. *I don't know,* he thought, *what difference does it make? I'm* not *over there where I should be, I'm here.* But he said, "Yes, I would."

Rein was quiet for a moment, and then he said, "Then I'm sorry you're not the royal commander anymore—some of my men might actually survive under those circumstances. No, the royals will open fire on us the moment they get one piece of artillery in range. They'll do it as soon as they can. I don't think they'll care about losing more of their soldiers at this point."

"You don't?" Wunic said, and Rein shook his head. "I don't follow, General. Why not?"

"Because," Rein said, "the officers aren't in charge, the war's nearly over for them. Even if you're right—and you probably are; even if they think as you and I do—your officers aren't ultimately giving orders anymore. How many generals were commanding the entire military when you were there?"

Wunic swallowed uncomfortably. "I was given command."

"Just you?"

"Yes."

"And now that you're gone, who will the officers receive their orders from? It would be the king, wouldn't it?" When Wunic remained silent, Rein continued grimly, "Not the king. Of course not, he's just a kid, but every order will have the boy's seal on it. Lord Denon has control of the royal army." Rein said. "And that means we're not fighting soldiers or officers, we're fighting *him.* Casualties will be different."

"I know," Wunic said, and Rein took out a folded dispatch and offered it to Jak. She read it, and Rein said to Jak, "Let him read it."

She nodded and handed him the single sheet, with a broken blue circle seal.

"This was intercepted," Rein said.

Wunic recognized the writing.

This letter is to be spread among the company commanders.

The pocket of enemy resistance has been breached in seven places, and the rebels are being forced into a steady retreat. In the coming days, the artillery should be used only under my direct orders that have been countersigned by the Church. The Executive Council has been suspended until the current crisis is resolved, and the king has been moved to a secured location. As many of you already know, the labor representative on the council, Orik, has defected.

What many of you do not know is that General Wunic, a former member of the Executive Council, has also defected. It is with great sorrow that I relate these events to you, as General Wunic was personally responsible for the destruction of an entire corps in the field as part of a larger plan of rebellion that could only have been premeditated and coordinated with the opposition. The general also ordered an attempt on the king's life. General Wunic should be taken alive if possible.

With this dispatch, I urge each commander to continue the offensive that has begun and to finish this war as quickly as possible, so that we can begin to rebuild what has already been lost. I also regret to inform you that rations must be cut by ten percent, as several food supplies have been destroyed by the rebels.

LORD DENON

Wunic closed his fist around the paper, and his arm began to shake. *Calm down,* he told himself. *I knew this would happen, I anticipated this, calm down.* Jak touched his shoulder and started to say something, when Wunic said, "Denon."

Rein said, "Yes."

"This is over," Wunic said, distracted.

"That's why they're going to hit us when they can," Rein said. " 'Countersigned by the Church'."

Wunic rose, still holding the paper. His vision flashed red, and he grabbed the chair as his leg started to give out. Jak grabbed him, easing his arm over her shoulder as she tried to steady him.

"Easy, General," Jak said. "Take it easy."

Rein asked, "What do you think, General? Can we do anything?"

"No," Wunic said. "Of course not."

Jak said, "Steady, General, I don't think you're—"

"Let go of me," Wunic said, the pain in his ankle lancing through him, and Jak helped him sit again. "I don't want your help." He glared at Jak, then to Rein, "What do you want me to do?"

This isn't possible, Wunic thought. *Pretending that I can get to him; Denon's won.*

Rein thought about it, and then he leaned closer, elbows on the table. "What do you think of an operation to take one or two pieces of artillery, and bring them here? Would that be possible with what you know about the royal army?"

"No," Wunic said. "No, you'll lose too many men trying to take the artillery."

"If all of my men were concentrated on those two artillery units?" Rein asked.

"Too many men," Wunic said again. "You'll lose too many men, General."

"If I had that artillery, I think we could hold out from this position indefinitely." Wunic was shaking his head, but Rein continued, "Or the captured artillery could be moved. I could knock out more of their artillery in the open, maybe even capture them if I had a piece of my own. If my men were spread into raiding parties, with guerrilla—"

"No, General," Wunic said. "It won't work." *Why not surrender now,* Wunic thought, *take my chances with the 'royals'? Hope a unit sides with me against Lord Denon? They won't—Denon is supposed to be working with the king, and those boys won't pick me over their king: That's what this is about, after all.* "General," Wunic said, "your only chance at this point is to pull everything back and then break through where they're weakest."

"All right General Wunic—and then?"

"And then you hit the palace," Wunic said. "You take Lord Denon and the king—capture both of them—the king agrees to your terms, and the war ends." Rein looked skeptical, but Wunic continued, "Take the palace, the king creates a new council, and the war ends."

"What will have changed—what will have been the point of this if I let him make another council, if the king is still in charge?"

"I'm sorry, but that's the only way you can win. The king will win a long war, he has more food, he can always draft more soldiers than you—and he has artillery now so he won't have to make it long. This will be over very soon unless your strategy changes. You have to be flexible here, General."

Rein said, "Taking artillery of my own is more important, I think."

"Can you take that artillery *and* hold the Southern Garr?" Wunic asked.

"If we wait to be encircled, we won't be able to break out again," Rein said evenly. "Water, food, morale. My men will die in a breakout charge, that would be our only obvious option at that point, and

I don't care how complacent your officers are—they'll anticipate it."

"Yes," Wunic said, "but they can't concentrate their surrounding forces everywhere—you can focus everything, and if it's timed . . . General, I know this isn't plausible. I know it seems that way, but the only other option is surrender and execution. Every one of your men will need a pardon from the king himself—and," Wunic said, "you *might* break through."

"No, I don't think so," Rein said.

Of course you won't, Wunic thought, *but what else are you going to do, you timid bastard? War requires action; stay in one place too long and you die. Fight or give up and stop wasting my Goddamn time.* But Wunic said, "Divide these boys up, and they'll run out of food, they'll either desert or be killed."

Rein slid out of his chair, heading for the door. "Thank you for your help, General Wunic. As I'm sure you appreciate, we don't have unlimited time here. I'm sorry we don't agree on this. Honestly, I hoped we would."

Jak frowned. "Rein—"

Wunic didn't answer, and Rein left them alone, shutting the door behind him. *Did he remember something or make a decision?* Wunic wondered. General Rein left so quickly.

"Sorry," Jak said, and she went to one of the beds. "I shouldn't have brought you here."

Wunic got to his feet behind her, and he grabbed one of Jak's arms, twisted it behind her back, his other forearm pressed to her throat—he slammed Jak to the wall. She was trembling, rasping, her cheeks turning a bright red, eyes tearing from the pain in her arm. If Wunic pushed harder, the joint would snap backwards.

"How do I get out of here?" he asked and loosened the throat hold enough for her to speak.

". . . what do you—"

"Tell me how I can get out of here. Can I walk out? Am I still a prisoner?"

"You're still . . . General Wunic."

They'll recognize me, he thought, and said, "I have no problem killing you, do I make myself clear?"

". . . yes."

"Good, now tell me how to get across the lines, back to the royals from here."

Jak coughed, started to fight, and he applied pressure to her arm—

she screamed a startled, frightened noise—and Wunic slammed her against the wall.

"Listen to me, bitch, I told you that I would kill you, and I meant it. You're not worth a bullet, so you'll understand if I just break your Goddamn neck—talk to me. Can I get back? Yes or no?"

Wincing, teeth clenched, Jak shook her head.

"No? Are you lying to me? Should I break your fingers to find out? Do you understand what I'm saying, am I being clear? I *will* ask soldiers for details. I'll find out if I can get out, and if I can, I will. And before I go, I'll make you very, very sorry you didn't kill me with the rest of my men. Do we understand each other?"

She tried to nod.

"Do anything to hurt me in any way and before I die, I promise, we'll be back like this again. Next time I won't let go. Is that clear?"

She rasped, ". . . yes."

"All right."

He released her, stepped away, and Jak doubled over, caught herself on the bed and started to gag, rubbing her arm where Wunic had nearly broken it.

"I'm sorry," she whispered. "God, I—"

"Don't regret what you do," he said, and he sat on the other bed—a lumpy, uncomfortable mattress, but Wunic didn't care.

"You're such a Goddamn asshole, General. I'm sorry. What do you want me to—"

"Nothing. Let's go to sleep." After a long silence, he said, "You and your General Rein, none of you are going to win this war. You never had a chance."

"We weren't getting enough to eat," Jak said quietly. "What did we have to lose?"

Wunic smiled and lay back on the bed, draping an arm over his face. *What did you have to lose?* he thought, and he chuckled softly.

"What's funny?"

"Try to kill me when I'm sleeping, try to go to the door without telling me first—and I'll hear your footsteps, do you understand?—do any of that, and I'll kill you."

"Yes, General," Jak said. "I understand. Should have listened to Murthus. I shouldn't have—"

"Shouldn't have done a lot of things," he said. And in Wunic's mind, he saw himself dragging Denon to the bottom of a river.

I can take it, Wunic thought. *And I will.*

chapter 13

Vel ran after Ulyu to the larger cavern, the blue light casting a faint circle of shadowy illumination around Vel, and they were back. Ulyu had stopped several feet away, his spear ready. Vel drew his own spear, holding it with both hands, and Vel strained to hear anything or spot any movement in the adjacent tunnels that fed into this large room.

"Where are they?" Vel whispered.

They are coming. Be quiet.

Will they talk to me? Vel thought. Like you do?

Yes.

And why are they coming to kill me?

Because you are trespassing.

Is that why you killed the men who were with me?

I did not—they did. It is part of the reason.

Why didn't they get me then?

Please, just be still.

Vel waited, his palms sweating on the smooth, heavy metal, and he walked in a slow circle. The carvings here were untouched. All of the walls and ceiling were filled with Frill writing that no person had ever carved over.

People didn't find these rooms? Vel wondered.

They found them.

What's wrong with trespassing? Vel thought. The last time I was here, I had somebody with me.

The other Frill were occupied during most of the time you were here. We found you, they did not.

So, I've never seen them before?

You have, but not like this.

Vel paced nervously. "What will they do?"

Quiet.

Sorry, he thought, what are they going to do? Are they going to fight you?

No.

Why not?

Because I will leave you.

"What?" Vel said.

Please, be—

"No," Vel said, "I thought you were here to protect me. You said that I'm your savior, right?"

There will be another time.

"Not if they kill me!"

You will not die.

"Because I have *this*?" Vel shook the spear at him. "I can't move like you do. What am I supposed to do with this, fight them?"

Yes.

"Goddamn it," Vel said, and he tried to steady the nausea in his stomach and throat. "You're just going to leave me here—"

Ulyu was gone.

Vel spun, scanning the corridors for any sign of movement. No sound, except his irregular breathing and the beat of his pulse in his ears. *I'm going to die in this room,* Vel thought, *because some God-damn Frill left me here as some kind of sacrifice, because he thinks I'm some kind of god.* Vel thought about the bone he had touched, about the story, and he tried to connect it with this. *The Frill have been abandoned here for centuries, and now I'm supposed to*—red slits in one of the corridors, gone again, and now more red flashes, and Frill advanced from one of the corridors, and then another, and another, and they closed on him in a full circle, all bearing spears, all dressed exactly as Ulyu had been dressed.

Their slit-eyes glared crimson at him, and then darkened again as they crept noiselessly closer. *Not moving as quickly as Ulyu had,* he thought, and then one was suddenly standing an arm's length away, spear levelled across its chest.

But we can.

Vel backed away, and more behind him, random red flashes from the corridors as the room filled with Frill. *Too many,* he thought, *hundreds of them, just like the last time.*

A deal was made, and we were betrayed.

"What deal?" Vel said, spinning to keep the spear pointed at them. "Tell me what's going on, please, I don't want to fight you."

Your leader promised us the soul of a human to be linked with our own.

"Who made that deal?"

You wear his coat.

Vel rubbed the sleeve of his black overcoat, the same coat Justice Hillor had worn. "I don't understand—what did he do? He agreed to let you mix a human and a Frill?"

You are not Frill, and if you were, it does not matter.

"You don't think it worked?" Vel said.

They pressed their spears closer, forcing him to walk, pushing him toward one of the tunnels.

We are damned, and the prophecy cannot be fulfilled. Our gods left us here.

"I know," Vel said. "How did he combine a person with a Frill?"

You are no Frill.

It began to make a kind of sense in Vel's mind. Hillor must have had his reasons, but, yes, it *did* fit in a way. *Link me—the successor to the king—with the Frill, and if you can control me I am the perfect tool to handle both the human city—Hope—and the Frill, to keep them all in line. If it worked.*

Into the tunnel, and they passed more unscratched Frill carvings, the passage gently turning, Frill surrounding Vel as they continued.

"Why wasn't I killed before?" Vel asked. "Why am I still alive?"

Don't worry, boy. You'll die very soon. We have our own traditions, and the weakling Frill who allowed you to come here cannot stop it.

"You don't believe in the Frill prophecies?" Vel asked.

Do you believe in your own mortality?

"What?"

You believe, but you do not understand, and when it happens, when you die, then you will know. Not before then.

"So you'll believe it when it happens?" Vel said. "When they're fulfilled, you'll believe the prophecies?" *Whatever the hell they are,* Vel thought uncomfortably.

You will die, but you do not really believe that. And so you do not live as if you know you will die. Because you are still young.

"And you believe whatever the prophecies are—you don't believe they'll be answered?"

You will not answer them, boy. You belong to us, and you are no savior.

They arrived at a cavern where the floor was made of half-crushed bones and skulls, a round table set into the center of the mess. Bits of decaying clothing still hung on a crumbling ribcage nearby, and the Frill silently filed into the room, around Vel, circling the table, pushing Vel closer to it. He remembered Guin's head, set on a platform that looked exactly like this. Bones crunched under his boots, and Vel turned on the Frill, his spear ready.

Vel shook his head, refusing to back any closer to the table. There were dozens of Frill in the room and more in the nearby corridor, seeming to drift noiselessly inside, over the mounds of dead skeletons.

Vel said, "No."

SISHA SWALLOWED more of the water in the mug they had left her, and she pressed her sinuses, trying to ease the ringing inside her skull. A soldier-priest in a white uniform with a swastika armband stood quietly in front of the door, armed with a rifle. He wasn't even looking at her. She lay on the king's bed, half-awake, but not really sleeping.

They switched guards every few hours, and Sisha had counted twelve rotations now. *Twelve times, but how often would they be switching? How long have I been in this room?* she wondered. *How long since Denon—how long have I been in this Goddamn room?*

Sisha had eaten four meals . . . or had it been three? She had fallen asleep several times, each time awakened by a new guard loudly opening the door to rotate positions. Footsteps outside, but it was still too soon for another replacement guard. Sisha forced herself to sit up, and she shivered involuntarily as Lord Denon entered, flanked by a pair of soldier-priests, both armed only with swords.

Denon looked at her as if she were a disappointing stain on the bed sheet. Then he folded his hands, and, looking at his fingers rather than at her, he said, "Sisha, you are accused of conspiracy in the murder of our king."

Sisha stared at him, unable to respond, and the Religious Guard near him moved forward.

"Secure her," Denon said, "and take her to the prison below."

"Why?" she said.

"You assisted a group of rebels who have assassinated the king. The penalty for treason is death."

Sisha thought about charging him, and she imagined her fingernails clawing away the flesh of his throat, exposing weak pulp and blood vessels. She noticed the sword and pistol at Denon's side. He hadn't been wearing them the last time she had seen him, when he had . . .

"Vel's dead?" she asked, and the religious soldiers took her arms. Sisha allowed them to pull her up and guide her toward the door.

Denon nodded. "He and his personal guard were killed shortly after leaving the palace."

"Vel's dead?" Sisha said again.

"Yes," Denon said shortly, and he stepped aside to let the men take her away.

Sisha dug her heels into the carpet, slowing them, and she said, "You're not a judge. . . . you can't sentence—"

"The Executive Council has been disbanded," Denon said. "We are in a state of emergency."

"Disbanded?" she said, catching the doorjamb with one hand, and the men began to pry her fingers away.

"I didn't do anything," Sisha said, forcing herself not to panic, not to cry or fight these men too openly. "I didn't have anything to do with the king's—"

"It is not a question of whether or not you did it," Denon said. "I *know* you did it. If you confess, it's true, I might consider an alternate sentence. But, there is no question as to your guilt—that's not the issue."

"Goddamn it," she said, and Denon stepped closer to her, and she said, "Stay away from me! Don't touch me!"

Denon said, "You need to calm down." And to the Religious Guard: "Get her out of here."

Sisha's shoulders shook; exhaustion and fear. Vel had been killed—no, Denon had been lying. Vel wasn't dead, he was the king, he had to be alive. Denon released her, and the priests kicked her down, yanking both hands behind her back, and Sisha heard herself crying as they wound a cord around her wrists.

"Lord Denon," she said. "Please . . ."

They forced her into the hallway—Sisha said, "Denon . . ." They paused.

"Yes?" Denon said.

"Why?" she said, tears rolling down her cheeks so that she could taste them, salty on her tongue.

"I know you are guilty," he said.

She shook her head. "No. Why you? Why are *you* doing this?"

He motioned to the Religious Guard, and they carried her away, her feet dragging limply behind her, and Sisha shouted, "*Why?*" Sisha heard Denon following them down the hall, and she continued, "Denon . . . you'll burn—you'll burn in hell. There's no reason for any of this. . . ."

Denon approached in the hall, and he waved at the soldiers.

"Stand her up," he said, and they raised Sisha to face him.

Denon drew close to her. His breath was hot and smelled of old grassfruit. "You will *not* presume to teach theology to me," he said quietly. And then he kissed her on the lips, and as she struggled, Denon pulled away and hit her hard, smashing her nose. Blood ran down her lips, and Sisha tasted it, warm on her tongue. She slumped, spitting blood, trying to talk, the priests still holding both of her arms, suspending her.

"There's nothing more I can do for her," Denon said. "Take her below."

The Religious Guard did as they were told.

Blakes floated through the abdomen of the *Australia*, and one of his crewmen—a soldier who had remained loyal to Blakes at the end, Michael—sat in a solitary chair at a console in a room ahead of him. The *Australia* was divided into three abdomens—long corridors connecting a series of rooms on all four walls—and each abdomen also linked with the other, parallel abdomens via a series of crawl spaces and ladders. Blakes thought of it as an engineered insect, not a spaceship.

Blakes drifted out of the abdomen into a small control room, where Michael sat working at a monitor, typing command after command into the console. The *Australia* contained one computer, an actual living organism that had maintained the space-sleep so well for all of them, and that ran the ship just as any electric computer would have, millions of times faster. Blakes caught himself on the back of Michael's chair and hung there, above him. Michael was strapped into the seat, his hair dancing in slow waves above him, rubbing against Blakes's chin. Blakes saw half of the screen was a series of technical commands—line after line—and the other was a black-and-white closeup of the planet Hera.

Eight different squares were on-screen, each a mess of gray and black and white smudges, and each surrounded by technical jargon and numbers.

"Eight quadrants," Michael said.

"You told me you would have it ready in twenty minutes."

"It is ready, sir," Michael said, and he stopping typing long enough to point out several things on the little smudge-squares. "These are the eight quadrants of Hera. Six of them are seventy-five percent or greater water. Strings of islands in those six, but they could be unstable, and I would suggest two possible landing sites in the other remaining quadrants."

"Where are they?" Blakes asked.

"Here," Michael said, pointing to a gray smudge on one of the squares, "and here." He indicated another gray area on a different square. "There's something near one of these that I think might make it worthwhile."

"But we can't take off and land again, can we?" Blakes asked.

"No," Michael said.

So wherever we go, that's where we live, Blakes thought.

"What's worthwhile?" Blakes asked.

"Well, it's all a matter of statistics. I think there's some cleared land—prairie possibly—near this one. That might make growing crops easier than landing in a hilly or forested area. And *here*, here there's something else."

"What?"

"I don't know exactly—it's just showing up as a regular cluster of stones. Could be nothing. The rocks are probably too big to be anything, or they wouldn't be showing up at all. But they seemed to be arranged."

Blakes cleared his throat. "Like what? Like a circle of stones, a Hera Stonehenge?"

"No," Michael said, "like a city. There are a few spots where there might be other configurations on the planet too; all of this is very imprecise because of what they equipped the *Australia* with. I can't really tell. But *this* one, the one near the prairie, might be perfect. There's a river there too, running right through the middle of it."

Blakes nodded. "We'll land there."

"Should I—"

"Yes," Blakes said, "that's where I want to land."

He turned to leave the room, floating over a table with a fresh white blanket and pillow—an emergency operating table—and past a poster one of his crew had mounted on the adjacent wall. Bright flames licked at blackness under the words TWENTY-FIRST CENTURY NIGHTMARE. Donna—the woman who had put it up—had been one of Blakes's mistresses on Earth, and she had smuggled it onboard. When Donna had showed Blakes the poster, he had made love to her frantically in his zero gravity bedroom. "Twenty-first Century Nightmare" was the title of a poem Blakes had written when he was still living in New York, and Donna explained that she had found it one night in his bedroom, on the floor.

Back in the abdomen, several of the crew—both women—saluted him, and Blakes nodded, using their bodies for leverage as he swam past. They laughed, and he thought about asking them to come to his room that night. As soon as he had woken, Blakes knew that all of these women were his, and he had told them all to choose husbands, but he had also made it clear what their duties would be when their Führer called on them. And everyone present, men included, had saluted him.

Blakes grabbed one of the ladders and pulled himself up into one of the adjoining abdomens. He pushed off of one wall and drifted into another room with two chairs, rows of monitors and consoles and a ladder leading up to several of the living quarters. A man and a woman sat in the chair, and several other people drifted in the air, talking. Blakes saluted, and they greeted him.

"Sieg heil."

"—eil."

"Michael's chosen a landing site," Blakes said, holding onto the chair behind the redheaded woman at the console. She nodded and watched words scroll down the screen.

Blakes said, "I don't know how long it will take, so just have the computer synchronize the landing sequence with Michael's orders."

"Yes, my Führer," the woman said, and the man nodded, continuing to work.

Blakes floated through the room, taking the ladder up to another floor, where a table and chairs had been temporarily attached to one floor, three posters mounted across from them. Another hallway led to the bedrooms.

The first poster was one of Blakes's own. It had been stolen from Germany following the Second World War, circulated through several rich families of antique collectors, and then Blakes had seized it, along with all of their collections, when he took power: a red swastika on a black background above the words

Deutschland
Was bietet Deutschland?

This is our Deutschland, Blakes thought, and he tried to imagine the stone city on the planet below. The second poster was propaganda with a giant photo of Mao Tse Tung surrounded by Chinese characters, and the third was a black-and-white picture of the mushroom cloud that had risen over a destroyed Nagasaki.

Blakes drifted past several people into the bedrooms, and he knocked on Donna's door.

"Yes?"

Blakes opened the door, and she smiled, her long brown hair swirling in the air around her face.

"We'll be landing soon," Blakes said, and he shut the door behind him.

"That's good."

"And then gravity will take over again," Blakes said, playing with her floating breasts. Donna smiled shyly, and Blakes began to kiss her.

"Whatever you want, my Führer."

"You."

Donna put her arms around him. "Then I am yours."

Five hours later, they landed, and Blakes's body felt as if someone had lined his bones with a thin coating of lead. He ordered them to uncover the smuggled weapons and supplies—and yes, they were really there. The Nazi standards had even been brought on-board; the gold staffs with eagle and swastika. Blakes grinned as they carefully opened one of the crates of antique—twentieth-century—rifles and replicas of late nineteenth-century artillery designed to be stored and later reassembled. Other boxes were being gathered together in the large, open abdomens, and Blakes listened to the metal of the *Australia* pop and hiss around him, whining as it adjusted to Hera's gravity.

Blakes found the books he told them to bring, a giant stack, and then they opened a huge, green plastic box that filled half of an abdomen. It had been stored, along with all of the rest of his supplies, between the rooms and the *Australia's* skin, in the organs of the ship's cargo bays. Opening the green box, they found rows of seeds, and Blakes sighed—at least the rifles and standards had been . . . —

and then he saw more boxes, hidden beneath several rows of seeds and farming equipment and tools and rations. In those boxes, Blakes found another portable container, specially designed, masses of wires, a black box and several columns of huge, black metal coffins. But they weren't coffins.

"Sir," someone said, "this should be food. This isn't—"

"It is," Blakes said. "I asked for it."

"But we need food. Where are the plows and the bricks—"

"We don't need them," Blakes said, and he glared at the man who had spoken. Blakes didn't know his name. "We *do* need these."

"What are they?" someone else asked.

"Our second chance," Blakes said, and then he found another box in another crate that contained layers of needles and containers of drugs. Small, white machines that looked like square refrigerators were set in white foam beside the drugs, and Blakes saw that some of his crew had begun to open the rations, distributing them. For the moment, he ignored them, examining the "refrigerators," making sure they had not been damaged, and they hadn't. *Not refrigerators,* Blakes thought, and he smiled, setting one back in the box. Genetic manipulators and cloning machines. With several of these, Blakes could mix the DNA of a human with any other species that bled, and he could grow newborns—mutants and human—from conception to birth in the womb of an "icebox."

When they had finished checking the supplies, Blakes ordered Michael to run a thorough analysis of Hera's atmosphere, pressure, gravity quotient, and on and on, until finally, he was satisfied that the planet was indeed close enough to Earth in both size and composition to be statistically identical. Blakes divided up his crew into groups of roughly twenty people, and then two of the groups—one led by Blakes, the other by Michael—chose an assortment of weapons from the illegal cargo Blakes had managed to smuggle aboard.

Blakes found a tiny replica of a human skull that had been carved by one of Pol Pot's advisors as a joke, and a stiletto with B. MUSSOLINI engraved on its handle. It had been carved in 1938 by a master craftsman in Florence, who had later been killed in the last days of the Second World War. Blakes pocketed both, offered Michael a gold crucifix that had once belonged to a long-dead conquistador, and said to his crew, "We are messengers of God's justice. Let us rediscover Eden."

They opened the ramps, and Blakes stepped off first, a woman behind him carrying a long pole with a huge black and red swastika flag hanging from it. The air was very dry, and it took a moment for Blakes's eyes to adjust to the bright yellow light—and as the world came into focus, Blakes saw the ruins.

They had, indeed, landed on the edge of a dead city of giant black stones. Some as large as skyscrapers, the mountains of rock were aligned in organized streets, and wiry trees and vines covered them. Rocks crunched under Blakes's boot, and he nodded to the woman behind him, who fell to her knees, planting the Nazi flag in the center of the dirt street so that its swastika flapped loudly in the light breeze. Blakes smiled, and took a deep breath of the clean, dry air, licking his lips. *Much better than the chemicals from the* Australia's *bowels,* he thought. His group fanned out through the street, rifles and pistols ready, as they jogged to crouch behind areas of crumbling rock walls.

Michael approached behind Blakes, and without turning Blakes asked, "What year is it now?"

Michael said, "2402 C.E., according to the computer. Three hundred and one years in transit."

"Not the common era," Blakes said, spitting into the dirt. "We are *God's* people. 2402 A.D." He walked down the street, to the edge of the ruins. Some looked as if they were on the verge of collapse, their tops cracked and tilting, and others had obviously already fallen, large bits of rock smashed all across the dirt. Blakes pointed out the spiralled, intricate carvings on the buildings he passed.

"Someone once lived here," Blakes said.

Michael nodded, followed several paces behind him. The rest of Blakes's crew began to get out of the *Australia*, standing in large groups in the street around it. The *Australia* seemed pitifully small, scraped and rusted and discolored, dormant and gently smoking between the rows of massive, carved rocks. Blakes saw what might have once been windows and doorways on the structures, and huge gaps where entire sections had broken away, cluttering the street.

At the edge of the ruins, high grasses—eight feet high—waved in an unending field.

"Prairie," Blakes said, and Michael stepped beside him.

"Yes, sir," Michael said.

"What kind of things live in a prairie?"

"Birds," Michael said, and they both looked at the blue, cloudless sky. "Rodents, maybe. Insects."

"Nothing very large, though," Blakes said quietly.

Michael nodded. "No, of course not. Why?"

Blakes didn't say that he thought he had seen something—a long shadow?—in the grasses, like the outline of giant fish deep below the clear surface of the Pacific Ocean. Blakes drew Mussolini's knife and carefully drew a large swastika over the curling writing of one of the nearest buildings. He then carved a fist, and below that, the words: *Hera—2402 A.D.*

"This is not to be touched," Blakes said. "I want this rock preserved."

"Yes, sir."

Blakes and Michael returned to their crew, clustered at the base of the *Australia*, all armed. Blakes saluted them with an open hand, and as one they responded—*"Sieg heil!" They're tired,* Blakes thought, as he drew nearer. *But they are still my people, my chosen ones.*

"We will build a city here, among these ruins. We will make these our own, and we will call the city Hope. Hope on a new Eden, in God's land, in Hera."

Blakes ordered the groups to begin exploring in rotations. The supplies could wait on the ship until they were certain they knew the layout. Michael explained that the remnants of a forest stood nearby, actually growing into and beyond the ruins. The *remnants,* because something—probably a fire or drought—had killed and permanently wilted most of the trees. None of the them grew leaves. Blakes wandered through the ruins to the edge of the woods. Instead of leaves, tough strands of moss—almost like hair—hung from the bark.

Outside the ruined city in this direction, trees grew from gray trunks to writhing, brown and discolored branches—draped in tufts of dirty moss, almost fur—and as Blakes walked, the ground clanked under his boots. And there, just below the dirt of the forest floor, was layer after layer of crude metal—waiting to be melted and shaped.

"God's will," Blakes said, as they began to collect some of the metal, and one of the older women came running from the ruins, her hair streaked gray on both sides.

"My Führer!" she shouted, breathlessly, cheeks red and panting.

"Yes?"

"The *Australia*," she said, "the *Australia* . . ."

Blakes was already moving, back into the empty ruins, his rifle ready. Other crew members followed, dropping the shiny metal deposits back to the soil.

"What?" Blakes said.

"She's gone," the woman said, and they ran—back to the street, where Blakes's flag still hung on its post, where the dirt was still shaped in the grooved pattern of the *Australia*'s belly. A large crowd had begun to gather, all looking at Blakes for a sign, an order.

He stomped through the empty space where the *Australia* had been. *No,* he thought, *it has to be here. This doesn't make sense. There's no place it can be. It must be here.*

"There were people on it," Michael said, hurrying to Blakes's side. "Sir, there were people—"

"I heard you," Blakes said. "Where the *hell* is it?"

"Not enough fuel to have moved."

"They couldn't have *rolled* it," Blakes said, and the crowd fell silent as Blakes began to pace. "They couldn't have rolled the Goddamn ship away, could they? It *must* be here. It cannot have moved. How many were on board?"

"Thirteen," someone said, and Blakes shook his head, sweat on his brow.

"No," he said, "it's here. It has to be here."

"Sir, we should divide up," Michael said. "They must have found a way to re-route power into one of the engines, to drive away."

But there are no marks in the dirt, Blakes thought, glaring at the dust that rose from the feet of several hundred people congregating around him, in the open path between the enormous rocks. *Something else is going on here,* Blakes thought, *and*—thousands of dark shadows appeared on the overlooking ruins, their tiny eyes flashing red from where they stood, hundreds of feet above Blakes's crew, and the sunlight glinted on their wickedly curled spears—metal faces and chests, black bodies.

"Devils," Blakes whispered, and people started screaming.

The figures were all around them, standing high overhead, looking down from every side, from the ruined windows and ledges of the black rocks, and people were shouting and pointing, waving rifles at the devils. And then Blakes saw it too, a line of thirteen people, kneeling on a giant ruin, between a group of the devils—the crew from the *Australia.* Blakes could almost see their faces as they gestured down at the crowd and at Blakes, as the devils kept their spears ready. *Alive,* Blakes thought, *they're alive, but where is the Goddamn ship?*

Michael was mumbling something in Latin, and a devil suddenly stood behind a crumbling rock thirty feet from Blakes, armed with the same long, glinting spear, its face a narrow mask with two dark eyeslits—they flashed red—and long hair from the top, and tubes from the mask to the chestplate, and the too-long arms and legs. Blakes pointed his rifle at the monster and clicked off the safety. There were too many of the things to count; thousands, covering the nearby ruins, all with spears—and they had some of Blakes's crew.

"Sir," Michael said quietly, "should we—"

"Kill them," Blakes said, and he aimed his rifle. The demon mocked him, remaining exactly as it was, daring him to fire. "I cast you out, devil," Blakes said.

"But our men are—"

"Kill them," Blakes said, more loudly, and then he waved one arm at his crew. "Kill them—*open fire!*"

They did, shooting in irregular bursts in every direction, blasting clouds of black smoke from the ruins, and Blakes shot the demon closest to him—the devils were gone. All of them: one moment there, the next gone. Slowly, the cracks of rifle fire stopped, and Blakes studied the empty rock-buildings—his thirteen had vanished along with the demons.

"Our war has begun," Blakes said, and he silenced the noise of his crew, walking directly through them. They moved aside, creating a path. "For every light, there is darkness. We did not come here for peace, but for a second hope. God has brought us here to revive His justice, and now you've seen the reason, just as I have—our purpose in coming here. Just as God is real, so too is Satan. We are God's warriors." Blakes stopped beside the limp Nazi flag. Wind ruffled it, and Blakes raised his arm high. "Fire and death to any who oppose God's law! *Sieg heil!*"

"—ieg heil!"

"NO," WUNIC said, looking at the dispatches Rein had handed him. "No, this is no use. I'm sorry, General, it's too late."

Murthus stood at the door, his rifle in hand, angled at the floor, ready to aim at General Wunic. Rein sat across from Wunic, Jak sat in the third chair around the table—she was flipping through more dispatches. Through the walls, a low rumbling droned on and off, on and off.

"That's it?" Rein asked. "Please, General . . ."

Wunic slid the dispatch across the table, back to Rein. Wunic tried to ignore the itching pain in his feet—it felt like a hot splinter was lodged where his toes should have been and when he put pressure on the leg, the splinters turned to flames, burning the tendons and muscles up and down his calf and thigh. *Damn all of you,* Wunic thought. *It's over.*

Rein was still waiting, and Wunic closed his eyes tiredly. He had begun to understand why the general looked as terrible as he did. Those are eyes that fight a losing war; the deep, almost-purple discoloration around them, the sagging flesh beneath. *How long before I look like that?* Wunic wondered. *Do I already?*

"That's my opinion," Wunic said at last.

"Be honest, General."

"Yes. I have been. I'm sorry if it's not what you wanted to hear."

Rein said, "You didn't think this could be done, and now it makes no difference that it has been? General, you're not being entirely honest with me."

"I told you my opinion," Wunic said. "No. I'm sorry, it doesn't change the only basic strategy you still have." He had begun to get very tired of the patient game of 'Ask General Wunic Questions While Murthus Stands in the Doorway with a Gun'. Wunic said, "You have to break out."

General Rein waited. "That's it?"

Wunic ran his fingers through his sticky hair, and his stomach growled uncomfortably. "Can I have something to eat please, General?"

"We've taken the piece," Rein said, as if making sure Wunic had actually read the dispatch.

"Yes, General, I know," Wunic said.

"It's below, in the yard right now."

Wunic sighed. "Great. I need to eat something. As far as I can tell, this doesn't change your situation significantly. You're still outnumbered and outgunned, and your supply lines are being cut."

Jak said, "Please, General Wunic—"

"You need those supply lines too right now, General," Colonel Murthus said to Wunic quietly, unmoving.

"Please," Rein said, picking up the dispatch and scratching his lower lip as he continued, "I'm open to the break-out idea, the push for the palace. We can talk about it." Rein checked his dispatches. "About one thousand units can be withdrawn to this Garr, and we now have a piece of artillery to punch a hole."

"Most of your soldiers don't have rifles," Wunic said. "Do they? Or if they have guns, they're almost entirely out of ammunition. Is that accurate? How many small arms do you have left, General?"

"I don't have the numbers," Rein said, and it was obvious that he did. *He knows just as well as I do what this is worth,* Wunic thought. *How easy it can be to lose a single offensive.* Rein said, "Do you have figures, General Wunic? How many units do the royals have?"

Wunic imagined the room falling apart. He saw the stone roof and walls exploding in a spray of debris, and the floor collapsing with a great cracking that would open a hole where the beds were arranged. It would be a spectacular end to the rebellion; the annihilation of a Garr. Something that could not be done—and Denon would do it, he would blast this building into rubble.

"The number everyone knows is six thousand," Wunic said, "I had over six thousand units: now that included the Garrs and the palace. But that's just the regular military before heavy casualties. I don't know what kind of damage you've done, but frankly, they still probably outnumber you five to one. And just before I was captured, one of the last things I saw was the instatement of a full draft."

Wunic didn't have to explain the consequences of a full military draft. Everyone between the ages of sixteen and thirty-five was automatically conscripted for the duration of the war. Everyone living in the shelters and the Garrs, waiting for the war to end, the rations to increase, and the snow to stop had suddenly become a part of the military. That meant another two thousand to three thousand soldiers at least—there were only a total of around twenty thousand people in Hope, after all.

"Six thousand," Jak said softly.

"No," Murthus said.

"Why didn't you say this earlier?" Rein asked, ignoring Murthus. There was fear in the perfect calm of Rein's voice.

Wunic said, "You knew, General. You had to have known what you were up against."

Rein didn't answer, and Murthus casually pointed his gun at Wunic. "He's lying. The general is a spy, sent to make us surrender."

Wunic said, "Tell me why Lord Denon would circulate a dispatch to the company commanders that I had defected."

"It must have been faked," Murthus said, stepping closer to Wunic. "Obviously something in the dispatch—some phrase—was a code that the commanders should ignore it. No," he said, "no, that dispatch was just for us. It could have even been set up: all the commanders might not really even have gotten it."

Jak said, "Colonel, General Wunic is a dick, but that doesn't—"

"I don't understand," Rein said, leaning heavily back in his chair, looking ten years older than he probably was. "*Why*, General? Why doesn't the artillery help us?"

"It might," Wunic said, the questioning and irritation in his foot culminating in adrenaline. "Of course it might, General. What I'm saying is if you're going to break out, you will. They will always have more—you can't rely on the artillery to change the outcome. You lost four hundred men taking one piece of artillery, and that's irrelevant too, in a way. We know this—I refuse to believe that you haven't seen this. Breaking out against these odds . . ." *It's suicide,* but he said, "If your men can do it, they won't need artillery. Some lives might be saved, but that's not ultimately the way success is measured. Capture the government, force a compromise."

"You knew we wouldn't agree with you," Murthus said.

Wunic's voice rose, "I think you do agree with me, *Colonel.* You don't forget how to be a soldier by deserting, regardless of how much you might stop acting like one."

Murthus tensed, and Wunic stared into the barrel, still sitting.

Rein remained calm, and he said, "I don't know. You might be right, you might not be. There are still different methods, General. You understand if I'm a bit paranoid, don't you? You would be in my position." He paused and said slowly, "After all, we *are* killing each other, aren't we?"

"Yes, General," Wunic said, without looking away from Murthus.

"What I don't understand," Rein said, motioning to Jak, "is you."

"She's with him, she's a part of this," Murthus said.

Jak rose—Rein drew a pistol, cocked it, and pointed it at her chest, still sitting passively in his chair.

"General . . ." Jak shook her head. "What the hell is wrong with you?"

Rein said, "Sit down, Jak."

She didn't move. "You can stop pointing the gun at me."

"You're going to defend him?" Murthus said, glancing at Rein for support. "You're with him, aren't you?"

"Colonel, how long have you been in the military?" Wunic asked. "Do you—"

"Quiet," Murthus said. "General, your time as any kind of advisor is over."

Murthus advanced—Jak tossed Wunic a rifle—and Wunic was on his feet in one movement, his own weapon aimed back at Murthus.

"Thank you," Wunic said to Jak, still glaring at Murthus. The pain in his feet had become a single entity, something he could focus and repress when he had to—like now.

"Don't do this," Jak said, and General Rein rose methodically from the table, keeping his pistol aimed at Jak. Jak dropped one hand to her pistol, and Rein cleared his throat.

"Don't," he said. "I don't want to shoot you, Jak."

She backed away from him, toward the beds. "Why are you doing this? You really think General Wunic is lying?"

"He is," Murthus said.

"Son, I'd ask you to keep in mind that you're speaking to a general, and the supreme military commander of the police force of Hope," Wunic said to Murthus. "Watch your mouth."

"Drop your rifle, General Wunic," Rein said, his pistol still pointed at Jak. "Drop it, or I shoot her."

Wunic said, "You're threatening me with taking someone else's life, General?"

"Jak goes down," Rein said, "and you have two guns pointed at you, not one."

Wunic listened to his pulse, wondering how long it would be before someone shouted for help from the rebels who filled the halls of the Garr. As soon as that happened, Wunic would be dead—along with the colonel, if things went well. Except that Lord Denon was still alive. *I can't die yet,* Wunic thought. *Not in this room.*

"In a situation such as this," Wunic said. "One man fires, everyone else fires. I'd ask you to count the guns, before speaking, Colonel Murthus."

Rein approached Jak, she edged away, and Wunic pivoted slightly, keeping both Rein and Murthus in his vision.

"Do you think I care if you shoot me, General Wunic? Don't they teach us not to care? If I kill you, what difference does it make? That's more than a fair trade, isn't it?" Murthus said. "You just finished telling us how Goddamn important you are."

"Then shoot," Wunic said. "Or put the gun down. I know you were one of the nominations for the Executive Council. But they didn't vote for you, did they?"

Actually, Wunic didn't know, but there was a good chance Murthus had been nominated. A young colonel with connections higher in the military, with a family that controlled several of the commodity factories—he probably even expected that he would win. And Wunic had beaten him, just as he had beaten the half-dozen other people who had run for the Executive Council seat Justice Hillor had left empty when he died.

Rein frowned at Murthus, and suddenly Wunic saw it. The way Murthus reddened, the way his eyes narrowed, all of this wasn't just wartime suspicion. Murthus resented Wunic because Wunic had gone to the Executive Council and Murthus hadn't even gotten enough votes to register in Wunic's memory. It had been a guess—and just like that it made sense.

"So you're not a politician," Wunic said, drawing slightly closer to Murthus. Pain flowed through his leg like broken pieces of glass, and his knee trembled, threatening to give. "Is that what this is about, son? You're still young, and if you don't waste it, there's a lot you can do with your life. You've still got time."

"Drop your weapon, General Wunic," Murthus said softly.

Rein was watching Murthus, and Jak's hand slid to the handle of her pistol.

"No," Wunic said.

"Let's all sit back down," Rein said.

Murthus ignored him. "You're not ready to die, General Wunic. You're too important."

"Colonel . . ." Rein said, but still Murthus ignored him.

"You ready, Wunic?" Murthus said.

"Colonel!"

Murthus's grip tightened on his rifle—Rein shouted again, but still Murthus did not respond.

"Are you ready?" Murthus said quietly. "Say you are, General."

Attack and counterstrike, Wunic thought. *I fire, he fires—no. No, not now. I still have things to do; I'm not afraid of dying, I'm afraid of running out of time. I will not die here,* Wunic thought, *for nothing.*

"Murthus—" Rein said, and out of the corner of his eye, Wunic saw Rein turn, raising his pistol—Wunic dropped into a roll, pain blinding him—Murthus's rifle bucked, and Rein shot Murthus in the side of the head. Wunic sat up, growling at the pain in his feet, holes smoking in the black stone inches from his face. Half of Murthus's head had sprayed across the door and wall and floor, and his body lay on its back, staring at the ceiling with what was left of his face.

Jak advanced quickly on Rein, pistol trained to his head. "Weapon down, General."

Rein tossed it onto the table and forced a smile. The door opened, rebels rushing into the room with more guns, slipping on the bloody mess around the door. One of them started to retch, and Rein said, "It's all right." Jak still had her pistol pointed at him.

One of the rebels said, "What—"

"Suicide, Major Selan," General Rein said. "Colonel Murthus committed suicide."

Selan studied the bullet holes near Wunic, and the still-smoking rifle in Murthus's dead hand. Wunic groped back to his feet, nodding to the major shortly.

"Can I—"

"You can stay or you can leave," Rein said, and Selan hesitated. "Why don't you leave, then?"

Selan nodded, noticed that Jak still had her weapon aimed at Rein, and started to say something.

"Thank you," Rein said, more loudly. "That will be all, Major."

"Yes, sir." Selan led the other soldiers out, closing the door behind them.

"I apologize," Rein said.

Jak holstered her pistol, and Wunic shrugged his rifle onto his shoulder, sitting painfully at the table again.

"Thank you, General," Wunic said.

Rein sat, putting his pistol away as well. "I don't usually carry one of these."

"Lucky us," Jak said, still standing.

"I think we've wasted enough time here," Rein said. "General Wunic, if I gave you command now—with all of the resources I have—what would you do?"

Reluctantly, Jak sat beside Wunic, put her pistol away, and leaned close to him.

"It doesn't bother either of you that there's a body on the floor over there?" Jak said.

"No," Wunic said, and he smiled.

"What would you do, General?" Rein said again.

"I would have your men train with the artillery as I withdrew everything from the field," Wunic said. "I would wait for the encirclement, pick a weak point . . ." Wunic paused. "And I would break out."

"Why wait?" Rein said. "Why not go for the palace now, before I'm surrounded?"

"Because it won't work now. Once you're encircled, the royals won't be defending the palace—they'll be preparing to accept your surrender." *Or to massacre everyone you've got left,* Wunic thought. *Or both.*

Rein thought about it, and then he leaned closer to Wunic. "With what we have, can we do that?"

We've had this conversation before, Wunic thought. *But why is it my pronouncement, General Rein? You know as much about this as I do, probably more. Do you want me to confirm what you're thinking? Will your men charge into artillery fire knowing they're going to die, knowing that only a handful will live to sack the palace, and that they could have surrendered or defected and had a chance to live? Will* you *do that?*

Why can't this be simple? But it is. That's the problem, Wunic thought. *It's* too *simple, and whatever I say, Rein knows that, has probably already made up his mind.* Wunic looked up.

"No," he said. "You won't win."

Rein nodded grimly: Wunic was pointing out an obvious, uncomfortable truth. "Then what can we do, the three of us, to stay alive?"

Wunic smiled. *This is what it's been leading up to, he's been thinking this the entire time. For once,* Wunic thought, *General Rein was thinking realistically.*

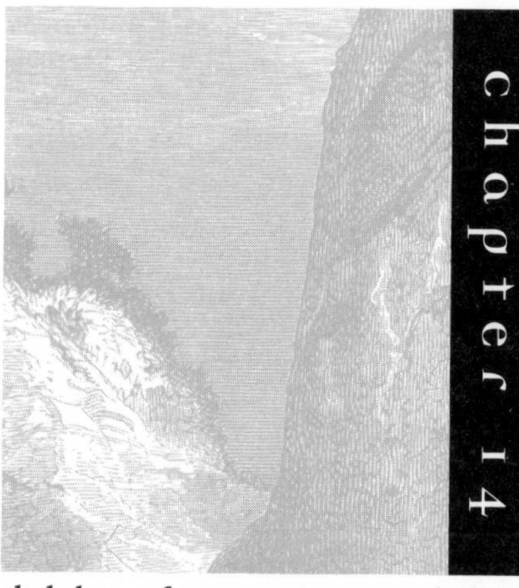

chapter 14

Vel planted his feet evenly in the ground bits of old bone, his spear in both hands, the curled, pointed end aimed at one of the closest Frill. They surrounded him, the table directly behind Vel. *Put me on the table,* Vel thought, *and then kill me, and leave my head like Guin's. I'm not a trophy,* he thought, his heart beating faster inside his rib cage, aching slightly, as if it was trying to push through his lungs and surrounding tissue.

You are an agent of the murderer.

"Stay where you are," Vel said, but the Frill had not tried to move. They filled the room, and he could see several more in the hallway, their eyeslits dark. Movement in the hall, beyond the extent of the blue light—and then Vel saw the Frill stepping aside, making way for a trio of Frill; a short Frill without a spear was locked between a pair of armed, taller Frill.

"Ulyu," Vel said, and the unarmed Frill cocked its head slightly.

You are still alive.

There *was* a slight difference in Ulyu's tone. The words came a beat slower than the voices of the other Frill. Ulyu was led into the room and walked around the table, finally stopping nearby, back to the table—four armed Frill separating him from Vel.

"What's going on?" Vel asked.

The armed Frill said, *The end of the weak, as well as the death of their prophecy.*

"You're going to kill us both."

Ulyu said, *Yes.*

The Frill edged closer to Vel, and he swung for their spears—they flicked out of the way—and Vel backed away, his lower back nearly touching the edge of the stone table. Ulyu remained perfectly still.

"Stop," Vel said, and the Frill swayed closer, their weapons still ready, but not attacking.

They will not kill you, Ulyu said.

"*Really?*" Vel said, and he slid onto the table, never turning away from the Frill that advanced—behind him, more Frill waited, their weapons within reach—but they weren't attacking. "You just said they would—what's stopping them?"

Even if they do not believe the truth of the prophecy, they still know that you might *be sent to test them. This is why you are still alive.*

Vel crouched on the table, turning in a slow circle to face the Frill, his spear poised. Ulyu remained where he was, and the Frill remained several feet from him on every side.

"Then what the hell is—"

The walls began to move. At first, Vel thought the circle of blue light was constricting, falling away from the walls, but then he realized that the light remained exactly as it was—it no longer reached the walls—and now there was a gap all around the perimeter, leaving room without bones—smooth, dark stone floor—for more Frill. The round room grew, the walls darkening as they slid silently away from him, and more Frill flicked noiselessly into the room from the corridor.

"Ulyu . . ."

They cannot kill you directly. If you were as the gods were, vengeance would be brought upon all of the Frill. Our prophecies forbid your direct death.

"Direct," Vel said, and he watched as the room continued to grow, the Frill forming circular row after identical row of dark masks and spears. "What does that mean?"

I will be killed along with you, Ulyu said.

"Because you're part of the group that isn't psychotic."

Because I believe you can become our god.

That's a yes, Vel thought, and he said, "What do you mean they can't directly kill me?"

The walls were black outlines now, barely visible, but still more Frill filled the room, hundreds of them now.

It is forbidden for their spears to pierce you or their limbs to crush you if you are our savior—they do not want to risk the possibilities if they are wrong.

"But they're still going to kill me."

They're going to try, yes.

"How?" Vel said, and his legs began to cramp as he continued to crouch on the table, facing the unending masses of Frill in every direction. "If they can't . . ."

The Frill parted, and an enormous suit of armor stepped through the crowd. The armor shined in a silvery blue, its head a narrow snout, its arms triple-jointed, ending in round clumps, and its two legs split into four stalks that each split again into another quad of metal supports. The thing stood twenty feet high, and it slid and squeaked as it stepped closer, the Frill moving out the way, leaving a wide path directly to the table—to Vel.

At least it makes noise, Vel thought, backing to the far end of the table. He had seen one of these things, motionless and dead, the last time he had come to the tunnels. Skeletons and clumps of old bones cracked and smashed under its heavy, multi-jointed legs. Ten feet from the table, the armor stopped and fluidly raised both arms, pointing the stumped ends at Vel.

Vel whispered, "This is how they do it indirectly?"

Ulyu said, *Yes.*

"What the hell is this thing?"

It is a builder, a digger.

A digger, Vel thought, and he raised they spear in his right hand at the digger. "What do you—"

And his left arm was ripped cleanly from his shoulder socket—it floated, bleeding, through the air—and hung suspended less than a foot from Vel's face. It took a heartbeat for the pain to register, and when it did, he fell screaming to the table, blood pumping from his open shoulder, Ulyu shouting from somewhere very far away, *No! You cannot be broken—you are as the gods were!* In a daze of pain and bright spots, Vel watched his severed arm glide away.

LIKE THEY were toys, Wunic thought. *Toys waiting to be broken into bloody, infected pieces.* Wunic stood outside the Garr, beside Jak, General Rein and Major Selan, watching a group of rebel wounded as they were carried through the inner wall to the rows of snow-covered cots and tents huddled around the base of the Garr.

Men and women were carried in unconscious, some screaming, without arms, without legs, some with huge pieces of their torsos missing, the gaps filled with discolored bandages. The snow all around the cots was a messy red and black slush. Withdrawing from the field meant bringing all of the wounded from wherever they had been hiding on the lines here, to the yard outside the Garr. There were a handful of doctors, who paced through the vomit stench with heavy swords covered in dried, frozen blood. Fires smoked and hissed beneath several of the tents, and the snow continued to fall, burying the exposed wounded who had stopped moving.

Hundreds of them, Wunic thought—he had been on his way out to inspect the artillery with Rein, Jak and Selan, but they had paused to let the flow of prisoners through the gates. The artillery was being kept in the "killing zone" between the walls on the opposite side of the Garr, away from the gates. Some of the wounded, those not expected to recover, were actually piled onto one another. A pretty girl with black hair sat up on one of the cots and said something to Wunic. Wunic stepped closer—*What was wrong with the girl; she was in her early twenties, both arms on the sheet in front of her. . . .* A line of stretchers waited at one of the tents, and Wunic saw a stretcher full of pale, frozen limbs being carried out of it. *A doctor's in there,* he thought, and another stretcher emerged bearing a man missing his right arm. Wunic looked back at the girl. Someone was screaming for water.

God, he thought, *why is she looking at me like that?*

"General," Rein said when there was a pause in the flow of incoming wounded, but Wunic ignored him.

Another man was dragged in missing half of his jaw and one arm—he gurgled something, blood running wetly through the bandages wrapped over him, dripping across the snow. *This is wrong,* Wunic thought. *I've seen casualties, wounded, but nothing like this. Swords and arrows cannot do this. They move as fast as the man using them, they depend on skill and honor, and they can kill and maim, but not like* this. *Not this completely, this lethally. It's never been like this. These are cowards' weapons,* Wunic thought. *And just like that the professional soldier is obsolete. Why learn discipline or swordsmanship if anyone can use a gun? I'm part of the past now, like all of my boys, everyone I taught; we don't matter anymore.*

And then Wunic saw it: The girl was missing both of her legs below the knees. Someone on a passing stretcher grabbed Wunic's overcoat, shouting and waving at him with the stump of an arm. Wunic shook the wounded man away, shivering, as he returned to Rein. *Not even people,* Wunic thought, and he swallowed, forcing the emotion away—*they aren't people, they're* units, *and guns did this, not people: machines. This rifles worked too quickly, and maybe the prophet Blakes had been right to bury them underneath the Church, to hide them and make people forget.*

"I'm sorry," Wunic said, and he glanced back at the legless girl.

"Husband," she said, and more of the wounded were shouting at Wunic, struggling to stand. "Children. Can't remember their names."

Jak took Wunic's shoulder, and they followed Rein and Selan out of the gate, into the narrow space between the walls, walking around, past bleary-eyed sentries. The rebels saluted General Rein weakly, and he patted each of them as they passed, boots crunching in the dirt. Artillery coughed through the snow. Wunic had begun to get used to it, as if that thumping noise should always be there, as if Hope's heart had begun to beat.

"I . . . the wounded," Wunic said, and Jak walked beside him, looking at the ground.

"It's bad," she said.

"It shouldn't be like this. We shouldn't be using these weapons."

Jak said, "Heard they have artillery shots that can vaporize a man, leave nothing but his feet or legs standing where he used to be." She smiled grimly. "Like he wasn't even there."

"I'm lucky to have any wounded at all," Rein said briefly, and their captured artillery was visible ahead: a long turret-tube, mounted on a black platform and sturdy wheels built into curls of traction, linked to a series of fuses and round hatches—where Wunic supposed they put the ammunition. It didn't look large enough or terrible enough to be causing what he had just seen. Five rebel soldiers stood guard around the artillery, and it was pointed up, at a forty-five degree angle over the outer wall, a pile of cumbersome metal boxes in the snow beside it, all marked ARTILLERY PARCEL.

I authorized this, Wunic thought. *I gave them permission to use it, to train, to learn to use the artillery. As soon as something like this exists, the rules change, because there aren't any more rules of conduct, codes of engagement. Single-squad advancements and man-to-man swordfights with crossbow support . . . that can vaporize a man . . .*

"Fully armed," Selan said, and the soldiers at the artillery saluted as Major Selan patted the cold metal barrel.

Rein looked at Wunic. "What do you think?"

"I don't know," Wunic said.

"Takes four or five men to transport," Selan said.

"How many rounds do you have?" Wunic said.

Selan motioned to the boxes. "Five in each." There were six boxes.

"Thirty might not be enough," Wunic said.

Rein said, "Probably not, no. But, if it's timed right . . ." He asked Jak, "What do *you* think?"

Jak studied the artillery, refusing to move any closer to it. "How do you aim it?"

"Not exactly sure," Selan said stiffly. "We haven't used any of our ammunition to test it."

"Do you have an estimate on the range?" Wunic asked.

Again, Selan said, "Not yet, sir. Best guesses come from the field, from reports based on how far the enemy is shooting—and that might be around five thousand feet maximum distance. Maybe longer, maybe shorter."

Five thousand feet, Wunic thought numbly. No one had told him it could shoot that far.

"You don't know," Rein said, and then to Wunic, "General, now you've seen it."

Wunic rubbed his gloved hands together, snow blowing in his face. *Five thousand feet means my boys can't see the people they're killing. Dying without honor, these rebels—these soldiers—are being slaughtered by invisible—this is wrong. This is not what combat should be.*

"It's intact," Wunic said at last.

Jak said, "It's just a big piece of metal."

Selan shifted uncomfortably in the snow. "Sir, we're fairly certain that the artillery *can* fire from inside the walls."

"Thank you," Rein said, and he thanked Selan, dismissing him, along with the other soldiers, until Rein, Jak and Wunic remained, staring uncomfortably at the single piece of artillery. Rein perched on the barrel, kicking the nearby inner wall thoughtfully with one boot.

"Supply lines have almost all been cut now," Rein said.

Wunic shrugged. "How much water do you have?"

"Enough for a couple more days," Rein said. "I doubt we'll have to wait that long."

They sat in silence for a long time.

"Damn it," Jak said, glaring at the artillery. "What can we do with one against fourteen of these things? They have . . ."

The rumblings in the distance stopped, and in the sudden silence, Wunic looked up at the gray sky and falling snow.

"Something's wrong," Wunic said quietly, and Rein backed away from the artillery toward Jak.

"They won't wait," Jak said.

"General, I think we're out of time," Wunic said. *Just a lapse in the artillery,* he told himself. But Wunic had had these feelings before—combat had a tendency to focus a man's instincts, and Wunic knew that something terrible was coming by the tingling along the back of his neck, the surreal, adrenaline anticipation. "Prepare the breakout now."

"Now?" Rein said. "We've got time."

"You feel that, don't you, General?" Wunic said, paling.

"It will start again," Rein said quietly.

Five thousand feet, Wunic thought. "If they can shoot five thousand feet, all they have to do is turn the artillery around. They might not even have to move it from where they are now."

Jak said, more to herself than to Rein, "I feel . . . he's right, at the front this happened the last time."

"It doesn't matter," Rein said, as if trying to convince himself. "My men aren't ready. You know that, Wunic. If I mobilize now—"

"You won't have another chance." Wunic went to him, and he put his hand on Rein's shoulder. "Please, General, you know this feeling—I know you see it too. I wouldn't subscribe to any of this, except that anyone who's been in combat knows that *this,* this moment, is what saves lives. Start moving now. Pick a position in the direction of the palace—you have to do it now, General."

Rein touched the artillery, thought about it, and then nodded to Jak. "Prep the company commanders. Go." She glanced at Wunic, and Rein said, "Go Jak—now."

Jak wiped the snow from her face and ran.

"If you open fire, my boys will return the volley," Wunic said.

Rein sighed. "I still have units in the field, General. It's possible that an extra fifty men might be the difference between winning and losing this."

"I think you may be encircled now," Wunic said. "It's possible the royals have left gaps to keep you from getting desperate—they've cut all of your supply lines, haven't they?"

"Yes."

"I know this is half-blind, you don't have intelligence, but—rather than risk waiting for the bombardment—you need to push now with everything you have."

"Not enough," Rein said. "I need more time to regroup, General."

Wunic said, "No." *Your men are going to be butchered,* he thought. Fourteen pieces of artillery focused on one place. The breakout will begin with this artillery trying to weaken the royals' position, but as soon as the thirty shots are gone, the royals will have all fourteen of their pieces concentrated on the gap. Nobody will get through. *Defect and I'm a traitor, charge and I die.*

Rein said, smiling sadly, "This is not an encirclement; that applies to crossbow entrapment. This is just a large-scale execution."

I know, Wunic thought, and he said, "Only if we don't get out." And Rein didn't answer—a soldier, one of the men who had been guarding the artillery—ran through the killing zone toward them.

"General," the soldier shouted to Rein, "General, we have refugees at the rear entrance—asking for admittance."

"Refugees," Rein said. "Why did they come here? How did they get through?"

"I've been told that the royals are forcing all refugees onto different sides of the encirclement. Evacuated from the nearby blocks, but the royals wouldn't let them out—so they came here."

"How many?" Wunic asked.

The soldier said, "Several hundred at least, General."

"Piss on the royals," Rein said.

Wunic swallowed. "This doesn't make sense—"

"What the hell am I supposed to do with several hundred refugees? Use their bodies as walls? Don't they know what's happening here?"

"I want to speak with them," Wunic said, approaching the soldier. "They're at the rear entrance?"

"Yes, sir," the soldier said.

"We can't take them," Rein said.

"I know, General."

"Now is not the time for this."

"I know," Wunic said again. "But if we're encircled, the refugees will know. They may have seen the artillery moving." That same adrenaline-discomfort stirred in Wunic's stomach. *Something about this is wrong. Why would the royals force refugees* this *way? They must all be sick and crippled,* Wunic thought. *But even then, why wouldn't they go to a shelter? Why move all of them here? It didn't make sense.*

"We *are* about to be hit," Rein said, and his hand began to shake as he clenched it into a fist. "The refugees are a distraction. I can't waste bullets on them, and they're not soldiers. The royals want me to waste time with the people whose homes we're fighting over. This is to keep me from moving."

"It's possible," Wunic said. "How soon will your men be ready?"

"I don't know," Rein said. "An hour?"

"You have to get rid of them," Wunic said. "I want to find out if they know anything. Then I'll make them leave." And Rein finally agreed, waving Wunic away—he hurried after the soldier, to the rear gate.

Why now? he thought. *God help me, we may have to mow them down if they refuse to leave. And they won't know anything. The royals sent them here to delay us; I might have done the same thing. Civilians used as tripwire. They might be slaughtered once the royal bombardment begins or they might simply be here to distract Rein's men until the encirclement is entirely ready and all of the artillery is in place, so that Rein is cornered into a dishonorable surrender and execution or suicide charge. And that's already what will happen, but I have to find Denon. I must stay alive long enough to make sure the king is alive and the government intact. And then Denon will pay for this: I may forget a friend, but I never forget an enemy.*

VEL CURLED into a fetal position, his right hand wrapped tightly around the Frill spear, his left . . . a numb space where it should have been, as if the circulation had been cut. Ulyu was saying something about how it was impossible; the savior could not be wounded like this. The Frill watched silently as the digger kept its arms pointed at Vel. *To take something else,* Vel thought, his vision clouding again. He rolled on the table. *Not die,* he thought, *not going to die . . .* and he threw himself into a sitting position, his lost arm still hovering over the edge of the table, blood pouring out of it, splattering the stone.

Sacrifice . . . the Frill said.

"No," Vel said, his knuckles whitening as he tried to heave himself into a kneeling position with the Frill spear. A wound opened around the top of his right thigh, bleeding out—the leg separating—Vel threw the spear at the digger's head, and it hit perfectly, slicing straight through, and the digger was bleeding, falling backwards—Vel's left arm dropped—and he rolled off of the table, the Frill backing away from him. Vel crawled, hand bleeding on the jagged bones—to the corridor. *Past the Frill,* he thought, *get out.* Skulls, fingers slipping in the eyesockets, and the Frill surrounded him. White slivers cutting his palm, shredding the skin. The Frill stepped closer, weapons to Vel's head.

You belong to us, boy. You are not our savior.

Ulyu said something desperate, but too softly, and Vel's vision blurred, blood soaking his coat, across his pants, down his legs—*my blood,* Vel thought, grabbing at the open gash, pressing the soft fleshy wound with his right hand.

Ulyu was saying, *Kill them. Prophecy even they will respect . . .*

Not die like this, he thought, and Vel vomited bile and salty blood. *Not yours.* Vel coughed blood; he breathed it, hot and stinging into his lungs.

Everything you will ever love.

One of the Frill stepped away from the rest.

Everything you will ever be.

Vel imagined himself without a head. "Please . . ."

Everything you will ever have.

"No . . ." The Frill raised its spear.

Will die.

Refugees, Wunic thought, and he hurried past rebel soldiers, frozen and shivering at their stations along the perimeter walls of the Garr. Some walked along narrow railings set into the back of both walls eleven feet in the air, and others crouched at the sniper holes, their rifles and crossbows resting on the cold stone. *Will they have any idea how close we are to being entirely encircled?* Wunic wondered as he tried to form a conversation in his mind. He approached the huge rear gate: It was an enormous wooden door, more than three feet thick and fifteen high. There were identical gates on both of the two perimeter walls, and the rebels clustered on the railing of the outer wall on either side of its gate waved at Wunic as he came closer. Major Selan was waiting for Wunic with a group of thirty rebels, most armed with rifles.

"How many did you say there are?" Wunic asked.

"Several hundred," Selan said. "No exact count, but they have one spokesman—who wants to be let inside."

A spokesman, Wunic thought. *Probably whoever came from the richest, most influential family in that crowd. He would be ready to bargain, to pull strings. Except that this is a war,* Wunic thought, *and in a very short time there's going to be nothing left here unless we take the initiative. And that means this has to be quick.* Wunic waved at the soldiers on either side of the gate.

"Let him through," Wunic said. "Just the leader."

I have to find out what they know and move on, Wunic thought.

The soldiers at the top of the wall waved their rifles over, and Wunic heard shouting from the other side.

"Back!" the soldiers yelled. "Back away from the gate—only he enters now. No! Get back."

"How many hundreds are there over there, soldier?" Wunic asked Selan.

"Don't know, sir—"

"Take a guess," Wunic said.

"Four hundred, maybe. I honestly don't know, sir."

Four hundred refugees, Wunic thought. *God, there are fewer than one thousand rebels in this Garr who aren't mortally wounded or incapacitated. What do these people expect us to do with them?*

Three rebels slid the complex lock away from where it linked the outer gate with the wall. Wunic glanced back at the interior gate, partially opened twenty feet away, leading to the courtyard of wounded and the Garr. The outer gate creaked, the soldiers on the outer wall shouting that the refugees would be killed if they tried to force their way inside.

Through the sliver of open gate, Wunic glimpsed a mass of people in long, baggy clothing, streaked with snow. *My leg is feeling better,* Wunic realized. *I didn't even use a cane when I ran here from the artillery. But it's probably not healing: the snow is numbing my lost toes.* A refugee with a thick beard stepped through the gate, a soldier grabbed him by one arm and threw him inside, and the gate slammed again, the lock snapping closed. They escorted the refugee to Wunic and Selan. He wore layers of discolored, bulky clothing, and there was a white scar below his right eye.

"Major Selan," one of the soldiers said, and Selan shook the refugee's hand.

Selan motioned to Wunic. "This is General Wunic."

"Hello, General," the refugee said, offering Wunic his calloused hand. A group of three soldiers waited behind the refugee, the rest of the soldiers talking quietly near the outer wall.

"Hello," Wunic said, shaking his hand.

"You were on the council," the refugee said, smiling. There were gaps where he had lost most of his front teeth.

"Yes, that's right."

"Weren't you a royal?" the refugee said. "Don't understand, I thought—"

"How many are with you?" Wunic asked.

"A few hundred. Don't know—we going to be admitted?"

I was wrong, Wunic thought. *This man isn't a factory owner or a politician. Why would the refugees choose* him *to talk for them? Why is he their spokesman?*

"Your homes were destroyed?" Wunic asked.

"Or occupied. We can't get to them—who can?"

"Have you seen many royal units since then?"

Why would they send this man inside? Wunic thought again. This was wrong. There had to be members of the aristocracy in the crowd—this man might have been a tavern owner or a sewage worker. He wasn't a businessman. His hands . . .

"People are freezing out there—" the man said.

"I know," Wunic said. "People are freezing in here too. I understand those people outside chose you to speak for them."

"No," the man said. "The rebs just asked for a representative—I came."

"Where are the royals on our flanks? Did you see artillery units?" Wunic asked.

"I don't know about your flanks or the artillery, but the royals were maybe a half an hour behind us."

"How many units did you see?"

"Don't know, several hundred?" The man wiped snow from his beard. "We going to be able to come in?"

"Is there anyone else out there who might have seen more of the royal positions? Did you all come here the same way?" Wunic said.

Selan said to the refugee, "Sir, you wouldn't want to be inside here. Believe me."

The three soldiers behind the refugee now paced near the exterior wall, talking to the rebels stationed on the railings.

"Nowhere else to go," the refugee said. "You guys at least have a roof."

"Is there anyone else—" Wunic said—and artillery growled nearby.

Thump thump, and then a pause, and the sound repeated. *No*, Wunic thought, and he backed away from the refugee, staring past the masses of confused rebel soldiers. *Goddamn it, Rein*, Wunic thought. *What are you doing?* The artillery shots had come from inside the Garr.

Movement in the corner of Wunic's eye—a dagger flicked past his throat, and Wunic stumbled backwards, off-balance—the refugee stabbed at Selan, slicing a gash in Selan's chest, and then he charged the outer gate, his knife dropping. He drew two pistols and started killing the soldiers on the outer wall—rifles pointed at the refugee as soldiers fell from their posts—a high pitched whine dropped from the sky, and a chunk of the outer wall near the gate suddenly wasn't there anymore. The low growl shook Wunic's rib cage, tossed him through the air, and bits of masonry hissed and smoked, peppering the snow.

Wunic landed hard, deep in the snow, and at first his vision was shaking—now he saw waves of refugees pushing through the gap in the outer wall, killing the rebels with concealed rifles. *Not refugees,* Wunic thought, his mind working slowly, and the refugees were ripped apart by the snipers from the second wall, bodies piling in the outer wall gap. *I was tired, distracted,* Wunic thought. *No excuse, I should have anticipated this.*

Bodies already cluttered the snow, and Wunic heard someone shouting to him that the inner gate was closing, sealing off the "killing zone," and Wunic found his rifle—the bearded refugee somehow still alive nearby and killing the rebels with his pistols, shooting them in the back as they tried to fire into the mass of attacking refugees—and Wunic killed the bearded man with a short burst and lunged to his feet—hot irons inside his feet—and someone pulled him through the second gate. Behind him, Wunic heard the outer gate crash, as the lock was blasted away.

"—inside!" someone screamed into Wunic's ear, and he was dragged through the courtyard by a pair of rebels, toward the Garr entrance. Wunic looked back—men lined the sniper positions of the inner wall, their rifles flashing loudly into the killing zone on the other side, and some dropped from returned fire—and a column of rebels strained at the inner gate, and it shut.

A terrible whining sent the men at the gate flying blindly into the air, and suddenly the gate wasn't there anymore, and all of the soldiers immediately around it were screaming and dying, and now Wunic saw the refugees rushing through the second wall, killing the soldiers in their path. Debris rained across the snow, and another blast took apart another section of the inner wall, rocking the ground, and Wunic shook free of the soldiers who were pulling him—bullets hissed over his shoulder and one snapped at his coat, punching a hole near his right thigh.

Wunic threw himself to the ground, the wet snow forming around his body, and he began to shoot down the refugees, killing the first wave with a long burst, and now more soldiers were outside, catching the refugees in a crossfire. And Wunic was out of ammunition—he crawled back, bullets raking the snow around him, and Wunic limped around the wall of the Garr, past rows of soldiers, half-concealed by stretchers and overturned tents, all firing into the broken gate and wall.

Pieces of wood smoked and burned, and more of the rebels were killed, the refugees charging into the open yard again—and Wunic was around the corner of the Garr. Ahead, the main doors of the Garr were wide, soldiers hurrying out with crossbows and swords. *They're already running out of guns,* Wunic thought. Wounded were dragged screaming to this side of the Garr, away from the fighting, and piled in huge masses of bloody stretchers, tents and dirty snow.

Jak stood at the far end of the yard, shouting at a company of ten soldiers, three of whom had rifles—Wunic ran to her.

"No!" Jak was saying. "Can't keep abandoning the interior defenses!"

"They've broken through the rear entrance," Wunic said, panting.

Jak nodded. "We know." To the soldiers: "Keep those soldiers where they are!"

"Can't," one of the soldiers said. "Snow makes their positions useless inside the Garr."

"I don't give a damn about the snow!" Jak shouted at him. "They go out there, they die."

The ground heaved as artillery blew apart something else on the opposite side of the Garr.

"Where's General Rein?" Wunic asked.

"Don't know," Jak said.

"We can't stay here," Wunic said. "I'm ordering the doors sealed, the re—your soldiers—"

"Can't seal the doors," one of the soldiers said.

"No?" Wunic said, and he waved his sword at a group of soldiers just outside the main entrance. "Tell everyone in the rear of the Garr to get inside *now*! We're sealing the doors!"

"—can't do that!"

Wunic spun and pointed his rifle at the soldier's chest. "You're not in charge, son. Get inside the Garr."

The other soldiers levelled their guns back at Wunic, and Jak swivelled her rifle, aiming it at the side of the nearest one's head.

"No," the soldier said, refusing to back down.

"Seal the Goddamn doors!" Wunic shouted.

Jak said, "Do it!"

"Ignore that order!" the soldier said.

A wave of soldiers rushed around the side of the Garr, tripping, and one fell in the snow. The nearest one was bleeding from his gut and held only a sword.

"—compromised!" he shouted, hurrying for the main entrance of the Garr.

Wunic grabbed Jak and yanked her up the yard, toward the stone doors.

"—courtyard's compromised!"

Wunic was inside, the narrow hall packed with soldiers running in either direction, and the soldier outside was shouting, "—fight for the courtyard! Not inside! Keep the doors open!"

Wunic forced his way through the mass of people in the hall, ordering them all up to the higher level.

"Go up! Up!" he said. "Make room! Come on, son, make way! Let's defend this Goddamn rock! Move!"

When the crowd swayed away, beginning to clear the hall, Wunic caught himself on one wall, spinning and heading back for the door. That same bastard soldier stood in the doorway, blocking it, and shouting, "Come back! Outside, not in here—"

Wunic snapped the butt of his rifle up, knocking the soldier aside, and blood splattered across the soldier's face—the soldier reached for his sword, royals charging Wunic from outside, and Jak crouched behind him, her rifle aimed around his torso. Wunic grabbed the doors, throwing all of his weight against it, and Jak fired past him, dropping one of the soldiers in the yard, return fire whistled and rang, ricocheting off the stone, and the wounded rebel drew his sword, lunging at Wunic—Jak kicked him hard in the back, and then again—and the front doors slowly shut. Then they stopped, and shouting from outside; someone was pressing from the other side—a rifle pushed inside, through the doors, angled at Wunic.

Rapid volley of gunfire from the yard, and blood sprayed through the opening, the rifle fell, and Jak ran to Wunic's side, helping to close the entrance. She kicked the rifle out of the way, and the doors shut.

"Lock it," Wunic panted, and they heaved the heavy stone bar into place.

"*Refugees*," Jak said. "How did this happen? I don't understand. . . ." The wounded soldier moaned and clutched his back and face, blood still slopping out of his nose and mouth—where Wunic hit him with his rifle. Gunfire above them: the rebel soldiers were firing out of the tiny windows, picking off "refugees" in the open yard outside.

"They hit us from the east," Wunic said, and he tried to make sense of it. *Warfare's changed, and I can't keep up,* a part of him said. *I'm getting sloppy, careless. I should have seen this coming.* "I should have seen this, but it was too fast. Too well-organized." Wunic shook his head, leaning over to catch his breath, hands on his knees. Popping cracks outside, return fire. The sealed stone door jerked and thunked.

"They'll break in," Jak said, and a female soldier hurried down the stairs at the end of the hall, running toward them. The soldier paused when she saw that the main entrance was closed.

"Thank God," the soldier said. "I was sent down to make sure they haven't—"

"Yes," Wunic said. "Get back up there and fight, soldier." And to Jak: "They had *immediate* artillery support. As soon as that 'refugee' started firing, artillery targeted the gate and the wall, and the 'refugees' outside were ready. It was perfectly timed." As the soldier turned to head back upstairs, Wunic called after her, "How many are up there?"

"Three hundred or so?" she shouted back. "Don't know, sir."

"Where's General Rein?"

"Haven't seen him, sir."

"Major Selan?"

"I don't know."

Wunic grabbed the wounded soldier by his shoulder. "Take this one upstairs with you—put him at one of the windows, make him a sniper."

"Yes, sir," the woman said, and she accepted the wounded man, dragging him down the hall, to the stairs.

The front doors rattled again, but they held.

"They won't shoot through," Wunic said.

A muffled whine, and the floor trembled—screaming and chaotic yelling from the floors above them. Wunic grabbed the stone wall, catching his balance. Jak put a hand on his shoulder.

"Bad idea," she said. "This is a bad idea."

The building shook again, black dust falling from the low ceiling, and soldiers appeared at the top of the distant stairs, hurrying down. "You're right," Wunic said. "The Garr won't hold."

"Walls breached," one of the soldiers shouted at Wunic.

"Stay in your Goddamn positions!" Wunic shouted at the men, and they paused. "Go back up there and take some of these royals with you!" He said to Jak, "There was someone on the inside. This happened too quickly." Jak glanced at the ceiling uncomfortably, as if it no longer mattered.

The corridor shook, and larger bits of stone fell from the ceiling.

"Sir," one of the soldiers said, drawing closer, and more rebels filled the stairs, pushing down, trying to get to the exit—*there's only one,* Wunic thought, *and I'm guarding it.* "Walls coming apart, sir . . ."

"We can't go out there, now get back to your—"

A low rumbling that rattled Wunic's eardrums shook the corridor violently—and this time it didn't stop. Jak grabbed Wunic's arm, a section of the ceiling collapsed behind them, crushing the staircase and everyone on it in an avalanche of falling black stone and dust. Wailing above them, and Wunic heard the walls grinding—gunfire outside, the walls continuing to toss—and the soldiers behind them in the hall, now a dead end, ran closer.

"Move!" Wunic shouted, and another section of the hall behind them collapsed, soldiers disappearing in the waves of falling stone, tossing thick clouds of smoke through the corridor, and Wunic grabbed blindly at the stone bolt—Jak at his side, fighting to lift it—and the rest of the hall ceiling began to fall, from the far end of the remaining corridor, sections breaking, each faster than the one before it, approaching the main entrance—and Wunic glanced back: a group of three soldiers diving and screaming as the ceiling fell on them in flashes of heavy rock. The bolt began to lift, and Wunic cursed loudly, his knees slipping with the increased pressure. The ceiling collapsed thirty feet away, the last soldiers in the hall disappearing under it. Wunic slipped, blades lancing through his feet, and the bolt fell away, the doors swaying gradually open—Wunic's vision flashed brightly as he tried to crawl through. Jak was pulling hard on one of his wrists. Five feet to the snow outside, and the ceiling dropped twenty feet behind him.

Jak yelled in his ear, "—the hell up, General!"

She grabbed his armpits, hauling him toward the snow. "Refugees"—royal soldiers out of uniform—lined the yard, rifles aimed at both of them. Ten feet. Sharp bits of stone blew into Wunic's hair, and smoke curled forward, enveloping him, blacking out the world—Jak pulled, and Wunic heard the rocks breaking above him, falling on the backs of his legs—and then he hit cold snow and rolled painfully down a slight embankment, the last of the Garr crumbling in huge gusts of black dust. It was an enormous mound of heavy black rubble, and somehow the front doorway still stood, snow already beginning to cover its edges.

Wunic coughed shards of black stone out of his throat and rolled onto his side, hot pulse in both legs. Jak stood in front of him, her sword and rifle in the deep snow at her feet, and Wunic shivered, hands and legs going numb again, his ears ringing. Jak raised her hands over her head, and Wunic looked briefly around—about thirty royals had formed a circle around them, all armed with rifles and dressed as refugees.

"Weapons down, General," one said to him. "Now."

Wunic realized that he was still holding his rifle with both freezing hands. He tossed it away weakly, and it barely moved, still within reach.

"—sword."

Wunic didn't try to stand as he unhooked his sword and removed his pistol, throwing them both away. He glanced at the remains of the Garr: a doorway and an uneven pile of smoking black rock. *Three hundred people buried in there,* he thought tiredly. *Goddamn it, just like that it's over. The rebs never had a chance.*

"Stand up," someone said, and Wunic paused for a moment, wondering just how much it would hurt—and then he hauled himself up, and yes, it hurt every bit as much as he was afraid it might.

The royals were silent, and more gathered, staring at Wunic, Jak beside him.

"General Wunic," one said.

"Didn't believe it," another soldier said. "They told us you had defected—I thought you were dead."

Wunic stared at them coldly, unanswering.

"Bind the prisoners," one of the officers said.

They tied Jak's hands, and then pushed her away, through another row of royals.

"Lord Denon," Wunic said, as they approached, preparing to bind him as well.

"I'm sorry, sir?" the soldier said.

"Don't listen to him, Private," an officer said. "Tie the bastard up."

"I want to see Lord Denon," Wunic said, and the soldier began to wrap sturdy cords of rope around his wrists. Wunic stared at the private, keeping his fists perfectly aligned, not letting his wrists press together completely; they were still sore from the last time, and the private finished without noticing.

"Shut up," the officer said to Wunic when the private had returned to the line of soldiers.

Wunic said, "Denon—"

"I don't give a damn who you want to see." And he punched Wunic hard in the stomach—Wunic doubled over, catching his breath, keeping his balance. "You don't give orders, got that?"

Wunic straightened, breathing painfully, and the officer hit him again. This time Wunic fell, and the officer kicked Wunic in the gut with the point of his boot. Jak watched from the edge of the circle of royals. Wunic tossed, bleeding, but he made no sound. Now more soldiers began to help, kicking Wunic hard, not letting him get up. Jak shuddered and looked away, her hair wet with falling snow. Ruined walls and piles of dead, and Jak thought, *I'm no different than them. I'm the reason he limps.*

Blakes sat inside his new house, on the side of a wooden cot, softened by several inches of tree fur. The temporary house was just one room that rattled and shook with each gust of wind. The house was made of strips of wood they had carried from the southern forest and erected on a cleared spread of grassland along the river. Hope was seven days old now: each day just under twenty-five hours, *almost* exactly *identical to Earth,* Blakes thought. And the years are even about the same. Three hundred and fifty-nine days or so, the *Australia's* computer had told them, before they had landed.

Now about half of the crew had a place to stay: long barracks that they just shared until better, sturdier buildings could be built. *But we need something,* Blakes thought. And they had discovered that underground, attached to every blade of the high grass, grew small, green fruit. Like a bland version of cantaloupe with a bitter aftertaste. They had settled a mile and a half—perhaps two miles—from the ruins, following the river north until Blakes decided on a spot. One day to clear the grasses, and another six to transport logs and begin building houses and basic lodgings.

Donna stepped in through the fabric Blakes had hung over the open doorway of his house. She smiled and brushed the dirt off her pants, opened her mouth, and Blakes said, "Where have you been?"

"Collecting fruits," she said, frowning and unbuttoning her coat. Blakes watched her, deep lines under both of his reddened eyes. There had been no sign of the thirteen or of the demons since they had landed.

"Don't lie to me," he said.

"Blakes, I was collecting—"

"I said don't lie to me." He folded his hands on top of a notebook in his lap. "You were with that kid, Charles." Donna shook her head, laughing, and Blakes said, "*Be quiet.*"

She stared at him, panic in her eyes, and she set her coat on the ground. "Blakes—"

"Now tell me," he said, "where you were."

Donna fell on her knees in front of him, taking his hands. He kept his fists tight.

"I swear," she said, "I wasn't—"

"I'll let it go," he said softly. "But only this time. Again, and both of you die, understand? We can't allow divisions."

"I didn't—"

"*I said* I would let it go."

Donna nodded, bowing her head. "Yes, Blakes."

"Good," he said, and patted her head. "Now go to sleep." And he got up without turning around and left the room. Blakes walked across the empty yard to one of the long, crude barracks, passing a guard—Fred?—at the perimeter with a rifle pointed at the high grasses that surrounded them. Blakes knocked on the barracks door, and said, "Michael?"

A moment later the door opened, and Michael stepped out, his hair dishevelled. "Sir?"

"Come with me," Blakes said.

"My rifle, sir, I—"

"Yes, go get it," Blakes said, and Michael ran back inside, past rows of identical cots, all lined with tree fur. He returned with his black coat—swastika armband—and rifle.

Blakes started walking, Michael hurrying into step beside him.

"One week."

"Sir?"

"Hope is one week old."

"Yes, sir."

"And they still hold our hostages. That's unacceptable."

"Yes, sir."

Blakes paused at the edge of the clearing of Hope, dark grasses shaking in the cool night air, several paces away.

"Damn them," Blakes said, and then he nodded, tapping his rifle and pistol. "We will bring them vengeance." Blakes started walking into the grasses.

"Sir, shouldn't we wake the others—"

"No," Blakes said, and he stomped through the blinding stalks. "You and I are perfectly capable of this, Michael. I have faith in you."

"Sir, the demons—"

"The demons will be smashed in the light of God's righteous glory."

"Yes, sir," Michael said, hurrying after him. "But shouldn't we—"

"No. Now, don't ask again."

They walked in silence for a time, the grass tugging at their coats, slicing at Blakes's hair and cheek.

"Ships do not disappear or cease to exist," Blakes said.

"Yes, sir."

"Do you know what I think?"

"No, sir."

"I think Donna has been with that boy Charles."

"Charles is married to Julie, sir."

Blakes began to jog, tearing more quickly through the field. "Tell me things I already know. Of course he is, Michael. Marriages do not concern me. There is a smile of deceit."

"Why do you suspect her, sir?"

"I can see into her mind, Michael. I see it all as plainly as if I was there as a witness. Just as I understand your loyalty, I understand her infidelity. You understand?"

"Yes, sir."

"Good," Blakes said, and they went the rest of the trip without talking, until finally, the grasses ended at the huge blocks of ruins. "Now. It is here." Blakes approached one of the smaller, square structures that lay nearby—probably a piece of a larger building that had fallen away. "You see? I understand *these.*" He ran his fingers across a wall of worn, spiral Frill writings. "They are in league with Satan's dark purpose, Michael."

"Yes, sir."

"I understand it now." Blakes began to climb, his boot slipping in and out of irregularities in the stone. "When we first explored, I climbed up here." And suddenly Blakes was on the top, smiling down at Michael with red cheeks, Hera's moon a bright crescent overhead. "Come on."

Fifteen minutes later, Michael reached the top as well, rolling panting onto the flat roof, full of untouched writing. At the far side, a blue circle had been inscribed among the words.

"You see?" Blakes said, excitedly, and he fell to a crouch, running his fingers along the surface, crawling quickly to the opposite end. "*Here* it speaks of their covenant. I hear it, as if I were spying on their wicked councils, Michael. Listen: 'Tho divided by the cross and nails and thorns and spear, in cruelties of Rahab and Tirzah, permanent endure . . .' "

Michael walked after him slowly, rubbing his eyes. "Yes, sir. You're reading that?"

Blakes didn't hear him, nearing the circle as he continued to wave his palm across the curled carvings. " 'Thus was the Covering Cherub revealed, majestic image of selfhood, body put off, the Antichrist accursed, covered with precious stones, a human dragon terrible and bright stretched over Europe and Asia gorgeous.' " Blakes kneeled on the blue circle, and he glanced up at Michael, as if to be certain that Michael was following all of this. "You see?"

"Yes, sir," Michael said, but he obviously did not see, and Blakes smiled.

"You will, I think," Blakes said, and he began to crawl off of the opposite end of the circle carving, toward the edge of the roof. " 'In three nights he devoured the rejected corpse of death—' " And Blakes was gone. Michael ran after him, stepped onto the circle, calling out for him, and then Michael backed away, off of the circle, and he was suddenly in a round, domed cavern, filled with sickly, blue light.

Blakes was standing at one of the round walls—a doorway on the wall near him—and more of the spiral writing was on every wall.

"The demons wrote this," Blakes said, without turning.

"Where are we, sir?"

"We are in the first pouch of the Malbolgia."

"Sir?"

"We are in hell, Michael." Blakes drew a cutting knife, and he began to write on the walls, carving over the intricate circle-writing. Michael approached behind him, and Blakes finished, grabbing Michael by the shoulder and leading him toward the doorway. The blue light followed them.

Blakes smiled and said, "Ready your sword."

"Sir, have you been here before? Do you know—"

"No," Blakes said. "Only in my mind. This place is evil," Blakes said, walking ahead of Michael into a quiet, rounded corridor of blue-black stone, the light following them. "You see this? Our souls cast light in the Devil's dream."

"Yes sir, I see. We need to call for more of our crew."

"Why?" Blakes said, and he paused, glaring back at the darkened room behind them.

"There was another blue circle in that room, sir. Must be a link between it and the one on the roof that you disc—"

"You want to go back?" Blakes said, and he shook his head sadly. "You cannot go back, Michael. God's vengeance comes with us. We are only his messengers; we are nothing in this, you see? I will bring the demons' blood to the soil of Hope." Blakes drew his knife again, and he drew a swastika on the wall, scraping away the old, illegible writing that was already there. "*Our* will. *Our* justice, Michael. Not theirs. This world belongs to us, and I will drink their blood."

Michael's eyes hardened, and his hands tightened on the handle of his rifle. "Yes, sir."

Blakes nodded, smiling. "For when our souls have learned the heat to bear, the cloud will vanish; we shall hear his voice, saying: 'Come out from the grove my love and care, and round my golden tent like lambs rejoice'." Blakes started walking again, his rifle perfectly steady. "The *Australia* is here."

The hall turned, splitting into a four-way intersection, and Blakes continued down the center corridor, the light following him—red slits in the darkness ahead—and now only blackness. Blakes paused. "We have come for your damnation, weak monsters."

Michael's breathing was loud in Blakes's ear, and he stepped closer, spotting one of the demons at the edge of his circle of blue light. It stood there, holding a wicked spear, its thin body entirely quiet, its face and chest mechanical, Blakes thought.

"*You are sin*!" Blakes shouted, and he walked closer to the demon. "This is our time, our place—not yours!" He pointed his rifle at the demon's head. "Back!" The rifle snapped, and the demon stood to the side of the hall, untouched. "*Back*!" Blakes fired again, and the demon flicked away, remaining the same distance away, and now Blakes was ten feet away.

Behind him, Michael said, "Sir, please—"

Blakes screamed, "*Dues, cui proprium est misereri semper, et par-*

cere, suscipe deprecationem nostram, ut hunc famulum tuum, vel famulam tuam, quem, vel quam delictorum catena constringit, miseratio tuae pietatis clementer adsolvat! I am your God and you *will* obey!"

Blakes stopped an arm's length from the demon, and he spat onto its metal face, the demon entirely still, glaring with black openings where its eyes should have been.

"*Obey!*" Blakes said, and he pressed the barrel of his rifle into the demon's soft, black stomach. "I *am* your God!"

The demon flicked away, and Blakes said, "*Domine sancte, Pater omnipotens, aeterne Deus, Pater Domini nostri Jesu Chrsti, qui illum refugam tiranum, et apostatam gehennae ignibus deputasti!* The Church of Hope, of God's glory on Hera and His power over the wicked and the damned begins now, with me." Blakes stepped close to the demon again, and this time he forced his rifle to the plate of metal that was its face. "God's vision on Earth is brought here. It could not thrive in America or Europe or Asia, but it will flourish here, do you hear me, scum? I . . . am . . . God."

The demon lowered its head and set its spear at Blakes's feet. A mass of identical demons appeared from the blackness of the tunnel, and in one motion they stopped behind the first, and they dropped their weapons.

"I am the minister of God's justice," Blakes said, and he picked up the closest spear, and then motioned for one of the demons to step forward. It remained where it was. "Now." Still, it did not move, and Blakes walked to the line of demons, and handed the spear to it, grabbing the demon by its strong, wiry shoulder and urging it forward. The demon obeyed, flicking to Blakes's side, and Blakes motioned to the demon that had first approached him, showing the demon with the spear that it should sever the first demon's head.

"We must have blood in birth. Kill him."

Michael waited behind Blakes, his rifle poised, aimed at the mass of devils in the hallway ahead.

"Christ did not die for mercy, he died in the name of God's justice, that would show the glory of death—*kill him.*" Blakes demonstrated again, using one of the discarded spears, and acting in slow motion the slice that would sever the first demon's head. "Now."

Blur, and the first demon still stood, red blood gurgling from its open, black throat—no head—the mass of pipes hissing and spouting white air and yellow and black fluid—its head rolling to the wall—and the spear-demon stood beside Blakes. The headless demon quivered and fell. Blakes nodded to them, and then he knelt in the hall and dipped his hands into the puddle of blood flowing from the demon's neck, wiping it into his skin.

Blakes stood again, and now he raised his rifle over his head with one hand and the spear-demon dropped his weapon.

"Where is my ship?" Blakes asked. No response from them, and Blakes stepped through the crowd, Michael followed a few paces behind him, and the demons parted. *"Where?"*

"My God . . ." Michael said. "How did you—"

Blakes glared at him briefly, and said, "It's down here, isn't it? You brought it underground somehow, to your pit." He continued on, the ranks of demons continuing, all with their spears at their feet, all staring coldly as Blakes passed them.

At the end of the hall, they found part of the *Australia*, one of the control decks, wedged into the rock, with a tunnel leading perfectly to its entrance.

The demons showed Blakes their machines, large knights with beaks, who squeaked and walked heavily through the tunnels, molding the walls with their rounded hands. *Dissolving the bonds between elements,* Blakes thought, as he watched the demon-machines change the shape of the corridor, and as the corridor leading to the *Australia* receded, forms appeared—human bodies built into the rock, like statues—and Blakes shouted for them to stop, leaving the people partially buried.

My crew, he thought, *become trees in the path of suicides.* Michael paced in the hall, demons lingering—weaponless—just beyond their blue glow, and the demon-machine stood by, huge and shiny, its arms waiting for a command. *There's power in the* Australia, Blakes thought, *which means that the cells are still intact—even if they break apart, they can still transmit.*

Blakes left the *Australia* buried under the ruins, and over the next few days, his crew collected all of the supplies from the ship—Blakes ordering the demon-machines to arrange the compartments of the ship so that they were all accessible through the same entrance with different codes. It took hours of commands and another demon was killed before they had it the way he wanted it. Demon-machines waiting inside the rock, just waiting for a code to be entered, and then they would shift the atomic structure of the underground, pulling up whatever part of the *Australia* was desired from where it was lodged deep underground and connecting it with the entrance.

In the months that followed, Blakes used the demon-machines to separate huge chunks of stone from the ruins, shape them into buildings—a palace, a church, and large piles for whatever else was needed later—all arranged in the new city of Hope. The demons' tunnels and corridors ran for miles underground, some beneath the very city of Hope. Blakes arranged for several of the demons' rooms beneath the palace and the church to be used for basements of the buildings, cut off from the rest of the demon-tunnels, but bound to one another with blue transporters. Old tunnels from the city to the ruins let him travel back and forth without moving through the grassfields. On the one month anniversary of their landing, Blakes carved a plaque from a piece of metal taken from the *Australia*'s hull with something he remembered Shakespeare saying and mounted it in the first street of Hope, where his first one-room house had been built:

HOPE—FOUNDED 2402
WHEN I HAVE SEEN BY TIME'S FELL HAND DEFACED
THE RICH PROUD COST OF OUTWORN BURIED AGE.

They built elaborate buildings from the wood of the southern forest, and Blakes executed more of the demons—they let themselves die at the hands of other demons—and after three months, the demons would not come when Blakes called for them, their machines were gone, and Hope was suddenly alone. A group was sent to the ruins, but they did not return. Blakes had begun to quietly grow clones of several of the crew, including himself, and he ruled as dictator from his stone palace.

Blakes wrote a law that was signed by all of the crew still living: two hundred and five people, and they agreed to his judgment, his laws, his rule. Every woman was ordered to bear as many children as possible, on pain of death to the wife and husband. The extra problem; the murderous frill at the edge of their settlement—the demons—would be destroyed: They would destroy the demons completely for their sudden betrayal of the Church of Hope. The tunnels would be flooded with napalm, and the planet would be cleansed.

Three days later, Blakes had recovered the ship's computer from the tunnels and transferred it to the black box he had brought, where the computer was automatically treated with nutrients and vaccinated. Theoretically, the pulsing pink blob, lined with blue veins, like some independent kidney or spleen—the ship's genetically engineered computer—would never die if properly cared for. When Blakes returned to Hope with the box, he ordered a population tally: one hundred and thirty-seven people left, only forty-eight women known to be pregnant.

The demons—the Frill, as people had begun to call them after Blakes's speech—remained under the ruins, and Blakes ordered a wall built around the city, to keep them out. Also, to keep everyone in. Census was taken every two days, and deserters were hunted down, tortured publicly and hung. But not all of them were found. One week later, there were one hundred and twenty people in the city. *We will not be cast out,* Blakes thought one night, Donna sleeping beside him in the enormous, empty palace. *The serpent will tempt, his red tongue licking the blood of the poison I am meant to eat—but I will not leave.* Blakes thought about the demons, the Frill, sitting under their ruins, waiting for people to trespass, and he wrote.

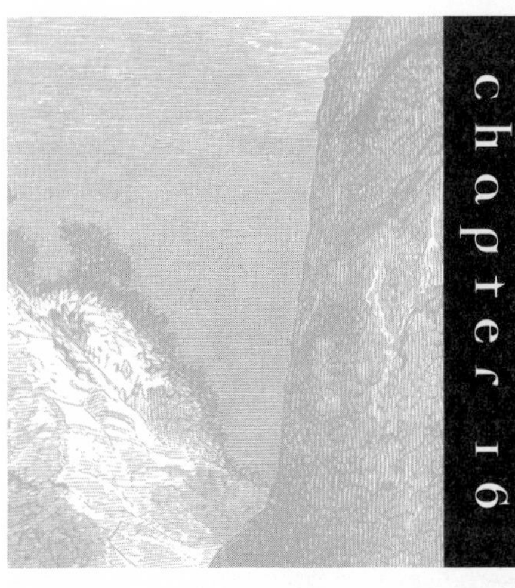

chapter 16

Vel tensed, the Frill standing over him. *Die,* he thought, *I'm going to die.*

"Stop . . ."

End and beginning are the same.

A piece of the wall dilated open, and Vel tried to focus, his vision blurring when he moved—more Frill in the new corridor—flicking into the room. Chaos-movement, spear thrusts and counters all too fast, Vel's mind struggled to sort out what was happening, and Frill bodies fell, piled, spears clattered; the new Frill were fighting with the ones already inside the room. *Fighting,* Vel thought too slowly—and the Frill swung at his head.

Vel was standing out of the spear's reach. *I moved,* he thought, staring at the Frill that had attacked him. *The thrust had been slow—no, fast—just looked slow because I was jumping out of the way.* I *was moving that quickly too,* Vel thought, and a part of him said that it was impossible, that he couldn't move that quickly, that no one could, and the Frill were all perfectly still, watching him with black slits.

The other Frill—Ulyu's Frill—attacking, Vel thought, his irregular breathing seeming to echo in the stone room, *trying to save me, to stop them from killing me.*

Yes, Ulyu said.

Vel's severed arm lifted from the ground, and he remained perfectly still, surrealistic adrenaline shaking him, as the arm aligned itself where it belonged—Vel felt it touch, and then suddenly his left arm began to tingle. The shoulder of his coat and shirt were ripped cleanly where the arm had broken away, but the skin was sealed again, as if it had never been cut, and Vel squeezed his restored arm, watching color return to the skin, wincing as sensation returned.

Another one of their machines, Vel thought. *One of the suits of armor, the diggers, that belongs to Ulyu's Frill must have done—*

Yes, Ulyu said again.

Vel glanced at him, all of the Frill waiting.

"What do I . . . ?"

You are one of us. Now you will fulfill your obligation, your place.

"How?"

The Frill that had attacked Vel stepped closer—and now Vel could follow the movement, his mind somehow sorting out the fast steps, making it coherent, so that the Frill was no longer flicking from place to place, but walking quickly.

You are not what they say, the Frill said, its spear lowered, ready to attack.

Vel thought, *Why is this—*

You are our savior, Ulyu said. *You are the meeting of shadow and sky.*

No, the approaching Frill said, and it lunged, twisting its blade for Vel's stomach—he slid away—the spear grazing him, cutting a perfect line of blood across Vel's navel. Vel stumbled away, toward the dead armor. The Frill parted around him, and Vel pulled his spear cleanly from the armor's head.

You belong to us, boy, the spear Frill said, circling Vel, and now the other Frill had formed a loose circle around them, the armor's body in the center.

All of them are watching, Vel thought, and he spun, trying to find Ulyu in the crowd of identical masks. *Ulyu's Frill and the others who wanted me dead—why don't they help me?*

You are already dead, the attacking Frill said, and it slashed again, and again Vel tried to dodge—it cut his new left arm lightly, sparks of hot pain in the wound. *But at least I feel,* Vel thought.

He said, "I don't want to be your savior—I want food. Didn't come here to—"

The Frill hit him again, deeper this time, in the leg, and Vel stumbled and almost fell. He had tried to block with his spear, too slowly.

"Stop it," Vel shouted, and the Frill cut his leg again, blood soaking into his torn pants.

Kill him, boy, Ulyu said.

The Frill circled, and now Vel was moving too, frustration pulling his muscles taut. He levelled his spear.

"That's not my name," Vel said quietly, and he charged the Frill, swinging for the mass of pipes at its throat—the Frill sidestepped and slashed Vel across the back, and again, in the back of his leg, and Vel spun—screaming—as he swung again, and this time the

Frill blocked. The spears clanged together, and Vel pushed the Frill off-balance and swung again—again the weapons connected, and again, and now Vel pulled back, and as the Frill prepared to circle, Vel hit it again—fake left, and he stabbed it in the stomach.

Dark red blood pumping out of the wound, and the Frill began to pulse rhythmically, shaking as it tried to circle Vel again. Vel attacked, spears hitting, again—locked together—and Vel kicked the Frill in its open stomach, and the Frill's spear slipped, and Vel cut open its tubes. The Frill made a wet, sucking sound as yellow and black liquids sprayed and hissed from the open pipes, and then Vel struck again, through the severed pipes, into flesh, chopping its head off.

The body quivered and went down, bleeding. Vel tried to wipe the filth from his face and hands—he was trembling with adrenaline—and all of the Frill had fallen to their knees, weapons on the ground.

Vel started to say something, and then Ulyu said,

> Words of the murderer, his words—but it is our
> prophecy:
> Born of Shadow and Sky.
> Without understanding, all is lost.
> Heat binds wounds that separate,
> And snow feels like cold ash.

WUNIC'S FACE WAS swollen, and he rolled his head to one side, licking at his cut lip. He sat in a chair between two of the Religious Guard in a small stone room under the palace, a candle glowing a faint blue from the dirty floor. Two more Religious Guard came into the room—all four were armed with rifles—and then Lord Denon stepped in behind them. Denon wore a white robe and an elaborate green vestment with intricate swastikas embroidered into it.

"Lord Denon," Wunic said, and he swallowed blood, his gums pulsing where the soldiers had kicked out his teeth. "What do you want?"

Denon stepped closer casually. "Hello, General Wunic. How do you feel?"

In Wunic's mind, he broke free, knocked the Religious Guard against the wall, a rifle in his hand, and Wunic pinned Denon's head to the wall, the rifle barrel inside Denon's mouth. "Know that you are about to die." And Wunic emptied the rifle in a bloody spray.

Wunic was bound, bleeding, and he thought about who he was and wondered why Denon would have wanted to see him personally before the execution.

"I'm fine," Wunic said.

Denon said, "You've been injured."

"No. I'm fine."

Once Wunic had crushed the Religious Guard, he might shoot off Denon's fingers and force them down his throat, watch him choke on them—"No, General, please"—and then Wunic would laugh and start on his torso. His rifle would be too quick. *I am General Wunic, I am supreme military commander of the police force of Hope and you do not push me.*

"I wasn't certain I would see you again, General," Denon said.

"Why?" When Denon didn't answer, Wunic frowned. "Does that make you feel better? I still don't know why, why all of this? I wouldn't have lost the war." *This was my war, not yours.* "Why did you issue those orders?"

"What orders?"

"You issued a dispatch, ordering an attack," Wunic said. "I'm not saying it wasn't well-planned. If I came back it would be as a traitor, if I died then that wouldn't be an issue." Denon's eyes hardened slightly, but he remained quiet, and Wunic continued, "Some people think evil doesn't have motivations, but I don't believe that. Is it power or something that infantile? Did I do something to slight you? This is all I don't understand: why?"

Denon said quietly, "You *did* defect, General."

Wunic stopped smiling. *Why am I alive?* he thought. *Some perverse kind of guilt? Are you sorry, would you like me to confess and humiliate myself, would that make you feel better? Did you have some last pronouncement? Do you want forgiveness?*

Wunic had been brought to the palace with the other survivors, herded into cells with the rest of them, told that his sentence was execution without trial. *And now I'm here,* Wunic thought. *I was ordered to come here, so that Denon can have the last word. Somehow I expected this, somehow this seems natural.*

"The council doesn't exist anymore, does it?" Wunic asked.

"General, this is a time of crisis."

"Where's the king?"

Denon paused, as if he expected Wunic to already know that. "Dead. The king was assassinated by a company of your rebels."

Wunic felt empty. He had expected this too. Denon was all that remained of the government, and no one would oppose the Church—at least not right away. *There's no one to act, no one to stop you now, is there, Lord Denon? And I let it happen; I didn't see it until it was too late.*

"What do you want?" Wunic said.

"What do you mean?"

"Why am I here?"

Denon nodded. "Of course. I want to offer you a chance at saving your immortal soul, General. Your past service has earned you this chance; you *did* serve the city once. Confess treason, and you will be welcomed into God's kingdom when you die."

Wunic smiled, and one of the Religious Guard hit him hard. *This is not my time,* Wunic thought, still smiling.

"My soul has nothing to do with this," he said. "Let's cut out the bullshit, all right?"

One of the Religious Guard pointed his rifle at Wunic's head. "Blasphemy, traitor."

"Don't threaten me anymore," Wunic said, staring at Lord Denon. "I won't go quietly. You know I won't, so what is this really about?"

"Will you confess?"

Someone knocked on the door behind Denon, and two more prisoners were brought in: General Rein and the younger officer, Major Selan. Denon motioned that they should kneel in front of Wunic, and the Religious Guard forced them both down. *So they interrogate us as a group,* Wunic thought. *This still doesn't explain why I'm not dead.*

"Lord Denon," Selan said, bowing slightly.

Denon nodded, and Rein glanced back at Wunic. One of Rein's eyes was swollen completely shut, and the entire left side of his face was a puffy, discolored mess.

"To the side," Denon said to Selan, and Selan stood, moving to the right wall.

Rein glared at Selan. *So there's the traitor among traitors,* Wunic thought. *Selan had helped to engineer that "refugee" attack. He must have started firing the artillery as soon as Rein left it, and now Rein and I*—Denon pointed at General Rein.

"You've confessed your heresy," Denon said. "An act against the government is an act against God. We live under divine law, inseparable from the teachings of our founder and prophet, Blakes. His law is God's law is our law. You admit that you betrayed God in your rebellion of the state?"

Rein stared numbly up at Denon. "I admit that I rebelled against this government's *justice*."

"You will be welcomed into the kingdom of Heaven for your confession," Denon said.

One of the Religious Guard pointed his rifle to the back of Rein's head.

Rein said, "I admit that we needed food, that—"

Crack of gunfire, and Rein fell forward, his blood across Wunic's legs and pants, splattered across the floor. Denon bowed his head, and Selan was staring at Wunic uncomfortably from the adjacent wall.

"Now," Denon said, and he motioned to Selan. "Please fall to your knees, my son."

Selan crouched uncomfortably, watching Rein's body. *What did they give you?* Wunic wondered. *What did Lord Denon promise you? Were you ever really a rebel?*

"You will be accepted into God's order," Denon said. "Please bow your head and close your eyes."

You wanted to be part of the Religious Guard, Wunic thought, and Denon nodded to another of the soldier-priests, who stepped silently behind Selan, rifle down, almost touching the back of Selan's neck.

"Thank you, Lord Denon," Selan said. "I will uphold God's law in my life."

"Yes, you will," Denon said. "You will carry His sword, and God's enemies shall be your enemies." Wunic wanted to look away, but he found himself staring—Denon motioned to the priest and said, "Welcome to God's order." The rifle fired, and Wunic jumped at the noise, closing his eyes. He could smell burning hair, more blood on his boots.

Denon put his hand on Wunic's shoulder. "You should know, General, that I am granting you this special privilege because of who you used to be. You will be processed with the rest of your rebels, but should you want the Lord's absolution, it will be given to you. The Lord forgives, and you can still escape damnation."

"It's too late," Wunic said softly, and they lifted him out of his chair.

"I'm sorry," Denon said.

So am I, Wunic thought. They dragged him away. *I'm sorry that you made this mistake, I'm sorry for your sake, Lord Denon, that I'm still alive. You won't live to see this end. I'm sorry all of these young people had to die, and that I don't care about consequences anymore. If there is still such a thing as honor—and there is—I'm going to kill you. I'm sorry I can't do it now.*

IN A deeper cell, alone in a blackness that consumed the shapes of her own body, Sisha was dreaming. Bright light. Sisha saw herself dancing in a field that was green, not cold and snowy. *It was green!* The women from the streets who had taught Sisha to dance stood all around her, watching Sisha spin in the green field, the tiny grass kissing her bare feet.

"Sisha," one said of the women said, "we believe you'll see this someday."

She stopped dancing, and a cool breeze ruffled her hair, stroked her neck. She wanted to make love. Not fuck, make love.

"Children," Sisha said, "I want to have children. I want to grow with them inside me, and I want to feel them living, I want to love them."

The women nodded patiently. "Yes," one said, "and we believe that will happen too."

"You love the boy," said another. "Though you barely know him, you want to take his pain away."

"Yes," Sisha said.

"If you live, you must save him."

"Save him?" Sisha said.

"Yes. His journey will not be easy."

Ripples passed through the grass, and she took a deep breath that seemed to open her skin, making each breath a pleasure.

"I love Vel," Sisha said.

"Good," they said. "If you love him, you will be the one to keep him from death. He is very strong, but he cannot survive alone. You know that."

"Yes," she said, "I do."

"Thank you, Sisha," the women said, and they began to leave. "We'll count on you. The boy needs you. And so do we."

The green faded. The colors darkened into black.

"Thank you," Sisha said, rolling on the cold stone. She was back in the cell, and the door clicked, creaking as it opened. Sisha stared at the gray light that spread around the outline of a soldier in the doorway.

"You are number two-forty-three," he said.

She did not move. "What?"

"Two-forty-three," he said. "Your execution number. Numbers seventy through eighty are being taken now. You'll be sent for when it is your time."

"Oh," Sisha said softly, and the door closed again, clicking loudly as the lock shut. Her body began to shake, and she knew that she was about to cry. The dream was still so fresh, the darkness complete. Sisha rolled onto her side, the tears suddenly forgotten. And she slept.

vel said, "We need food. In the city, we're almost out of food."

The Frill remained on their "knees"—triple-jointed legs, so they weren't technically knees—and Vel slid his spear back into his belt. The Frill blood under his fingernails would not come out, and he said, "Did you hear me?"

Yes, Ulyu said.

"Where are you, Ulyu?"

One of the Frill in the first row around Vel stood, thin arms at its sides.

"What's happening?" Vel asked.

You have fulfilled your place. We are yours to command.

"What, because I killed him?"

Yes. And both Frill have seen it—you are *our savior. You are Frill, but not Frill.*

"Tell them to get up," Vel said.

Why don't you tell them?

Vel swallowed and rubbed at the cuts in his leg. "All right—get up. All of you, come on, stop that."

As one, the Frill rose, their spears still on the ground.

"I want food taken to Hope."

They have already begun to do as you ask.

"They're already getting the food?"

Yes.

"They look like they're still just standing here listening to me."

There are thousands more Frill who hear you.

"What about the cure for the Pox? The plants that bleed medicine? Do you have those?"

We grow them. They cleanse all disease, my Lord.

"I'm not your lord."

Yes, you are. You were created to be. We made you this way, to end our suffering.

"You didn't want to wait for a savior to come, so you *made* one?" Vel asked. "That's what you were talking about before, wasn't it? You used some of—whatever the founders had—and you mixed a human with a Frill. And Hillor was the one who let you do it, because he thought he could control me, to control you. He wanted to keep you from attacking the city."

Yes, and the Age of Darkness is ended.

"What do you mean?"

You will bring the gods back to us.

Vel thought about the bone.

Yes, Ulyu said. *That is further confirmation—you could not have communed except through the work of the divine. Every Frill belongs to you now.*

"The Nerago, the gods, made you—they made the Frill somehow—and you think I'm one of them?"

No, Ulyu said. *You are not one of the old gods. We created you ourselves to bind the shadow and sky. Yes, we were created in their shadow, but they were forced to leave. Our prophecies say that in the time of the next winter, shadow and sky shall meet and then we will be brought back to the gods.*

"So you knew the seasons were going to change? You *knew* winter was coming when it wasn't supposed to?"

Yes.

"Goddamn it," Vel said. "Why the hell didn't you tell any of the people that?"

We do not speak directly with anyone but our own.

"What? You mean you can talk to me because I'm half-Frill, but you can't talk to anyone else?"

Yes.

"Then how did you make a deal at all?"

There are other ways to communicate.

"Yes, and I suppose you understand enish. You just won't speak it."

My Lord, we—

"Stop calling me that," Vel said, and he sat on the side of the table. "It doesn't matter. I have to go back." He pointed at the bones along the floor. "What is this room?"

Many people have died in this room, sacrificed.

I'm going to unite you with the gods, Vel thought.

Ulyu said, *Yes.*

And who wrote these prophecies?

The gods.

I knew you were going to say that. So they must be right, huh?

They have never been wrong.

It doesn't hurt to actively help them come true, though, does it? Vel thought. You *made* someone to fulfill the gods' prophecies, you didn't just wait for it to happen.

The prophecy is fulfilled.

I see, Vel thought, but he wasn't sure that he did. I have to take food and the plant-cures back to Hope. There's a war going on there, and I was supposed to get dispatches here. God knows how they would have gotten to me without you killing the messenger.

We did intercept two humans carrying messages.

Terrific. I suppose you killed them?

Yes.

Why don't you let people move freely through your tunnels?

We remember.

What? Remember what?

Would you like the messages?

Sure, Vel thought. Why not? Vel motioned to the Frill standing motionless in the room.

"Don't they have something else they could be doing right now?" Vel asked.

Ulyu said, *They are yours. As I am.*

"Tell them to—" Vel paused. "Never mind, I'll tell them myself. . . ." And he sat up, waving one arm at the Frill. "Go. Disperse, wait for orders someplace else."

The Frill filed silently out of the room through the two tunnels.

"They'll hear me other places?" Vel asked.

Yes, Ulyu said, and they were alone with the body of the headless

Frill and the dead armor and the piles of bones. *Your thoughts are heard by Frill everywhere. And you will be obeyed—from this time on, you are our leader. You will unite us with the gods.*

Great, Vel thought. Just what I want: Frill listening to my daydreams.

Even gods doubt, Ulyu said. *We know that.*

"Glad you know that," Vel said, and he shifted uncomfortably on the table. He nodded to the dead armor. "What is that thing?"

A tool of the gods. They left us their blessings, to tend their city, to watch over it.

"Been a little busy, haven't you?"

War between the two factions. War for centuries, and then humans came and we thought at first that they had been sent by the gods, to bring us together again. To bring them back.

And they didn't.

No.

How many Frill are there?

Thousands. Every time a Frill dies, another takes his place.

"You can have baby Frill?" Vel asked.

We are born inside the wombs of the gods' walls, just as you grew in a human birthing chamber.

The gods left you in charge of their city?

Yes.

And they wrote you prophecies, but when they were gone and they didn't immediately come back, the Frill split into two groups. One bad, one good.

Not bad or good. Some Frill believed—

I know, Vel thought. Some hated the gods for leaving and decided that they were damned, and the rest wanted to wait it out.

It is more complicated than that.

But that's it basically, isn't it?

Yes.

Another Frill brought two dispatches and left.

> *This letter is to inform the king that the rebels have been repelled from the immediate vicinity of the palace and some have been captured. They still hold areas all around my location, and our safety is at great risk. Stay away from the palace; the area is not secure, and although the artillery is on-*

line, it has done little or nothing to break the rebels' ranks. Remain where you are, and I will keep you informed as to the situation.
LORD DENON

Vel set the paper aside, and he looked at the second one.

This was later, Ulyu said. *This dispatch was received several hours ago.*

This letter is to inform the king that the rebels are still inflicting heavy casualties and have captured the majority of our artillery positions. We have held the palace, but more forces are defecting, and I fear that the rebels may again threaten us with an actual siege. We have taken a sizeable number of prisoners in the recent offensives and counteroffensives, and among them is General Wunic. He has offered a truce in exchange for his own life and dictatorial control of the government. The offer would appoint me his personal advisor, and also outlined plans for your capture and execution. Naturally I have refused it, placing Wunic in class five status in our prisons. His execution will be forthcoming.

Your Majesty, I have done everything in my power to keep your throne from being lost. It has been brought to my attention that Orik, the vocal minority leader on the Executive Council, was recently killed at Wunic's hand. I believe that the rebels are moving into position for another attack on your palace. For that reason, I ask that you remain in the ruins. The city is not safe, and there is still no guarantee that we will win this war. I will continue to do what I can, and I advise you to do the same. Stay away for now, Your Highness, as the opposition still remains strong.
LORD DENON

Vel stood, putting the papers into his pockets. "Where are my weapons?"

Your human weapons?

"That's right."

They are intact.

"I'm going back," Vel said, "and you're coming with me."

Ulyu hesitated, and then said, *My Lord—*

"Vel."

Vel, returning may be very dangerous.

"Really?" Vel said, and he sighed in sarcastic amazement. "How do you know, Ulyu—what makes you say that?"

Our prophecies are somewhat ambiguous, but there are some who believe that the savior may be killed . . . in a situation very much like what you are now planning to do.

"What? You have a prophecy that says not to go back to Hope during a civil war?"

They might be interpreted in that way, yes.

"What do they actually say?"

It would take more than eighty years for you hear them all only once.

"What about the ones specifically relating to me returning to Hope?"

They can be retrieved, if you command it.

"You don't just *know* what they say?"

No.

"Ulyu," Vel said, smiling, and he patted the Frill on the shoulder, "I expected more."

I am sorry. I did not—

"And that's why you're coming with me." Vel started walking again, the blue light following him, and now Ulyu was a step behind him. Vel's boots crunched bone, and Ulyu glided after him, its body either too light or too fast to make sound. "If I needed them, how long would it take the Frill to come to Hope through the tunnels?"

Not long.

"How long is not long? Or should I even ask?"

You probably should not.

"So, they'd be there if I needed them?"

Yes. Why are we returning to your city?

Vel thought about it. "One, they need food; two, they need a cure for the Pox; three," another Frill was waiting in the hall ahead with Vel's pistol and sword, "I've got a war to win."

chapter 17

Blakes stumbled through the tunnel, his old hands sliding along the walls, rasping along the Frill writing. He paused, and sat in the dim blueness with his back to the wall, closed his eyes and said, "My spectre around me night and day, like a wild beast guards my way. My emanation far within, weeps incessantly for my sin."

Blakes shook his head and pressed one fist to his forehead, and he said, "Never ever . . . no, no . . ." He wrapped his fingers around the rifle on his chest. "Never, never I return, Still for . . . victory I burn. Living thee alone I'll have, and when dead I'll be thy grave."

Sixty-seven years old now, today was to be the day they returned to Earth for vengeance. Ship's computer had located a power supply, radioactive, deep underground, and now it was being drilled, automatically sent up to the disjointed sections of the *Australia*, where it slowly incorporated itself into the ship's drive. Theoretically, it had all been worked out: still possible to blast out from underground, still possible for the *Australia* to be re-assembled once it hit the surface, not hard really. The computer, which Blakes now carried in a black pouch, in a black box, could do all of the calculations, could arrange everything itself.

Blakes sat in the tunnels just outside Hope, but not yet far enough away to be in the ruins, and he tried to remember another line from the poem—what was the *name*? *No Goddamned name*, he thought, *what was it*? Right now, a group of seven to ten, most first generation Herans, would be reaching the *Australia*, they would be preparing to launch. Except that the ship's living computer was now in Blakes's box, and even if the computer did manage to link into the systems onboard the *Australia*—which it could do through wave emissions—there would not be enough fuel stored yet to shoot the *Australia* out of the ground, let alone reassemble her and return her to Earth.

The name's gone, Blakes decided at last. *I can't remember the Goddamn name, and that's that.* He stood, pausing to let the joints in his legs adjust to the pressure, so that they wouldn't ache like they did in the wintertime. Hera's weather was worse than Earth's had been, after the global average temperature had increased by more than ten degrees in the twenty-first century. Twenty years of seasonal weather that seemed to flow annually rather than trimonthly—Hera-years were nearly identical to Earth's; in the short-term it made no difference. *Still,* Blakes thought, *twenty-fifth century on Earth now. God, so much time that anything could have happened.*

On the *Australia,* Blakes knew that the new crew probably would not even reach the seats in the control rooms. He hadn't given them the codes the Frill had set up to move the ship compartments through the stone ground, and it made no real difference anyway, because the Frill would be waiting for them to trespass. And the crew would all be killed. Blakes was supposedly there now himself, helping them. Except that he wasn't, and he had never intended to be.

The drill Blakes had had smuggled aboard the *Australia* would take centuries to accumulate enough fuel for a return to Earth, but it would keep working until it was finished. Blakes had come to the tunnels to think and to hide, until it was safe to return to Hope and breathlessly tell them what had happened. Horrible—a, a massacre. The Frill . . . and so forth.

Blakes opened his bag and took out the computer-box. He drew the wire he had managed to graft into the skin of the organ-computer, a single black wire that wound out of a perfect hole in the back of the box. Chemicals flowing through the wire—which was really more of a biochemical tube Blakes had cut from the *Australia's* setup—and now Blakes opened a small bandage on the back of his left arm, picked off a scab, and let the end of the wire suck away his blood, mixing some of its own into the wound. The computer needed to align itself with Blakes's brainwaves using his "signature" communicated through his DNA, and likewise, the process wouldn't work unless Blakes's own brain output was slightly altered using some of the computer's blood.

A moment later, Blakes spoke with the computer in his mind, his body still limp and hibernating quietly in the tunnel. As he continued to talk with the black box, a pair of red slits flashed in the darkness, and then a single shadow stepped closer, the perfect curled point of a spear almost visible in the blue glow.

The computer explained to Blakes that the crew were already dead, all killed by the Frill, but the ship was more or less intact. One of the crew recorded a message, the computer told Blakes, but he didn't care: no one would ever find the message and survive long enough to return with it. When he was finished, Blakes woke, blinking and breathing deeply—and a Frill stood over him, its spear held calmly, ready to cut his torso in half. It made no noise, just watched, as if curious about the black box.

Blakes stared, not really frightened, not even surprised.

"What?" he said at last. He held up a combination of fingers rapidly to spell the idea of a question—that he didn't understand; in the months that he had worked with the Frill they had learned to communicate through numerical finger combinations. For whatever reason, the Frill had refused to speak sign language with anyone else—only with Blakes—and they had never progressed beyond basic commands. Although Blakes had tried to explain the concept of letters to them, it hadn't worked.

The Frill's hand flashed up, its five fingers dancing, and it spelled back, "We know." It might also mean "We understand" or "We believe."

"You do?" Blakes muttered, and he signed "What" again.

The Frill signed a letter. Blakes had taught them letters—years ago, and he had only done it once, for the entire English alphabet, but he had stopped when it became obviously too complicated to try to teach them the entire language phonetically. And now the Goddamn thing was doing it, it was spelling letters exactly as Blakes had taught it to.

"A-B-O-U-T" the Frill spelled, and then it paused.

You know about, Blakes thought, and he shivered, a chill running up the length of his spine. The hairs on the back of his neck stood as the Frill continued to sign.

"No," Blakes said, shaking. "Get away from me." There were tears in his eyes. "You *fucking* stop it!" He lunged at the Frill, and it was standing several feet away, out of reach—but it had already finished the word: A-D-R-I-A.

The Frill signed, "W-H-Y."

"Go to hell."

"W-H-Y."

Blakes turned away from it, methodically put his black box away, closed his bag, and stood to leave, his knees and fingers constricting with arthritis, as if his bones had become stiff, hot sticks and twigs. Glancing back, the Frill was gone. Blakes walked slowly back to the city.

At Hope, Blakes explained that the Frill could not be trusted, had murdered more of the city, and now—more than ever—people must stay within the city limits. Blakes had formed a small police force precisely for that purpose, and he was in the process of finishing the basics for a court system. The Church of Hope used Blakes's own works for guidance, and civil law was the same as divine law—Hope was God's city.

That night, as Blakes walked uncomfortably to the top of the long staircase to the second floor, a passing soldier nodded and saluted him with the familiar "Sieg heil!" Blakes weakly returned the gesture. In his room, the young blonde he had been sleeping with—she was nineteen, named Jessica—was waiting for him, already in bed. She was dressed in a black nightgown made of soft tree fur.

Blakes placed his bag at one wall, and Jessica said, "How are you?"

Blakes didn't answer her, sitting at the bedside, exhausted. He wanted to cry, for no reason. This had never happened in sixty-seven years—or three hundred and sixty-eight, if you counted relative time.

"Do you want me to take off my gown?" Jessica asked softly, rubbing Blakes's sore back.

He shook his head. "Going to sleep alone tonight."

Jessica's hands stopped, still touching his back. "Are you—"

"Please, leave me alone. I'm very tired."

"Yes, my Führer," Jessica said, and she kissed his cheek before leaving.

Blakes sat for a long time, but he didn't cry.

He said to himself, "I was angry with my friend: I told my wrath, my wrath did end. I was angry with my foe: I told it not, my wrath did grow."

Blakes paused, and then he sat slowly forward, closing his eyes and pressing both hands to cover them. He knew the words:

> And it grew both day and night.
> Till it bore an apple bright.

And my foe beheld it shine,
And he knew that it was mine.

Blakes whispered, "And she knew that it was mine." He left the palace and walked to the cemetery that had just begun to grow, with several rows of headstones, all fresh and clean stone. Hope's night streets were empty and small, with few buildings, most wooden and clustered together to remain standing, their curling pillars and gutters looking uneven and crude in the moonlight.

Blakes went to the cemetery, and he found the pile of unmarked stones waiting for more deaths, behind the rows of more than one hundred graves, many of them children. He carved on the tombstone:

Adria you were safe
This is not my first life
And will not be my last
I will see you again.

That night, Blakes buried a Frill spear deep in the ground where he set the memorial.

"The demons we'll see together," Blakes said, and he kissed the cold stone as the sky began to brighten. And that morning, Blakes left Hope. He wrote a brief note to the city that God had called him, that he should be thought of as dead, and that his five children—four boys, one girl—should inherit his throne, and his blood should rule eternally. Blakes took only a black box with him: everything else was already in place.

A crowd of cold, hungry people filled the Church pews, their loose-fitting layers of baggy clothing streaked and covered in melting snow. Lord Denon smiled at them from where he stood behind the altar at the front of the large stone room. The Religious Guard waited, unarmed, between the high candleholders at the walls and swastika tapestries. Denon walked quietly around the altar dressed in an elaborate white robe with a black swastika on his chest, his hair neatly braided and long. As he reached the front of the congregation, the people stood, quieting, except for several babies and children, crying at the back of the room.

"And we know that a fire came from the sky," Denon said, his voice resonating. "And with that fire came the prophet Blakes, and thus man and woman opened themselves to Hera, giving the planet their bodies, so that humanity might grow." Denon waited, and in one voice the assembly said,

"*Amen.*"

"Belief," Denon said, folding his hands fluidly, "is more important than any virtue you might ever learn. When you believe, energy grows inside you that cannot be taken away and cannot be removed." Denon spotted a company of soldiers in ragged gray coats, standing with their families in several of the rear pews.

"Please be seated," Denon said, and they all sat with a loud ruffling of fabric and clicking of boots. The crowd looked thin and very pale, some of their eyes rounded by dark sunken, hungry spaces. Rations had been cut again and again, as the last of the city's food supplies dwindled.

"An excerpt from the prophet's *Rebirth*," Denon said, "chapter thirteen." He was not reading, he was speaking from memory. But the book sat on the table behind him, thick and closed. "Once I saw a Devil in a flame of fire, who arose before an Angel that sat on a cloud, and the Devil uttered these words:

" 'The worship of God is: Honoring his gifts in other men, each according to his genius, and loving the greatest men best. Those who envy or calumniate great men hate God, for there is no other God.' God has brought his light to humanity's second hope, on Hera. The Angel told me this:

" 'A star fell to Hera, and with it fell our hope. We dropped into darkness and brought light. Each star is brighter than the one before it, and each dimming light struggles with the new brightness for its place in the sky, until the darkest light is gone, and a new bright glimmer appears. And then the first brightness begins to grow dark, knowing all the while that it was once more brilliant than the new star, yet it cannot understand the reason for its weakness.' "

Denon paused, thought for a moment, and then he continued:

" 'When that star dies, another new star appears and this star cannot even remember the first glow that once brightened the sky as it now does. Nothing is learned in this, and, in truth, nothing should be learned.' Nothing should be learned," Denon said again. "Some day the last star will go out, and then there will be only darkness. And nothing will exist to remember them at all.

"Life over Lies, my friends. Our lives may seem difficult. We may want to look around, to stare at the devastation, at the freezing dirt and snow—at our lost houses and lost husbands, friends, fathers, wives, sons and daughters—we may be tempted to look and to question our most basic truths.

"We may question everything in our desperation. You may even hear some say that we are damned, that life here will end because those who set the first fires, who began the killing, did not remember our prophet's words: *Life over Lies.* But it is in our hands to return to God's law. He has provided us with our city, and we will provide him with hope.

"Believe," Denon said, "that is all you need to do now. Believe. Do not look at what is happening with questions. My challenge to you all is to exist and to believe in that existence. I have done, and I will continue to do all that I can in this time of crisis. There *is* real danger, but it is not fatal. We *will* survive, so long as we do not question and we never lose faith. God provides us with answers through the prophet's laws. You are all my people, and I love with you with my soul. Know that, and we will be saved."

The congregation seemed to relax slightly, some closing their eyes calmly, others watching Denon with complete trust, desperation turned to hope. Denon faced the altar and said, "Let us return to the glory of our past."

The crowd stood, and Denon bowed low to the altar, the Religious Guard bowed, and as Denon turned back to the assembly they said again in one voice,

"*Amen.*"

"This celebration is ended," Denon said. "Go in peace."

Conversation began slowly, people filing solemnly out of their pews, and the Religious Guard opened the front doors, letting the people back into the snow. Wind whipped into the church, and one of the guards nearly lost his grip on the door as the snow blew down the aisle. Outside, the snow was deeper now, some drifts higher than a man's waist, and all of the houses on the opposite side of the street were buried, their roofs gone, long since collapsed.

People approached Lord Denon, and he thanked them for coming, giving group blessings. They asked about the king, about the government, and Denon told them that there would be new elections—the king was dead, gone to God—and some of the people cried. Others, too hungry and tired, simply thanked Denon for his help and led their families back outside, back to the government shelters and the Garrs, where they had been living in shacks and slowly freezing for weeks now.

When the last of them had gone, Denon sat quietly in the first row of pews and motioned one of the Religious Guard to join him.

"Lord Denon?"

"Most recent execution numbers?" Denon said.

"Numbers one-ninety through two hundred, I believe. Should be finishing that now."

"Issue the following dispatch," Denon said, and the Religious Guard drew a piece of stationery and a stalk of thin, black chalk. Denon began, "Dispatch to unit and company commanders. They are to locate any remaining rebels and have them executed as soon as possible, without trial. Due to the overcrowding of the prisons, rebels should be dealt with in the field as much as possible." Denon paused. "New dispatch."

"Yes, Lord Denon."

"A dispatch for the extension and continuance of mandatory universal conscription. Every man and woman between the ages of twelve and forty are now to be drafted into the military, except in cases of extreme physical deformities and women in the last months of pregnancy. The new draftees will live in the government facilities of the Garrs and palace, and they will receive standard government rations."

The soldier-priest nodded, finishing the dispatch. "Is that all, Lord Denon? Do you have orders concerning those people whose homes were destroyed in the fighting?"

"If they are between twelve and forty—and most of the city is—then they have a new home now," Denon said. "We'll feed them, just as we do the rest of the military. If they do not fall within those ages, their rations are to be cut, and they will rely on the generosity of their family members who qualify for the draft."

The priest hesitated. "Lord Denon, are you—"

"Those are my orders." Denon waved him away. "See that they are carried out."

"Yes, sir."

Denon watched the soldier-priest depart, and then he got up to leave, heading down the main aisle. Most of the Religious Guard in the room followed him out.

"The palace," Denon said, as they reached the doors, and wind hissed into the room, making the bulges of Denon's sword and pistol very pronounced under his robe. When Denon glanced back, all of the Church candles were dark.

A pair of soldiers tossed Wunic into Jak's cell. He hit the floor loudly, coughing and wincing, a small candle flickering in one of the rear corners. The cell was disproportionately tall, and there were faded markings on the black stone walls.

"Numbers two eighty-two and two eighty-three," one of the soldiers said, glaring at Wunic as if he had put up a fight.

Jak asked, "What number are they on now?"

The soldier shrugged and began to shut the heavy cell door again. "Around two hundred or two-ten, I think." The door shut and locked loudly.

Wunic's face was matted with dried blood, and he shifted on the floor and cleared his throat. "Is he gone?"

Jak sat beside him and put one hand to the back of his head carefully. "They're gone."

Wunic opened his eyes and sat up easily, popping the joints in his shoulders and picking away the blood from his face with one hand. Wunic's hands were still bound together, just as Jak's were.

"They'll bring a plate of food," Wunic said, and he kicked the heel of one boot against the floor hard, wincing with the sudden pain that lanced into him.

"What did they do to you?" Jak said.

He shrugged. "Nothing." Wunic hit the floor with his boot again, harder this time. "General Rein's dead. Selan's dead."

Jak took an uneven breath, as if he had just slapped her. "You saw the general?"

"Yes," Wunic said, continuing to stomp on the stone. "Selan was the traitor."

"Selan—you mean the major running the artillery?"

Wunic nodded. "Yes." And he glared at his boot, frustrated. "Damn it."

"What are you doing?"

Wunic hit the stone again, the boot popped, and the heel slid out of place, revealing a small compartment inside the lining of the shoe. A pair of thin stilettos fell to the floor. Jak stared at the knives, and Wunic knocked the heel back into place.

"You—"

"Yes," Wunic said, and he sawed through his wrist bindings.

"How'd you get those by them?"

"How do you think?"

"Why didn't you use them when we had you?"

Wunic said, "You took off my boots and tied me to a chair." She stiffened and Wunic's hands were free. He started on Jak's. "I designed the last renovations on this prison, I authorized the sentry placements and set up the defenses on this floor." He shook his head and finished with her ropes—she was free. "They have too many prisoners to use metal wrist clamps on all of us," Wunic said.

Wunic stood, absently licking the blood from his lower lip.

"Did they hurt you?" Jak said, amazed at how quickly their situation had changed.

He rolled the knife across his knuckles. "Yes. I can do this alone, but it *will* be easier with two people. You have to do exactly as I say, do you understand?"

"You're not going to kill me?"

Wunic frowned, as if that hadn't occurred to him, and he said, "I could, yes."

"You need me—"

"No," he said. "Don't think for a moment that I need you. You're going to be executed here too. Do as I say, and we might get out."

"And once we're out?"

He smiled. "For now, we focus on getting to that point. Understand?"

"Yes."

"Will you do what I tell you to do?"

"Yes."

He tossed her the second stiletto. "Here. Have you used a stiletto before?"

She nodded and palmed the blade, rising to her feet. "I take it you have a plan?"

"Yes, of course. It only works one way—"

"I know, if I listen to you. I will, General."

Wunic hesitated, then said, "The guard who brings our food won't be armed with a rifle. That's done deliberately, so that if any prisoner *did* manage to overpower him, the only weapon that prisoner would have is a sword. Now, we were put into the same room because we were captured together, we're both considered level five prisoners, and they're running out of cells."

"Level five?"

"It means I would be dangerous, if they didn't think I was wounded. And you're dangerous, but you're not a soldier."

"And I'm a woman," Jak said, flicking the stilleto lightly against her fingers.

Wunic shrugged. "That may be part of the reason—that's irrelevant. Because I was a general, they'll bring us a last meal on a metal plate. The plates are large enough and strong enough to jam the reinforcement gates at the end of the hall. Now, pay attention: Once soldiers start dying on this floor, the guards on the other three prison levels, and maybe even four floors up—in the palace—they'll all be ordered down here to seal off the compromised prison section.

"Their access depends on a reinforcement gate at the end of the hall. It isn't a solid gate—they will still be able to fire through the gaps in the bars, but they won't be able to enter the hallway if the lock's jammed. They could shoot off the lock, but they might not want to—they might want to keep us down here—and even if they did, blowing the lock off will take time."

Wunic was talking faster, his gestures sharper and more animated. "I'm going to run to the end of the hall, force the plate into the lock, then slam the gate—the lock will break and they will be stuck on the other side."

"That would defeat the purpose of this, wouldn't it? Won't we be stuck down here?"

"No," Wunic said. "There are other ways in and out of every floor, all hidden. In the cell on the opposite side of the hall there's a hidden stairwell built into the rear wall. That cell is always empty because there's always the fear that a prisoner might accidentally discover the stairs."

"Do the soldiers know about it?"

"Yes," Wunic said. "The ones who have been here longest know, but with everything that's happened, the guards here might be new. Even if they know what we're planning, we'll be at the top on the main floor of the palace before word spreads that there's been a breakout. Am I making this clear?"

"Yes. Do the stairs lead right up to the palace, past the other prison levels?"

"Yes."

"Are you sure—"

"Just do as I tell you," Wunic said, and he began to pace with a slight limp. "Yes, it will work."

"I'm sorry for what I did, General."

He shook his head absently. "This will only work if we focus. Stop talking about the past. Focus on now. If we die, we die. They're going to kill us anyway. But this *will* work if you follow my instructions. Can you do that?"

"Yes, General. I told you—"

"When they start firing, you won't fall back in the cell and act like this was my plan? I don't regret what I do, I don't live with guilt, and I don't lose because of other peoples' mistakes. If this is too much for you, it's all right, but I need to know now."

Jak said, "You can trust me with this."

He met her eyes, twirling the stiletto in one hand, distracted. She had worked with him at the Garr, when it mattered—Jak had been at his side, hadn't she? *I have to try,* he thought. *If I give up, I prove them right: The man who was General Wunic will have disappeared, defected or dead; it doesn't matter. I am still the commanding officer of this army. I choose what happens, not them, not Denon. I am still General Wunic and my war isn't over.*

He nodded at last and looked away from her. "We don't have much time. Are you ready?"

Jak held her stiletto down, the blade concealed in her palm. "Yes, General. Tell me what to do. Let's get the hell out of here."

VEL AND Ulyu returned to the cemetery, and then they walked to the palace, Vel struggling and fighting with the deep snow. *Always snowing,* he thought. At the palace, the rows of soldiers and refugees inside ragged tents and boxes of wood that cluttered all across the front courtyard stared at Vel and at the Frill.

"—our Majesty?"

"—is that thing with the king?"

"—dead?"

Vel waved at them briefly, heading inside. No refugees inside. *They have to sleep outside?* Vel thought, as he walked past more soldiers, down the main entrance hall, toward the staircase to the second floor. *Why the hell aren't there refugees staying in here?* Vel wondered, and he led Ulyu past the statues and star and swastika tapestries, up the stairs, and into his bedroom: empty.

Vel walked back into the hall and called to one of the nearest soldiers, "Where's Lord Denon?"

"Your Majesty," the soldier said, staring at Ulyu. "You were pronounced, you were—"

"What?"

"Thank God you're alive, sir."

"Of course I'm alive," Vel said, the soldier still watching Ulyu, one hand on his rifle. "Keep that weapon where it is—this is a Frill, we had a frank discussion, and we're friends now."

Denon's voice from the top of the stairs, and Vel hurried down the hall, Ulyu silent behind him—Denon reached the top of the stairs, still speaking softly to a group of Religious Guard—and froze when he saw Vel.

And now they're all carrying rifles too, Vel thought, noticing the guns the Religious Guard held. Denon glanced at Ulyu, then a slow smile formed as he approached Vel.

"Your Majesty," Denon said, and the Religious Guard left, heading back down the stairs. Vel and Denon embraced at the top of the stairs, and Denon walked beside Vel, leading Vel and Ulyu back to Vel's room.

"This is unexpected, Your Majesty," Denon said. "Did you get my dispatches?"

"You've kept this from falling apart," Vel said, examining the hall and the soldiers that moved less frantically through the palace than Vel remembered. "Thank you, I appreciate that."

"Everything has been done in your interest," Denon said, and he motioned to Ulyu. "What is that?"

"The Frill," Vel said. "You know—"

"You brought one here."

Vel said, "They've changed—they aren't warring anymore."

"I don't believe it."

"It's happened, Lord Denon. They've united behind me." Vel smiled. "So long as I don't have to start dressing like them, I have no problem with it."

Denon put one arm on Vel's shoulder, turning him away from Ulyu, drawing him close. "*United*? Vel, you cannot trust them."

"What are you talking about?"

"The Frill want nothing more than to destroy everyone in Hope. They are godless, and they are ruthless. Please listen to me: Never trust them, Vel—they're using you."

Vel said, "Denon, I *do* trust them. They want to stop the fighting between us. They want—"

"They want," Denon said, "to annihilate us." He looked back at Ulyu nervously. "Your Majesty, you must make them leave. The Frill want to kill us, and they're using you to do it. *That's* why Justice Hillor took you away from them as a child. They're using you, Vel."

"How do you know? I think the situation's changed."

"Your Majesty, surely you know how dangerous they are. Why would they want peace between us? The Frill can survive without humans, and they know that," Denon said. "They want us gone from this planet—this was their world before it was ours."

Vel thought about it, and then he said tiredly, "I don't want to argue about this. I want to see that girl, Sisha. I never apologized."

Denon swallowed, stiffening. "The Frill should leave as soon as possible."

"Sisha," Vel said, "did you hear me? I need to see her. Where is she?" Denon was quiet, and Vel asked, "What is it?"

"Please, Your Majesty, order the Frill away."

"Denon, what's wrong? What's happened?"

"Sir, you should know that I tried to stop—"

"What are you talking about?"

"I tried," Denon said, his fingers tightening as he pressed his hands together. "I didn't want to be the one to tell you . . . and so soon after you've returned."

Naturally this is going to fall apart, Vel thought. He tried not to think about all of the people who had been destroyed because they knew him. *No,* he thought. *No, Goddamn it. This is not happening—whatever it is, it isn't going to happen to* her, *a girl I don't even know.*

"Tell me," Vel said quietly.

"Order it away."

Vel turned to Ulyu, and he shouted loud enough for the soldiers to hear, "Leave, Ulyu. I want everyone to leave."

Vel?

Leave, he thought. Wait in the tunnel under the cemetery with the rest of the Frill. There are things I have to take care of.

Vel, I must protect you—

"I told you to leave," Vel said again, and when Ulyu remained, he shouted, "Get out of here."

Vel, we're—

"I said get the hell out of here!" Vel said. "Now, Ulyu."

Ulyu flashed down the hall, and was gone.

"Perhaps we should discuss this in private," Denon began.

Vel said, "We can discuss it now. I understand that you're reluctant—I know you want to protect me, but I have to know: what happened?"

"I didn't want to tell you now." Vel waited, and Denon went on, "Sisha was . . ." Denon forced the words, "she was raped, Vel."

As if it had been waiting under his skin for this moment, anger rushed to the surface in an instant, adrenaline flooding his arms, and Vel tightened both fists.

"Who?"

No, he thought. *Don't tell me, I don't want to know—I don't want this to happen.*

"General Wunic."

Vel backed away from Denon. *Goddamn it,* Vel thought. *I know how to hurt you now. I'll make you bleed, you arrogant bastard. Now it's you, Wunic. Now, you're the one to find the weak places. This time I can act.*

Vel said, "Where is he?"

"Vel—"

"*Stop it,*" Vel shouted, and Denon paled. "You tell me where he is." Denon didn't answer, and Vel touched his pistol. "Listen to me very carefully, Denon. I don't give a damn who you're trying to keep alive. He can't do that. I'm in charge now. I'm not going to let it happen, do you understand? Where is he?"

I'm not human anymore, Vel thought. *I'm going to make you wish I was, General. Slit your Goddamn throat and see if you bleed red. You buried me, but you didn't do what you should have. You didn't kill me. The only way to fix this now is to destroy it. Whatever this is that keeps destroying pieces of my life, it will end. Now. One of us is going to die, Wunic.*

"Where is he?" Vel said again.

Denon told him.

The cell door opened, and a soldier entered with a small plate of grassfruit. Two mugs of water jostled from the tray, and at the far wall, Jak lay on her side, not moving.

"Your food," the soldier said—Wunic stepped out from beside the door, put his hand over the soldier's mouth, and neatly cut his throat. The soldier jerked, tried to draw his sword, bit into Wunic's palm, and a moment later it was over. Wunic lowered the body to the floor, and Jak stood, her stiletto catching light as she approached him. Wunic took the soldier's sword. *Quiet,* he thought. *This has to stay quiet as long as it can.*

Jak removed both mugs from the plate, took a brief drink from one, and then dumped the grassfruit beside the soldier's body, handing Wunic the plate. *Remember,* he thought. *Two soldiers. One at each end.*

Into the hall back to back, and they flicked stilettos at the soldiers on duty—a third man behind Wunic's target—and Wunic hit his soldier in the forehead, Jak caught hers in the throat, both dropped, and Wunic charged the third, sword raised. The third soldier didn't have a rifle, and he drew his sword in time to block Wunic's thrust, and then they clanked again, before Wunic pushed the soldier into the wall and stabbed him twice in the chest. Jak's soldier spit blood, gurgling as he raised a rifle at her—she rolled under the volley, kicked his rifle away and stomped her stiletto deeper into his throat.

Wunic reached the gate—through the doorway a small crowd of soldiers obliviously approached, talking. Somehow they hadn't heard the gunshots. Wunic shoved the metal plate into the lock and slammed the gate door—it didn't close. The soldiers beyond stopped, staring at him. Wunic slammed the door again, harder, and still it wouldn't close—behind him, Jak opened fire, bullets sparking the bars as she fired past Wunic, and one of the soldiers went down, grabbing at his stomach as it spilled open. The soldiers returned fire, and Wunic slammed the gate a third time. The bars rattled and shook as bullets ricocheted against them, hissing past Wunic's face. Again, the gate didn't close.

"Close!" Wunic shouted, and Jak hurried beside him, pushing the barrel of her gun through the bars as she fired into the soldiers, killing all of them so that their bodies piled around the base of the stairs—shouting came from the floors above them.

"Goddamn it," Wunic said. Still the gate wouldn't shut.

"General . . ." Jak said, aiming her rifle at the stairs.

Wunic kicked the plate and pulled again. It whined, and there was a crunching sound as the plate caught in its lock. The gate shut.

"I never doubted you, sir," Jak said, and she shot a soldier starting down the stairs.

"Quickly," Wunic said, and they hurried for the cell across the hall. The door wouldn't open, and Jak shot off the lock, kicking it open. The cell was identical to the one they'd been kept in, and Wunic went immediately to the opposite wall, his hands tracing the cracks and grooves in the stone. Wunic's fingernails blackened from the stone, and there was shouting from the hall outside.

"Reinforcements," Jak said, without looking.

"I'll find it," he said, and Wunic sheathed the sword he'd taken from the soldier, using both hands. *Goddamn it, don't do this,* he thought. *Where the hell is it?* Wunic moved his fingers more frantically, and Jak went back to the door, pivoted briefly into the hall and fired at the soldiers behind the barred gate. She ducked back as they returned fire, the doorway flashing and ringing as bullets snapped at it.

A section of the wall swung back to expose a narrow, spiral staircase. The steps were wooden, and Wunic smiled.

"Will they hold? How old is this?" Jak said. Wunic started up, and the wooden beams creaked loudly.

"Shut the door," he said, and Jak did, swinging her rifle onto her back as she followed him up. The passage was entirely dark, and Wunic coughed at the thick smell of dust and mold.

"Stairs *should* support us," Wunic said.

"How much farther?" Jak said, and they walked up in silence for a time—Jak slipped on one of the beams, catching herself on the low stone ceiling. "God, this is narrow."

"This was added later," Wunic said from above her. "It wasn't in the original plans."

"Can't see anything."

"Yes, I know," Wunic said. "We're almost there."

They kept moving, and the stairs ended at another wall. *Where are you, Denon?* Wunic thought. *Where would you be?* The wall opened, and Wunic stepped into one of the rear rooms of the palace. Jak followed, and several soldiers stopped in the near distance, pointing at them. The room was dark, with empty weapon racks on all four walls, and large circles spaced on the floor, connected with complex series of lines. *A training room,* Wunic thought, and then he stopped: Through the far doorway, Wunic saw the king, walking quietly. Vel had not seen them, and he wasn't looking up.

"It's him," Wunic said softly. *Denon, you bastard.*

Jak smiled. "He's not dead. Means Denon isn't—"

"I know," Wunic said, starting toward Vel. "Vel!" he called out. "Vel, it's General Wunic!"

Vel froze in mid-step, and he looked up, hair falling into his eyes.

Wunic smiled. "You're alive, thank God, Your Majesty. You have to stop the executions, sir."

Soldiers approached, rifles raised, but Wunic didn't care. Vel changed everything. With Vel alive, Denon hadn't won, it wasn't over. The king was alive! The soldiers surrounded Wunic and Jak.

"Drop your rifle," one said to Jak. "Back away from each other."

She glanced at Wunic, and he shrugged and said, "Doesn't matter now. Do as they say."

Vel walked closer, his sword drawn, and Jak let her rifle drop.

"Now your sword," one said to Wunic, and Vel reached them, stepping past the circle of soldiers without looking up.

"No," Vel said. "Let him keep the sword."

Vel still wore the coat that had once belonged to Justice Hillor. That long, dark overcoat flapped behind him as he drew nearer, and Wunic extended a hand.

"Thank God, Vel."

Vel drew closer, unanswering.

"Hello, Vel," Jak said.

Vel said, "Take Jak out of here. She's free—let her go."

Wunic said, "What's—"

And Vel shouted at the soldiers, "*Do it now*!"

They closed on Jak, escorting her away without another word, leaving only a handful of soldiers.

Wunic said, "Your Majesty—" And Vel attacked.

chapter 18

Their swords met once, and Vel hit again, striking low in two quick thrusts that Wunic knocked away, stepping back slowly. *Why can't I move like I did before?* Vel thought, frustrated. *I fought the Frill, and I was one of them.* Wunic raised his sword defensively across his torso, and Vel began to circle, swinging for Wunic's head. Wunic knocked away Vel's sword without moving—his arm snapping up sharply to stop the attacks.

"Please—what are you doing, sir?" Wunic said.

Vel swung again, this time with a quick series of thrusts; right, left, right, center, left, and the swords met each time, resonating loudly.

"Your Majesty, please—"

Vel went faster, and Wunic used both hands to catch the attacks now, stopping all of them. As Vel circled again, Wunic slowly turned, pain in his feet—Vel saw it and swung for Wunic's leg. Instead of parrying, Wunic backed away and raised his sword to Vel's throat, the blade poised against Vel's skin. Vel knocked Wunic's sword away, and attacked again, and each time Wunic met the thrusts. Vel stepped back, breathing hard, sweat on his forehead.

"Your Majesty, you don't understand," Wunic said softly. "I didn't defect. Why are you doing this? Why?"

Vel lowered his sword, one hand dropping to the pistol at his belt. *To hell with it,* he thought, and he drew the gun, clicking the safety off.

"Wait—" Wunic said, and the gun flashed, blowing away part of his leg. Wunic staggered, blood running from his wounded thigh, and he fell, somehow still holding onto the sword. "No," Wunic said softly, and he pressed at the wound, blood pumping over his fingers.

Vel walked closer. "Get up."

Wunic stared at him. "What the hell are you doing?"

"Get up," Vel said again, and he leveled the pistol at Wunic's head, still holding his sword in one hand.

Wunic's face contorted as he grabbed his uninjured leg, struggling to rise. He growled, and stood, his weight focused on his good leg, the wounded leg hanging limply, a dark puddle pooling around his boot.

"What are you doing, sir? I can't . . ."

"What you couldn't do to me," Vel said, sliding the pistol back into his belt. The soldiers watched silently.

"I don't understand, Your Majesty."

Vel attacked again, and Wunic raised his sword, still blocking each swing. Wunic's arm reacted perfectly, as if disconnected from his wounded body, and he stared numbly at Vel as their swords met again and again.

"What?" Wunic said, pushing Vel away. "I don't understand."

Vel continued to attack. *Stop it,* he thought. *Just die.*

"Stop, Your Majesty."

Vel circled, forcing Wunic to turn. Wunic slipped as he put weight on his wounded leg, and Vel tried to push Wunic off balance. Wunic stopped the thrust, and then again—and now Wunic pulled back hard, locking their swords together, and he twisted his wrist—Vel's sword spun away, across the room. Vel backed away, and Wunic remained where he was, blood drenching his pants and boots.

"Need a medic," Wunic said quietly to the soldiers.

Vel picked up the sword, and again he advanced on Wunic.

"Stop it," Wunic said. "I don't want to hurt you."

"You won't anymore," Vel said, stopping just out of Wunic's reach. "I want you to remember me as the last thing you see, General. Lord Denon told me."

Chills ran through Wunic, and he held up both hands, offering the sword to Vel. *Oh no.* "Your Majesty, Lord Denon is a traitor. I swear to you, whatever he told you, while you were gone—"

"Be quiet, General."

"You don't—"

"Be quiet."

Vel shot him. Wunic dropped, and Vel went to stand over him, lowered the pistol—Wunic gurgled softly—and shot him twice more.

Vel looked away from the mess and said to the soldiers, "Have him removed."

They did as they were told, and one soldier said quietly, "He was a traitor, Your Majesty."

"I know," Vel said, holstering his pistol. He watched them take the body from the room and thought, *It's done. It's done, but I don't feel any better,* Vel thought as he returned to the main entrance hall and staircase, walking for his room.

"Your Majesty." Denon stood behind him in the hall, the Religious Guard passing him, moving down the stairs, some of them heading up. *So many of them here,* Vel thought.

"I just heard what happened," Denon said.

"Where's Sisha?" Vel said.

"The girl's still somewhat traumatized."

"Just tell me where she is."

Denon nodded to a door behind him. "She's in the room across from yours, under medical supervision."

Vel started past him, and Denon caught his arm. "Be careful, Your Highness. The girl's gone through a lot."

Vel nodded. "Thank you, Denon."

As he approached the door, Vel heard Ulyu:

You cannot move without escort, it's too dangerous.

Stop it, Ulyu, Vel thought, and he nodded to the soldiers posted on either side of Sisha's door. "How is she?"

"Don't know, sir," one said.

You will be guarded. We cannot risk this now.

Vel thought about what Denon had told him—

No, Ulyu said, *you must not trust that man.*

Why? Vel thought. You want to tell me why I should trust you more than him?

You are our—

Enough of that, Vel thought, and he reached for the doorknob.

You will return us to our gods.

Vel said, "And how the hell am I supposed to do that?" The soldiers stared at him, and Vel walked past them, into the room.

Listen to me—

No.

We will protect you.

I don't want your protection, I want you to leave me alone, Vel thought. You want to follow my orders: Then I'll tell you when you're needed. Now, get out of my head.

When was the last time you slept?

Shut the hell up, Vel thought. He approached the side of Sisha's bed, waving her doctor away.

You're making a mistake, Vel.

You're making a mistake if you don't stop bothering me. I swear to God, Ulyu, I'll order all of you Frill into a mass suicide if you don't knock it off. Now go away.

Sisha's head was tilted back, her eyelids moving rapidly, and there were bruises across her cheeks. *Why Wunic?* Vel thought. *Why did you do this?* Vel had wanted to kill the general with the sword, to move like the Frill had moved, and it hadn't worked. *Of course it hadn't worked,* he thought, and knelt beside her bed.

Sisha mumbled something, and she shifted under the bedcovers. Vel drew closer, smelling something bitter. . . . What was it? Sisha's eyes fluttered open, and she blinked, talking softly to herself, and she rolled to face him.

"It's over," she rasped. "All over now . . . isn't it?"

"Yes," Vel said, and he recognized the smell: dulling oil. They'd drugged Sisha to make her numb. *Was it better or worse this way?* he wondered. Numbed she would feel nothing, but that meant her mind would be fogged as well.

"I'm dead," Sisha said.

Vel rubbed her shoulder. "No. You're being taken care of."

"My number's been called?"

Vel said, "It's all right. Just lay back. I'm back from the tunnels." *What number?*

Sisha kissed his hand weakly, her breath halting and weak. "Don't remember it . . ."

"What?"

She smiled calmly. "Dying. I don't remember it."

"You haven't died," Vel said, and he wondered just how badly Wunic had hurt her that they would give her dulling oil?

"But, this isn't the prison," Sisha said. "Why not the prison if I'm alive?"

"What prison?" Vel said. "What are you talking about?"

"Oh, Vel," she said, taking his hands. Her fingers were cold, and he could feel the bones in each joint. *God, what had happened to her?* "I'm sorry—I care about you."

"I care about you, Sisha." Vel held her hands more tightly. "You've been through a lot, and it's time for you to rest. Don't think about it right now."

"Thank you, Vel," she said softly. "You're so . . ." She sat up stiffly, her eyes widening, her face pale. "Why haven't I died? Vel?"

"Sisha, it's all right, I'm here."

"Kill him," she said. "Kill him as quickly as you can."

Vel nodded. "It's done."

She hesitated, struggling to blink back the drug. "He's dead? You've done it already?"

"Yes," Vel said. "Now, don't worry. We'll be all right."

Sisha relaxed, and she closed her eyes for a long time, her breathing becoming very regular. Vel lingered by her side, unsure of whether she was still awake. They hadn't asked him if she should be drugged . . . procedure, but they hadn't asked him, hadn't even mentioned it. *I need to talk to her,* he thought. More than anything he wanted to know that she understood him, so that he could explain that they were safe now.

And then, without moving, Sisha said clearly, "Denon."

Vel squeezed her hand again. "What?"

Sisha was silent, and he watched her face. *God,* Vel thought, *she was beautiful, the face of an angel.* Perfect except for the splotches under her skin where he had hit her. Her skin was tanned and glowing in the candlelight, the color of gold.

"Watch him," she said.

"What, Sisha? What are you talking about?"

"Denon," she said, without moving, "watch him."

"What about Denon?" She didn't answer. "What about Denon?" Vel said again, his voice rising.

"Stop," Sisha said softly.

"What did you mean?" No reply. "Sisha?"

"Yes, Vel."

"Talk to me. Why did you say Denon's name?"

She rolled onto her side, away from him, letting go of Vel's hand. Vel got up to leave, staring at her. *Drugged,* he thought, *must be drugged.* It was as simple as that. The drugs were talking to him, not her. Denon's name hadn't meant a thing. But Wunic had said something too—*Stop it,* Vel told himself.

"Sisha?" he said, but she was asleep, so Vel blew out the candles, kissed her forehead, and left her alone.

"I heard," Jak said simply. She stood defiantly, her hands bound behind her back.

Vel motioned Denon and the soldiers to back away from her. They did, moving out of earshot.

"What?" Vel said.

"About the general. You were wrong," she said. "Wunic wanted to save you." Her blonde hair was streaked with dirt, and a single wooden window rattled and hissed with the snow outside. "I don't think anyone can now."

"I want to talk to you about a compromise," Vel said.

Jak rolled her head in a circle, neck popping. "Compromise? Now is not the time to ask me for favors, Vel."

"I want you to be a spokesman—I want you to talk to the rebels for me," Vel said. "You do that, I'll let you go."

Jak smirked, waiting for the punch line. "Why don't you do it yourself?"

"I can't—"

"You're serious?"

"Jak—"

"Don't you have any idea what's going on?"

"The rebels, Jak. You'll talk to them, convince as many units as you can to surrender. They'll be given—"

"Vel," she said, "it's over."

"You don't want to help me," Vel said. "I know that. Please, Jak—if you don't, you'll be treated like the rest of them."

"You mean I'll be killed."

Vel glanced at Denon, a line of soldiers and several Religious Guard standing behind him, waiting for a signal from Vel.

"Look," Jak said, "you forget that I saved your life? You think you could've stopped Hillor without my arrows?"

"That's past."

"So is the war. You've already won. Now what the hell kind of game is this?"

Denon raised his eyebrows, and Vel shook his head. *No*, he thought, *I'll handle this. I can handle Jak.*

"You know I've been out of the city," Vel said, "but Goddamn it, Jak, I'm not stupid. I'm offering you a deal—agree to speak to the rebels, and you'll live."

"Untie me." When Vel hesitated, she turned to show him her wrists. "Untie me," she said again.

Ten soldiers, two Religious Guard and Lord Denon, Vel thought, *She's not planning an escape, she just wants to be able to move her hands.* Vel drew his sword and cut her bindings.

She said, "That's better. Thank you."

"You agree?"

Jak extended her hand. "I suppose so—I don't have much choice, do I?"

"Not really, no."

"Still, there is no war, Vel, so I'm not sure who you want me to talk to."

Vel forced a smile, and he shook her hand. "Thanks for the—" And Jak twisted his arm behind his back and grabbed his sword, raising it to his throat. Vel's elbow was locked, and the joint burned as she applied pressure—Jak turned to face the soldiers, using Vel as a shield against their rifles.

Lord Denon sighed, as if she had stained the carpet. "What are you doing?"

"Quiet," Jak said. "Open that door."

None of them moved, and Jak pressed the sword harder into Vel's neck, beginning to break the skin.

"Do it," Vel said. "Open the—"

Denon said, "No." The soldiers kept their rifles trained on Jak, and Denon continued, "Let go of him."

"Don't think so," Jak said. "Now, open the door or I cut him open—you want to watch it happen? You don't think I'll end him?"

"No," Denon said. "I don't."

"This little bastard murdered General Wunic. You know what Wunic meant to this city? He was the only one—"

"Let him go," Denon said again.

"Swear to God, Denon," Jak said, and Vel winced as the blade drew a slow trickle of blood. "You open the Goddamn door, and you do it now. Want to see him die?"

Vel motioned to the soldiers weakly with his free hand. "Do what she says . . ."

Two soldiers went for the door, and Denon said, "Open the doors." And then to Jak, "You can't leave. Where are you going to go?"

"Maybe I took the wrong hostage," Jak said.

"Release him."

Vel said, "Jak, you can't—"

"Shut up Vel," she said. Jak approached the door, keeping Vel between her body and Denon and the soldiers. "Move to that wall," she said, but they didn't get out of her way. "Get against the God-damn wall." No one moved. More soldiers stepped into the doorway, behind them more of the Religious Guard. "I'll kill him," she said, "I swear to God."

"Kill him and you die," Denon said. "You know that."

"And what happens if I let him go? I suppose you'll just forget this?"

Vel said, "Jak, they won't let you—"

"Shut up." Jak backed to the rear wall, away from the door, and she motioned to one of the closest soldiers. "You. Drop all of your weapons and step forward." The soldier tossed his rifle, sword and a pair of knives to the floor, and stepped closer—Jak shouted, "*All* of them—those little blades in your sleeves, under your coat and in your legs and boot, I want to see them all on the floor there. Drop them all." He did, and she pressed her back to the wall, Vel still between her and the rest of them. "Anyone else moves, and he's dead before I am."

"Gentle with the sword," Denon said. "Watch his throat."

Jak ignored him and said to the unarmed soldier, "The window: Open it and step away." The wooden window might have been large enough for a small child to squeeze through, and when the soldier drew the shutters aside, it only exposed a row of metal bars. Snow beyond, and the dark night.

"All right," Jak said, and she looked unhappily at Denon. "Will I die if I release him?"

Denon didn't answer, and Vel said, "No."

Jak grinned. "Thank you, Vel. I'm sure you have something other than your own neck in mind when you say that." And to Denon again, "I'll be sent to the firing squad? I'll be killed, won't I?"

Denon thought about it and said, "No."

"Come on," Jak said, "say it again. Like you believe it this time."

"No," Denon said, "if you release Vel right now you will not be killed."

"Better," she said, and several of the soldiers edged closer. "Watch it, assholes, or I might sever a major artery by accident." She nodded to Denon again. "I want a promise."

"You have it," Denon said. "You will not be killed if he is released now."

Jak said, "They're not going to let me out of here, are they?"

Denon said, "No, they won't."

"Well, I think we're about out of options, aren't we?"

"Let him go, Jak."

She hesitated. "Fine." And then Jak withdrew the sword, a dark red line across Vel's throat, and as she released his arm, the soldiers fell on her fast, knocking her sword away, and they smashed her face with the butts of their rifles, quickly beating her to the floor.

Denon put a hand on Vel's shoulder and guided him away. "I suggest you rest, Your Majesty."

"Stop," Vel said to the soldiers, but they seemed not to hear him. They blocked Jak's body, and only the wet sound of them hitting her told him that she was there. "Stop."

Denon pulled him away. "It's done."

"Let her go. Tell them to stop."

"Your Majesty, I'll escort you to your quarters."

Vel caught a glimpse of Jak's battered, swollen face, the skin discolored and bloody. She wasn't making any noise.

"Enough," Vel said, and several of the soldiers paused, noticing Vel.

"Please," Denon said, and reluctantly Vel followed him out of the room. Vel felt numb. *I knew Jak,* Vel thought, *and she was right—she did save me. Jak was the one who killed Hillor, not me. Why would she do that?* he wondered. *What have I done? I offered to save her.*

"You were right," Vel said. "She *was* desperate."

Four of the Religious Guard trailed after them as they made their way through the stone hallways, past black-and-white portraits of long-dead kings.

"And what did she say?" Denon asked.

"That the war had ended, that the rebels had already been beaten." Vel blinked, and his eyes wanted to remain shut. *God, I'm tired,* he thought, *why haven't I noticed it before now?* "Agreed so I would cut her bindings, so she could get my sword."

"You should get some sleep," Denon said, and they reached the main entrance hall, mounting the stairs to the second floor. "If conditions do not improve by morning, you may need to leave for the ruins again for your own safety—it's possible that the rebels might sack the palace again."

Vel nodded. "Thank you, Denon." When Denon didn't respond, Vel said, "You've kept all of this together better than I could have. I don't think I could do this without you. I'd probably be dead without your help."

"I do what I think is best."

"Thank you," Vel said.

"You're welcome." They reached Vel's bedroom, and Denon started back to the stairs with the Religious Guard. As he left he said, "Now, sleep. Whatever happens, I'll keep you informed. Remember, there's still a war to be won."

chapter 19

They were coming for him. Blakes crouched in the blue darkness, his back to the stone wall, the bag with the black box and several of his writings on the tunnel floor behind him. Further back, just beyond the limits of the blue glow, was the hall of encased people—the thirteen from the *Australia*, from the first days on Hera—and beyond that was the doorway and the hall that could lead to any section of the *Australia* through the demons' technological sin.

Blakes heard their voices, approaching in the dimness ahead, coming from the direction of Hope. He backed away, down the hall. They had read his note, and now they would demand that he return to lead them, rather than leave management in the hands of his young children. *Well, this is a dynasty*, Blakes thought, *and I must be allowed to leave when I have finished God's work. And Hope is their city now, not mine.*

They saw him—a huge group, perhaps fifty or more; more people than he had thought would come—and Blakes hurried for the door and hallway, the people running after him, shouting for him to stop, to wait and listen to them. They wanted to honor him, they said, to ask why he was leaving—questions about the judicial system, about the harvest, about the perimeter wall and the Garrs and—Blakes ran inside the hall to the opposite door.

"Identification number, please."

"One, three, two, one," Blakes said, and then he added, "second entry." That code could lead two places, to one of the control rooms or to an empty storage compartment. Blakes chose the storage compartment. He left the door open, and inside, he grabbed a crude breathing mask from the plastic floor. Several refrigeration canisters installed in the walls were already chilling the air, and as the people rushed in after him, Blakes waited beside the door, allowing them all inside.

"—prophet, what are you—"

"—some challenge your law—"

And when the last were inside, Blakes smiled at them through the breathing mask, shut the door, and raised his hand for silence.

An old woman in the front of the group stepped forward and said, "Führer Blakes, you must not leave us now, when your children are still so young." Odorless, invisible gas began to fill the room with a low whisper. "There are people in the city who don't want your children to rule unchecked. They aren't old enough yet, and we believe in you."

"I wanted to be left alone," Blakes said softly. "I told you that in my note. I told you not to come after me, not to break the perimeter law."

"Yes, but . . ." Several of them slumped to the ground, and the woman closed her eyes, staggering, and she continued, "Blakes, please, we need . . ." And she dropped. In another moment, they were all motionless. Blakes called out the code to leave the room and ordered the computer—via the black box—to remove the air from the room and begin the sacrifice. Three minutes later, the computer reported that the poison was gone, and large metal hooks, hooks made from Frill spears Blakes had stolen, dropped from the ceiling. One by one, Blakes stripped the bodies and hung them in neat rows, spitted on the hooks. As he left the room, Blakes set the temperature low enough that they would be frozen, permanently preserved.

Blakes collected grassfruit from the surface at night, and during the day he wrote and slowly carved large buildings out of the rock of a Frill cavern. Years passed, and Blakes continued to work on his memorial to the perversion of the future on the past; he worked to build his own Auschwitz, so that its eventual ruin would always be remembered. *Meaning traded for petty emotion*, Blakes thought, as he worked, using a Frill spear to carve out the smokestack building. He managed to dismantle the core of one of the *Australia*'s engines and install it to create an oven that would burn for centuries.

How old am I? Blakes wondered one day, as his memory of human perversion in the face of courage and vision neared completion. *Seventy? Eighty?* Without the sinful medicines of Earth, he was lucky to still be alive. But they had inoculated and medicated him when he was younger. They had designed him to be a resilient cow in the stock of humanity. That night, Blakes saw his Angel.

The Angel looked as he always had, and he said, "Lead us not to read the Bible, but let our Bible be Virgil and Shakespeare, and deliver us from poverty in Jesus, that Evil One. For thine is the Kingship, or Allegoric Godship, and the Power, or War, and the Glory, or Law, Ages after Ages, in thy Descendants; for God is only an Allegory of Kings and nothing Else. Amen."

"Amen," Blakes said, and he looked around, at the museum–death camp he had created in the Frill ruins. *Why don't they come and kill me?* he wondered for perhaps the ten thousandth time.

"Because you were the first to come here."

"I'm going to die."

"Yes," the Angel said, and it smiled calmly. "It could be worse. After everything, it could be worse."

"I will not die," Blakes said.

"Oh yes, you will."

Blakes stood very weakly, his chest aching, and he picked up the bag with the black box. "Walk with me."

The Angel fell into step beside him, and Blakes wandered away from Auschwitz, back toward the *Australia*'s grave. They passed the frozen thirteen, entered the passage to the *Australia*'s passages, and Blakes said, "You know I haven't seen them in years."

"I know."

"The Frill, I mean."

"I know."

"Why haven't they come to bother me?"

"They've been watching," the Angel said, and Blakes touched the second door.

"Identification number please."

"Three, seven, seven, nine," Blakes said, and the door opened to one of the smaller control rooms, where somebody had posted that damned poster: TWENTY-FIRST-CENTURY NIGHTMARE. *My poem*, Blakes thought, but he couldn't remember the words. He walked slowly to the chair and sat down at the console and began to type, his fingers flaring with pain at the movements.

Blakes read the words on the screen, and the Angel whistled.

"Four centuries to finish drilling," the Angel said.

"Four centuries or more before we have enough to go back," Blakes said, and he typed, bringing up another complicated series of messages. "Enough to make them burn."

"You're still angry."

"Yes," Blakes said.

"Why? You fought them all, and you won for awhile, and—"

"They sent me here."

"Yes. They gave you another chance."

"Another chance," Blakes said. He had taken all of the technology from Hope, buried it in locked vaults under the Church or deep inside the tunnels to keep the people pure. Before Blakes had left he had been careful to outlaw all books not sanctioned by the Church and government and to make sure that the only people who would learn to read would be those controlling the presses.

"Why did you leave?" the Angel asked.

Final lines of text came on-screen:

Authorize computer separation /auto-run: (Y/N)?

If Yes: Tyger remaining in stasis, cerebral cleansing, collection process proceeding indefinitely, transfer(s) upon request.

Blakes typed "Y", and the screen flickered and went dark.

"What did you do?" asked the Angel.

"You'll see."

Blakes left the room, and back in the hall he paused at several rows of black metal set into the stone walls. Nearly transparent in the blue light, Blakes saw the outlines of ten different people—the last one on his right was a young teenager, growing slowly inside the metal coffin. When he reached twenty-nine years of age, he would stop growing and remain untouched.

"Looks like you," said the Angel.

Blakes started back down the hall, toward Hope.

"This is finished," he said.

"Finished? You mean you're ready to die now?"

"Yes."

"I'm surprised."

"I should not go quietly?" Blakes asked, and they both smiled. "This life, I've had enough."

" 'What immortal hand or eye, dare frame thy fearful symmetry?' "

"Yours," Blakes said, and when they were closer to Hope, he sat against the wall and set the black box in front of him. "I'll see you again."

"I'm afraid of what you'll do to them."

"They called me an animal," Blakes said. "A murderer. I'm sorry, but I won't forget or forgive that. You're right; I will kill all of them if I can. I am an animal."

"A tiger."

"Feel more like a very sick old man." Blakes took the wire from the black box and drew a small blade.

"Down the wrists, not across."

"Thank you," Blakes said. He cut open his arms, and as he died, Blakes pressed the computer wire to his open muscle, the pumping blood mixing with the computer's own. "I am . . ."

Blakes stopped moving.

The Angel glanced uncomfortably at the black box and said softly, "Yes. I see you."

vel.

He kept his eyes shut.

"I'm sleeping," Vel said. "Can't hear you."

Something is happening.

Vel glared at his dark bedroom, at the candle that was ready to go out on his bedside table. "What?"

You must leave the city.

"When I wake up we'll talk about it."

There will not be time. Please, Vel.

Vel tried to ignore Ulyu and go back to sleep.

You and everyone else are in danger.

"What kind of danger, exactly?" Vel asked, without opening his eyes.

There isn't time, Vel. Please, you must listen. There isn't—

"Much time." Vel wiped one of his eyes and yawned. "I know, Ulyu. I need to sleep now."

You can sleep in the ruins.

"Doubt it," Vel said. "The floors look pretty hard."

You must kill that man and leave.

Vel sat up uncomfortably. "Who?"

Lord Denon. Frill are waiting for you in the tunnels—call them now, and they will be with you—

"No," Vel said. "I don't think I will."

Vel, you are our link with the gods—

"Enough about the gods for one day," he said. "I want you to leave me alone."

Your Frill are here. Something very bad is happening.

"That's sufficiently vague as to be meaningless. I'm not worried, unless you want to tell me what the hell you're talking about."

I can't.

"Why not?"

No answer, and Vel said it again, "Why not, Ulyu? Why can't you tell me what is so important?" Vel waited, and when Ulyu didn't answer, he rolled onto his side, grumbled to himself and tried to go back to sleep.

The door opened.

A strained, barely audible voice said, "Vel?"

Vel sprang to his feet, grabbing his sword from the bedside table—Sisha stared at him, her eyes large and white. She wore a torn black dress, the same dress she'd been wearing when he'd taken her into his bed. How long ago had that been?

"I'm here, Sisha," Vel said, willing his pulse to slow down. "What is it?"

"How did you move like that? Didn't even see you—too fast . . ." She was tapping the doorknob with one hand, and Vel put his sword away.

"Not sure," Vel said, and he thought about how it hadn't worked against Wunic. "You're awake. Are you feeling better?"

Sisha said, "You're not safe," in a stage whisper, as if she knew someone was listening in the hall. "Guards are switching, and they'll be back any minute. I wanted to tell you. Get out of here as quickly as you can. You aren't safe here, Vel."

Not talking as if she's drugged, Vel thought. *Then why is she saying this?*

"What do you mean, Sisha?"

"Lord Denon," she said. "Vel, you have to get away from him. He . . ." She swallowed painfully. "He . . ."

"What?" Vel said, approaching her. "I don't understand."

"Don't come to my room," she said. "They'll drug me again. Denon did things while you were gone. . . ."

"What things?" he said.

"I have to go."

"What things?"

She didn't look at him, opening the door again. "I love you."

"Talk to me, Sisha. I'm king here. You don't have to run like this—"

"Vel, he raped me." Sisha's voice cracked, and she shook, holding herself up on the door. "I didn't . . . you just . . . I shouldn't have let it happen."

Vel felt like someone had slapped him, and his stomach rolled uneasily. *I made a mistake.*

"No," Vel said. "It wasn't Denon."

"It was."

"No," Vel said again, stepping closer to her, his voice rising, "it was not Denon. It was General Wunic." Sisha shook her head and started to say something. "No!" Vel said. "It was Wunic. Don't let those drugs mess with you. *Stop it, Sisha.*"

"Please, Vel . . ." She started to cry.

Vel backed away from her. Lord Denon wouldn't do that. Denon had wanted Vel to become king, Denon was his friend, Denon had helped him win, had saved the city. "You're drugged. Go back to your room like you said you would."

"Vel, I'm sorry."

He sat at the foot of the bed, and Sisha didn't move.

"I trust Denon," Vel said softly, looking at her. "I'm going to forget that you brought this up. It wasn't him. It was General Wunic." Vel shivered. "I know about it. I've handled it."

"No," Sisha said, and she drew the door open. "You don't, you—"

"Go back to your room."

"They'll drug me again, and you're going to die if you don't leave. Listen to me, Vel."

"I know they've drugged you," Vel said. "I know what dulling oil does. It's all right. Go back to your room."

"*Don't talk to me like that!*" Sisha shouted suddenly, and Vel put his hands over his face, trying to forget what she had said. *I killed the wrong man: this isn't real, this is a dream or something.*

"I didn't forget about you," he said. "Just go away right now."

"No. God, do you think—"

"Leave, Sisha."

"Please, it isn't—"

"*Leave.*" She backed into the hall, and Vel said quietly, "I care about you. I'm sorry, I'm just tired."

"Get out of here," Sisha whispered.

He nodded, forcing a smile. "Get some rest."

Vel heard her door close across the hall, and a soldier passed outside, wearing the white markings of a messenger.

Vel called after him, "Dispatches?"

The messenger paused, and Vel motioned him to come into the room—Vel met him in the doorway.

"Yes, sir. For Lord Denon," the messenger said, "but you have clearance if you want to read them."

Sleep is overrated, after all, Vel thought. "Let me see."

Vel watched the messenger leave, toward the main staircase—and there stood Lord Denon at the top of the stairs with six of the Religious Guard surrounding him. Vel broke the seal and read:

> This dispatch is to inform Lord Denon that sentences for prisoners numbered 1 through 346 have been carried out. The remaining prisoners are being interrogated now . . .

The letter continued—Denon approached, the Religious Guard behind him—and Vel read more:

> Also, in light of His Majesty's recent victory over the rebels and their unconditional surrender, refugees who do not fit the requirements for conscription are requesting that their homes be . . .

Vel stopped reading, the rest of the page continued meaninglessly. *And their unconditional surrender. My fault. I've been . . .* Vel realized that he was holding the paper tightly with both hands, and he backed into the bedroom, toward the bedside table—toward his pistol and sword. *And their unconditional surrender. How do I deal with this? All this time . . .*

Vel reached his weapons, and Denon stepped into the room. "Dispatches?"

"Yes," Vel said. "I've taken care of it."

Denon watched him calmly. "What were they?" The Religious Guard moved beside him, rifles ready.

"Questions about the refugees," Vel said.

"Are the dispatches intended for me?" Denon asked casually, pointing to the broken blue-circle seal.

"Yes," Vel said, and he slipped his sword and pistol, along with the Frill spear into his belt. Without turning he asked, "How's the front?"

Denon stepped closer, more of the Religious Guard slowly moving into the bedroom. "You hold the most recent dispatch. Tell me, Your Highness." When Vel didn't answer, he continued, "Can I see it, Vel?"

Vel's hand dropped to his pistol—Denon said, "Please, don't." And their rifles clicked, already aimed.

Vel frowned. "Have we lost ground?"

Six rifles, Vel thought. *Don't think about what this means, think about staying alive.*

"We have," Denon said. "I suggest that you leave as soon as possible, Your Highness." No change in his voice. No emotion, no restraint, nothing.

I trusted you from the beginning because you brought me here. Didn't know what I was doing and you . . . you, Vel thought. And he could think nothing else. *You.* The word repeated in his mind, over and over and over again. *You.*

"Maybe I should leave for the ruins," Vel said.

Denon nodded. "Yes."

Vel dropped the dispatch. "Why are their guns pointed at me?"

"You were reaching for your pistol," Denon said. "You do not look well. Have you slept?"

"No."

"That's unfortunate."

"How about you, Lord Denon? How are you sleeping?"

Denon said, "As well as can be expected."

"It's strange that General Wunic would defect, isn't it?"

Denon crossed his arms, one hand sliding under his robe. "Is it? I don't think so."

"He was in charge of the entire army—I thought I could trust him," Vel said. "Until he tried to have me buried alive."

"Yes."

"Until he betrayed me while I was gone. And raped the girl across the hall."

"Sisha," Denon said. "That's her name, isn't it?"

"Yes," Vel said. "That's her name."

"Can I see the dispatch, Vel?"

Vel nodded. "Go ahead." He didn't move. Vel waited, and when Denon didn't act, Vel said, "Would you die for me, Lord Denon?"

Denon's cheek tightened slightly. "If your life was in danger, yes, I would."

"Would you?" Vel said. "What happened to the Executive Council? Why haven't I seen any of the council members?"

"General Wunic and a number of the representatives are dead. Obviously there must be new elections."

"You know, I used to think that everything here is created for a purpose," Vel said. "Somebody told me that once, that everything on Hope has a purpose."

Denon nodded. "Everything does."

"Problem is, I'm not sure it's always a good purpose. If I draw my gun," he said, "will they shoot me?"

Denon was silent.

"I don't understand. Why are their guns drawn? Aren't I the king?" The Religious Guard edged closer, slowly surrounding him, and Vel made no attempt to get away. "If I died, if I fell down the stairs or committed suicide, what would happen? Wouldn't the military react? I'm sorry, Lord Denon, but wouldn't they? How would you survive?"

"Vel, we've lost ground," Denon said, his voice flat. "I suggest you return to the ruins for your own safety."

"I want you to talk to me about this first. I want to talk to you before it's over. Tell me why you're doing this."

Denon carefully drew a pistol from inside his robe, but he didn't point it at Vel. "No."

"Tell me why."

Denon raised one hand, and the Religious Guard steadied their rifles.

"Isn't this dangerous for you?" Vel said. "If you kill me, wouldn't the soldiers stop you?"

"Statistics," Denon said quietly. "There are now more members of the Religious Guard protecting Your Highness than there are military personnel at this moment."

A hole opened in the side wall, and the Frill entered, spears raised, red slits flashing briefly. Vel saw the outline of a digger in the new tunnel behind them: ten Frill flashed into the room, more behind them, and Ulyu raised his spear to Vel.

Tell them that if they do not lower their weapons, they are all going to die.

"Lord Denon," Vel said, "you had better pray that there is no such place as hell."

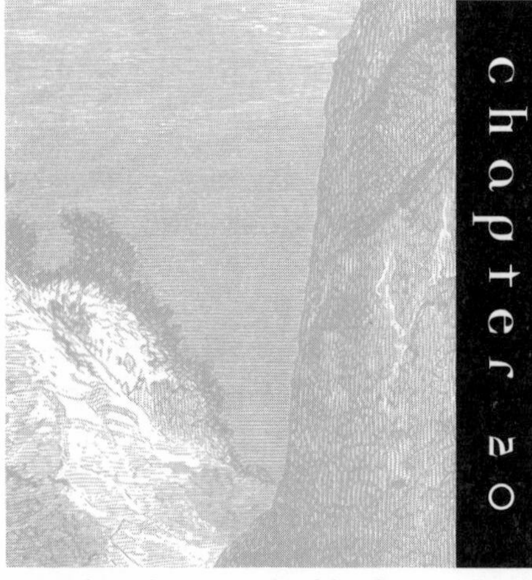

chapter 20

"Order them away or she dies," Denon said, remaining perfectly still. The Religious Guard looked from Vel to the Frill. Yes, Vel thought, *that's terror I see in their faces.*

"What?" Vel said, and more Frill flicked into the room.

"If I yell," Denon said slowly, "Sisha will be killed. There is a man standing in the shadows of her room, armed with a pistol. If he hears my voice, he'll fire. Do you understand?"

"I don't believe you."

"Lord Denon, they only have long swords," one of the Religious Guard said. "We—"

Denon ignored the man and said, "Vel, order them away."

"And after she dies," Vel said, "what will you do? You have a burial plot picked out for yourself?"

"If you do not order the Frill away, Sisha will die."

"I don't believe you, Denon."

"Then test me," Denon said. "And you can die knowing that both of us, along with the girl, have gone to a better place. My soul is ready, but I'd prefer not to die unless there is no other option." He paused. "There is always another way. Order them to leave."

Vel said, "Order your Religious Guard to lower their rifles."

"This is not a negotiation—"

"Yes," Vel said, and a part of him wanted to take out his pistol anyway. *But I won't kill you with a pistol,* Vel thought. *You'll wish that I had, but you won't die like that, Denon.* "It *is* a negotiation. That's exactly what this is. Now tell them to lower their rifles, and I'll order the Frill to back away."

"Sir, we can—"

Denon glared at the priest who had spoken, silencing him. *You're still human, aren't you?* Vel smiled without meaning to, as he thought, *I'm not. I brought this on, and I'm going to fix it.*

"All right," Denon said, and they began to lower their rifles, and Denon started to say something else, but Vel was already reaching for his pistol—a guard shouted, Denon rushed for the door, and the Frill blurred forward. The Religious Guard raised their rifles, and three went down, heads rolling onto the floor. Denon reached the doorway—a fourth Guard decapitated, and a fifth, his rifle flashing uselessly, and Vel shot at Denon, blasting away the wall behind him—and the sixth Guard fired at Vel before the Frill cut him down.

Vel rolled, the room swimming together, and the bullets burned against his skin, snapping hard into the floor and bed around him. But they didn't hit him. Vel's shirt was ripped in several places, but the bullets hadn't drawn blood—Denon was shouting in the hall outside.

"Now," Vel said. "Kill him." And the Frill flashed through the doorway, after Denon. Vel dashed across the hall—a mass of the Religious Guard were blocking the Frill nearby, their rifles firing uselessly as they were butchered—and Vel threw open Sisha's door. She was sitting up, frightened in the bed.

"What's happened?"

"You're—" Vel said, and he backed into the hall. "Stay here. Don't leave."

Dozens of bodies piled headless in the hall as the Frill broke through the rows of Religious Guard, staining the walls and carpet. *You,* Vel thought, and his heart pounded, shaking his vision—he advanced on the blurring shapes of the Frill, and then threw himself in the air, tightening his body into a ball as he jumped over them and fell among the Religious Guard, his outstretched arm catching one by the throat, his pistol blasting a second through the chest. One hit the ground hard, and Vel fired again, shooting down two more.

Denon was at the top of the stairs, and Vel shot at him, missing as Denon descended to the main floor. Denon's voice echoed through the palace, calling the Religious Guard to stop the rebel king, and Vel drew his Frill spear as a hot bullet tapped his pants. *No longer moving as a person,* Vel thought. *I'm not one of you anymore,* and he charged toward the stairs, slicing through the guards that stood in his way. The men tried to block, but Vel was moving too quickly, knocking them back in a fast clanking of metal that opened their stomachs and split their throats.

A spray of bullets went by his head, and Vel vaulted forward, firing his pistol behind him in midair, taking another man down—

the Frill had almost finished with the rest, and Vel ran in fast steps that seemed to miss the ground—to the stairs. Religious Guard hurried through the main entrance hall to one of the passages on the left. *Following you,* Vel thought. *You. You know you can't win this. You're retreating. You're going back to your Church.*

Vel took several steps, and he jumped past the stairs. *No,* he thought. *No, you're not.* The stairs shot by in a flurry of horizontal lines, and the wooden floor flew forward. Vel hit on his side, rolling to his feet as if he'd been trained to freefall. *They made me this way,* Vel thought. *I'm what they created, and Goddamn it, I'm going to fix this.* Still gunshots from the second floor as the Religious Guard somehow managed to hold out for several more moments against the Frill.

A burst of gunfire shredded the floor around Vel, and he bounded toward it, his Frill spear and pistol still drawn—a soldier-priest was half-covered at the corner of the passage, his rifle flashing at Vel—and Vel dodged, shooting back twice. The wall exploded in a black mist around the priest, but he continued to fire.

"I hit you . . ." the priest shouted, and another Religious Guard stepped behind him, his rifle also aimed.

Vel stepped to the side of the corridor doorway, and they continued to fire out, blasting the empty entrance hall and staircase past Vel. Now Vel noticed the dead police soldiers and Religious Guard scattered through the area. *My soldiers,* Vel thought, *he had them killed.* Frill flicked down the main staircase to stand around Vel.

The girl is safe.

"There are at least two of them," Vel said, panting, and a Frill slipped past Vel into the hallway without stopping—bursts of gunfire, a scream, and the sound of bones snapping. Twice.

More Frill appeared at the top of the staircase.

"Go outside," Vel said. "Make sure they don't leave." Vel motioned to the heavy double doors at the other end of the entrance hall. A group of Frill went for the doors, and another group came to Vel's side, Ulyu at the lead.

"How many did you lose?"

None.

"Good." Vel turned the corner, a single Frill standing over a pair of decapitated Religious Guard at the end of the hall. The coronation room beyond was empty except for a line of chairs set against one wall and a table at the far end. Three doorways led out of that room, and Ulyu followed Vel in.

"Where is he?" Vel said. "Can you, I don't know . . . sense them or something?"

No.

"Rear exit and several side doors. That way . . ." Vel motioned to the right door. "Go that way, Ulyu. The rest of you, that way . . ." Vel pointed left, and he started toward the doorway in the center. Three Frill followed him. The rest did as they were told.

We'll find him, one of the Frill said.

Vel didn't respond. The dark, wooden walls of the hall forked ahead, and there were several closed rooms on either side. A soldier's body cluttered the fork in the passage, ripped apart by gunfire.

Vel nodded left. "Two of you that way."

He turned right, and one Frill followed.

More doors passed on either side, quarters for some of the highest military personnel, and there were more bodies in the hallway ahead, one of the doors half-closed on an aged officer, an unused sword in his limp palm.

They've been this way.

"Really." Vel kept his pistol pointed ahead, his spear lowered to one side. "*Someone's* been this way."

The hall opened into a small room with benches along the walls—Vel shot down two Religious Guard—and the Frill flashed past Vel, into the room, killing more soldier-priests who had been hiding along the walls. Two more passages left the small room, and when Vel reached the room, he said, "We have to split up."

That's not possible.

More bodies at an intersection down the right hall.

"If Denon gets away," Vel said, "we won't have another chance. We have to find him."

You cannot—

"There isn't time for this." Vel started left. "You go that way." The Frill began to follow him instead. "Goddamn it, do you or do you not follow my orders?"

If you order yourself to be placed into risks—

"Bullshit," Vel said. "You do what I tell you to do, and you don't question it. If I tell you to cut off my head, you cut it off."

It isn't safe.

"None of this is safe. Now, go that way." Vel started moving again, more quickly, and when he glanced back the Frill was gone. *Don't I have any soldiers?* Vel wondered, and the hall turned: more soldiers' bodies on the floor, with several Religious Guard piled among them. Another corner, and Vel turned—into a Religious Guard, three feet away, staring at his bloody hand.

"Stop," Vel said, he didn't, and Vel shot him in the head twice—another Religious Guard further down the hall.

"Lord—" the man started, and Vel blew apart his chest, dropping him. And there he was.

Lord Denon stood in front of a small group of Religious Guard, and they hurried to protect their leader, firing at Vel, and he stepped around the bullets, shooting them down. Denon opened a side door, and Vel studied the hall for a moment before following him. No more Religious Guard here. These rooms were barracks for officers, not exits. No way out.

Vel drew closer, and he thought about Sisha, about—*die,* Vel thought. *It doesn't even matter how anymore. I just want you to die. Choke. Bleed. Spit. I want to hear you beg. This is my problem, and I'm going to fix it.* Vel reached the door. It snapped back into him violently, and Denon tried to rush him, a pistol in one hand. Vel sidestepped the door, Denon's gun flashing, and Vel spun, batting the weapon away from Denon with his spear, and knocking him back into the room.

It *was* a bedroom, set with a neatly made bed, a small table, wrinkled clothes on top, and a black-and-white drawing of Hope's river mounted on the wall. Denon drew his sword and backed away. *Nowhere to go,* Vel thought. He stood less than ten feet from Denon—and he pointed his pistol at Denon's head.

"Do you remember what I told you?" Denon said. Vel waited. Denon ignored the pistol, watching Vel. "I'm your friend in this."

Vel's finger tensed on the trigger. *Just make his life go out. Just end it like this. Just finish it.*

"No," Vel said. "I don't care about *why* anymore, I just want it—I want you to stop."

Denon remained where he was. "You're going to shoot me?"

Vel nodded. "That's right."

"You can't kill me," Denon said, stepping closer to the pistol.

Vel tightened his grip. "No?" And pulled the trigger.

Click.

Denon put both hands on his sword and nodded calmly, as if he'd been counting each shot. As if he'd waited for Vel to realize what he already had.

"No," Denon said.

Vel let the gun drop and steadied his spear. "You'll wish there had been more bullets."

The room shook.

The floor rattled, and the bed vibrated. Vel stepped back, grabbing the doorway, and Denon lowered to a half-crouch, steadying himself as the ceiling began to spit black dust. The room and hall were filled in a sudden dark cloud, and Vel gagged on it, holding onto the stone as the building continued to shake. His eyes watered, his throat burned, and Denon sliced him across the cheek, slamming Vel's head back, into the wall. His ears rang.

The world flashed, and warm liquid splattered down Vel's face—he struggled to rise. Through the dimness, he saw Denon running. The bastard had slashed his face. Denon disappeared in the smoke. No. Another black cloud fell from the ceiling as the building rocked violently, and Vel saw several large pieces of the ceiling fall away after Denon. Vel ran after him, stumbling against the walls, choking in the darkness. The ceiling collapsed just ahead of him, and Vel stopped, the passage suddenly blocked, his lungs refusing to work. He turned, his head on fire, and the hall went by in a haze as he hurried in the opposite direction. Intersections, and more of the ceiling fell, throwing more of the black dust onto him.

A hand took Vel's shoulder, and he was moving more quickly, rooms passing, and then they were outside, cold, cleansing air hurrying into his lungs. Vel collapsed into the snow, his body retching as he choked.

"Getting away," Vel said, gasping. "He's gone. We have to stop him."

No, Vel thought. *This time I will not stop: I will not shrink and fall away and give up. I made mistakes, and I will fix them.*

Vel, Ulyu said.

"Not over." They were outside. Part of the palace had collapsed, smoking.

Vel, please look up.

He heard Sisha's voice, "Vel, thank God!"

Sisha took his shoulders, and pulled herself to his shaking back.

"Beat me," Vel said. "This is different—I'm not letting him get away."

This is different, Vel thought. *Because I've been through this before, and I used to be afraid, I used to wonder what to do, how to cope with the world without someone telling me what to do: That's over. I'm alive now, I'm in charge.*

Stand up, Vel.

He opened his eyes, blinking back tears, and forced himself to rise, Sisha beside him, her arm over his shoulders. The snow still fell, but for the moment it no longer fell in thick gusts. Vel stared away from the palace, into the courtyard and the nearby streets, except he couldn't see the buildings. Something was blocking them, and Vel saw the word, *Australia.*

epilogue

Vel stumbled to his feet, Ulyu and Sisha behind him. Soldiers surrounded the metal . . . *thing* that filled the street. Closer, and now soldiers were rushing to his side, talking very quickly about Lord Denon and the Religious Guard—and no, it had just appeared in the sky, and as it landed, it had shaken down the buildings.

Vel stepped out of the courtyard. *What is it?* he thought, and he moved past the soldiers and civilians who surrounded the thing. It was organized like a random series of metal boxes and strange-looking pipes and enormous compartments, all built into three central bodies or torsos. *Like abdomens of some giant monster,* Vel thought. The thing snapped and tocked as snow continued to settle on it, and steam rose in thick wafts from its sides and top. And written on the front was the single, gigantic word that was really just gibberish, *Australia.*

A part of the thing's underbelly creaked and whirred, and then it lowered, and the soldiers started shouting, aiming rifles. A ramp came down, and a man in black, wearing the red swastika armband, slightly different and more precise than the Church's, walked slowly down. He shivered and blinked at the surroundings, his skin pale. His hair was receding and unkempt and his eyes glanced intensely at Vel. He paused in the snowfall, closed his eyes and smiled broadly as the snow swirled around him.

Vel kept one hand on his spear and tried to remain calm. Denon was still alive, still—the man stepped closer and offered Vel his hand.

"Hello Vel," he said, "I'm Blakes."